IN ELLEN'S SHOES

BASED ON THE INSPIRING TRUE STORY OF
ELLEN BREAKELL AND ALEXANDER NEIBAUR

EMILY BEESON

HOMESPUN LIGHT PUBLISHING

*But lay up for yourselves treasures in heaven, where neither
moth nor rust doth corrupt, and where thieves do not break
through nor steal:
For where your treasure is, there will your heart be also.
Matthew 6:20-21*

To my mom for sharing pioneer stories
and to my dad for reading Dr. Seuss to us so many times, he could
recite the books by heart.

1

Preston, England 1834

The Breakell family moved to their rented pew on the right side of St. John's Minster and filed in one by one. Ellen pulled her embroidered skirts and petticoats close to fit between the benches. While flattering to her waistline, the style was rather cumbersome. Once seated, she was obliged to deflate one of her sleeves a bit in order to make way for her younger brother's view of the pulpit.

Her dearest friend, Patience, turned, placing her gloved hand on the back of the pew in front of Ellen. "I am so pleased to see you," she whispered.

Ellen covered Patience's hand with her own and smiled. "Am I not always here?"

"Indeed. But whether or not you desire to be here is another matter. You do like to keep up appearances, though." She laughed softly, drawing the reproach of her husband of two weeks, who put a finger to his lips. In position, they were the perfect match, but as to their temperaments, time would be the judge.

Patience knew Ellen well, but she was wrong. This was one time Ellen would have much preferred not to keep up appearances.

With an utter lack of discretion, Patience gestured in the direction of Mr. Neibaur.

Ellen instinctively knew where he was seated in the room, sensing his presence. She lowered her gaze to her trembling fingers.

Patience dipped her head to catch Ellen's eye. "Something has happened between the two of you." She squeezed Ellen's hand. "If Preston's latest Beauty Contest winner cannot keep the man of her dreams, what hope is there for anyone? How long has it been since you've spoken with him?"

Ellen shrugged, as if she had not counted every moment since their last meeting.

How many times had Mr. Neibaur ridden to their secret spot by the river and waited for her? Had he given up? Did she want him to? She pictured him alone on the far side of the chapel, the usually jovial countenance smitten from his bearded face. To be still and quiet suited him ill. Knowing it was in her power to resurrect his happiness did little to put her at ease. She could not face him again after what he had done.

What they had done together.

Mr. Cole stepped to the pulpit, and Patience turned to face the front, to the clear relief of her dear Mr. Walker. "God bless you on this warm Sabbath day. I am compelled to speak of morality and our infinite need for the Lord Almighty. Brothers and sisters, we are nothing. I repeat, nothing. I quote from Romans, seventh chapter. 'For we know that the law is spiritual, but I am carnal, sold under sin, O wretched man that I am." He clutched the front of his double-breasted jacket.

Ellen's own hand clutched at her bosom, not in mockery as it ordinarily might have been, but in true distress. She could not abide a lecture on morality today.

Mr. Cole's stern face contracted. "Who shall deliver me from the body of this death?"

She almost wanted to peek at Mr. Neibaur but could not bring herself to lift her head in his direction and witness his stooped frame. His mind would likely be on her during this torturous sermon, as well, but with what attitude did he think on her? Was he relieved they had parted? Did he miss her? Did guilt scorch his conscience? Or had he, unlike her, been able to put the whole miserable business behind him?

Her youngest brother, Richard, pulled on her sleeve. "I must leave, Ellen."

"Oh hush." At the age of ten, Richard should be able to sit quietly through a sermon. He stared up at her, pulling on his collar, and she softened her expression. As the baby of the family, he had never been expected to act his age. Having his twin taken to Heaven had only solidified his position as the one to be doted upon.

The vicar's heavy voice vibrated through the thick, damp air as Ellen peeked past Richard to their brother, William, his eyes straining to stay open. It distracted her from her own distress. "Can you not stay awake for the Lord?" she teased.

"I am awake." William shook his head and opened his eyes unnaturally wide.

Beyond him, the rest of the family sat perfectly still. Mama was focused on the preacher, piety written into every line of her face. Dear Mama. Would Ellen ever be filled with such faith and love of the Church? Did it even matter? She squeezed her eyes closed. Her mother had had much to worry about these past months. Mama's open criticism of Mr. Neibaur had turned Ellen to lies, deceit, and now this guilt-ridden heartbreak. Part of her wanted to scream and blame Mama for all of it, but something inside would not let her rest her guilt on anyone other than herself. Not even Mr. Neibaur.

Her mind wandered to the day she met him in this very

church. She had been intrigued by his foreign air and vibrant smile. Unlike anyone else in her acquaintance, he alone had stolen her heart.

Mr. Cole's voice dropped deep as the grave. "As Adam and Eve were expelled from the Garden of Eden, so shall we be expelled from God's presence if we do not live a life of utmost purity." He pounded the pulpit, and the sound reverberated in her chest.

She was tempted to arise and leave, but she could scarcely move. Maybe an angel of God would swoop down from the heavens and cast her out like Eve from the garden. She lifted her eyes to the gothic-arched windows, pillars, and rose window, constructed to instill awe in the church's parishioners. They weighed upon her, mocking the sinner within.

Her mind flashed back to the blackened day, seared into her mind for ill.

"Miss Breakell," Mr. Neibaur had said one afternoon as they sat on a patchwork quilt by the River Darwen, not far from the Breakell's country home, "I..."

She watched his deep brown eyes, darker even than his curly hair and beard, with expectation bubbling within her.

He rarely addressed her with such formality anymore when they stole away to the river. He started again, "Dear, dear Ellen."

She encouraged him with an expectant smile, and when that was not enough to prod him along, she kissed his puckered mouth. "I like the sound of my Christian name on these lips."

His eyes twinkled. "My parents did not give me a Christian name."

She laughed. "No. I would not expect your Jewish parents to bless you with a Christian name, but you do have a name other than Mr. Neibaur, of course. May I call you Alexander?"

"I would like that."

"Very well. Do you have something pressing to say, Alexander?" She batted her eyes as his name rolled from her tongue, sweet as an apple.

Trying not to focus on the way his muscles stretched the fabric of his suit when he rolled up onto his knees, she averted her eyes.

"Ellen, will you have me to be your husband?"

She squealed with glee and threw her arms around his neck, nearly knocking him over.

"Does that mean yes?"

She grabbed his face and kissed him again. "Yes. Yes. Yes."

"Three yeses?"

He smiled, and his whiskers tickled her palms. "A thousand yeses."

"A thousand? Good heavens." He waggled his eyebrows, then cleared his throat. "Let me be serious for a moment. I will earn a comfortable living for you..." He smiled mischievously. "And for our children. I will love you deeply, kindly, fully. I will be your proper English gentleman."

Though his words were English, his German accent and manner were decidedly foreign. She nudged him for his boldness. "No. I do not wish you to be any different than you are, my Jewish-Christian Prussian dental-surgeon."

He kissed her fingers one at a time without breaking eye contact. "We will be partners in life. You will be my ezer."

"Pardon?" She twirled one of her loose curls around her fingers and let it fall to her shoulder. "Your what?"

"My ezer. It is a Hebrew word. Sometimes the English Bible loses meaning in its translation from the perfect Hebrew."

She tilted her head in a teasing manner. "Perfect Hebrew, you say?"

"Ja. I do not boast. Hebrew is the original language of the Bible, and as it has been translated again and again, some truth and meaning is lost. It cannot be otherwise."

She gazed up at the cotton clouds and pondered his blasphemous words.

He squinted. "Are you angry with me?"

The mixture of love and anxiety, knowledge and innocence, softened her. "Of course not. I am surprised to hear those words coming from a religious man, such as yourself, but I find they make sense. Tell me how to be your ezer."

"Two are named ezer in the Books of Moses—Eve and God. In the sacred stories, the Children of Israel are in great danger at times, and God is ezer when he arrives in power and comes to their aid."

Fascinated by his words but even more entranced by each expression, each mannerism, each movement of those lips, framed by long dark whiskers, she said, "I shall come to your aid whenever you need an ezer." She straightened up and tried to sound powerful.

With intensity in his unbreaking gaze, he stood and offered his hand, lifting her into his embrace. "Shall we walk along the river?" He kissed her cheek, which warmed to his touch, then tugged her hand along the winding path beside the river. "Your parents will not approve."

She poked him, wrinkling her nose as if the thought smelled of manure. "Do not spoil the moment with such talk."

"It will need to be dealt with soon."

She nudged him harder, and he stepped one foot into the shallow depth of the river's edge. When she giggled, he dipped his hand low into the water and splashed it toward her.

"Alexander," she cried, and without thought, she followed him into the frigid water, scarlet slippers and all, and swept her arm through it, throwing a wave at him.

Chuckling, he grabbed her around the waist and, dripping wet, pulled her close. "I love you. You make me the happiest man on Earth."

They pressed into each other, and since Alexander was stronger than Ellen, she found herself stepping backward until she felt a solid tree trunk against her back. As she could no longer move, the slight separation between them vanished. He kissed her neck, cheeks, and ears. Her arms clutched at him, her hands moving along his back and into his coarse, curly hair.

His hands traveled down both sides of her ribs and waist, stopping on her hips as they kissed, alternating between soft, damp kisses and deeper ones, full of longing.

He leaned his head back. "I should take you home."

"Yes, you most definitely should." Her heart pounded against his chest. They stared into each other's eyes, breathing heavily, love passing from one to the other in a way no words could express. They should not be alone. It was improper, dangerous, but her feet refused to take her away.

Their lips met again, moving together more deeply and passionately than before. She knew they should stop. She knew that he knew it.

But knowing one should do something and doing it are two very different things.

When she had returned home that day, she did not float in as usual. Feeling as heavy as her soaked scarlet slippers, she was a tangle of confusion. Her elation when Mr. Neibaur proposed marriage had turned into a frenzied longing. Before he left, he mentioned asking her father for her hand in marriage.

"Not tonight," she had answered, leaving him hidden in the trees, just out of view of her home at Darwen Park.

Now, what did she feel? They had let their passions run away with them, leaving her empty. It was not the former emptiness of longing for his return. It was a new emptiness.

Regret.

Richard leaned into her sleeve and its underlying puff,

where he dozed off, his face enveloped in the folds of fabric, only to start a moment later. "Is the sermon almost over?"

Sympathy—balanced with a pang of piety—chastised her. "Yes. I believe so." She returned her attention to the vicar.

Mr. Cole pursed his lips before continuing. "The Bible says, 'But I keep under my body, and bring it into subjection: lest that by any means, when I have preached to others, I myself should be a castaway.'" Mr. Cole shook his head. "We must not give in to the father of lies and suffer that eternal torment that awaits all who follow him."

Richard snickered into her ear. "This sermon is eternal torment."

She raised her eyebrows. "Maybe attending church prepares us for purgatory."

Richard nodded, and Mama scowled at them.

"Truly, we must be quiet." Ellen straightened her posture. "Do you not remember the time I had to stand on a stool at the front of the congregation wearing a white garb?"

He laughed, but she bit her lip against the memory.

"I do not see the humor in that." She pointed to the front with her chin. "Mr. Cole is finishing up now. It appears you have survived, and though the sermon was tormenting, it was not quite eternal."

Anxious to make her escape, she was one of the first to stand, and out of the corner of her eye, she saw Mr. Neibaur do the same. Her gaze involuntarily moved to his, her heart pounding in her chest.

In only a breath of time, the room fell away, and his eyes pleaded with hers, his lips parting as if to call out. She longed to dash into his arms, to forget.

But the moment passed. The congregation rose, filling the space between them, leaving only emptiness within her.

She would never forget, nor would she ever be forgiven.

2

Ellen retired to her bedchamber where her sister, Beth, helped her change into her shift. She had scarcely spoken a word to her family all week, other than a mumbled remark about the weather or a request to pass a dish at dinner. It had not taken long for the Breakells to allow her the privacy she required. Her legs dangled from the side of her bed while she glanced out the window, watching a gentle breeze rattle the vibrant green leaves of the elms.

Beth sat beside Ellen on their bed. "Tell me what the matter is. Are you ill?"

Ellen sighed. "I am not ill."

"Are you heartsick?" She smirked. "Did something happen with Mr. Neibaur during your last rendezvous?"

Ellen smiled without humor. Beth and dear Patience were the only people in the world she had been frank with about her secret meetings with Mr. Neibaur. "Yes and no."

Beth squinted in confusion, so Ellen clarified. "He asked for my hand."

Beth gasped. "Is that not what you wanted?"

"It is what I wanted, and I accepted him."

"That is wonderful." She clapped her hands but, observing Ellen's expression, blew out a slow breath. "Is it not?"

Ellen shook her head. "I shall have to tell him I have changed my mind."

Beth scrunched her nose. "You need not tell me anything, but you know I am in your confidence should you need a listening ear."

Ellen squeezed her sister's hand, and in doing so, discovered a folded paper enclosed there. She lifted her brows in question, and Beth opened her palm, offering the paper. "It is a letter from Mr. Neibaur. Do you wish me to find someone to read it to you?"

Ellen shook her head forcefully, knowing the letter could contain ruinous information and be her undoing. "No. Set it on the table there, please."

Beth obeyed and left their room.

Ellen hurried over and unfolded the paper, staring at Mr. Neibaur's neat, slanted script, and willed the letters to form into words and sentiments, but the effort was in vain. Folding it back along the creases, she tucked it under her pillow. She had never wished to be able to read more than in that moment.

She plopped herself into her chair. The fault was as much hers as his. Her mind had been churning for days. She wanted to marry a man who would bring out the best in her, so how could she marry someone with whom she had made the most reprehensible choice of her entire life? She was being hypocritical, but she did not want to settle with the kind of man who took a girl's virtue and left it by the river like a fallen leaf to wither and die.

But he was not that kind of man. He was a good, deeply spiritual person who had let the natural urges of a fallen world overpower spirit and belief, if only for an evening.

Of course, he had not acted against her will. She had participated in the scandal as much as he had.

But would he do it again? Was he filled with remorse? Was he upset because of what they had done or only because of her repeated refusals to see him?

They had both been raised better than this. Their parents and pastors had taught them to save themselves for the marriage bed. Had he not been taught to protect a lady's virtue at all costs? Even the appearance of virtue must be protected. As vastly different as their upbringings were, she could not imagine he had not been taught to save himself for his wife and to marry one who had saved herself for him.

She needed a man who believed those things and lived them. She could not marry him *now* and have her groom be a daily reminder of her treachery and ruin. While she could not deny the part she played, she may be able to forever bury her guilt.

But what if she did not marry him? Would she tell another potential suitor about what had occurred between Mr. Neibaur and herself? Who would marry her then? She paled at the thought and squirmed back into bed, pulling the bedsheets over her head and cradling her knees.

After some time, she flopped onto her back, tossing the bedsheets off, and paused, unmoving, arms sprawled out to her sides. She had to speak with Mr. Neibaur.

The next morning, she rode her midnight black stallion, Counterpoint, into Preston with his letter tucked carefully into her bodice. She came to the row of townhouses on Avenham Road in which he lived and found the appropriate door as soon as the hour permitted, determination in every step. She tied Counterpoint nearby.

Alexander opened the door himself and let out a great sigh when he saw her, as if he had been holding his breath until her appearance.

A small, metal tool was clutched in his hand. Why did she not think before making a fool of herself? He must be working on a patient. "I apologize for calling unexpectedly. I can return at your earliest convenience." She was turning toward the street when he reached for her. Before his hand touched her arm, he yanked it back, wiping it on the handkerchief from his coat pocket. "Please, come in. Will you wait in the sitting room? I will not be but a few more minutes."

She dared not meet his alluring eyes, but she nodded. "I will wait outside."

He let her turn and walk away.

Pacing the street, she watched small groups of people move in and out of the Preston Main Street shops and the post office. A horse and carriage clip-clopped on the cobblestones before she dashed across the street. When Mr. Neibaur emerged from his townhouse, he led a man who was rubbing his jaw. They shook hands, and the stranger waddled down the road toward the row of open-air fish carts. Mr. Neibaur's eyes moved along the road until he spotted Ellen. He waved and sprinted her direction, coattails taking flight behind him.

She meandered back across the street, inadvertently kicking pebbles with her shuffling feet and fingering the hanging ribbons of her bonnet.

"Please, come in," he said, pointing toward his home.

She glanced side to side to see if anyone was near enough to overhear their conversation. "That would be improper."

He raised an eyebrow and whispered, "Seems a little late to worry about propriety."

"Be that as it may, will you walk with me instead? The weather is most agreeable."

He nodded slowly and offered his elbow. "Of course."

She considered whether or not to take his arm, not wanting to give false hope that their relationship could go on as before. But it *was* proper to take a gentleman's arm, so she curled her fingers into the crook of his elbow, mindlessly squeezing as she had so many times before and ignoring the small flutter of her heart.

As they followed a path through the trees, the only sound came from the crunching of the leaves beneath their feet. Ellen paid little attention to their direction as her thoughts swirled with the breeze, refusing to form into words. The lush romance of summer was ending, changing with the leaves before blowing into the bleak loneliness of winter.

At length, she began to speak, but Mr. Neibaur commenced at the same time. She dipped her head to allow him to talk first.

"I assume you read my letter, but I would like to reiterate the sentiments therein."

Ellen, embarrassed to admit that she was unable to read, allowed him to proceed uninterrupted.

"Miss Breakell," he said, as her heart beat a foreboding tune. "I am very sorry for...what I did. I am not saying I would make a better decision if the same situation arose, but I want to be your husband, to have you for my wife." He punctuated each word. "I am everlastingly sorry that we did things in the wrong order." His eyes locked onto hers. "Please marry me, Ellen."

A familiar shiver moved up her spine, but the heavy guilt outweighed everything she felt and desired. She shifted her gaze to the Square, now some distance away, allowing herself to be distracted by a mother retying the ribbons on her young daughter's bonnet before meeting his eyes. "I did not read your letter, Mr. Neibaur, and you were foolish to send it. I have not been taught to read, and fearing your written words would condemn us both, I was unable to have another read it to me. You placed me in a most distressing position."

His face could not have appeared more surprised if she had slapped him. "Once again, I am sorry. As a landowner's daughter, I never imagined you would not have your letters." He shook his head, as if he could scarcely believe the mess he had gotten himself into. "It seems a grave omission from your education, ja?"

Indignation rose in her throat. "As one of the feminine sex, my father and mother did not see the need to teach me to read or write. While my father's traditional views on the matter may be out of fashion, they are by no means unheard of."

"Ja," agreed Mr. Neibaur, nodding vigorously. With his nose scrunched, he rubbed his beard and threw up his hands. "I will keep apologizing until you beg me to stop." He lifted his bearded chin, his gaze following a passing cloud. Lowering his deep set eyes to hers again, he said, "Miss Breakell, do you by chance have the letter with you?"

"I do. I could not very well leave it where it might be discovered by unsuspecting eyes."

Relief relaxed his features. "Would you be so kind as to return it to me?"

She angled away from him and glanced around to make sure she could be discreet before reaching into her bodice and retrieving the folded paper. Ensuring that she was not compromised in any way, she spun around and raised his missive out to him.

"Thank you." He took it and proceeded further along the path.

She stared blankly at his retreating back. While the letter would not do her any good, she still wondered about its contents. Now, he was moving away with it.

Counterpoint awaited her in front of the townhomes. Assuming he was leaving her alone, she blinked back tears and stepped in that direction when Mr. Neibaur turned on his heel, holding his arm out to her. "Are you not joining me?"

The infuriating man. Perhaps their different cultural understandings were incompatible as her mother had repeatedly expressed. Ellen grabbed handfuls of her skirts and caught up with him. They strolled side by side until they reached a steel park bench. Mr. Neibaur motioned for her to sit before seating himself beside her.

He unfolded the letter, the paper crinkling in his hands, and dipped his face toward hers.

Dear Miss Ellen,

Please excuse my actions. It is very difficult to keep my thoughts and actions appropriate around you. Minutes after promising to be an English gentleman, I broke your trust and behaved abominably. I hope you are not ill, but I find myself afraid to think that if you are not ill, you are avoiding me. I can only hope that my actions toward you--with you--have not changed your feelings for me and your desire to marry me. Please allow me to express these feelings in person. Please let me see you again.

With deepest affections,

A.N.

His fingers rubbed the paper before he refolded it and squeezed it in his palm.

The tree branches swayed in the breeze. "They are pretty words, but I find that I should have spoken first to save you from such a speech. I loved who I was with you until..." Tears pricked at her eyes. "Until the last time we were together."

He grimaced, but she pressed forward. "I know the blame rests on my shoulders as surely as yours. I feel it keenly. The guilt is so heavy, in fact, that I can no longer feel the blissful stirrings of love I felt before." A growing ache filled her chest, and she arose, stepping away to clear her mind. What did she want? Part of her wanted to set things right with him but the rest wanted to bolt like a spooked horse.

He gave her a few minutes before shortening the distance between them again. "Please do not do this to me, to us. Marry my imperfect self. In Jewish law, we make restitution for our sins by returning whatever we have taken plus more. That is why murder and immoral acts are the most grievous sins of all. There is no restitution that gives back what is lost, but I will live my life making it up to you. You have my word." His longing expression pleaded with her.

She exhaled. "Enough about your strange religious ideas. I do not wish for you to marry me out of some obligation to the law of restitution."

He stepped back, his shoulders falling. "That is not fair." He angled his face into her line of sight. "You know that is not why I desire to marry you. I proposed first, remember? I love you."

She tried to hide behind the brim of her bonnet, but he cupped her cheeks in his hands, and turned her face to him. She pushed his arms away. "Let us not talk of marriage any more today. I need some time to sort out my feelings, Mr. Neibaur." Her formality and finality seemed to wound him again, and his eyes glistened.

What did she mean to this man? Had any gentleman cried over her before? Certainly not. She was moved by his tears and pulled him into an embrace. A few of her own tears landed on his shoulder, which shook as he cried silently in her arms. A deeper desire to end his sorrow swarmed inside her, but that was not reason enough. She would not marry for pity.

"I love you, Ellen," he said again.

She nodded and stepped back.

His hand took hold of her arm and squeezed, but she shook her head, and he released her.

On the way to her horse, she refused to allow herself another glance at his solemn face, focusing determinedly on the path ahead.

3

Days passed with only silence from Mr. Neibaur. Ellen's heart was ripped in two, like Darwen Park's old maple tree that had been split by a strike of lightning. Part of her wished to be reconciled with him, but would it not be in their best interests to move on? Her mind told her this was so, but her heart was less sure.

She was sorely tempted to fake a toothache and show up at his doorstep once more.

"Ellen, are you not hungry tonight?"

Upon their mother's words, Beth narrowed her eyes, suspecting where Ellen's thoughts had been.

"Yes, Mama. I am, actually." She dipped her spoon into her white soup.

Beth, sitting beside her, gave her a little squeeze on the arm. She was a true comfort. Ellen could scarcely imagine living a life without Beth. They had eaten, slept, and grown up in one another's company.

Young Richard sat on the other side of Beth. He had not wanted to let Ellen out of his sight lately, as if she might become a wife at any moment and move away as their older siblings had done.

William, becoming a strapping young man, was eating his second bowl of soup with vigor, but he paused to cough. "What is the matter, Ellen?" he said.

"Nothing."

William went back to the business of his dinner. Helping in the stables had tanned his face and broadened his shoulders. It looked good on him, and she smirked as the pleasant thought that he and Patience's younger sister would make a stunning match went through her mind.

"What?" he asked again with a groan.

She shrugged. "What do you think of Patience's sister, Charity? She is becoming quite the town beauty."

He smiled as if he had noticed the same thing. Redness spread from his cheeks to the tops of his ears, and he made a show of focusing on his meal.

"Yes," Ellen said, clapping her hands. If she could not settle the matter of her own heart, she could enjoy making matches for others. "Who else shall I match up today?"

Richard huffed. "James. He is older than William, and if he moves away, he will no longer torture me. Do you know what he did today?"

Ellen shook her head with a dramatic frown.

"He pressed me down on the bench in the park and hung spittle from his mouth, and before it touched my face, he sucked it back in."

William chuckled. "Would you have preferred he let it fall?"

Richard scowled and sent a pleading glance to Ellen. "That was not all. James did that twice, but the third time, he did not suck it up fast enough, and it landed in my eye."

That caught Mama's full attention. "Oh, James, you must never behave in such a way. Never do that again." She turned to young Richard, exasperation written on her face. "How will we ever find an advantageous match for him if he behaves so abominably? Did you hear what he did, Mr. Breakell?"

"Hmmm?" Mr. Breakell's eyes remained glued to his agricultural book until they all laughed. "What?"

Ellen saved him. "Nothing, Papa. We were discussing the usual family squabbles that occurred today."

"Hmmm." He returned his attention to his book, causing more giggles to erupt around the table.

William cleared his throat. "I know who James hopes to marry."

Ellen and Beth satisfied him with eager *oohs* and *aahs*, and Beth leaned toward him. "Do tell."

"I shall only say her Christian name." William wiggled his fork in the air. "You will have to guess to whom I am referring. It starts with a J, and she is thirteen, same as me."

James huffed. "I have not noticed any girls so young."

"Ha!" William said before coughing. "You are only two years my elder."

Papa set his book next to his plate and joined in. "Does she have a Bible name, perhaps? Jemima, maybe? Jewel? Jochebed?"

William wrinkled his nose. "I do not believe this particular Christian name is found in the Holy Book, Father. Any other guesses?" He waved his arms around at everyone.

A spark of recognition filled Ellen's face. "I know. Does her name start with J-A, William?"

"Right you are, Ellen," he said, slapping his hand against the table. The excitement made him cough, and there was a hollow ring to it.

Understanding moved around the table as each member of the Breakell household figured out who William was talking about.

Mama nodded vigorously. "Miss Jane would be a lovely match for you."

James grunted. "Beth's turn."

"Me? I would rather not."

"I have a feeling her match might start with a J, as well, and quite possibly come from the Bible," Ellen said.

Beth kicked her under the table, and Ellen giggled.

Mama raised her brows. "Really, ladies. Behave yourselves. What would the Preston gentlemen think of your behavior? As you are older than your brothers, you must act like ladies."

Ellen tried not to chuckle aloud. The family moved to the sitting room while the cook began to clear the dishes. Ellen crossed to the pianoforte but stopped short at the clopping of horse hooves pounding outside the house. A thrill shot across her skin as she saw Mr. Neibaur riding up to Darwen Park, looking smart in his brown coat and tan pants. He was riding so fast, he had to swing his hand up to hold his top hat on.

Her heart ached at the sight of him as he yanked on the reins and jumped down in a single motion. Something about his eagerness was contagious. She had made up her mind not to react to him this way, but her heart betrayed her. He dismounted and practically sprinted to the door, but then he stopped abruptly as if unsure whether or not to proceed.

Ellen backed away and plopped herself onto the settee beside her sister.

"Who is it, Ellen?" Mama called.

She flinched, knowing the answer would be unpleasant to her mother. "It is Mr. Neibaur."

"Oh, heavens," said Mama. "Send him off at once."

Ellen scowled, and Mama threw her arms up in apparent defeat.

Her three brothers congregated by the window.

"What is he doing?" Ellen said, fearing he would leave but questioning whether she wanted him to stay.

Richard glanced over his shoulder and shrugged. "Pacing. He has come to the door and gone away thrice."

William snorted. "Make that four times."

Ellen leaned into Beth. "Shall I rescue him?"

Beth wrapped her arm around Ellen. "Let him make up his own mind."

William and James took to waving dramatically at Mr. Neibaur through the window.

"You are acting younger than Richard," Ellen said. "Nearly grown men making fools of yourselves."

William smirked. "He will have to come in now, for he knows we have discovered him. And you will have to stop moping about as if the sun forgot to shine."

A knock sounded against the door.

"It worked," he said smugly.

Ellen smoothed her dress and stood in unison with Beth.

One of the servants directed Mr. Neibaur into the room. Ellen had not seen him this nervous since the first time he had called on her at Darwen Park. She sighed. With their history, was it any wonder? He avoided her gaze and bowed to Mama. "Mrs. Breakell, I hope you are well."

Mama pursed her lips and made little pretense of civility in return.

Despite Mama's coldness, Mr. Neibaur faced Ellen, and though his smile did not falter, his grip on the handle of his cane tightened. "Miss Breakell, will you take a turn through Darwen Park with me?"

Mama stepped between them. "She is feeling ill, Mr. Neibaur, and is unable to go out of doors at present."

"Mama," Ellen protested, "I am quite well."

Mama huffed. "You may visit for a *short* time here in the sitting room."

Despite all they had been through, Ellen's desire to see Alexander only increased as she watched him endure the scornful eye of her mother. He must care for her very much to show up where he was unwelcome.

Standing behind her mother, she waited for eye contact with Mr. Neibaur. When he glanced in her direction, she ran her fingers across her other hand, attempting to mimic the motions of horse's hooves.

He squinted, then raised an eyebrow, and she tried to contain her grin.

She made the motion again, and he tilted his head with an expression of concentration.

Mama whipped around in Ellen's direction. Mr. Neibaur took the opportunity to move his cane between his legs and made a brief but exuberant galloping motion.

Ellen burst into laughter, but, by the time Mama returned her gaze to the man, he stood erect, looking innocent. And particularly handsome. Ellen wrapped her lips around her teeth and bit down to keep from chuckling. She nodded, indicating that she had indeed been trying to make a horse with her fingers.

Triumph and understanding lit his face, but then confusion returned.

"Well, that was a nice little visit, Mr. Neibaur. Off you go. I am sure we will see you at St. John's on Sunday." Mama directed him toward the front door.

He glanced over his shoulder as he was swept away.

She mouthed, "Ride with me," and hoped he was decent at reading lips. The thought brought a blush to her cheeks.

Beth's brows knit together in an expression of compassion. "Are you well?"

"I hardly know." They sat back down, Ellen folding her hands in her lap and wondering how long she need wait before going for a ride without raising the suspicion of her mother.

Beth winked at her. "Mama," she called, "I have something to show you in the library. Come."

Beth and Mama exited down the hall, and Ellen knew a pang of guilt. She had hoped the days of deception were behind her. How many times had she ridden away on her horse to secretly meet the handsome foreigner her parents disapproved of? Had she learned nothing at all?

"I am going for a ride," she told the boys. "William, would you mind preparing Counterpoint while I change into my riding habit?"

William puckered his lips before nodding. Did he suspect? Either way, he did not stop her.

Counterpoint was ready by the time she went out, and she mounted him like a soldier running from battle, albeit sidesaddle, directing him toward the usual rendezvous spot by the river.

Wind whipped her bonnet behind her, and as she neared the thicket, she spotted Mr. Neibaur cantering ahead. Digging in her heels, she flew right past him, but, as the river came into view, a sickening knot tied in her stomach at the memories they shared there, and she leaned back, yanking on the reins. "Let us ride somewhere else today." She hesitated to lift her gaze to his.

Understanding sparked in his dark eyes.

Her most beloved spot in all the world was blemished. Blemished like her, like a dress with a hem soiled so deeply it could no longer be cleaned. To remove the stain would require more scrubbing than the fibers could handle, and it would simply fall to pieces and become a rag.

Mr. Neibaur skimmed the horizon. "There may be time to reach Beacon Fell by sunset, and if we hurry, we can have you home before dark."

She nodded, grateful. "The fall foliage is stunning this time of year, and I can scarcely imagine anywhere greener."

"Berlin may outdo it, but I will let you know." He smiled, his cheeks rising up to his eyes, and he angled his chestnut mare, Rachel, toward the distant hill.

She nudged her heels in and shook her reins to encourage Counterpoint to catch up. They rode in silence but for the cheeky sounds of the nesting sparrows in the tops of the dogwood trees and the soft crunching of the horses' steps in the autumn grass.

Mr. Neibaur cleared his throat and halted when they reached the top of the hill overlooking Preston and the Forest of Bowland. Ellen turned Counterpoint parallel to Mr. Neibaur and his horse and admired the landscape.

"Breathtaking," she said.

"Yes, you are."

She half-smiled and patted Counterpoint's warm, moist neck. "You are feeling emboldened today, Mr. Neibaur." She laughed and redirected his thoughts. "Are the moors quite as green as Berlin?"

"Ja, but I have not come for a tête-à-tête about the local flora. I wrote a poem for you in another attempt to express my adoration. Nevertheless, if you do not want to hear of my affections now or ever again, I shall relinquish the subject forevermore."

She shrugged, feeling incapable of discerning right from wrong regarding him. The ability disappeared the moment she had allowed herself to be lost in his arms. Nay. She supposed her discernment had first led her astray when she agreed to meet him by the river though her parents forbade her to be courted by him. Her hesitancy wiped the hope from his face, so she straightened. "I would hear your poem." She tried to make her expression appear encouraging.

He did not reach into his pocket but dismounted and stepped toward her until she could feel his chest against her knees. He gazed up at her with his big, brown eyes and recited the words of his heart.

You burst into my life
Like a sunny morning
After weeks of rain.

Like dew
On the desert sand.
Elegant as a swan,
Delicate as a tulip,
Genteel as a lamb,
And I,
I who should have
Protected,
Nurtured,
Adored,
I left you wounded
And scared.
But I will not
Abandon you.
I will
From this moment forward,
Protect you as a swan,
Nurture you as a tulip,
Adore you as a lamb,
Allow you to be my sun and dew.

Her voice came out in a whisper. "Oh, Alexander."

"Dear Ellen." Moisture welled up in his eyes.

She watched him without a word, her feelings wadding up in her throat.

He wrapped her hand in his palms, and she slipped from her mount, closing the distance between them.

He gulped. "I love you. I love you more than anything, save for one thing only. The Law says, 'Now, O Israel, what does God ask of you? Only to fear God, to go in all His ways and to love Him, and to serve God with all your heart and with all your soul, to observe the commandments of God and His decrees.' I love and respect you, and I love and respect our God. I am ever remorseful that I let anything stand above those ultimate treasures of my heart, mind, body, and soul. Please forgive me, and if you can find it in your strength to do so, please marry me."

"Stop, Alexander. What a speech!" Her hand moved between them to her heart and clutched the fabric there.

She inclined her head toward him, and he moved his lips to hers eagerly. Too eagerly. She gave in to her feelings of longing for but a moment before she pressed back against her horse's warm side. All that had passed between them flooded into her mind. He would falter again. She felt how much he desired her, and it frightened her to the core.

His remorse must not be as deep as her own. "I do love you, Alexander, and I do not blame you any more than I blame myself. I only wonder if we are good for one another."

"We are." He wrapped his arms around her trembling body, linking his hands behind her, but she pushed against him, and he released her.

"I should go," she said.

He shook his head but offered his hand and helped her mount.

Silence surrounded them as if nature waited to breathe. Not a bird chirped nor a leaf rustled in the quiet of that moment. She stared into his eyes and felt the breadth of the difficulties between them, then kicked Counterpoint and turned him toward Darwen Park.

Tears streaked down her face and evaporated on the wind as she rode away. "Lord, I am not worthy of an answer, but I know not what to do."

When crying made it impossible to view the path ahead, she dismounted and was sick in the trees.

4

Ellen swooned and clutched her stomach. "I am sorry," she said to the maid, "but I need to sit a spell."

The maid, still holding Ellen's dress over one arm, helped her to the edge of the bed.

Ellen had been fighting some type of illness for several days now, as well as a nagging feeling that something may be amiss.

It could be this dreadful summer heat. Meals had simply not been as satisfying, and each one left her unsettled, but the nausea was somehow worse when her stomach was empty. She could hardly abide her corset and felt immense relief upon its removal each night, as if she could finally breathe again after a day of shallow inhales and exhales.

If she was honest with herself, she had to admit she had been eating a bit more than usual. That must be the cause of the restricting of her corset.

Perhaps a meal would do her good. "I am ready to dress now," she told the maid.

During breakfast, Ellen set down her fork and shifted her focus to those around her. "You look pale, William. I have not been feeling well myself. I wonder if we are afflicted with the same malady."

"I am well enough," he said, but his body betrayed him, and he coughed violently. He stood but, before leaving the room, doubled over with whooping coughs.

"William is getting sicker, Mama," Richard said.

"I fear he is quite ill." She pursed her lips. "His coughing has grown severe quickly, and, from the sound of it, I would wager the sickness is settling into his lungs."

Ellen had not realized how concerned everyone was about William. Ashamed at her own self-centeredness, she tried to console them. "I am sure he will be well again soon."

Mama nodded but pushed the pork around on her plate without eating another bite.

William spent the rest of the day reclining in the sitting room. Every time Ellen passed by, he reminded her of a barking dog. On one such occasion, Mama was exiting the room to refill his cup of ale. Upon seeing Ellen, she put on a brave face. "He will be better in the next couple days. He is a strong, healthy young man, not some street urchin." Mama sounded like she was trying to convince herself.

Ellen crossed the space to William's side. "We are all worried needlessly, are we not? Tell me this is a common cold."

He smiled but only answered with a series of coughs.

She placed her hand gently on his shoulder. "Shall I call on Mr. Neibaur?"

Since her abrupt departure from Beacon Fell, Mr. Neibaur had not attempted to call on her again. He was giving her the space her mind knew she needed. Her heart still belonged to him, but she felt humiliated every time she remembered their stolen evening together on the banks of the River Darwen.

"Is the illness in my teeth?" He opened his mouth wide for her to look, which prompted yet another fit of coughing.

Grateful she had not been any closer, she waited for him to

catch his breath. "Your wit seems unaffected." She nudged him. "As you know, Mr. Neibaur has some knowledge gained at the University of Berlin that may help. He is a doctor of sorts." She glanced at the pale sky through the open window. "He is quite smart, not to mention handsome and funny and..." She shook her head and returned her attention to William.

He cleared his throat hard and said in a raspy voice, "Do you love him?"

Ellen looked at the ceiling, not wanting him to see the distress on her face. She drew a breath and stilled her features, sensing his observant eyes upon her. "Very well, Will. I love him, but it is complicated."

"Is it?" He half-laughed, half-coughed. "I hope I am around to see you marry at St. John's."

Ellen rested her cheek in her hand. "What has you talking that way? If we are to marry, you must be there...or, well, I simply cannot marry without you." The half-circles under his eyes reminded her of storm-clouds, but she was determined to be strong for him no matter how concerned she became. "Anyway, I hope to marry at St. Laurence."

"All the same." He cleared the roughness from his throat, and his chest rattled. "I may get better. On the other hand, I may be the first to lie next to our dear brother Thomas at St. Andrews. Do you think Richard will be jealous if I am the first to see his twin again?" More whooping coughs racked through him, and he clutched his middle, closing his eyes.

Feeling ever the more disconcerted, she told Mama she would call on Mr. Neibaur that he might assess William's condition and advise them. She could not bear to stand idly by.

It was a testament to the severity of William's illness that Mama did not object. "Have one of the servants drive you, and take Richard along."

She located Richard in haste and filled him in on the task at hand.

A short while later, Ellen and Richard arrived in town and were shown in by Mr. Neibaur's servant. Through an arched opening, they saw Mr. Neibaur hovering over a man on the parlor settee. Mr. Neibaur's fingers pressed into the man's open mouth as he reached his other hand toward the assorted dental tools arranged in a soft leather case on the small table.

His eyes lifted as he fingered the instruments, and he caught sight of Ellen and Richard. He froze, causing a blush to heat Ellen's cheeks, but this was no time to play the flirt. She moved in his direction. "I apologize for showing up unannounced once again, and I see that you are occupied, but William is quite ill. He has had an increasing cough over the last several days, and we are growing concerned. We fear it may be the chincough. I wondered if you might come, and tell us what you think."

He turned back to his patient. "Of course," he said, bowing above the man. "Mr. Smalley was on his way out." Mr. Neibaur patted his patient's shoulder. "Try to keep the area clean of bits of food. The pain should subside over the next few days. You may find it more comfortable to eat soft foods until you feel better." With that, he directed the man out the front door.

She smirked. "Your patients always look as miserable as unsheared sheep on a summer's day."

"I suspect he is thinking that his toothache was less painful than his lack-of-tooth ache." He shrugged. "It will be better in time."

Richard laughed, and Ellen put her arm around his shoulders.

Mr. Neibaur glanced at her out of the corner of his eye. "Shall we go to Darwen Park and attend to your brother?"

"Yes," Ellen replied, although there was so much more to say. "Thank you." And sorry and a dozen other things.

"Shall I ready my horse?"

"That is not necessary. We would be honored to have you ride with us."

Outside, Alexander offered his hand to help her into the carriage, and she felt him run his thumb across her knuckle through her delicate glove as he lifted her up. She wished it did not send a shiver to her spine, reminding her of the dangerous charge between them.

Once the three were settled with Richard and Ellen on one side of the carriage facing Alexander, the journey home commenced. The ride was shortened in their haste, but the stress of the day must have exhausted Richard, whose head began to bob.

"The motion of the carriage has often put him to sleep ever since he was little. I do not know how he can be comfortable enough to rest," Ellen said, gingerly easing his head to her shoulder. "I feel as though I could be sick at any moment." She swallowed, hoping her nausea would settle.

Concern creased Mr. Neibaur's brow. "You do look pale. Shall we stop?" He scooted forward until she felt his knees bump hers.

"No. To be honest, I have not been well myself." She gulped the extra moisture in her mouth and felt a gag rise out of nowhere. "Blasted road." Her stomach heaved. "Perhaps we ought to stop, after all." She gagged again, waking Richard, and Mr. Neibaur sought the attention of the driver. Attempting to maintain her modesty, she leaned down and lifted a corner of her hem as the contents of her stomach found their way out of her mouth into a cupped piece of the bottom of her dress. Mr. Neibaur wiped a small bit from his sleeve with his handkerchief, folded it over, and handed it to her as the carriage came to an abrupt halt.

Ellen covered her mouth in shock.

Mr. Neibaur's eyes widened. "Are you going to be sick again?"

A laugh at the horror in his expression she was sure mirrored her own, burst from her lips despite the overwhelming stench and absurdity of the situation.

When she had cleaned herself as well as could be done in such circumstances, she allowed her eyes to meet Mr. Neibaur's. Mortified, but hoping to find a light in the darkness, she said, "I suppose we need not stop any longer."

He pulled out his pocket watch.

With the awkward turning into downright awful, he was surely anxious to make his escape from the carriage. "Sorry," she said.

"Do not apologize. If I was squeamish, I would not have gone to medical school." His smile eased her mortification a bit. "I only wonder if you are fit to continue this journey. Based on the time, I believe we are closer to your home than mine but only just."

She nodded, feeling weak, embarrassed, and ill. "What choice have I? Besides, William's condition is more important than my present discomfort." She shifted. "Sorry about the odor."

He waved it away. "Once again, you forget that I am a surgeon."

Richard snorted. "Unless surgeons do not have a sense of smell, that cannot make much of a difference."

Ellen bit her lip. "I am also sorry for abandoning you at Beacon Fell."

He swallowed visibly. "There are worse places to be abandoned." His serious tone did not match his light-hearted remark, nor did the yearning in his dark eyes, which reflected the orange light of the sunset.

Once at Darwen Park, after Ellen hastily changed her gown, they found William sleeping fitfully. A bout of coughing awoke him, and he caught sight of them looming over his makeshift sickbed on the chaise longue. Beth joined the little congregation there.

Alexander knelt beside William, feeling his head and limbs. While William coughed, he listened, worry drawing his heavy brows together. "He has a wan appearance, and, while his head is warm, his limbs are cold. Have someone mix a drink of hyssop with rue and honey. I will help administer it."

Beth ran off to speak with the cook.

"Ellen," Mr. Neibaur whispered as he rose and stepped to her, taking her hand. "I do not want to give hope where little can be found. He may recover, but you should steel yourself against a different outcome."

She savored his closeness and the intimacy of his hand in hers before slipping back to William's side. She fought back tears while she ran her fingers through his unkempt hair as Mr. Neibaur helped him sip his tincture.

Papa came in and helped William to his bedchamber. Ellen offered to stay with him through the night, but when Mr. Neibaur pointed out that she had not been feeling well either, Mama sent her directly to bed.

The following day and night were spent with the whole family fretting over William, and Ellen insisted on staying at his side at every possible moment.

By the third night, Ellen complied when James insisted she take a break from her watch and sleep in her bed, though she dreaded the prospect of being separated from William, knowing any breath may be his last.

Sometime during the blackness of night, whilst James sat watch, Ellen awoke to see a candle floating above the bed where she and Beth slept. She attempted to focus on the figure holding the candle and heard Mama's shuffling feet. "Ellen, Beth, my dear girls." She made a choking sound. "William is gone to be with God and Thomas." She tucked a loose strand of

Ellen's hair behind her ear, her fingers lingering briefly before she reached over Ellen and patted Beth's shoulder.

Ellen buried her head into her pillow, wrapping her arms around it, unready for her bubble of remaining hope to pop. Nausea pumped from her stomach to her pounding head. Would her illness not allow her a moment to grieve?

Perhaps she would be next.

"There is nothing to be done," Mama said. "I thought you would want to know right away, but go back to sleep, girls."

The welcome peace of sleep did not return.

A rising sun warmed the earth traitorously, without a care for the mourners dressed in black, keeping vigil by dear William's lifeless body day and night, each in their turn. The undertaker came to hang William's chamber with heavy, dark drapes, making it a blackened heart, no longer beating in the center of the Breakell home.

Tallow candles flickered in ghostly patterns in a room otherwise dark as a moonless midnight. Perhaps her own brother's ghost danced around with the flashes of candlelight.

Beth whispered, "Has there been any change?"

"No," said Ellen. "Hope is lost. His body is an empty shell whose occupant has moved on to a finer home. I have not the smallest hope at this point that he is only unconscious."

Beth nodded, clearly expecting this response. "Allow me a turn. Get some rest."

Ellen started to protest, but Beth continued. "You are not the only one who needs to say her goodbyes."

With a nod so subtle she doubted Beth noticed, Ellen headed back to her bedchamber. Every blessed memory with William swirled through her mind as she stood on the cliff's edge of sleep, neither falling into it, nor fully awakening. She remembered teasing him about Patience's sister, Charity. Now he would never have the chance to find love, marry, or have children. His light was snuffed out at the cusp of manhood.

Remembering his teasing about Mr. Neibaur only days ago ached. It seemed years somehow, far away and long ago.

Mr. Neibaur had been so kind and helpful that evening. She wondered if her parents had softened to him at all, but it had all come to naught either way.

Dear William was gone.

Mama and Papa entered her room, and she welcomed the diversion, sitting up and propping herself against her pillow.

"Can I be of service? What do you need?" Ellen asked.

Their answering gesture was to sit on her bed and encircle her in their arms. She feared the moment when her tears would start, knowing they would be as difficult to contain as the River Ribble.

When they left with scarcely a word, she felt nauseated and more alone than ever and bolted outside to deliver the contents of her stomach into the hedge.

THE FUNERAL WAS A MODEST AFFAIR. Mama had chosen to travel the short distance to St. Andrew's Church in Longton to bury William beside their brother, Thomas. The church was draped in darkness. In the front of the chapel rested a dreadful elm coffin enveloped in velvet so black, it sucked the light from everything around it. Inside, the body, dressed and washed, reposed on a sheet of white, too nearly matching the pallor of the bloodless face.

Thin beams of light streamed through the stained glass, contrasting with the general gloom and darkness surrounding them. At the center of the colorful windows stood the Resurrected Lord, risen above his own gray stone tomb draped with white linen.

Ellen could not believe the reality of her brother's death, yet here he rested, lifeless. Memories of another day flooded her mind, when a different minister led a service for one of her dear brothers in this same, heartbreaking spot years ago. Perhaps she might slip through the floor into nothingness.

Ellen supported her mother, walking her to the front where the Breakells sat together. "Do you truly believe in life after death?" Ellen asked her. "That Jesus lives and has raised William and Thomas?"

Tears filled Mama's eyes. "Yes, Ellen. I do."

"How can you be sure?"

"I feel it here," she said, pointing to her chest. Tipping her head and pointing to it, she added, "And it makes sense here."

Ellen grimaced.

"What?"

"I fear I will never see them again."

Mama squeezed Ellen's hand. "You will, darling. You will."

But Ellen knew that even if Heaven existed, she would not be welcome there. She had squandered all hope of happiness in a heap of hopelessness by the River Darwen. Her hands shook as she lifted her eyes back up to the depiction of Jesus, then lowered them in shame at her own grievous sin, a ball of grief roiling in her gut.

Why must there be funerals anyway? Ellen wished she could ride all alone and get lost far away somewhere instead of being surrounded by people in a stuffy church, but she feared she lacked the energy for such a ride.

Ellen spotted Patience across the room and lifted her hand in an unenthusiastic wave. Patience came and sat beside her, enclosing Ellen in her arms. "I am so sorry. We all loved the dear boy." Patience could not speak further, and tears began to spill out. Ellen's own tears did not come, for which she was grateful. She hoped William would understand if he was watching her. Would he feel unloved knowing her cheeks were dry?

Mr. Neibaur stood in the far corner in conversation with the vicar. He dipped his head in her direction, silently asking her what she wanted him to do, so she motioned for him to approach her. She did not attempt to rise to her feet but allowed him to take her hand when he stood before her and Patience and offered his condolences. He was the only one in the room who might have the smallest glimpse into the depth of her sorrows, knowing the loss of a family member would be permanent for a sinner such as her.

He looked into her eyes and swallowed, rubbing his thumb under her palm and holding her gaze.

Her hand tingled, both bringing her into the present and reminding her of the grave consequences of their actions. She tightened her fist around his hand to stop the tingling sensation which taunted her.

Dear William. She had given up her chance to ever be with him again. In the midst of comforting those she loved, there would be no comfort for her.

That night, beside Beth's shaking form, the well of Ellen's tears opened up. She cried, only ceasing long enough to slip to the floor and empty the contents of her slightly swollen stomach into the chamber pot. The bitter taste remained potent in her mouth as she curled up on the ground and held herself.

It felt like hours later when she sat up and stretched her back. Beth was asleep. Ellen clutched her middle, focusing on breathing in and out when a thought came uninvited into her mind.

How long had it been since her monthly sickness?

It could not be as long as it seemed.

5

The leaves of the wheatley elms were shining gold when Ellen met Mr. Neibaur near the Square one Sabbath afternoon after services. As she had been occupied with the busy drudgery of mourning, she had not seen him since the funeral.

She sat erect on the bench, stilling her shaking fingers, but it did little to quell her nerves when she motioned for Mr. Neibaur to join her.

"I am so pleased to see you," he said heartily, though his smile seemed hesitant. He took her hand. "You can scarcely imagine the relief I felt in receiving your message after all this time."

Ellen stared at their interlocked fingers. "I hope your sentiments remain unchanged at the end of our conversation." She bit her lip. "I need to tell you something." Her voice quavered.

He inched closer until she could feel his leg against hers through her floral morning gown. "Ja?"

"I am not sure how to speak to you of this particular something, which is just dreadful, yet a little bit wonderful. Mostly I feel we must be cursed to be dealt such a hand. I feel immense guilt to have to say it in the first place, but I also feel horrible for wishing it away." She released all the air from her chest until her head swam and focused on his tan face. "I fear you will not like what I am about to tell you."

He furrowed his brow and brought his face very close. "I haven't a clue of what you speak, but nothing you could say would change the way I feel about you."

Although she did not doubt his sincerity, he clearly did not know how completely she was about to shatter his world. She laughed without joy. "Do not be so sure."

Alexander cupped both hands around Ellen's cheeks and did not break her gaze.

She tilted her head forward until her forehead rested against his. "I have thought about this for some time."

He wrinkled his nose. "You do not wish to marry me." He sounded so depressingly certain.

A lump filled her throat, and it took all her strength to speak. "I do. I really do."

"Then," said Alexander with obvious relief, "we will deal with whatever it is together."

Ellen heard Alexander's words but could not believe them. "You still want me after all I have put you through?"

"With all my heart."

It was nice to hear, though it was still for naught. He could run away from this, return to his homeland or go anywhere else in the world, and she would be left alone. This was not a problem she could flee. It was within her and only her. A sob escaped as she stood. Thoughts burned in her mind, but she could not figure out how to move her tongue and lips to form the words she needed to speak.

Loving concern poured from his deep, dark eyes. "Ellen, talk to me."

"Let us walk. I am too agitated to be still."

He rose, offering his arm, and they ambled in silence along

the winding path beside the riverbank. When they reached Walton Bridge, Ellen released his arm and leaned over the rough wooden rail to watch the river roar beneath their feet. She longed to be swept into the current. Anything would be easier than this moment. In the distance, the Enterprise steamed downriver, headed to a distance thoroughly unknown to her.

Alexander waited patiently at her side, casting sidelong glances in her direction.

Ellen's gaze swept the area once more to be sure they were completely alone. Their nearest company, besides a small flock of ducks, were a couple fishermen, but they were far out of earshot. She watched the ducks while her mind and stomach settled, then tried to speak.

Time would not heal this wound.

"I am with child."

Surprise and understanding lit in his eyes. His jaw slackened, and his mouth hung open. "I..." he began, but nothing followed.

"I know," she said, analyzing his face.

He placed his hand gently atop hers on the rail, then withdrew. "I need a moment. I must think about this. And pray." He crossed to the far end of the bridge, glancing over his shoulder before disappearing into the trees beyond.

Wind whipped a loose, dark curl into her face, and she brushed it away, along with a stray tear. What did he mean by leaving her here? She waited, no longer focusing on anything in her view, her mind empty and numb.

The descending sun glowed yellow in a magenta sky, and still Alexander did not return. She shivered, whether from the cool evening breeze floating atop the water or from fear, she could not tell.

Why did life take everything? Thomas, William, Mr. Neibaur.

Thomas, William, *Alexander.*

Dear Thomas, dear William, *dear Alex.*

But staying here alone was neither pleasant nor safe in the growing cold and darkness, so she determined to follow him across the bridge and into the trees. "Mr. Neibaur," she called.

A gust of wind answered, swaying through the elms.

Doubt and loneliness ached in her bosom as she rubbed at the front of her neck. "Alexander?" she called again.

Had he left her? She deserved to be left alone, husbandless, and with a child to care for. What did she expect to happen? A sob burst into her throat, and she collapsed to the ground from the force of it.

She was ruined. Nobody would want her now. Nobody would look after her or the child. The baby would be an urchin.

If only it would disappear. The thought tore through her, and she squeezed her eyes closed against the pain. She scooted toward the nearest tree trunk and steadied herself against it. How could she wish harm to a child? Unlike her, it had done no wrong.

She screamed out into the engulfing forest. "Alexander!"

He emerged from the forest, lifted her up, and crushed her against him. "Are you well? No. You are not. I should never have left you." He wrinkled his eyes, pulled his hand-kerchief from his pocket and tenderly wiped the tears from her cheeks.

Her head shook without her telling it to. "I thought you left me. You should. You still can. I do not wish to tie you down like a boat at the dock. You do not have to take part in my ruin." Her stomach heaved, and she curled into him. "You left. I was alone."

He tucked her head into his hand and pulled it to his shoulder. "Shhh. I have been thinking, Ellen. Thinking and praying. I could never abandon you now, nor did I ever wish to be parted from you." He held her away, still holding her arms, and his eyes darted to her middle and back up to her face. "Are you certain there will be a child?"

She nodded. "I scarcely believed it myself, but there have been signs I must not, as a lady, discuss."

"I am a surgeon, remember?" He grinned and pulled her into his shoulder once more. "We should marry soon. Will you have me? After all we have been through, Ellen Breakell, will you be my wife?" He rubbed the back of her head and neck.

A relief she had barely hoped for, cleansed her from head to foot. "If you will have me." The corners of her lips curved into a pained smile, blinking back tears and feeling her lashes brush against his neck. "If you will have us, then yes."

"Only one yes this time?"

Ellen blinked her tear-clouded eyes. "Yes, yes, yes."

He raised his hands and tilted his head one way and the other. "Three yeses is not a thousand, but I will take what I can get. Shall we pay the ten shillings or wait for the banns and marry in three weeks time?"

"I believe we have waited far too long as it is."

With a grunt, Alexander agreed. He lifted her up and twirled her before setting her down gently. "Sorry," he said, patting her stomach.

"Yes, well, we better not spin anymore if you do not like to see a lady get sick."

"Sorry again. Have you been very ill? Oh." He raised a finger. "The carriage."

A genuine laugh burst forth, surprising her. "I have become well-acquainted with the flora around Darwen Park, as well as a couple other places between here and there."

He grimaced. "I am sorry."

She shoved him playfully. "Stop apologizing. Proposing marriage is a much more pleasant occupation." She bathed in the delight of being with a man who cared enough to save her. The very man she loved most dearly in all the world.

"I may have to spend my life apologizing. Sorry."

"You are to blame, I suppose."

Alexander opened his mouth and closed it again.

She placed a gloved finger to his lips. "One innocent little kiss to celebrate our most recent engagement is probably in order." She closed her eyes and puckered her lips, waiting for him to oblige, which he did with great tenderness. His soft lips moved with hers, even as the bristles of his beard tickled her chin.

"I love you," he said as his lips brushed her cheek.

"And I love you, Alex."

They separated, grasping hands and emerging from the shelter of the trees, where Alexander again came to a halt.

Her eyebrows shot up. "Have you changed your mind already?"

He shook his head. "I only dread telling your parents."

"As do I."

"What if they refuse me?"

She kissed his cheek. "Then you shall have to steal me away to Scotland."

His eyes opened wide, but then resolution filled them, and he nodded once.

"Mama?" Ellen called when they entered her home at Darwen Park. "Papa?"

Mama's footsteps clipped toward them, stopping the moment she laid eyes on Alexander and Ellen standing arm in arm. Her brows knit together. "Mr. Breakell!" she called shrilly.

Mr. Breakell, however, was the last person in the family to make an appearance, after James, Beth, and Richard. Even the maid peeked around the corner.

Alexander had questions in his eyes, but there was no

turning back, and Ellen would not make a different choice even
if another path presented itself. She nodded her encouragement.

Alexander cleared his throat. "Mr. Breakell, may I speak
with you privately?"

Mama's eyes narrowed at him, but Papa nodded, directing
him toward his study.

Placing hands on hips, Mama said, "What is this about,
Ellen?"

Ellen squared her shoulders. "He is asking for my hand,
Mama," she said when the men closed the door.

Beth's smile took over her face, and she embraced Ellen. "I
am so happy for you. It is what you want, is it not?"

Ellen's cheeks warmed. "It is."

Beth embraced her again. "What wonderful news."

James patted her on the shoulder and nodded as Richard
threw his arms tightly around her waist. When Richard tipped his
head up, his eyes were wet. Ellen pushed the hair out of his face
and kissed his forehead. "Trust me. It is for the best," she told him.

Mama folded her arms across her chest. "Run along, everyone. I need to speak with Ellen."

Beth squeezed Ellen's hand once more before vacating the
entryway with James and Richard.

Ellen wrapped her arm around her mother's shoulders, and
they moved to the pair of floral chairs in the sitting room.

Mama pursed her lips. "I will not allow you to throw your
life away with this man. I know you can find a more advantageous match."

"At three and twenty I have already met every eligible
gentleman in Preston. Besides, no one more suitable would
have me."

Mama reached out to one of Ellen's curls and wrapped it
around her finger. "How can you say that with your beauty?

And what of your family? Do you not care to help your siblings by making a smart match? I do not believe your Mr. Neibaur even owns a carriage."

A giggle forced its way from Ellen's lips before she could stop it. Of all the ridiculous things to worry about. "He is an educated gentleman, as well as the son and grandson of educated gentlemen. He went to University and desires to do something truly valuable with his life. And he wants me at his side." One side of Ellen's mouth curved up. "With or without a carriage."

Mama shook her head, refusing to listen. "That only brings up my other major objection to the man, which I have spoken of repeatedly. Your different cultures will not be a blessing to you. Marriage is difficult enough without coming from opposite parts of the world. He grew up a Jew in Prussia, whatever he claims to be now. He could not be as civilized as an English gentleman. Do these things not matter despite all I have taught you?"

"No." Ellen rose from her seat, but a wave of nausea coursed through her, and she was obliged to sit back down. "I will marry him. If you knew what had passed between us, you would understand." She swallowed her spittle and covered her mouth.

Mama narrowed her eyes. "Are you well?"

Ellen tilted her head to one side and raised her eyebrows as if daring her mother to guess what Ellen would not speak.

The study door creaked as it swung open, and the men emerged.

Mama and Ellen rose before their seats and waited breathlessly.

Papa pressed his lips together and gave Ellen the briefest nod. It seemed that he had given permission.

Mama noted the exchange and redoubled her protests.

"Say not a word, Mrs. Breakell. Mr. Neibaur must wed our Ellen."

Mama appeared confused. "But..."

Papa raised his hand and looked pointedly at her. "Mrs. Breakell. They MUST marry."

Mama gasped as realization hit, and her eyes grew round as saucers while she fell backward into her chair. She turned from Papa to Ellen to Alexander and back to Ellen before she lowered her forehead into the palm of her hand and groaned.

6

Sunlight beamed through the parted curtains and shone directly on Ellen's closed eyelids, which shot open as her mind recollected the occurrences of the previous evening. She rolled to her side and cradled the almost imperceptible roundness of her stomach in both arms. Today would be a flurry of preparation. She scarcely believed the time had arrived when she and Alexander could openly prepare to wed.

Beth shifted in the bed beside her and awoke to Ellen's contented gaze upon her. They both grinned.

With a yawn, Beth said, "How can I help today?"

"First, we shall send letters to our older siblings to persuade them to join us at Darwen Park. I daresay Margaret will be the least pleased as she has not yet found a match of her own, but I think she will come along with John and Mary and Alice and her husband, Will, nonetheless. I must also tell Patience. Perhaps Patience will be able to accompany us to the dressmaker on Church Street this afternoon to ascertain whether a dress can be made special for the event."

"You make it difficult since you are hurrying the process,

not even allowing time to read the banns. Must it all happen in such haste?"

Ellen nodded against her pillow. "I shall miss having you as my bedmate."

Beth tightened her lips and pulled the quilt up to her chin. "Do not speak so. This is a time for joy."

Ellen snorted. "Mama would not agree."

"You must not blame her for her hopes, especially since you were fine with her ambitions for you until Mr. Neibaur, with his curly beard and crisp German accent, strolled into St. John's Minster."

"You will have to fulfill all her hopes and dreams instead."

After dressing, the girls joined the others at the breakfast table. Papa was reading, and Mama was fussing about James's rushed appearance. To an outsider, the meal may have appeared ordinary, but to Ellen, the very air weighed as heavily as an English fog. Mama avoided her gaze, and Papa stared at his book without ever turning a page.

Richard sulked and cut his hot cakes to bits. "Why are you in such a hurry to leave us, Ellen?"

Her shoulders sagged, knowing she could not discuss the reason nor ease his disappointment. "I will not be far."

Richard, stuck in the space between a small child and a young man, was too old to whine or cry, but the loss of William continued to make separation that much harder for all of them. "Alice and John are not far, either, but we do not see them often. When you are married, you will not come to breakfast with us."

James patted his shoulder. "At least you will not be the *only* child left for a few years hence."

Papa set down his book, stared at the wall, then rose to leave without looking upon anyone. Before sweeping out the door, he addressed himself to Mama. "I shall be in my study. Let me know if you require anything from me."

Mama did not lift her eyes from her fork when she

responded. "I will make certain the church is available for a wedding in one week on Tuesday morning."

"Thank you. Beth and I are hoping to take the carriage into town today."

Mama nodded, focused on her plate.

A rush of exhaustion and nausea spread through Ellen. "Very well."

Later, when the sun and the damp air competed for intensity, Ellen and Beth called on Patience, who, despite the lack of forewarning, was delighted to join them on their outings.

As the carriage turned onto Church Street, Beth leaned close to Patience, pretending to be in her confidence. "Ellen needs a bit of cheering up."

"Oh?" Patience said. "Are you nervous to wed? Have we a blushing bride?" she teased.

Ellen's cheeks grew hot at the description, though not for the reason her companions may have guessed.

They stopped in front of the dressmaker's, and Beth shook her head. "I was referring to Ellen's confrontations with our mother, who is less than pleased with Ellen's choice."

"Ah," Patience said. "We knew she would not support the notion."

Ellen laughed. "That is putting it lightly."

"Then why does she allow the match at all?"

Beth and Patience waited for an explanation, but Ellen shrugged. "Perhaps she does not loathe him as we suspected."

The girls eyed her suspiciously as the carriage stopped, and the door opened. Ellen gratefully stumbled out, and the girls trailed her into the shop.

Miss Mary, a stylish red-headed woman in her mid-thirties, greeted them. "How can I help you today, ladies?"

Patience and Beth turned to Ellen, waiting for her to speak. "Miss Mary, I am preparing to be married."

Miss Mary clapped her hands. "You are in need of a dress?

Do you require anything else for your trousseau? A bridal handkerchief, perhaps?"

"Just a dress, which I fear is more than enough, and some ribbons for the wedding party, please." Ellen scrunched her cheeks up to her eyes in apology. "We are planning the ceremony for Tuesday."

Miss Mary nodded slowly. "One week? Hmm. Well, if you choose from my current stock of fabrics and lace, I should be able to put something together in time. Mind you, it will not be fancy enough for Queen Adelaide, but it will be elegant in its simplicity."

Ellen placed a hand over her heart. "I would be ever grateful."

"It is my honor to make a dress for such a beautiful bride." She smiled warmly.

The girls fawned over the silks and intricate lace much longer than necessary until all of the decisions had been made.

Patience elbowed Ellen. "I think you *will* be a blushing bride when Mr. Neibaur sets his sights on you."

Ellen set a hand to her middle without thought.

Miss Mary approached them with a tape measure. "May I?" she asked.

Apprehension churned in Ellen, but she arose. Would the seamstress notice growth in Ellen's stomach, and in combination with the speedy wedding, guess what was concealed there? Miss Mary started by measuring the distance from one shoulder to another and from the nape of her neck to her heels. A bead of sweat trickled down her spine when Miss Mary wrapped her arms around Ellen's waist with the tape measure. Ellen stared at the ceiling until Miss Mary stepped back, humming as she walked away.

Ellen sighed. The sooner she married Mr. Neibaur, the better. With her hidden secret literally growing larger by the day, she needed to move past reproof.

"Thank you, Miss Mary." Ellen dipped her head in gratitude when they had completed their task. The ladies exited the shop. "I find I am not anxious to return to Darwen Park just yet. I would so enjoy sitting a spell with the two of you. Shall I buy you each a treat from the pastry-cook's for putting up with me today?"

Beth laughed. "You have not been difficult, but I am happy to pretend you were if it means I get one of those strawberry jam tarts."

"Have you tried the apricot ices?" Patience asked with a giggle. "Dear me."

Ellen linked arms with them and stepped in the direction of the pastry-cook's. "I may have to try one then. Miss Mary will have to let out my seams."

"Will you also be ordering a wedding cake?" Patience asked.

"We shall have one made at home."

The pastry shop was quaint and orderly, with a large table that filled most of the space in front of the cook-stove. An assortment of ladles and pots and pans lined the walls above the short shelves full of treats. Ellen ordered a small array of desserts, including tarts and ices. As she pulled the coins from her reticule, she said, "Where shall we have our small impromptu picnic?"

Patience and Beth glanced at one another, and Beth said, "Let us sit on the obelisk steps," so they headed to the Square with their goods.

"It seems we are not the only ones enjoying the temperate weather," Ellen said as they found a space to sit, and Ellen began to divvy up the treats.

Patience opened her mouth and took a generous bite of tart. Her eyes widened, causing Beth and Ellen to laugh. She held up a finger, signaling that she needed to speak once she finished chewing.

Ellen took a small bite of some orange cream while she

waited. The cool sweetness swept over her tongue, and she sighed.

Patience swallowed at last and lifted her chin to point at something. "Over there. Mr. Neibaur is speaking to my husband."

Ellen's head whipped around, and she found them immediately in the crowd. She wondered if Alexander sensed her gaze when he turned and locked eyes with her. Warmth spread through her cheeks as the crowds disappeared from view. His lips still moved as he spoke to the gentleman beside him, but he did not break his gaze with Ellen as he bowed to Mr. Walker, who waved to the ladies and headed in the opposite direction.

Beth and Patience giggled as Alexander approached them. He swept off his hat and ducked his head. The women rose to greet him, and Ellen smoothed her floral printed dress, grateful she had chosen a favorite for her errands. Patience reached up and brushed a crumb from Beth's chin.

Alexander's smile overtook his face. "Ladies. What a pleasure to see you. What brings you into town?"

"Secret wedding business," Beth said with a wink.

Alexander bowed with his characteristic smile. "Then I shall not ask." He leaned toward Ellen and whispered. "You are not doing more than you can handle, ja?" He directed a pointed glance at her stomach.

She did her best to hide the surprise from her face. If Alexander thought he was being subtle, he had a few things to learn.

Patience's smile did not reach her eyes. "Congratulations, Mr. Neibaur."

Did Ellen detect a hint of underlying suspicion in her tone?

Patience continued, "I only wonder what took so long." She tilted her head, as if daring them to respond.

But Alexander seemed oblivious to her unspoken inquiry. His jovial eyes danced along with his bearded lips. "As do I."

Ellen turned to Patience and Beth. "Please excuse us." She threaded her arm through Alexander's and tugged him around to the other side of the obelisk.

"Have I done wrong?" he asked, his eyes reminding her of a puppy asking for a scrap.

Her anger deflated. "Somehow, Patience and all of my sisters are still ignorant of my present situation, and I would prefer to keep it that way."

"Did I not speak softly?"

She patted his arm. "Not as softly as I would have liked, and do not look at my stomach."

"Did I?" He smiled. "I apologize. I find it difficult not to." His eyes darted down again.

She waved it away. "I suppose they will all know anyway when a baby comes all too quickly after the wedding."

"Nobody will count the days." He shuffled his feet, then stepped back in the direction of Patience and Ellen, who had seated themselves and were enjoying more taste testing.

"Wait," Ellen said, pulling him to a halt.

"Ja?"

"I only wondered what business you had with Mr. Walker."

His eyes grew excited, but he only said, "Like him, you will find me peculiar if I tell you."

"Now I am all the more intrigued." She waited. "Do tell."

His gaze was measured, and he rubbed his beard. "Very well. No more secrets." He grinned in a way that reminded her of the secret they shared. "I did not have business with the gentleman, but, while we spoke, I told him I was highly distracted by a dream I had last night."

"A dream?"

He nodded. "There was an angel dressed in white. It descended from the clouds until it came to stand before me." As if to demonstrate, Alexander's hands reached up and lowered. "The angel carried a golden book and told me it was a new Bible. I turned the pages, but I could not read the words."

Ellen blinked. "Save the angel, that is how books always are for me."

He chuckled, but his eyes brimmed with intensity. "We will have to do something about that."

"Perhaps," she said. "Grown women rarely work to become educated."

"This book—the one from my dream—was different. The words were like no words I have ever seen, and I was wrought with an intense desire to read them, but the scene disappeared, and I awoke."

"Peculiar, indeed." She surveyed the crowd and lifted her shoulders. "Dreams often are. I am not sure why you felt the need to speak to Mr. Walker about it."

He followed her lead toward Beth and Patience. "It is all I can think of today."

Ellen halted, her expression one of disbelief. "*All* you can think of?"

A roaring laugh burst from him. "I exaggerate. Our impending wedding is at the forefront, my love, I assure you."

Satisfaction permeated her, and she pulled him to keep moving.

"These dreams are not unusual for me."

She tugged him along. "Then why is this one so distressing?"

He swallowed. "It is difficult to explain, but these dreams feel special somehow, and they buzz around endlessly in my mind like a fly on a horse."

ON THE MORNING of the wedding, Ellen was grateful that styles had grown increasingly full and more concealing over the last few years. Miss Mary had outdone herself. Pale golden silk glimmered where early morning candlelight reflected upon it. Round, gathered sleeves were topped with bows at the ends of her almost-bare shoulders. A wide matching band wrapped around below her rib cage, and the dress cascaded down to her matching shoes, which were her favorite part of the ensemble. Her hair was pulled tightly back except for the ringlets the maid was putting the finishing touches on.

Something fluttered in her stomach, and her fingers went there instinctively.

"Are you well, Miss?"

Ellen blinked rapidly. "Indeed. Thank you." Another flutter. She bit back a smile.

The round lump of her belly hid under her dress like a pirate's stolen treasure. Would it be a Mr. Neibaur or a little Miss Neibaur? Was she prepared to be a wife and mother? Ready or not, she would be one all too soon.

With perfectly coiffed hair, she was swaying side to side in front of her small mirror when Mama stepped in. "You are an idyllic bride, dear, but we always knew you would be." Mama came up behind her, placing her hands on both of Ellen's shoulders.

Ellen half-smiled, meeting her eyes in the looking glass. "I am sorry to disappoint you."

She lifted her shoulders and let them fall. "Mothers always want what is best for their daughters. I would still try to persuade you to a more advantageous marriage if your father had not forbidden me to do so."

Ellen turned toward her mother, took her hand and placed it on her stomach. "Your first grandchild, Mama."

Pain registered on Mama's face. "If, unlike your first two nephews, it survives."

Ellen blanched at the unfeeling tone to the statement, but Mama's eyes went out of focus, staring at nothing before returning her attention to the bride. She swallowed hard. "I hope it takes after its mother."

A chuckle burst from Ellen's throat. "In stubbornness?"

"And beauty." With both hands on Ellen's stomach, Mama gently kissed Ellen's forehead.

Beth, Alice, and Margaret burst into the room. Mama whipped her hands from Ellen's middle, a look of guilt on her face.

Beth's hand flew to her mouth as Margaret raised a brow and said, "No wonder you are allowing her to marry the Hebrew. I cannot say I did not have my suspicions."

Alice and Beth stared at Ellen.

They all knew her secret now; she was no innocent, blushing bride. She was much more prepared for the marriage bed than she ought to be.

Deep sadness laced Mama's smile as she stepped toward Ellen's sisters. "Seldom do I have all my girls under my own roof anymore. Let us put such talk behind us and treasure up this day, shall we?"

The girls nodded, apparently still too stunned to utter a syllable, and followed her into the hall, but none of the girls could keep their appalled, accusatory eyes from her for long.

A short time later, when the wedding party had all received their favors of ribbons, and flowers had been pinned to their shoulders, they took their journey to St. Laurence in Chorley where Ellen had chosen to marry.

At the parish church, Ellen was filled with gratitude and anticipation as her focus flitted across the faces of her dearest friends and relations. Patience and Mr. Walker were present, of course. Ellen recalled talking to William about this very day and keenly felt his absence. Alexander, likewise, would be missing his family, to say nothing of his customs.

She discovered him seated at the front of the chapel, holding his top hat in his lap and kneading its brim in his hands. He rose and caught sight of her, his hands stopping in place. Everything save their love for one another fell away. Almost everything. They had made a grave mistake that could not be reversed, but they would do what they could to make restitution.

For the first time in months, her heart soared with the dream of good things to come.

Preston, England 1837

E llen scrubbed the mud from the stone porch of her town house where she lived with Alexander and their little ones. It was the first morning in a week that dawned clear, and the dirt was as thick as a riverbank. Many of the neighbors were about the same task of whitewashing.

Abigale Lewis, who was always anxious to share the latest gossip to a willing pair of ears, called out to Ellen, her orange hair flouncing with each word. "Have you heard about the two American preachers who came to Preston?"

"No," Ellen said, working at a tough bit of caked mud. If only she still had servants to do her cleaning. While Alexander's work paid for a maid of all work, there was too much for one young person to do.

"They are over at the Cockpit."

Ellen pictured the old building a block away, next to St. John's Minster. It was one of the largest public buildings in which a crowd could gather. How much space could a couple of American ministers require?

Abigale strolled over. "It is a strange thing of which they speak. They claim an angel brought them a golden Bible."

Ellen squinted against the sunlight, wondering why that idea sounded familiar, but then shook the thought free. "All the more reason to pay them no attention."

Abigale pouted. "I suppose."

Alexander's face popped through the open window. "What was that you said?"

Abigale, apparently thrilled to have a more willing audience, repeated her news. "I was talking about the odd preachings of the new American ministers at the Cockpit. They claim an angel of God brought them a gold Bible." She covered a laugh with her daintily gloved fingers.

Wide-eyed, Alexander threw his hands into the air. "I must find them. Are they in the Cockpit now?"

Abigale's brows shot up. "I know not."

Ellen stretched her back and placed her fists on her hips. What good could come from this? "You cannot be serious, Alex. You want to waste time listening to such nonsense?"

Alexander's head disappeared behind the curtains, and Ellen wrung out her rag over the edge of the rail, glad he had abandoned the notion. She was avoiding Abigale's curious stare when the front door swung open, and Alexander stepped out in his hat and coat. He lifted Ellen off her feet, then clasped her dirty hands, bringing his face close to hers, his boyish excitement leaving her breathless. "They may have the answer to my strange dreams! I must speak with them."

"Go, then." Her tone mirrored the doubts in her mind. How could American preachers know anything about his fantastic dreams?

Alexander practically skipped down the cobblestone street, his coat tails flapping behind him, into the cool morning. The amused faces of several neighbors followed him.

Satisfied that her porch was spotless, she straightened up,

holding her stomach. She returned into the house where she poured tepid water from the pitcher into a washbasin in the kitchen. She scrubbed the dirt from her hands and wondered about the strange things Alexander would hear. Surely he would realize that the preachers were telling fairy stories and come directly home.

Dreams had plagued Alexander long before she met him. Whether simply the illusions of night or heavenly visions, she could not be certain. In his early youth, he had had dreams that, according to him, felt different than the normal imaginings of the sleeping mind. Though they permeated his thoughts, he could not make sense of them. He would awake, agitated and sleepless.

Only a week ago, she had awakened in the middle of the night to find him observing her. In the darkness, she could make out the whites of his eyes.

"What is it?" she had said with a yawn.

He chuckled. "Just a dream. Sleep, dear."

But her mind had cleared somewhat, and she nestled into his arms, tucking her head under his chin. "Tell me."

"The angel with the golden book came back, and then he was replaced by a beautiful, new building on a distant hill. I ran toward it, knowing I needed to be inside. For hours, I tried to get to the building, but it seemed to be moving away from me."

"Strange." She shifted to a more comfortable position, feeling more concern at his restlessness than the unusual content of the dream. Were not all dreams a bit odd?

He stroked her hair. "When I at last entered the building on the hill, it was exploding with light."

"Hmm."

A few slow breaths later, she was asleep again in his arms.

She later suspected he had stayed awake for the better part of the night. When morning had come, he had a faraway look in his eyes.

Was it possible that the preachers from America had been given a golden Bible by an angel as he had envisioned? She shook the thought from her head. No. Alexander would come home disappointed. Dreams did not predict the future.

And their future was already decided by their past. She feared that nothing, not even a new religion with golden scriptures and heavenly messengers, could make her enough and cover her sins.

Little footsteps on the wooden floor planks pattered above her. "Good morning," she called to Joseph and Maggie, making her way to the bottom of the stairs to wait for them. Joseph came bounding down, and she gave him a big morning squeeze while Margaret slid backwards down the wooden staircase with surprising speed and agility, joining in on the morning ritual of an embrace. Ellen cuddled them until they pulled away, and Maggie rubbed Ellen's nose with her pointer finger. "Pet bunny. Pet bunny."

Ellen grinned and replied in kind by petting Maggie's nose. "Your hair is a rat's nest, Mags." She placed her on the floor and went in search of a comb.

While Ellen pulled at the snarls in Maggie's wispy hair, Joseph sat cross-legged beside her. "Where is Abba?"

"He is speaking with some ministers at the Cockpit, but he will be home soon, I should think. Perhaps we can peek in on him and see how he fares. After breakfast, shall we go out for a walk?"

"Watt," said Maggie, unable to pronounce her k's.

Joseph nodded, twiddling the stick he had saved in his pocket the day previous.

"We shall, then."

Later, Ellen stepped out onto the perfectly clean porch, pleased by the sparkling townhouses under the sunlit sky. She carried Maggie on her hip and held Joseph's pudgy hand as she directed the little party toward the old Cockpit.

The short distance might have been miles for the slow progress they made, but, when they arrived at length, she was surprised to find it relatively full of people in conversation, despite being able to hold several hundred people. The circular platform where cockfighting used to take place was topped with a pulpit, and right at the center of the crowd, Alexander, arms waving, stood speaking with a group of gentlemen.

When his head moved in her general direction, she waved, but his gaze returned to the men without seeing her.

Joseph tugged her hand in his father's direction.

Ellen imagined threading through the crowd with her little ones. "On second thought, we will see him when he comes home," she told Joseph, still clutching his hand, and leading him back into the sunshine.

They traversed the short distance to Saint John's along Church Street. The small graveyard there reminded her of her mother and brothers who were buried at the simpler chapel in Longton.

"What is the matter, Mama?" asked Joseph, perceptive and eager to help.

"I was only thinking of Grandmother Breakell, who adored you, as well as of the uncles you will never meet."

"Like Uncle Richard does?"

"Yes." She sighed. "And all of your other aunts and uncles, too."

"Even Abba's family?"

"I am sure your father's family would love you, too, but since they live all the way in Prussia, you are unlikely to ever know them. I am certain your Grandfather would be proud to meet the little man named after him." She squeezed his hand. He would likely be taller than his father one day, and, though he was named for Alexander's father, he looked English, with light blue eyes and freckles. He was a perfect little English gentleman. Margaret, on the other hand, had a darker complexion, although her light eyes matched Joseph's.

"Why am I named for someone I do not know?" Joseph said.

"Well, your father loves him. Besides, it is common practice to name the first son after his paternal grandfather."

"What is paternal?"

"So full of questions," she said. "It means on your father's side."

Maggie was walking, so they progressed at the pace of a snail through the bustling street, past the public-house and town shops.

"Shall we stop into the Weavers' Cottage and say hello to Uncle John and his family?"

"Yes, Mama," said Joseph, sounding grown up.

"Yeth. Yeth," agreed Maggie.

Ellen adored that lisp. She rubbed her thumbs on their soft hands and breathed in the moment. She smiled to herself, thinking about the third child that would soon join their growing family. Nothing new would ever make her what she needed to be.

But her family? They were all she needed right now. Was that not enough for Alexander?

While Joseph knocked on the front door of John's two story cottage, Ellen raised her eyes to the row of windows along the roofline. Nobody answered, so Ellen led the children around the side to the stairs and up to the shop where they found John and Mary working the large wooden loom.

Mary spotted them first and immediately ceased her work. John turned to see why Mary stopped, and both of them came over and embraced the children.

"What are you doing out today?" John asked Maggie as he lifted her onto his hip.

"Looking for Abba."

John turned his attention to Ellen. "Is he missing?"

"No." Ellen laughed. "Of course not."

Joseph said, "We saw him, but he did not see us. He was talking to the Americans."

John slowly lowered Maggie to the ground. "Americans?"

Ellen lifted her shoulders. "Just some street preachers he heard about. He is probably at home by now."

Mary shook her head. "I heard tell of these American preachers. Some people in town are quite displeased with the things they are teaching."

"Oh?" said Ellen.

John nodded. "Many are talking about their strange messages. I think we would all do well to steer clear of them."

Ellen smiled. "I am sure we will."

ELLEN and the children were hanging their hats when Alexander danced through the door. His face shone with excitement, and words spilled from his mouth in a blurred waterfall of sounds. Although Ellen understood him better than anyone despite his strong German accent, when he spoke with this much speed and enthusiasm, it could still be a challenge.

She smirked at him and placed a hand on his chest. "Slow down, Alexander."

He took a deep breath and started over, holding up a tan leather-bound book. "It is called The Book of Mormon, and it is more precious even than gold."

Maggie peeked around the folds of Ellen's dress, giggling.

Alexander hugged the book to his chest with both hands and rested his chin on the top of it. "The American preachers spoke of a man named Joseph Smith, a prophet like Moses. He saw God the Father and Jesus Christ, two separate glorious beings." He held up two fingers to emphasize his point. "Later, an angel came to him and gave him a book of golden plates. He translated them and published them as this book. An angel with a book, Ellen, precisely like my dream."

A wave of nausea boiled in her gut. "Find something else to do," she told the children before taking a seat on the settee in the parlor.

Alexander followed suit, sitting beside her.

Ellen swallowed her nausea. "How can you believe such wild stories?"

He lifted his brows as if he could not comprehend her lack of interest. "I feel it. The God of Abraham, Moses, and Jacob sent this blessed book to me. To us!"

Ellen was speechless.

After a moment's silence, he stood. "I will be in my study if you need me."

W hen it was time for dinner, Ellen and the children waited at the table for Alexander to join them. It was so unlike him to be late to a meal. His trusty pocket watch was as dear to him as Ellen herself. She grinned. Maybe not quite that dear, but he loved it, nonetheless, and he never failed to be punctual. She glanced at their maid for an explanation. "Where is Mr. Neibaur?"

Louise did not have an answer but went in search of one. A few moments later, she returned. "Mr. Neibaur will not be joining you this evening."

"Not joining us? Whatever do you mean?"

"He did not explain, Mrs. Neibaur. He only waved me away." She demonstrated the shooing motion with one hand.

Ellen glanced at the children before addressing Louise once more. "How peculiar. Did he appear ill?"

"No, ma'am."

"What *is* he doing then?"

"Reading, ma'am."

Ellen pursed her lips. "Very well. We shall eat without him if that is his desire."

Maggie started to cry.

"What is it, Maggie?"

"Abba," she sobbed.

Ellen stifled a frustrated groan. "You father is only in his office, Maggie."

After the meal, Ellen left Joseph and Maggie with Louisa and went to talk to Alexander. She rapped on the door, and after a short delay, he called her in.

Sitting at his desk, he was practically folded over the book. He waved her over but did not look up.

She placed her hands on his shoulders. "You missed dinner," she said. "You never miss dinner."

"Ja. I was not hungry."

She snorted. "You are always hungry, Alex."

He tore his gaze from the pages and smiled at her briefly. Holding his hand in his place a quarter of the way through the book, he flipped back to the beginning with his other hand. "Look at this." He shook his head in amazement and pointed to the page, as if to make sense of what he was witnessing. "Let me read it to you. Right here on the title page, it says, 'written to the Lamanites, which are a remnant of the House of Israel, and also to Jew and Gentile.' That is me and you." He motioned to the both of them. "And then down here, it says, 'to shew unto the remnant of the House of Israel how great things the Lord hath done for their fathers,' and He has, Ellen. I have been reading these miraculous stories." He ran a hand through his hair. "And here, 'that they may know the covenants of the Lord, that they are not cast off forever, and also to the convincing of the Jew and Gentile that Jesus is the Christ.' Can you believe it?"

Ellen's eyebrows knit together. "No. I cannot," she said simply. "Can you?"

"The Lord is telling us we are not cast off!" When she did not reciprocate his excitement, he flipped back to his place and continued reading silently.

"A book, written by a stranger on the other side of the world, cannot possibly tell us something so personal and, quite frankly, impossible as to the status of the salvation of our souls."

Alexander, focusing on the book, only grunted.

"Shall I have Louisa bring a tray to your office?"

"Hmm?"

"Never mind."

Ellen was not sure if Alexander had come to bed at all that night. In the morning, she found him in the same place and attitude as the previous evening. "I am really quite concerned. What vice has taken hold of you that you can neither eat nor sleep?"

"Do not worry yourself. All is well. Better than that. God is speaking to me through this book." He raised it above his head and lowered it again, then opened it and stared.

"Nonetheless, you must eat."

"This book tells me to feast on the words of Christ. That is what I am doing. Feasting!"

"Do you know how mad you sound?"

He did not respond before she stalked from the room.

For three days, Alexander scarcely emerged from his office, rarely touching the food brought to him. If he came out for a minute, he paced in a circle, holding the book up close to his face before returning to his study in silence.

At long last, he came out and shut the door behind him. Joseph and Maggie ran into his arms, and he scooped them both up.

Joseph leaned his head onto his father's shoulder. "Did you finish your book, Abba?"

"I did, but I am sorely tempted to start again right away."

Ellen dashed over. "We will not hear of it. Will we, children? You have not spoken to us for days."

"Very well," he said with a weak smile. "I do find that hunger and exhaustion are catching up with me. What shall a famished man eat around here?" He still had both Joseph and Maggie on his hips, and he started to nibble at their necks, ears, and noses.

"Not us, Abba. Not us!" squealed Joseph, but he was difficult to understand between giggles.

The following day, Alexander led his family to the Cockpit to meet the preachers and listen to their speeches. Ellen was again surprised to see the immense number of town parishioners attending the meeting. Alexander pointed out the five she had seen on the platform earlier in the week. "Those are the Americans: Heber Kimball, Willard Richards, Orson Hyde, Isaac Russell, and Joseph Fielding. Well, Mr. Russell is from England originally, so he is not American. The God of Abraham has brought them from a place called Kirtland, Ohio, through a prophet by the name of Smith. They are good men. You will see."

The Neibaur family located seats as near to the circular platform as they could. Mr. Russell waved and smiled at Alexander, who tipped his hat and glowed in return. Mr. Russell was a handsome, dark-haired man with a clean-shaven face, except a small patch of hair below his mouth.

It took some time before the crowd of hundreds settled. At length, Heber Kimball arose and took the pulpit. He had a strong nose and dark sideburns that extended down to his jaw bone. "I am not an eloquent man," he said. "When the Prophet Joseph Smith told me the Lord wanted me to serve a mission across the Atlantic, opening the door of salvation to this great nation, I was overwhelmed. What could I contribute, being the son of a blacksmith and so lacking in schooling as I was? But the Lord gave me strength to leave my family and travel here to a land famed throughout Christendom for learning, knowledge, and piety.

"When we landed in Liverpool and discussed where to go from there, the Lord directed us to Preston."

Alexander smiled at Ellen, his feet bouncing.

Mr. Kimball said, "I have also left the Kirtland temple to preach to you. Last year, the stately structure was completed, and I was present when it was dedicated. We sang 'The Spirit of God'. The Apostle Simon Peter appeared at the dedication on the twenty-seventh day of March, 1836 to accept the offering of the Lord's house."

Alexander took Ellen's arm and shook it gently, though his eyes remained glued to the speaker. "Do you hear what he is saying?"

She nodded, wary. "I am listening, Alex."

"One week later," Mr. Kimball said, "one thousand people gathered in the temple for another service. After a morning session, Brother Joseph and Oliver Cowdery received a series of heavenly visitors. These visitors were the ancient prophets: Moses, Elias, and Elijah."

Alexander, who was holding Ellen's hand, squeezed her fingers and scooted forward in his seat.

"Moses gave Brother Joseph power for the gathering of Israel from the four corners of the Earth. Elias gave him the keys to the Abrahamic Covenant for a great posterity. Elijah gave him the power to bind families together in the worlds to come."

Alexander crushed her hand until she yanked it from his grip, watching his intensely interested expression. What did he find so enthralling? Were Alexander and Ellen not beyond saving?

At the conclusion of Mr. Kimball's discourse, Alexander reached for her hand again, but with a measure of gentility, and led her to speak with the missionaries, trailed by the little ones. He introduced her, his features beaming with pride. "This is my estimable wife, Mrs. Ellen Neibaur, and our two children."

"How do you do?" they said, bowing and tipping their hats to her.

She returned their greeting. "How do you do?"

Seeing a line forming, all but one of the men excused themselves and dispersed to answer questions. Isaac Russell remained with them.

"Mr. Russell," Alexander began.

Mr. Russell placed a hand on Alexander's shoulder. "Call me Brother Isaac," he said, grinning.

"Very well, Brother Isaac." Alexander shrugged. "I cannot contain my excitement at hearing the message about the dedication of the American temple." His face shone with joy as he shook his hands in the air. "Do you know—does Brother Joseph know—the Jews have long foretold that Moses and Elijah would come together at the end of times to make way for the coming of the Messiah? As Christians, we believe the Messiah has already come once, as you know, but the appearance of the ancient prophets is a sign of the second coming of our Lord. This means the time is at hand."

Ellen tried to keep up with Alexander's explanations, but his culture was a world apart from hers. Time had helped bridge the gap, but there were moments like now, when it was difficult to fathom the differences in their upbringing.

Alexander balled up his hands. "Furthermore, you will not believe this, ja?" He paused and glanced at Ellen for encouragement.

She smiled, and he continued. "You stated that April the third of last year was the date of their appearance, correct?"

"I believe that is correct, sir," answered Mr. Russell, clearly amused by Alexander's eagerness.

"That was Passover season," said Alexander, throwing his hands up.

Each face in the group stared at Alexander blankly.

"Do you know about Passover?" Alexander asked.

Mr. Russell shook his head, but Ellen nodded. "You know I do, dear."

Alexander placed his palm on Ellen's shoulder. "Do you remember that we open a door for Elijah to dine with us at the Passover table? That we pour a glass of wine for him, full to the brim? And last year, our son, Joseph, opened the door as part of the ritual to see if Elijah would come in."

Ellen squinted as she began to make the connection. "Yes, I remember."

Alexander emphasized each of his words with his hands. "At the very time when my people celebrated Passover and watched for Elijah, he was appearing at the House of the Lord in America to his new Prophet." He brought his palms to his head, rubbed them down his cheeks, then shook his hands in front of him. "Since accepting Jesus Christ, I have seen many parallels between the Law of the Jews and the life of the Savior. This parallel, though, may be my favorite one. Is it not remarkable?"

She nodded. "It does sound too remarkable to be a mere coincidence."

Alexander shook Mr. Russell's hand with vigor. "I would like very much to talk to Mr. Joseph Smith." Alexander's eyes lit up again. "There is more." He touched Ellen's arm. "This is a second witness that these people have brought God's truth to us."

"What is?"

His face was exultant. "They have a temple. It is the beautiful building from my dreams. First the angel with the book and now the House of the Lord." Turning to Brother Isaac, he said abruptly, "We want to be baptized."

Ellen whipped her head to him, her jaw hanging open. "What are you talking about? We have already been baptized."

He nodded. "Ja, but we need to be baptized in *this* church. This is right, Ellen."

Mr. Russell appeared as dumbfounded as Ellen felt. "Mr. Neibaur, I am pleased by your abundant faith. Baptism is an important step, nay, an essential step, but I advise you to give it more time and thought before making this commitment."

"Why?" Alexander stepped back with a frown. "Many are being baptized. Is that not what you came to England to do? To baptize? I saw The Book of Mormon and the Holy Temple in my dreams and know they are from God. I want to start anew like Alma." His eyes flicked to Ellen, full of hope.

"Indeed," Mr. Russell said, shuffling his feet. He met Ellen's eyes and seemed to find camaraderie there. "I am not sure you and your family are ready."

"You are wrong. Follow me to the River Ribble, and dunk me now."

Mr. Russell chortled.

"I do not speak in jest, sir," Alexander said, seemingly affronted. "I wish to be baptized at your earliest convenience."

"I know, Mr. Neibaur. Nobody could doubt your sincerity." Mr. Russell clasped Alexander's shoulder. "All in good time. We shall bring you and your family to the River Ribble." Mr. Russell faced Ellen. "The first nine members in England were baptized there a few short months ago. That day will stand as one of the great days in the history of the Church. Quite a crowd came out to watch, some estimate there were as many as seven thousand. Did you hear of it?"

Alexander and Ellen both shook their heads. "It sounds wonderful," Alexander mumbled, his head hanging slightly down.

Ellen shook the gentleman's hand. "Thank you for your counsel to give this more time and consideration. I appreciate it."

Alexander scowled at her but then laughed with the rest.

"All in good time," Mr. Russell said. "All in good time."

As was the custom in the Neibaur home, Alexander read and discussed the Bible in the evenings following dinner. The children usually fidgeted, but it was a pleasant daily ritual. Ellen enjoyed listening while she took up the mending and sewing. Sometimes Alexander got so involved in what he was saying, it was as if he was having a heated discussion with himself. She wondered if he missed his family and homeland, his culture and schooling, more than he let on. Were his people all as vivacious as he?

"Tonight," he began, "I shall read from the new book given to me by the Americans and bestowed upon them by an angel."

Ellen nodded her encouragement, wanting to understand what had taken hold in his heart and mind.

As he read, he stumbled through the pronunciation of many of the names and some of the curious words. She mused that he probably made them sound too German or Hebrew or like one of the several other languages he knew.

"'Wherefore it came to pass, that my father Lehi, as he went forth, prayed unto the Lord, yea, even with all his heart, in behalf of his people. And it came to pass, as he prayed unto the Lord, there came a pillar of fire and dwelt upon a rock before him; and he saw and heard much; and because of the things which he saw and heard, he did quake and tremble exceedingly.' Holding the book open with one hand, he raised his head.

"Did you hear that part, Joseph? Who else did the God of Abraham, Isaac, and Jacob visit like a fire?"

"In the other Bible, Abba?" Joseph asked.

"Ja."

Joseph stood straighter. "Do you mean Moses? In the burning bush?"

"Ja," he exclaimed with a punch to the air. "Does this Lehi not remind you of Moses, Ellen?"

She nodded. "There are similarities, to be sure. Do you think Mr. Smith copied the Bible?"

Alexander shook his head vigorously. "They are completely different stories, but they fit together so well, like a hand in a glove." He winked. "Like you and me."

She felt a blush rise but was pleased. "Really, Alex."

OVER THE NEXT FEW MONTHS, Ellen's stomach grew once again. Alexander read to them from the Book of Mormon each evening. From the moment he laid eyes on that book, he had embraced it like a sailor to a lifeline. She enjoyed listening to him. It was a nice story, but it was not the same Bible her nanny had taught her. She still did not understand Alexander's obsession with everything the Americans taught, nor his desire to be baptized. For some reason, though the ministers had baptized over one hundred English parishioners since she met them, they hesitated to baptize Alexander. Could she be the reason they were holding him off?

Alexander needed to be sensible, though, and think of the family. They had already been baptized in the Church of England. Their children had been christened there. She put her hand to her round belly. Before long, their third would be christened. It would take place at Saint John's as the first two had. Was one church different from another?

And did any of it matter when she was irreparably damaged?

9

E llen bundled up the children for the Breakell family Christmas gathering. She tried to bend toward them to help with shoes and coats, but her protruding middle blocked the way, so she squatted. When that position strained her hips, she called to Alexander, who, after checking the time on his pocket watch, plopped onto the floor to be of assistance.

He was dusted in white powder from preparing the Challah loaves for the Sabbath. Ellen brushed some flour from his cheekbone and kissed him. With more force, she smacked flour from his coat sleeve. "Time to be less Jewish and a bit more Christian, dear."

During the bumpy carriage ride, Ellen dozed off on Alexander's shoulder. Sleeping at night did not come easily during this part of expectancy, yet somehow the stiff bench lulled her to dreamland, and, in what seemed an instant, they arrived at Darwen Park shortly following the families of her siblings.

The house was brimming with Breakells, but those who were missing were not forgotten. John and Mary had three children, and Will and Alice had Alice's little namesake, Alice; both mother and daughter had been named for Mama Breakell, who was laid to rest. Margaret was yet unmarried. Dear Beth and her husband, John, also had a little girl.

Maggie and Joseph were delighted to play with cousins. Their uncles, James and Richard, chased them through the house to explosive giggles and intermittent spurts of tears while the adults gathered in the sitting room.

Beth took a place beside Ellen in the floral chairs by the window. "How are you? What news from town?"

Alexander answered the question from across the room. "Tell her the exciting news." When Ellen cocked her head but did not respond, he continued, "We have been learning about a new religion, restored in America. They have given us new scripture!"

Tension sucked the air from the room, and Ellen swallowed hard. After all Alexander had been through in leaving the religion of his parents, surely he knew to proceed with more caution than this. The eyes of everyone in the room bored into her, waiting to hear her confirmation or rebuttal of what her husband had revealed.

Alexander started again. "They also have a..."

"Stop," Papa interrupted from his seat, holding his hand up toward Alexander and staring at Ellen. "Tell me he is not talking about the Mormons."

Ellen cradled her stomach, and her grimace must have given away the truth.

"I cannot believe you would listen to such nonsense." His eyes were like stones.

Alexander tried to speak again, but Papa silenced him with a glare, and Alexander stepped over to the fireplace, rubbing his mouth and beard.

Beth put an arm around Ellen's shoulders, sharing her strength, and Ellen answered. "He is referring to the Mormons,

Papa. The Book of Mormon is a nice book, and the ministers are kind gentlemen."

Alexander moved back to the center of the room. "The Book of Mormon is more than a nice book. It is the word of God, handed to a Prophet by an angel."

Papa huffed. "Oh! I have heard of them and their supposed prophet."

Ellen shook her head and watched her gloved fingers rub together.

"Blasphemy," Papa murmured. "Stay away from them and their lies."

"We cannot." Alexander, who would not drop the subject for which he had such an abundance of passion, said, "Let me explain. We were led to the Mormon ministers through a..."

Maggie and young Alice burst into the sitting room squealing ahead of Richard, who glanced around while he caught his breath. "Sorry to interrupt."

Alexander finished his sentence. "Through a series of powerful dreams."

John broke in. "Ellen, you told me you would not get involved with the Mormons and their strange teachings." His wife nodded in agreement. "It is dangerous."

"Forgive me," Ellen said. "I did not think we would at the time."

Beth rose abruptly. "Let us gather the family around the pianoforte for some carols."

Grateful, Ellen followed her lead, feigning more interest than she felt. She collected Alexander, urging him to drop the subject of religion, then helped round up the children.

When all were present, they sang "Oranges and Lemons", "The First Nowell", and "God Rest Ye Merry Gentlemen". Ellen played the lively tunes her mother had taught her while the others sang. Alexander gradually gave into his joy of singing, and his rich tenor voice rang out beautifully. When the children grew restless again, Richard taught them to play a game of Hunt the Slipper, which, of course, ended in tickles.

Ellen played the familiar tunes, reminiscing about Christmases with her mother and William, wondering what they would think about the teachings of the Americans, until Alexander made a show of checking his pocket watch and pointing toward the entryway with his head, hinting he was ready to head home.

After two more carols and long squeezing hugs with each of her family members, as well as a kiss—or two—from each of her nieces and nephews, she was willing to depart. She and Alexander came to her father last. The men shook hands but their faces remained impassive.

"Papa," Ellen said in pleading tones. "Perhaps if you joined us at the Cockpit tomorrow for the Christmas Conference, you would discover that there is nothing to be concerned about. Will you bring the boys and join us?"

Mr. Breakell's face grew harder still. "No, Ellen. We will not be joining the Mormons for one of their meetings."

James shook his head, warning Ellen against speaking any further on the matter.

Ellen nodded and smiled sadly. "Happy Christmas."

ALEXANDER'S EYES were alight as he waved an arm, indicating the crowd at the Old Cockpit. "I would guess there are three hundred in here from all over. We have branches in Walkerford, Alston, Bedford, Eccleston, Wrightington, Penwortham..."

"We?" She was unsurprised but still unsettled as she looked around at the Saints. Many appeared quite poor, and she wondered what she was doing in such company and whether it would not be more prudent for her little family to be with the rest of the Breakells at the traditional Christmas service at St. John's Minster.

Alexander greeted every person who caught his eye with an animated wave, and Ellen dipped her head politely, keeping a firm grasp on Joseph and Maggie.

They found seats near the center of the cavernous building. Though it was an impressive turnout and a testament to the success of the ministers, the old cock fights that used to take place here had audiences double the size.

After Mr. Kimball spoke, another man arose—a stranger with a light complexion and a friendly face. Moving to the pulpit, he said he felt moved upon by the Holy Ghost to speak. "Bereshit bara Elohim et hashamayim ve et ha arets..."

What was this?

Alexander stood up, as if entranced.

"What are you doing?" Ellen mumbled, yanking on his sleeve, but he pulled away from her and shuffled past the occupied seats to the aisle. He walked to the center platform and stopped directly in front of the speaker, who continued to speak unintelligibly.

Although Ellen did not understand what was being said, a curious joy burned within her chest. Others around her seemed to be feeling the same, the Spirit manifesting itself in various ways in their expressions. Still others looked confused, even disgusted.

As the speaker finished, a bearded, rough-looking man near the back of the crowd stood. "What was that rubbish?"

Alexander stepped to the pulpit. He raised his hands high above his head, and the crowd quieted. "Friends, my name is Alexander Neibaur. As you hear in my voice, I am not an English speaker by birth. I was raised learning many languages from my father, who served as a linguist and surgeon for Napoleon Bonaparte, but the two languages I know best are German and Hebrew."

Murmurs filled the room. He waited for a hush before continuing. "It has been a few years since I heard my beloved Hebrew spoken from a mouth other than my own. Naturally, it filled me with joy at the hearing and lifted me from my seat in praise."

Ellen placed a hand on her chest.

"Mama," Maggie said, but Ellen swatted the air to hush her. "Just a moment. Listen to your father."

"I testify to you that this man was not speaking gibberish, but the beautiful opening of the Torah, which you know as the Old Testament, along with some insights. I will translate, not as a gift of the Spirit, but as a natural-born Jew."

The light-complexioned speaker next to him seemed astonished. "I have never heard Hebrew in my life, let alone spoken it."

Alexander clapped him on the back. "Well, sir. You just did. You just did." Alexander proceeded to translate the man's teachings, telling the story of the creation of the world.

Later that evening, Ellen set aside her mending and cuddled beside Alexander while he read excerpts from the Book of Mormon. Her mind whirled around the events of the morning, so when Alexander stopped reading and flipped to another part of the book, she placed her hand on it to stop him. "I would like to ask you a question."

"Go on."

"What is the purpose of speaking in a language unknown to anyone in a crowded room?"

He pressed his lips together with his fingers. "But it was not unknown to all. I translated for him."

"But hundreds there did not understand until you did."

He nodded. "Did the Holy Spirit testify to you as he spoke?"

A corner of her mouth turned up. "I believe it did." Her smile grew.

"There is your purpose. To testify. In the Book of Alma," he said, flipping pages again, "it tells us, 'Behold a type was raised up in the wilderness, that whosoever would look upon it might live. And many did look and live.'" He turned to Joseph. "What story is this?"

"The children of Israel and the fiery flying serpents!"

"Right." He shifted back to Ellen. "The gift of tongues points us to the Messiah. Many in attendance today will not look any further. The teachings, prophesies, and gifts of the Spirit will be like the raised serpentine staff to which they do not raise their eyes. He sends us the signs to follow but does not force us to look.

"On this next page, Alma teaches, 'I would that ye would come forth and harden not your hearts any longer; for behold, now is the time, and the day of your salvation.'" Moisture welled up in his eyes, and he whispered so only she could hear. "We can still be saved, Ellen."

The words tickled her ear. She had given up on salvation long ago, but she could appreciate the moment. She whispered back, "I love you, and there is nothing more attractive than watching you teach my babies."

The children scooted closer to them on the wooden floor planks.

"Then my training to be a rabbi was worthwhile after all." He lifted his brows.

"What is Abba saying, Mama?" asked Maggie.

Ellen shook her head.

In a voice loud enough for the children to hear, Alexander said, "Please seek to know as I do, that this book is true."

She leaned into him, wondering whether the truthfulness of the book even mattered to sinners.

A fortnight later, Ellen awoke in a small puddle of moisture. Pangs of pain shot through her torso in time with great claps of thunder from above. Alexander was not in bed. With considerable difficulty, she rolled over like a carriage wheel in mud, and, using her elbows for leverage, sat upright.

Wind howled outside her frosted window, whistling through the imperceptible gaps in the house. She was thankful, once again, that Alexander's work kept them so well-situated in comparison to many. It would be a bitterly cold morning for most of the community.

She dressed in clean clothes and hobbled down the stairs. Halfway down, she clutched her belly, breathing heavily. When the pain subsided, she searched for Alexander. As usual, he was at his desk, surrounded by books and medical tools.

"Good morning," he said without glancing up.

She stepped behind him, pressing her fingers into his shoulders. His eyes rolled back, and his shoulders relaxed. She kneaded his neck with her hands, until her stomach tightened into a ball again. Her fingers stopped, and she doubled forward.

Alexander pulled her arms around him, kissing her fingertips before placing her hands back on his shoulder, silently asking for more with a waggle of his eyebrows.

When the contraction passed, she said, "I am afraid that will have to be enough for today." She sighed dramatically. "You need to call for the midwives."

It took a moment for comprehension to blossom on his face before he jumped up and embraced her, with her stomach protruding to one side. "Sorry. Did I hug you too hard? What do you need? I should be rubbing your shoulders!" He laughed and offered his elbow, directing her to the lavender sofa with its dark mahogany trim, knowing it was a favorite perch.

"Actually, will you help me back to bed?"

"Of course." He happily shuffled his feet in the other direction with her in tow.

"And will you take the children to Darwen Park as soon as they wake?'

"But I cannot leave you alone."

Putting one hand to her cheek, she said, "Call for the midwives first. Only what of this storm? Will it be safe to take the children out in the carriage?"

"I am more concerned about facing your father than the storm. Will the children be welcome there?"

"Of course. Papa and Margaret would never take their prejudices out on the little ones. Besides, the servants love Joseph and Maggie as they loved me. They shall be well cared for."

Though he appeared unconvinced, he said, "Shall I stay with you while the baby is born?"

"As I tell you every time, it would not be proper."

"I may know something from University that could be of use."

"No, Alex. The midwives know what they are about."

"As a matter of fact," he pressed his lips to one side, "I have been doing some reading."

"Oh?"

"I fear you will not like what I have to say."

"Uh-oh," Ellen said, both in response to Alexander and the tightening sensation she felt.

Alexander supported her the rest of the way to the bed and helped her climb in.

When Ellen's stomach softened a touch, she said, "What did you wish to speak to me about?"

"I know we have talked about it before, but the research shows it is best."

She let out a huff. "Alexander, I am not full of patience today."

"Ja. I wish you would reconsider breastfeeding and not use a wet nurse with this one."

Ellen sighed, but it turned into a groan of pain. "You want me to be an animal." She breathed heavily in and out. "And feed the child myself. Why? Joseph and Maggie did just fine with wet nurses."

He knelt beside the bed, placing his hands on her arm and meeting her gaze. "This is important to me. It is unnatural to send babies away. They are healthier with their parents."

Ellen stared at the ceiling, trying to picture such a thing. "What of the women who nurse because they need work?"

His eyes pleaded with her. "That is important, but I feel more responsibility regarding our babies."

"I do not know the first thing about it."

"Will you try? I can teach you."

"What do you know about it?" she snorted.

"My mother did it. And I have read about it." He lifted his shoulders. "Would it hurt so much to try?"

"It very well might." Ellen bit her bottom lip. "But I will try."

Alexander's face was exultant. "Thank you! You will not regret it."

She chuckled. "Do not be so sure. I already do."

Another tightening took her breath away as Joseph and Maggie came bounding into her bedchamber.

Joseph narrowed his eyes. "What is it?"

She breathed in and out and tried to maintain a normal tone. "Thank you for asking, my little gentleman. Your grandfather and Aunt Margaret want you for a visit. Abba will take you over in the carriage after breakfast." She stopped and held her breath before finishing. "You may be there for some time."

Their eyes lit up at the mention of a trip to Grandpa's, and Ellen hid her grimace from their view. Alexander caught her strained expression, and directed the children downstairs. They would be in the excellent care of the Breakells and their servants, and it would be good for their health to spend time at the country house. She only wished Mama could be there, too, to put Ellen's mind at ease.

It felt like hours of increasing pain before Miss Amelia and Miss Edith Davies arrived to care for her, after sweeping in from the swirling storm. She relaxed, grateful she was no longer alone. Childbirth was no afternoon at Beacon Fell, and it certainly did not come without its risks to both mother and child. The two Miss Davies helped her dress down to her undershirt, shirt waist, petticoat, and stockings and cleaned her abdomen, thighs, and other parts thoroughly.

They plaited her hair, lest it become entangled like a chaffinch nest, and rolled up an extra sheet, tying it to her bedpost. "When the time comes," Miss Amelia said, "you will pull on this sheet, like so."

Ellen stuck out her bottom lip. "You will recall that I have done this more than once before. And more than you at that."

"But we have performed as midwives a few dozen times." She smirked. "And a few reminders never hurt. Women forget what to do between children."

Ellen wrinkled her nose but quickly forgot the quarrel as

the pain intensified. She grabbed the sheet and strained against it, wailing through gritted teeth. "It hurts."

"Yes," answered Miss Edith. "It is meant to. The Good Book tells us, 'I will greatly multiply thy sorrow and thy conception. In sorrow thou shalt bring forth children, and thy desire shall be to thy husband, and he shall rule over thee.' Not to feel pain would be a sacrilege."

Ellen felt the urge to strike little Miss Edith, but the pain doubled, and she squealed instead, silencing the midwife midspeech. Ellen screamed again for good measure when it appeared Edith might resume her lecture, and the latter shut her mouth, pursing her lips.

It was Miss Amelia who reprimanded her next. "Really, Mrs. Neibaur, do you want all of the Old Cock Yard to hear you?"

Tempted to yell in the affirmative, she ground her teeth together and grunted in reply.

The pains grew closer and closer until she hardly had a breath's space between them. "Is it time yet?"

"Relax, Mrs. Neibaur. All is well. You are progressing, but you still have some time to go."

A knock sounded at the front door, and Ellen listened as the maid answered.

"Who would come at such a time as this?" Miss Amelia asked.

"I am not expecting anyone—besides the baby. It is," she stopped to catch her breath before speaking again, "likely one of the street urchins." She clenched her teeth and shut her eyes. "Surely they can leave me in peace today of all days."

Miss Edith crossed the small window. "For some, I fear waiting one day for a mouthful of bread is too long. They will not see another sunset with earthly eyes."

"Do not worry about the urchin. Mr. Neibaur is more than generous."

Miss Edith walked back to the bed. "But he is not present, so the child will go away hungry."

"That is not my greatest concern right now," Ellen said forcefully.

Miss Edith frowned at her.

"What do you want me to do about it?" Ellen said.

"It may help if you walk around anyway."

"You want me to go downstairs and help the urchin. Now?"

Miss Edith shrugged and lifted her shoulders. "It couldn't hurt."

"Why does everyone keep saying that? It surely will hurt." Ellen rose from the bed, and the midwives came to her sides to support her, but she waved them away. "If I am going to do this, I shall do it myself."

The ladies smiled and nodded at each other in triumph.

The maid was closing the door when Ellen called, "Wait, Louisa. Is it a child in search of food, even in this weather?"

Louisa dipped her head. "It is. A little waif of a girl."

"Let us find something to give her." Ellen moved painstakingly down the steps. "Call her back, and have her sit beside the fire while I find a morsel of bread and cheese."

The urchin was happily eating at the table with Louisa when Ellen returned to her bedchamber. Her pain continued to increase for the next few hours while the storm grew increasingly raucous. "Is something wrong?" she asked. "Should it not be quicker and easier by the third time?"

"Often it is, but sometimes it is not."

"Is something wrong when it is not?"

Edith shook her head. "Not necessarily."

Ellen breathed in and out, her exhaustion growing, and at long last, the two midwives said it was time to push the baby out. Ellen gave every last ounce of strength to the task and felt a rush of exultation as the baby was born.

Amelia cheered. "A boy. He is small, but his coloring is perfect."

Tears filled Ellen's eyes in relief as they handed her the little boy. "Isaac," she crooned. "Hello, little gentleman. I am so pleased to see you."

Miss Amelia admonished, "I know you like to be doing things, Mrs. Neibaur, but you must not. Take advantage of your confinement. Leave your other children at Darwen Park as long as you can. And do not descend the stairs for at least a week."

Ellen lifted her brows. "I know the routine. Thank you."

"I am telling you, I do not want you to move a muscle for a few hours, at least. Take care of yourself and baby, and let Louisa take care of you, you hear?"

Ellen smiled weakly. "Yes, Miss Davies. Thank you. I will do my best to obey." After they had cleaned and changed Ellen, they left and sent Alexander, who had recently returned from Darwen Park, in.

"Isaac, meet your abba."

Alexander raised the tiny bundle, cradled in both hands, toward his face. "Hello, little Neibaur. Welcome to the family." His eyes brimmed with love, and she felt she might float away into the clouds if she was not so blasted tired.

"Have you tried to feed him yet?" Alexander asked, not breaking his gaze from the baby's face.

"He was only just born."

"That is the best time to start," Alexander told her as he handed Isaac back.

"This might be a little awkward for the both of us," she told the baby, "but I promised your abba I would try."

"Nothing could be more natural, Ellen."

She exposed her breast and lifted the baby to her nipple. His tiny mouth moved over the tip of it, feeling it in his mouth. Ellen pulled him away. "I do not think we are ready." She covered herself back up and lifted Isaac to her face, so she could sniff him.

Alexander laughed and came in for a whiff. "Do not you worry. I am certain he will tell you when he is ready."

Ellen leaned her head back against the headboard and dozed until Isaac fussed some time later. "Are you hungry, little one?" She sighed and brought the angel to her breast, leaning her cheek to his fuzzy head and breathing in his sweetness.

Isaac latched on to her nipple, but pain shot through her, and she pulled him off. "Ow," she said. "No wonder mothers do not like to do this."

Isaac fussed louder, and she tried again. This time, he shifted his mouth further onto her breast, and, when he sucked, she felt a type of pressure but no pain. Half an hour later, they were both asleep again.

By Ellen's second week of confinement, she felt more than ready to leave her bedchamber. Carefully, she descended the stairs with little Isaac tucked against her neck.

Alexander came running, appearing anxious. "Are you well enough to come down? I am so glad to see you about," he said, coming to support her by the elbow for the final two steps. She leaned into him gratefully.

"Where do you want to go? The sofa?"

She nodded. "Do you think it is time to send for the children? I miss them so. They, on the other hand, are probably enjoying their time away from the hustle and bustle of town."

"If you are up to it, I will send for them at once. I guarantee they ask for their mama multiple times each day."

"And their abba," Ellen added.

Alexander took the baby, while she sat and arranged herself comfortably.

~

WHEN ELLEN WAS WELL ENOUGH, they recommenced their evening readings of the Bible and Book of Mormon and later attended the Latter-day Saint meetings at the Cockpit.

Temperatures warmed a little, and, as they walked to the first meeting in April, they admired the cuckoo flowers and forget-me-nots blooming along Church Street. Sunshine and crisp spring air renewed Ellen's spirit and filled her with awe. A chill breeze blew, and, seeing that it left little Isaac breathless, she bundled him in tighter. "He thinks he cannot breathe when a gust of wind hits his face."

Alexander held the hands of Joseph and Maggie, who seemed so grown up compared to the baby. They loved to help their mama. Sometimes their help was not at all helpful, but it was always endearing, such as when she asked Maggie to get clothes for Isaac, and Maggie grabbed a dirty sock of Alexander's instead.

At the meeting, another General Conference was announced in one week's time, after which the ministers would return to Kirtland, Ohio. Elder Willard Richards had returned from Bedford where he had established two new branches of the Church. Elder Hyde addressed the audience with such spiritual power that tears cascaded down Ellen's cheeks. Elder Hyde was so overcome himself, he clapped for joy. An equally compelling speech by Elder Kimball followed.

Alexander bent toward Ellen. "With you growing stronger and the weather improving, next week would be a good time to be baptized. It may, in fact, be our last opportunity for some time." His eyes were full to overflowing with hope and pleading.

"I will consider it. I promise."

Before climbing into bed that night, she knelt on the wood floor, and, desperate for an answer, she prayed. "Dear God, Thou knowest Alexander is determined to be baptized by the Latter-day Saint ministers. He wholeheartedly believes their words and book. While I find the Book of Mormon to be a nice story, I am not sure if it is sent from Thee.

"I have long believed that Alexander and I have been too sinful to be saved, so a baptism seems fruitless. Today, however, Thy Holy Spirit touched my soul as the brethren spoke, and, for the first time, I felt a spark of desire to enter the waters of baptism. Please confirm that this is the correct choice for our family. While hundreds have joined this American church, I fear what it may mean for our future, with opposition mounting alongside membership. I especially fear what it may do to my relationships with my family. Please place our footsteps, Lord. In Jesus' precious name, Amen."

She did not climb into bed immediately. She paused, listening, until Baby Isaac started to squirm. Still, she kept the prayer in her heart as she nursed him.

While she slept, she dreamed the blue sky was covered with small white clouds, which drifted together until they formed a giant circle and gradually transformed into a man's face—the face of Willard Richards. She gazed upon it for some time before each cloud dropped to the earth as snow.

Filled with warmth, Ellen awoke slowly, savoring the details of the dream. God had sent Brother Willard and the other ministers from America to find her. Her heart burst with joy, verifying her thoughts, and her understanding of Alexander's convictions grew. If God desired her to be baptized enough to send her a dream like unto the many dreams of her husband, maybe there was a glimmer of hope for her after all.

She tapped his shoulder, and, when that did little, she shook him awake. With tears in her eyes, she said, louder than necessary, "I want to be baptized."

ALEXANDER CHECKED his pocket watch again as they walked into the Cockpit the following Sunday. Several hundred people had gathered to hear the ministers, knowing their departure was imminent. A majority of those attracted to the gospel were the poorest of the poor, and there were plenty of those around after the preceding months of intense winter.

During the meeting, the brethren invited the children to come to the center platform to be blessed. Alexander walked Joseph and Maggie down for blessings from the Elders. They were promised health, prosperity, and strength in Christ the Lord. Ellen observed through grateful tears. She squeezed the children when they returned to their seats. "It reminds me of the Book of Mormon, when Jesus calls the children to Him one by one and blesses them."

As in the story, they felt surrounded by angels, and the Spirit of the Lord flooded the room.

Because the missionaries were preparing to leave, a new Presidency of the British Mission was established with Elder Joseph Fielding as president and Willard Richards and William Clayton as counselors. All, including Willard Richards himself, seemed surprised he would not be returning to America with the others.

The meetings went from nine in the morning until five in the evening without intermission. Ellen praised the children for doing remarkably well through the course of the long hours. When Alexander and Ellen greeted Mr. Russell and told him they wished to be baptized, he threw his arms around both of them at once.

"Tomorrow morning," he said, nodding repeatedly. "We will meet your family by the footbridge at the River Ribble, after which we will take our leave by way of coach to Liverpool."

"We will be there," said Alexander, sheer joy emanating from him.

"Yes, we will be there," repeated Ellen in quieter but equally joyful tones. She excused herself and stepped toward Brother Willard. "Pardon me," she said, "but I would like to tell you about my dream in which you were a prominent figure."

He listened with pleasure swelling in his expression and shook her hand vigorously. "Thank you for telling me. You have made my day."

THE FOLLOWING morning dawned bright and unseasonably warm. Great oaks sprouted with the bright green leaves of new life, and the hill down to the river was blanketed in deep pink and yellow wildflowers. A small congregation of new and old friends waited by the water's edge. Some were there for support and others to be baptized themselves. The Neibaurs walked down and stood next to the Snailhams, who were recent converts and old acquaintances of the Breakells from Saint John's. Her heart ached with longing, wishing her parents and siblings were there partaking in the ordinance and feeling the Lord's Spirit alongside her. Perhaps her mother was watching with less trepidation than she would have had on this side of the veil.

"What better day to be baptized?" said Alexander, with a smile that threatened to split his face.

Ellen peeked around the brim of her bonnet at him. "It is a lovely day, but I think you have more in mind than that, do you not?" She laughed. "Why is it the best day for a baptism?"

"You know me well," he chuckled. "In preparation for Passover, we cleanse our house of every bit of leaven, which represents evil or sin. On the Monday before Passover, Jesus cleansed the great temple of Jerusalem by throwing out the moneychangers. Today, we are baptized on the Monday before Easter and will cleanse our own bodily temples in preparation to know Messiah more deeply."

Ellen nodded, impressed but not surprised by his insights. She spoke softly. "But can we truly be cleansed of our sins, Alex? You know how grievous they are. Do you believe our baptisms will help?"

He pounded his chest with his fist. "With all my heart."

"I hope you are right." She kissed his scratchy cheek, and he waggled his thick brows.

"I love you, Ellen."

Maggie tried to imitate him. "Yub you!" She planted a kiss on Alexander's pant leg.

"Yub you, too, Maggie Moo," said Alexander, and to Ellen, "Shall I go first, or would you like to?"

"Go ahead, dear Alexander." She laughed. "You have waited long enough."

He kissed the back of her hand. "It turns out that the elders knew what they were doing when they did not allow my baptism last fall. I would not trade this experience with you for a dozen stallions."

Ellen and the children observed Alexander's baptism from the hill. When it was her turn, Ellen handed Isaac to Mrs. Snailham and left the children in her care before she trudged into the icy river. Her morning dress and underthings grew heavier with each step. Alexander, wrapped in a blanket at the water's edge, beamed at her.

Mr. Russell steadied her before placing her hand on his left forearm and raising his right arm in the air. "Ellen Breakell Neibaur. Having been commissioned of Jesus Christ, I baptize you in the name of the Father, and of the Son, and of the Holy Ghost. Amen."

He paused long enough for her to suck in a breath, lowered her into the cold water, and raised her back up, as if awakening her to new life. Ellen felt that her own face might split for joy. Though her teeth chattered, she felt warm and happy through and through. As quickly as her heavy skirts allowed, she raced from the water and embraced her husband, who opened the blanket and wrapped her in it with him like a chrysalis. Joseph and Maggie came over and snuck into the dripping blanket with them.

Brother Russell stuck a hand out of his own blanket and heartily shook each of their hands, including Maggie's. The little girl peeked out from behind Alexander's legs and giggled.

A long road lay ahead of Ellen, but she had to believe that the Lord had sent the missionaries for a reason, and that reason must include some measure of possibility for their ultimate redemption. This was an important step. She would do every-thing in her power to make up for her past. She would give her all, and maybe, just maybe, it would be enough.

The only thing that could make Ellen's joy full would be the approval of her family. Would her father reject her completely now that she was one of the Saints? She had not dared tell her family beforehand for fear they would try to stop her, but they were sure to find out soon enough.

A gorgeous autumn morning dawned, blowing leaves, crisp as the cool air. Ellen, Alexander, and the children bustled about, making preparations for a local celebration. The entire town was expected to turn out today, in addition to many of the ladies and gentlemen who lived in neighboring areas. Even those who generally opposed progress would attend. Nothing so exciting had ever happened in Preston before. The final railroad tracks had been laid, and the tram bridge across the River Ribble was complete, connecting their town twelve miles south to Wigan.

Everyone wanted to observe the first steam engine arriving on its trial run. When Ellen and the children were ready, the family walked to the station. Joseph was determined to push Isaac in the pram, and Maggie rode on Alexander's shoulders, so Ellen was free to stroll unencumbered and soak in Fishergate Street, which was steadily growing busier, not that that was a bad thing in all regards. Market Square was becoming more varied. Ellen enjoyed looking through the array of ribbons and wares sold there.

The yeasty smell of the bakery trickled through the hot,

fiery air billowing from the smithy. The train would, of course, add to the growth of the city, which some vehemently opposed, and others welcomed. Ellen was not as keen on it as Alexander, though a bigger town could mean more patients for him. Perhaps he was not as attached to the way Preston had always been since he had not been raised nearby.

The railway station was packed with onlookers despite the cavernous two-story room surrounding the platform. Too many bodies made it impossible to maneuver the pram through, so they found a parking spot for it, and Ellen lifted Isaac into her arms.

Alexander checked his pocket watch the moment they entered the building. "We have not arrived a minute too early." He set Maggie down and lifted Joseph up for a turn to see over the crowd. "Can you see the train approaching yet?"

Alexander was nearly knocked over by Joseph's flailing body squirming back and forth, trying to see past the crowds. "Not yet, Abba."

Maggie grabbed Alexander's trousers with one hand and Ellen's skirts with the other, pulling like a bellringer at the parish church. "I want to see. I want to see."

Alexander picked her up.

"I see it," she yelled.

"What do you see?" Ellen asked.

"The train," she said, but, when pressed, it turned out she was only seeing the tracks in the distance. The engine would come into view at any moment.

Ellen, surveying the crowd, spotted a cluster of ladies, acquaintances to her, standing not far distant. They seemed to be motioning toward Ellen, whispering and sniggering. She tried to shake the feeling that they were gossiping about her, telling herself they were likely talking about the train, but she failed to believe it. Ellen was about to point them out to Alexander when someone called, "The train is coming."

If the bodies were crammed together before, they found a way to be tight as basket weaving now, and every head faced down the track. Alexander raised Maggie back up with Joseph still on his shoulders. Nearby, some young men, about Richard's age, were lifting each other up to see, hooting and hollering. More ladies and gentlemen lined the tracks outside the structure.

Over the din of an energetic crowd, the train chugged and whistled. Ellen craned her neck to catch a momentary glimpse. People around them cheered, throwing their hands in the air in exultation. Through the jostling crowd, Alexander said, "This may not have been the best place to bring my young family." But he appeared as thrilled as the children.

The train squealed into view, although Ellen never did see the whole of it at once between all the hats and bonnets. The engineer stood in the back of the steam-propelled engine, air rushing into his face and hair. A smoke stack, twice as tall as the engineer, towered at the front of the shiny bronze engine. An enormous wooden barrel tipped on its side made up the body of the train. The covered station filled with curling fingers of smoke.

The engineer pulled the whistle cord, and the throng erupted in cheers, startling Isaac into a fit of wails. For all the noise, Ellen would not know he was crying without looking upon his moist rosy lips, curled out into a square of sobs. She tapped Alexander and pointed to the baby. "I need to step outside with Isaac," she yelled. "You have Joseph and Maggie."

Alexander smiled ear to ear and waved a hand for her to go.

Cutting through the crowd like a salmon swimming upstream took longer than it should have, but Isaac settled down as soon as the cool, fresh outdoor air touched his soft skin.

"Ellen," a voice called, and she turned to discover her father.

"Papa," she said with a smile he did not return.

He took Isaac from her arms, lifting him to his shoulder and patting his back. "You have not visited for a time."

Ellen nodded slowly. "Nor have you."

"I know why," he said with a scowl.

"You do?"

He stopped patting Isaac and swayed side to side. "You actually joined that Mormon cult, didn't you? I thought I made myself quite clear about how I felt about them."

She tilted her head, holding her neck in her hand. "Indeed. Do our feelings on the matter count for anything?"

He grunted, tugging her toward the side of the station as the crowd began to flow out like a river breaking through a dam. "People will not like it."

"You mean you do not like it," she retorted.

Alexander bounced toward them, carrying both of the children on his hips. "Have you ever seen anything so glorious?" he asked Ellen, lowering Joseph and Maggie to the ground and gripping their hands. He greeted Ellen's father and asked, "Did you see the steam engine?"

Papa nodded curtly. "I saw it before I followed Ellen and Isaac out."

Alexander's joyous face appeared oblivious to the tension between Ellen and her father, and he spoke to her again. "We must take a trip once it starts towing passengers. This is going to change our world, Ellen, perhaps more than we can comprehend."

"I believe you are right."

"Father! Ellen!" John and Mary joined the small, still gathering beside the dispersing sea of bodies. "It is a family reunion," John boomed.

Alexander slapped him on the back. "What do you think of the train?"

John glanced up at the building before answering. "It is a

spectacle to behold, but I fear what it may mean for our town and for me."

"What do you mean?" Ellen asked.

"It may be the nail in the coffin for our handlooms. More mills are coming in anyway, but, with a train stop, Preston will become more industrialized by the day."

Isaac began to fuss, and Papa handed him back to Ellen, saying, "I abhor change."

Alexander chuckled. "It is coming despite your feelings, so you might as well embrace it."

Papa poked Alexander in the chest. "It is your fault my daughter became a Mormon."

John and Mary looked simultaneously stunned and turned to Ellen, who stepped back in alarm. "Is it true?" Mary asked.

Ellen licked her lips and blew out a breath as she let her head fall in confirmation.

John swept his hat off and ran a hand through his hair. "I warned you about them, Ellen."

She nodded again. "I know."

"Multiple times. Yet you kept seeing them."

"They have the truth," Alexander said, placing an arm around John and squeezing his shoulder. "Let us tell you more about it."

"No," Papa butted in. "No more Mormons in this family."

That night, Ellen was reminded of the group of ladies at the station. She had seen Miss Taylor among them, one of Beth's most intimate friends. Her look of timidity as Ellen caught her eyes seemingly confirmed Ellen's suspicions. She told Alexander about it while she nursed Isaac in their bed and stroked his feather-soft hair. "I understand why my family is upset. They care about us and are worried about our future. But why must acquaintances bother themselves with our business?"

"Ellen, I have something of concern to discuss with you, and I believe it relates to the incident of which you speak."

"Go on."

He sat beside her on the bed, leaning his head back against the tufted fabric. "Word has spread about our baptisms. It is not only your father who is opposed to our conversion. It is affecting my work. Three ladies and a gentleman canceled appointments last week. It seems that they utterly refuse to be in the presence of a Mormon. And this week is the same."

She pursed her lips in disbelief. "This cannot be about our baptisms. Many are joining the church. Is there no other explanation?"

He shook his head. "It is *because* many are joining, which means they are leaving the churches of their birth. The preachers cannot allow it. Not only do the other churches believe strongly in their preaching, but the preachers need parishioners in order to make a living and are spreading lies about the Mormons."

Ellen nodded, remembering the image of her father's furious face. A wall was being built between her and her family, as if each step further into the Restored Church laid another brick between them. "They are not all lies. You must admit that some of the stories are peculiar."

He sighed. "It should not matter if your dentist believes a peculiar story or not."

Ellen switched Isaac to the other breast and continued nursing.

Alexander scooted closer to them and ran his fingers along Isaac's thin, bare arm. "I have known religious persecution from those I love. I am sorry you now know the same. I never wished this upon you or the children. It is not an easy thing, but it seems that the Lord's errand rarely is. There is more I must tell you."

"What is it?"

"I overheard, I believe on purpose," he hesitated before continuing, "Mr. Walker was attended to by a different dentist last week."

Ellen scrunched up her eyes. "That is odd."

"Is it? The gentleman speaking said Mr. Walker refuses to see a Mormon for any services."

"Surely not the Walkers. Patience is my dearest friend. I will speak with her. Perhaps it is a misunderstanding."

Alexander's smile did not reach his eyes. "I hope you are correct." He stretched both hands high, then rested them upon his head, staring at the ceiling. When he finally turned to her, his eyes shone with sincerity and warmth. "You know I will always take care of you, ja? You need not worry."

Ellen had never concerned herself over finances, but what if fewer and fewer patients sought her husband's services? Would it be a problem for them long-term? Of course it would. She could hardly imagine raising her children in a situation where there were not enough provisions to go around, as if they were street urchins.

Her children would never want for bread. Of this, she was certain. They might have to do without some comforts if business decreased, but Alexander's happiness was another matter. He would not be content without working with his hands.

ELLEN LEFT the children in the care of Louisa and called on the Walkers the very next day. She took the carriage since it was nearly half a mile's distance. Though a humble home, it was situated to its best advantage, and Patience seemed pleasantly settled.

The Walker's maid of all work greeted Ellen at the door and directed her to wait in the sitting room. When it took her friend longer than usual to make an appearance, Ellen squirmed.

What if Mr. Walker was firmly set against the Saints? Against her? Would her oldest and dearest friend abandon her because of this newfound religion?

Patience's appearance did not lessen Ellen's worries. Her stride was stiff, and her face firm. She sat erect, back straight, and, when she spoke, her tone was formal. "How is the weather? Were the roads suitable for your journey?"

Ellen squinted, unable to answer such an aloof question when her heart pounded so. This was Patience, and she would make bare her heart. She crossed the room to sit beside her and grasped her hand. That her friend allowed the action gave her a measure of courage. "I have come because Mr. Neibaur told me something he heard in town. He said that last week, Mr. Walker needed to see a dentist and sought out one other than my dear Alexander."

Patience's eyes were upon their clasped hands. "That is true."

Ellen dipped her head to meet Patience's lowered eyes. "But why, Patience? I must know the reason."

"You are a wise enough woman." She gulped. "You must have your suspicions."

Patience's curt answer seemed to be an attempt to quell her emotions.

"Mr. Neibaur has conjectured it is because we have joined the Latter-day Saints." She did not intend the accusatory words to come out harshly, but there they were, demanding to be addressed. As she waited, she thought about the more pleasant times they had reposed in this very parlor, with little more than idle gossip to worry their minds.

Patience watched her free hand run along the wood carvings of the sofa arm, then let out a long breath. "I would have liked to skirt around this, but I will speak if I must. Mr. Walker wishes me to cut off our association due to your new....religion."

The sound that escaped Ellen's lips was a strangled mix of a gasp and the word, "No!"

Patience's eyes dropped to the floral rug beneath their feet. "If you and Mr. Neibaur renounce the Mormons, I will be allowed to keep your acquaintance. If, however, you are determined to move forward on this ill-advised course, I am sure there will be more trouble for you than the loss of my friendship."

Ellen shut her eyes, removing her hand from Patience's, and covered her face. "Your friendship is one of the dearest things I have."

A glimmer of regret shone on Patience's countenance when Ellen opened her eyes again. "Had, dear Ellen. I can no longer be your friend. It is dangerous, and I cannot dismiss my husband's wishes if there is ever to be peace again in my home."

"Dangerous?"

"Yes. It is dangerous to our way of life in a myriad of ways."

"But why? After a lifetime of intimacy, I deserve more of an explanation than that."

Patience inched away on the sofa but angled herself to more fully look upon Ellen. "Opposition is mounting. Many hoped the departure of the Americans would end this movement, and all would return to its comfortable state, but Mr. Walker says the Mormons continue to increase in number, disregarding the passionate pleas of the pastors we have known and loved all our lives. He believes it is," she swallowed with an expression of disgust, "the devil's work, and that you are deceived." She blinked rapidly.

Shaking her head, Ellen refused to believe what she was hearing. "Patience, will you read a Book of Mormon if I procure one for you? Then you will know for yourself of its truthfulness. Alexander reads it to me, and I believe it! It took me some time, I admit, and I may have said things to you that were less than favorable at times, but it has been some time now that I have known for myself that these things indeed come from God."

Patience stood. "No, I cannot accept a Book of Mormon. Would you have me go around Mr. Walker's back to accept such a gift?"

"You could tell him." Ellen sounded sheepish to her own ears. "He could read it with you."

Patience laughed unhappily. "He would throw it in the nearest fire, and what good would that do either of us?" She towered over Ellen, appearing mournful but resolute. "Please do not call upon me again, Mrs. Neibaur." She abandoned the room without another glance at Ellen, who showed herself out.

12

E llen sat in the chair opposite Alexander's office desk and attempted to nurse Isaac while telling Alexander about her unpleasant visit with Patience, but she began sobbing, and Isaac was too distracted to suckle. He kept pulling off and staring up at her tear-stained face and batting at her.

Alexander came around the desk to stand beside her. He pulled her wearied head toward him while she cried.

As much as it pained Ellen to lose Patience, the growing distance from her family was just as hurtful. The Breakells ceased requesting their visits. Ellen was as restless as the children. Alexander, without much of the satisfaction of the work he loved, threw himself into reading and studying. Ellen took walks with the children, and sometimes Alexander accompanied them for a stroll through town.

On an unusually bright, clear morning, Ellen suggested they all take the carriage to the River Ribble for a day trip. They packed a basket with victuals and were preparing the children when Alexander said, "It looks like our adventure will have to wait. Look."

They all glanced toward the window. Foreboding clouds had filled the sky, and it was starting to drizzle. Maggie plopped onto the floor and started to cry as thunder rattled the house.

"Well," said Ellen as brightly as she could manage, "let us play a game instead."

Joseph and Maggie came to her and snuggled into her lap. She placed Isaac on the floor so she could hold them. "What game shall we play?"

Isaac was scooting toward the stairs, and Maggie watched him with apparent concern. "Isaac, Mama!"

"I know, Maggie." Ellen gingerly pulled Isaac back toward them. "Would you like to play charades or a card game?"

"Charades," they said in unison.

"Very well."

"Abba, will you play with us?"

"Ja. Shall I go first? I will act out one of the old stories."

They agreed.

Alexander stood and asked if they wanted to move into the parlor, but they were already comfortably enough situated on the floor. He pulled the lapels of his coat forward and strutted around the room. Then he pulled a frightened face and dramatically fell to the ground. Joseph giggled, but Maggie's eyes opened wide. She scooted over and poked at his face. He winked and smiled, so she snuggled in next to him. Joseph decided this would be a fun diversion, too, and he climbed onto Alexander's back. Ellen brought Isaac to them and laid him atop the pile, holding him up to prevent a spill.

Alexander, still flat on his stomach, mumbled. "What are your guesses? Do you know who I was pretending to be?" None of them did. "I was Alma when the angel appeared to him, and he fell to the earth."

Maggie climbed onto Alexander's head and pet his nose. "Pet the bunny," she said. Alexander carefully turned to his side. There was a slow avalanche of children before Alexander tucked his knees beneath himself into a squatting position and began to hop around like a bunny.

Joseph clung onto Alexander and rode the wild rabbit.

Ellen tickled Maggie's belly with one hand and protected Isaac with the other, kissing his chunky neck.

But then Joseph fell off the wild rabbit, landing on Maggie's finger, causing her to cry once again. She scooted to Ellen, who checked her finger and pulled her into her lap.

Isaac was overwhelmed by the noise and joined in the lamentations.

Joseph grew teary watching the others. Holding three crying children, Ellen and Alexander shrugged at one another in camaraderie, and held their little ones tighter.

"Sorry about all this," Alexander said, gesturing to the mound of tearful children. "Starting with that one." He pointed at sweet Joseph. Their precious one that should never have been. If they had waited to have a child after marriage, would he still have come to them?

Guilt still had a grasp on her heart, but she could not wish away what she now had. Perhaps the Lord could take the caterpillar she was and turn it into something beautiful.

Alexander's eyes grew quizzical, but she shook her head to say there was nothing to worry about, though there was plenty, if she was honest. They were starting anew. Their life had shifted, and it was unclear where the new road would lead.

At least they had each other. And that would have to be enough.

ALEXANDER ROLLED toward Ellen early one morning. "Are you awake?"

"Hmm?" she said, yawning.

"I have four patients scheduled today. As you know, I have

not seen so many in a day since, it seems, all of Preston has turned against us. It will be important to be efficient. Will you be able to manage the children and keep them from screaming or wandering underfoot?"

"To be sure. We will leave the house if we must." She yawned again and rested her head on his shoulder, but, as she was beginning to doze off again, Isaac started to wail and reach for her, so she moved him to her breast, between Alexander and herself.

She kissed the top of Isaac's head as Alexander wrapped his arm over both of them and whispered, "His name recalls the story of Abraham and Isaac. I could never sacrifice one of my dear sons."

"Or daughter, I suspect," added Ellen, knowing that Maggie had a firm place in Alexander's heart.

"Be careful. You do not want to draw my attention to your competition, ja? I might leave right now for a snuggle with her."

Ellen pulled a shocked face and grabbed onto him. "No. Don't leave me," and then letting go, "but if you must, I will understand. She is a beautiful little lady."

After a quick breakfast, while Mr. Neibaur was with his first patient, Joseph bumped the cabinet, causing Alexander's blue and white crock from his University of Berlin days to crash to the floor and shatter. Ellen peeked from the room and met Alexander's stern gaze in his office doorway. "I apologize," she told him. "I was with Isaac, but we will have this mess cleaned up straightaway."

He widened his eyes and disappeared from view. Clinking of his tools resumed, and Ellen silently prayed the rest of the day would progress without incident. She pulled a forlorn-looking Joseph into an embrace. "All is well. These things happen. Abba is stressed today. Let us clean this up." She lifted him up onto her hip, so he would not hurt himself on any bits of broken pottery.

"When did you grow into a little man? I can scarcely carry you anymore."

Joseph's tear-stained cheeks pulled up into a smile. "Abba told me that I am three AND a half now."

Ellen feigned shock. "Not possible. Were you not just three?"

He nodded, smug.

During Alexander's second appointment of the day, Maggie threw a colossal tantrum when Louisa served her a piece of challah that had been broken in half. Louisa tried to undo the damage by giving Maggie a new, whole piece of bread, but Maggie was too far gone. It took Louisa and Ellen a solid quarter of an hour to calm her.

While Alexander was working with his third patient, Ellen was peacefully breastfeeding in her bedchamber while the other children played quietly. Too quietly. She had not heard a single sound from them for several minutes. "Joseph?" she called. "Maggie?"

No answer.

She called louder but still heard silence in return, so she rose, holding Isaac to her breast while she searched for them. A banging sound downstairs followed by a long wail alerted her to their whereabouts.

Alexander poked his head out again and glared up the stairs. She pointed at Isaac and threw up her free hand to show there was not much she could do, but she called Joseph and Maggie to her. "I need you both to sit silently by me until Isaac is finished, then we will take a stroll through town. Right now, though, you are required to sit without making a single noise. Pretend we are in church. Do you understand?"

"Yes, ma'am."

"Yes, Mama."

To Ellen's relief, they obeyed, then excitedly but with little sound, prepared to step out.

It was a nice day for a walk, possibly one of the last warm days of the season. Isaac sat in the pram, with pillows and blankets around him, but now that he was semi-mobile, he kept pulling himself up along the side of it.

Ellen pushed the pram with one hand and hung onto Isaac with the other.

The most recent rains had washed pathways through the gravel, making the pram difficult to maneuver.

"Hey, Uncle John," Joseph yelled, dashing into the street without a glance. A horse and rider were moving at a quick clip toward him.

"Joseph!" Ellen screamed. Leaving the other children, she bolted toward her oldest just as the rider pulled the reins hard to one side and missed Joseph by inches. John grabbed Joseph's hand and led him across while Ellen went back to Isaac and Maggie, who was crying. Ellen, placing Maggie's hand firmly on the side of the pram, said, "Hold on," and walked across the small gravel road to John's cottage.

John embraced Ellen. "That was close." Holding her shoulders, he leaned back to observe her. "It has been far too long." He picked Isaac up from the pram and asked Maggie, "Who is this child?"

"Zaaaack," she said.

Joseph laughed. "You know Baby Isaac."

John shook his head, leading them up his shop. "Indeed I do, but this baby is twice as large as Isaac." He took the baby under the arms and moved him back and forth, inspecting him from every angle.

"It is Isaac," Joseph reassured him.

"You must be right." John threw his hands up in defeat. "He clearly is not Joseph, because you are Joseph, and he cannot be Margaret, because you are Margaret. Isaac is the only other possibility." He waved the children to the back of the weaving room. "Come here, children. I have something for you to do."

He directed them toward a table and brought out a large assortment of buttons. "Will you do me the favor of helping me sort these?"

Joseph nodded, feeling important.

John grabbed Ellen's hand with the arm not holding Isaac and led her to the corner opposite the little ones. "I would speak with you."

"I am glad to hear it. I daresay you may be the only member of our family who wishes to."

He shifted, but then squared his shoulders. "Ellen, renounce this new religion, and return to the safety of the Church of England."

"I will not, though I appreciate your concern." She faced away, as if the conversation was concluded, but he turned her gently back around.

"There are rumors of trouble for the Mormons. Do you have any idea what this decision could mean for you? For your children? Do you not care that their future will be tainted with this scandalous religious debacle?"

Her eyes swept the room, everywhere except John's eyes. "Preston will adjust. You will see. It will be like the locomotive. Many opposed it, but, once it all settled, we continued to plough forward as a town."

"There is talk about threatening anyone who continues to patronize Mormon businesses."

She reflected the pained expression on his face. "What talk?"

"At the public house. They figure the Mormons will leave if they cannot work."

Ellen waved a hand through the air. "That is the whiskey talking."

John did not pay attention to the finality in her voice. "How is business?"

"A lady does not discuss the financial affairs of her

husband," she said loftily. "Besides, it is probably no worse than yours. Have the mills put you out of business yet?"

"Ellen, I want to know how becoming a Mormon is blessing your life. Do you see a lack of friends, acquaintances, and business associates as a blessing?"

Isaac started to fuss, and she bounced him on her hip. The other children had stopped sorting buttons and were watching them, hands paused midair. "Those, of course, are not blessings," Ellen admitted, "but there are other blessings worth the lack of business and even worth the loss of friendship when it comes to that. Isaiah says, 'And the work of righteousness shall be peace; and the effect of righteousness quietness and assurance forever.' This is what my new religion brings me, despite the challenges of which you speak."

"Peace? Listen to yourself. How can you speak of peace? Will Alexander feel peace when he can no longer work? Will you feel peace when the town turns its back on you? Will your children have peace when they grow without friends and eventually are unable to make suitable matches? You may be willing to lose your friends and family, but will you inflict the same pain upon your children?"

Ellen's eyes betrayed her, filling with tears. She tried not to think about Alexander's loss of business, the coolness between herself and the Breakells, and her loss of dear Patience. It was too much.

John shuffled his foot against the ground. "I am sorry. I did not wish to make you cry. I want you to be happy."

"Do I not look happy?" She laughed through her tears.

He chuckled, pulling her to him. "Not particularly. I never thought to see the day when my little sister would preach to me. You *have* chosen a new life."

Ellen nodded into him as Maggie toddled over and grabbed hold of her skirts. "Let us go, Joseph and Maggie. Father should be done working." To John, she said, "We are fine. Alexander had four appointments today." If only she believed what she said.

John tipped his hat to her as she strolled out, head held high.

She made doubly sure Joseph and Maggie were holding the pram before crossing the street and decided it was easier to hold Isaac on one hip and push the empty pram with the other.

Maggie stepped in a mud puddle, instantly soaking her hem, and whimpered.

"We are almost home," Ellen told her.

Maggie began to wail.

As soon as they entered the house, Ellen crouched down, setting Isaac on the entry floor. He immediately headed toward the stairs while Ellen removed Maggie's shoes while she wailed louder than a steam engine. Ellen tossed the shoes aside and dove for Isaac as he reached for the fourth stair, high enough to take an injurious tumble.

Alexander stepped out of his study, shutting the door behind him. His chest rose and fell while he surveyed the chaotic scene around him. "I told you I needed quiet today, and all day, this is what you do," he hissed, whipping his hands through the air in front of him. He withdrew, closing the door harder than necessary, apparently still with a patient.

Ellen and the children sat, stunned, staring at the door. She shook her head, picked up Isaac, and straightened up the entry before taking the children to the kitchen to wash up.

They were still completing this task when Ellen heard Alexander escort his patient out. He stormed into the kitchen. "How could you?" he roared.

"How could I have done differently? Louisa was busy, and I was dreadfully outnumbered." Ducking her head, she hid her face behind the brim of her bonnet.

"I need to work, Ellen." His tone was hard but pleading.

"I know." Tears stung the corners of her eyes, but she

refused to look at Alexander. Her heart could not handle another layer of sadness today. It was already brittle.

Alexander would not be deterred by tears, though. He stomped toward her and took her by the shoulders. "Do you even care? This is important."

"I care. I am doing my best." She choked down the threatening sobs. "Perhaps if we moved to the country by Darwen Park, the children would have more room to explore and stay out of your way."

Alexander raised his voice. "We must stay in town. If I lack patients here, there is no way they will make the journey out to a country home to see me." He threw his fist at the wall. "Leaving is out of the question."

Ellen covered her mouth and ushered the children from the room, leaving a mess on the table and an angry husband rubbing his knuckles.

13

E llen felt Alexander's chill skin against hers when he came to bed.

"I am so sorry," he said. "I love you. How do I make restitution for this? What do you need? Time with friends?"

It was the worst possible suggestion. "I have no friends. Even my family is rejecting me."

He pulled her close, stroking her hair. "What then? A trip to the sea?"

"We both know that is not happening. It is too far a journey. I am not a world traveler like you. Besides, you need to work."

"It is not far. Most days I do not have any patients anyway."

She burrowed into him, knowing a holiday was not on the cards.

He kissed her forehead and lips tenderly, then with more passion and movement, he kissed her again.

She blew out the stress of the day in a long breath and allowed herself to get lost in his apologetic embrace.

THE WEATHER COOLED, and Ellen's middle started to round out. Though she loved being a mother, she wondered if she could handle another when she could scarcely contain the ones she had. There was not enough of her to go around, especially without a wet nurse. How had her mother had so many children? Ellen leaned her head into her palm, missing Mama. She needed to take the children to call upon Papa and Margaret. When Ellen announced the visit to Joseph and Maggie, they received the news with delight, but Ellen felt queasy. Nonetheless, she still hoped her family would accept their decision to join the Latter-day Saints with time.

She stepped out onto the stoop with the children, and Ellen spotted her neighbor and waved. "Good day, Miss Lewis."

Abigale's head shot up. She met Ellen's gaze for the briefest moment before entering her house without a word. She, who willingly chattered away to anyone with ears, had ignored Ellen. The irony was that Abigale was the one who first informed them about the missionaries from America. She had known their involvement from the start. Why did she choose to avoid Ellen now?

Joseph and Maggie, with fists full of her skirts, watched with curious expressions, and Isaac fidgeted in her arms. As if a great oak, Ellen stood stock-still, wondering if she could bear the further rejection of her family today. Joseph, tired of waiting, descended the steps and poked at a worm between two of the larger cobblestones.

Was this what it meant to be one of God's people? To be persecuted and alone for the sake of her faith?

"Mama," Maggie said, pulling on her dress. "Come."

Joseph agreed. "Yes, Mama. Let us go."

"Shall we take a trip to the bakery instead?" Ellen tried to fill her voice with enthusiasm.

"No," said Joseph. "I want to go to Darwen Park to play in the gardens. You said we could."

"Yes, I did, but I might have changed my mind on the matter."

"I want Grampa," Maggie piped up.

Ellen gritted her teeth, outvoted. "Very well."

WITH BETH and her older siblings, save Margaret, married off, and Mama, William and little Thomas buried, Darwen Park was a shadow of what it had once been. James, now twenty, would likely not reside there much longer. That would leave only Papa, Margaret, and Richard. Richard hurried out at the sound of the carriage and hugged each of the children as they climbed down.

When it was Ellen's turn, she embraced him, grateful her youngest sibling had not soured toward her. He had always been a favorite.

Richard took Isaac from her arms, setting him on his shoulders.

Her father came out with smiles and hugs for the children but did not meet Ellen's eyes. The children seemed oblivious to the neglect of their mother, which suited her fine. She took Isaac back from Richard so he was at liberty to give chase, erupting the tense silence with happy squeals.

When they were safely out of earshot, Papa nodded toward Ellen's once again swollen stomach. "Another one?" He narrowed his eyes and appeared less than pleased.

"Yes. Is that not good news?" Ellen's tone dared him to tell her how he felt.

His head moved back and forth, almost imperceptibly.

"You are not pleased to have another grandchild?" she said in disbelief. As deeply as her family's coolness had cut her, this newest revelation left her breathless.

Avoiding a confrontation, he waved Ellen toward the

house, but she would not allow him to leave without another word. "Tell me you are happy to have another grandchild," she pleaded. "I know you dearly love my children. Surely you will not let your prejudices turn you away from an innocent infant."

He cleared his throat. "Another baby, another Mormon." His eyes were on some distant bit of the wood beside the Park.

Ellen gasped, less because of the words, and more because of the venom with which they were spoken. She felt as if she might swoon, and she was not generally a fragile woman. Rooted to the spot, she was tempted to gather up her chicks and fly the coop for good. But if she did so, it would be more difficult to bridge the growing gap between them in the future. It was an impossibly long distance to bridge already.

She opted to stay for a brief visit. "Shall we go inside?" she said in a falsely civil tone.

Papa offered his arm and led her to her preferred chair in the drawing room and sat nearby without a word. Margaret was seated on the settee, stitching a patchwork quilt.

"How do you do?" Ellen said.

"We are well," Margaret said without shifting her focus from the task at hand. "You need not check in."

Ellen smoothed her skirts. "Forgive me, but I was not merely checking in. The children and I wanted to see you."

Margaret huffed and continued her needlework, folded in half over her work like a bedsheet.

A gust of wind brushed elm leaves against the window.

Papa caught her eye. "Winter is coming."

"Yes. We wanted to visit before the roads became more trying."

He nodded.

"But I see we are unwelcome."

He pursed his lips, staring at the tree rubbing against the window. "If your mother was here, she would know how to handle this, but I am glad she does not have to witness the path you and that Jew have chosen."

Ellen's jaw went slack. "That Jew?"

Papa clenched his teeth so tight, his cheeks caved in.

Ellen rose. "I would prefer to play the pianoforte over making unpleasant conversation with you while the children get some fresh air. We will leave shortly. If you want to talk civilly, you are welcome to interrupt my playing at any time." She staggered to the bench and played a mournful song for days gone by, filling the melancholy notes with the frustrations and disappointments of her heart.

He did not stop her.

Nor did he stop her when she realized the futility of the visit and said goodbye.

She hoped time would heal instead of scar their relationship.

When Ellen arrived home and saw the deep lines above Alexander's brows and an almost perceptible burden upon his shoulders, she kept her mouth shut. Their troubles were not swiftly blowing away on the wind with the golden leaves of autumn.

Bone-weary, but knowing she must prepare the children for bed, she put on a happy face and directed them to their bedchamber, leaving Alexander to his books and ledgers.

Joseph and Maggie, tired from a long day, were slow to obey, and it took more strength than remained to get everyone settled for the night.

After an extra drink of water for Joseph and two extra bedtime lullabies for Maggie, Ellen collapsed on the bed to nurse Isaac. She held him with one arm and stroked his wispy, brown hair, which curled up in the back like that of a duck, with the other. Though he was nearly one, his skin was still smooth to the touch. She rubbed his cheeks and stroked his arms.

He smiled, breaking his latch, and cupped her face before returning to his task with his cherubic hand resting on her breast.

Inclining her head, she kissed his hair. "Do not tell Abba," she whispered to him, "but he was right about breastfeeding. I will never again give up this chance to bond with my babies by employing a stranger to feed them."

Ellen rubbed her belly, thinking of the baby to come and recalling her father's reaction. His callousness toward the unborn child made Ellen feel like a garment, tossed into the street and trampled by horse-drawn carriages. Was this newfound religion worth the loss of her family? She did not desire to be separated from them as Alexander was from his family, whether by physical distance or by choice, but would continuing to reach out to them bear fruit? Remembering Richard's face as she had exited the carriage brought a small grin to her lips. For his sake, she would not give up on the Breakells.

Alexander wrote to his parents once in a while but never heard back. He wondered if he should stop writing altogether, but a glimmer of hope kept him doing it, as long as he thought his letters might be read. Joining the Saints would be of no consequence to them after what they considered Alexander's ultimate betrayal in becoming a Christian. He had left, nay, built upon the beliefs of his youth in a way his family could never understand, let alone support.

Isaac's brown eyes watched her, and he pulled off her breast once more, just enough to coo before suckling again..

When she laid him into his wooden cradle, he was still awake, wrapped in warm blankets for a brisk night. She sat on the edge of her bed and rocked the cradle with one foot to the beat of Lavender's Blue, which she hummed on repeat until he dozed off. She was tempted to kiss his forehead, but, knowing it might rouse him, she resisted, rocking the crib with slower and slower motion and carefully removing her foot. When she stopped rocking him, Isaac stirred, and she held still as the obelisk in Market Square, but he did not awaken, and she fell back into her bed and was instantly asleep.

"ALEX, COME SEE," Ellen hooted through their home in an unladylike fashion one day. Everyone in the household came running to the kitchen to see what the ruckus was about. "Look," she told them, pointing to the boys.

Joseph, kneeling on the cold wood floor, held Isaac under the arms. Ellen, seated on the floor a few feet away from them, reached toward Isaac. "Come on, Isaac. Show Abba what you can do."

Isaac, with arms up to steady himself, took a wobbly step, then another before diving into his mother's arms. They all cheered, and Maggie hugged him. "Hooray, Isaac! Hooray!"

Three weeks later, Ellen called out again, but this time she screamed in desperation.

14

The door flew open, and Alexander shot in as Isaac vomited and heaved over the chamber pot. Ellen supported him under his arms, steadying his soiled body.

Alexander's brows knit together, standing helplessly before dashing from sight again.

He returned with rags and a clean white gown for Isaac.

Ellen wiped the baby and removed the dirty clothing, changed him, and wrapped him in a blanket. She set down his half-awake form to clean herself off, but he soiled himself again the moment she arose.

Opting to leave his clothes off this time, she spot-cleaned the blanket and wrapped him snuggly against her.

All night his body purged its contents from both ends, and Ellen and Alexander grew increasingly distressed.

Ellen held Isaac through his eighth bout of vomiting. Or was it the ninth? She had lost count. "Could it be cholera?" Whatever plagued him had emptied his little body, and yellow spittle was all he had left to expunge. She held him over the pot while he heaved and hiccupped.

"It could be." Alexander reached for the pile of dirty blankets and clothes.

"No!" she yelled.

Alexander reeled back toward the door, surprised by her fervor.

"Sorry. I will handle everything," she said. "We cannot risk anyone else becoming ill. Leave the laundry. Take the children to Darwen Park as soon as they are up." Isaac retched again while Alexander stood framed in the doorway.

"What about you?" he asked.

"I must be the one to stay as I am the one to breastfeed him."

He clenched the doorframe. "I will return."

Shaking her head forcefully, she said, "Stay with Joseph and Maggie. I shall send word when it is safe to return."

Alexander stepped toward Ellen, but she raised a hand to stop him, and he stepped back once more. His eyes fixed on their little boy, whose head rested in Ellen's lap. "I have a patient coming."

"Alex," she said in exasperation. "You cannot see patients here."

He pursed his lips. "So I must rely on the good graces of your father."

She lifted her shoulders. "Where else are you to go?"

"Anywhere. How about John's?"

"They do not have extra room as my father does, and you know how the children love it there."

He grunted and disappeared.

All that day and the next, Ellen rested fitfully when Isaac slept curled against her, and she cared for him when he awoke for short periods. Within only a couple days, he seemed to have become an empty shell of himself with hollow, apathetic eyes encircled in blue shadows, his purple lips like a drooping bow on his pale face.

"Lord," she whispered. "Please do not take my son." Worry and exhaustion poured out with her teardrops, moistening Isaac's forehead, and she swept them into his dry skin with her thumb. Surely God would not take an innocent baby from the arms of his praying mother, especially after all she had given to His cause. The Good Lord would not take him from her.

But was it enough? Was she enough? Heaven knew how deeply flawed she was. Could she ever make up for the sins of her past?

Abraham was asked to sacrifice his beloved son, but the Lord did not make him follow through with it. "Please, Lord, do not send me through this hell. Allow me to raise my boy. I will do anything."

Isaac squirmed in her arms, likely tormented by aches in his legs and back, but he was unresponsive to her voice and touch. She gave him a spoonful of tepid water from a bowl provided by Louisa, but most of it dribbled from the corner of his mouth. "Come on, sweet boy. You need water. Have a little drink for Mama."

No response.

A sob erupted from her throat in one solid burst. "Please, God. Please save my baby."

Her head bobbed a dozen times that night, but rest did not come.

As bits of light streamed through the windows, brightening the room beyond the flickering of the candles, she stretched a hand to the back of her neck and massaged her tight, aching muscles. She carefully placed Isaac into his cradle, which he filled from one end to the other. Reaching one arm over the edge of the bed, she rocked his bassinet. His formerly round, soft cheeks were sunken and gray and trembled with each slow, shallow breath.

Ellen dozed with her arm still gripping the bassinet, but she startled when Isaac mumbled. Her arm prickled as she reached for him and brought him to her breast. His deep-set eyes remained closed, and, though his mouth formed a little O, he did not latch on to feed, so Ellen spoon-fed him until he sealed his lips and refused to open them again. She adjusted their bodies to a lying position, hoping they would be more comfortable and get some solid, healing rest.

Isaac shifted his head and squinted through heavily lidded eyes. "Mama," he whispered in a hoarse voice.

Her heart leaped into her throat. "I have you, baby." She swallowed. "Take some broth." She sat him up and guided his head toward the cup, bringing it to his lips. He took a sip, swallowed, and sipped again.

"Praise the Lord," she said, supporting his head and kissing it tenderly. "Do you feel a little better?" She gave him another drink, and he gulped it down before nestling into her. Would the Good Lord send her a miracle despite all her shortcomings?

They settled, and she eyed his chest, watching it move in and out as it whistled like an urchin's hut.

His breathing grew increasingly labored over the next hours, peppered with dry, weak, unproductive coughs, and her hope in his recovery slipped away. "Save my baby," she whimpered into the empty air.

Isaac opened one eye but refused to eat, so she squeezed his cheeks softly to open his mouth. She dipped her finger in the broth and rubbed the moisture along his chapped lips and into the side of his cheek. "Keep breathing, sweet boy." She rocked forward and back though every part of her ached.

She matched each breath to his and rested a hand lightly on his chest to feel the evidence of life still pulsing within, wondering if each inhale would be his last and end the beating of his heart.

She had not earned the right to live a happy life. God was taking her baby despite everything she had given up for Him.

Isaac gasped for air, then a whoosh of wind escaped his lips.

She stared, wide-eyed. Her fingers trembled against his still chest, creating a pulse that no longer existed. Becalming her hands, she willed his chest to rise once more, his glossy gaze to meet hers, his limp fingers to tighten around her hand.

To have his lifeless lips mouth the word "mama".

But nothing happened. Nothing at all.

He was gone.

And it was her fault.

She was a statue with no tears left to cry, leaving her as hollow as the baby's body in her arms.

Time passed, and she hardly blinked, afraid he would disappear.

Louisa came in, but Ellen did not budge. Louisa's hand flew to her heart, and she paused mid-step. Her arm reached toward Isaac, but Ellen rolled and wrapped herself around him, staring into his tiny expressionless face.

"I will send for Mr. Neibaur." Her sentence hung in the silent stillness as if she wanted to say more, but she shook her head and disappeared from the corner of Ellen's view.

DAYS LATER, Joseph pranced into the room to say good morning. The effort to raise her eyes was as strenuous as lifting a cotton loom. Part of her wanted to smile at her son—her only remaining son—but the edges of her mouth were stone.

Alexander stretched, climbed from the bed, and directed Joseph downstairs. "Ellen," he said.

She met him with silence. Her arm ached from hanging over the bed, but she could not stop running her fingers along the smooth wooden edge of Isaac's cradle. She rocked it, the lilting melody of Lavender Blue languishing in her mind.

Alexander sat beside her, placing his hand on her shoulder. "Ellen?" he tried again. He sniffed and rubbed his beard, and still she stared at the cradle. "You must keep living for the rest of us."

Though her thoughts swam in a sea of grief, words hung elusive.

Alexander hunched, picked up Isaac's bed, and stomped from the room with it. He came back after a period of time, empty-handed. Like her. Her eyes were still trained upon the bit of floor where the cradle had been. How could she keep breathing when her perfect son had not?

With the strength of a frail, old woman, Ellen faced Alexander, wrapping her palms into the front of his shirt as if it was a lifeline. "I thought God would heal him." Her cracking voice sounded mad. "Our Isaac is sacrificed. God did not send an angel to stop his death, because I am no Abraham. He left me alone and did not save my boy. I failed him. I failed him," she lamented, wetting his shirt with her tears. God was force feeding her the lesson she deserved. The sinner within would never be worthy of lasting joy.

Alexander gulped and drew her close. "No, Ellen. It is not your fault, and we have not been abandoned."

Her empty arms shook, and she craved the measure of peace Alexander seemed to have.

"I have felt my grandfather's presence," he said, stroking her hair.

It was a pretty notion, but all Ellen could see in her mind's eye was the expressionless face of her little one, who had just begun to speak and walk. "If that is true, then God sent his angel to steal my baby, not to save him."

He let out a sharp breath. "Listen." He touched her chin and adjusted her head to face his. "I know this is unconventional, but I desire to do something. Are you hearing me?"

She blinked her assent. It was all she could manage.

He swallowed again. "May we change Isaac's name to Samuel Peretz, after my maternal grandfather?"

She tried to clear her mind with a shake but could not make sense of what he was saying. "Change his name? Whatever for?"

He lifted his shoulders and glanced to the ceiling before answering. "It feels right. I know he has been watching over us. He was a handelsman by trade, a family man by passion. My opa will be proud and take care of him."

What did it matter? "I wanted to take care of him."

ANOTHER YEAR, another funeral. It would take place at the relatively new St. Paul's Church in town. The Latter-day Saints did not have a building for christenings and burials.

The usually white sandstone appeared fittingly gray on this sunless day. Gray as the world. Gray as her future without Isaac —nay—Samuel Peretz. She scrunched up her eyes. A foreign name after a man she would never know. Either way, both were gone.

Ellen's family attended the simple ceremony. Somehow her father managed to feel aloof even as he took her into his arms. Beth grasped her hand with clear emotion in her eyes, but Ellen could not reciprocate outward emotion.

Patience slipped into the back of the room a moment before the small service began. When it was over, she approached Ellen, holding something out in her palm. "I am so sorry. I hope it was not too presumptuous of me, but I called upon the undertaker and had this made for you."

An ebony brooch trimmed in gold rested on her open hand. Ellen took it, feeling its weight, and bringing it close for inspection. At the center, behind glass, was a little knot of Isaac's feathery hair. She fingered the glass with her pointer and middle finger, then her hand flew to cover her mouth against the sobs that would surely come.

Once they began, they may never stop. She would drown in them.

DAYS AND WEEKS rolled into a single tangle. The funeral had been the only event since Isaac's death. Mealtimes kept a pretense of structure to Ellen's otherwise languid hours. During dinner one evening, as Ellen swirled soup around in her bowl, Maggie climbed from her seat at the table and pranced around to where Ellen sat. She raised her arms above her head, so Ellen scooted her chair back and lifted Maggie into her lap. Maggie reached up to Ellen's cheeks, wiping them with her pudgy fingers. Ellen had not known she was crying until she felt the moisture at Maggie's gentle touch. She smiled at her little girl, hoping it looked genuine.

"Why are you sad, Mama?"

"I miss Baby Isaac."

Maggie squinted at her mother. "Is he sleeping?"

Ellen covered her mouth and gulped, waiting to respond once she could do so with a clear voice. "Yes, Maggie. He is sleeping in Heaven."

Maggie rested her head on Ellen's shoulder. "Where is Heaven?"

Ellen glanced at Alexander for support, but he only watched the scene with sympathy and concern written in his brow, so she answered. "Far away in a more beautiful place than you can imagine."

A place Ellen would never be.

"ELLEN," Alexander said in bed one morning. "Do you know what day it is?"

"The Lord's day, but I am not ready to attend services. Maybe next week."

"Shabbat. Ja; that is true. It is also Joseph's birthday."

Ellen's mind was dense as an English morning, and it was difficult to see anything as ordinary as a birthday through the mist, but something panged inside her at the realization she had forgotten such a significant day. She was failing her children. She had already failed Isaac-Samuel Peretz. "Is it the 6th of January already? That makes Isaac's birthday tomorrow, and yours on Tuesday."

"Ja. It should be a week of celebrations."

She stretched, then curled back up. "It *should* be, but things are not as they should be."

"We need to celebrate Joseph." He punctuated his statement with a hand on her shoulder. "We cannot give up on our little ones because of the one that is missing."

"God has abandoned us." Trying to shake the gloom, she allowed the hope of having something to celebrate renew her sense of purpose.

Samuel Peretz had required the most from her this past year. His job had been to grow while Ellen took care of every one of his wants. She had been his sustenance, transportation, love, his everything, and they had all adored him. At least he had not died—she flinched at the word—from lack of love.

Hundreds of thousands of mothers had experienced this same heartache. Her own brother, John, and his wife, Mary, had lost their first two sons, both named Richard. How did they move on? She had not shown them enough of the empathy she now needed.

As Ellen finished dressing, she heard Alexander call, "Joseph, Maggie."

The children shuffled in, cowering like mice in the corner of the bedroom. Ellen felt a deep pang of guilt. They needed their mother.

Alexander waved them over, and he and Ellen crouched onto the floor. The children ran over, nearly knocking them to the ground. Scooping their little ones up, the hole within Ellen partially filled as she embraced them.

Her family would soon have five members again. It was time to rejoin the living.

SPRING BLOSSOMED upon the bustling town of Preston, though Ellen was not ready for it to pierce her heart. When it was time for their afternoon stroll, she skirted to the closet to grab the pram before recalling that it was unnecessary. Her hand paused on the doorknob, and she tensed.

"What is it, Mama?" Joseph asked.

She steadied her heart. "Nothing. I quite forgot what I was about."

The street was full of the sights and sounds of people bargaining at the fish carts and the corn exchange and passing in carriages, but Ellen's ears honed in on the sound of a crying baby the moment she stepped out the door. She squeezed her children's hands and led them toward the Square. A brisk breeze whipping at her face reminded her to feel.

Ellen lifted her hand, along with Joseph's, to wave at the gentleman and lady who lived in the last home in the Old Cock Yard. They glanced at one another and scurried into their home before Ellen approached. Her stomach tightened. She had learned which shops to avoid to stay away from the mounting tension against her faith, but she would continue to wave at her neighbors. Perhaps over time, they would once again respect her family. Alexander needed the trust of the community if he was to continue to provide a living.

She would hold herself—and what was left of her family—

together. Joseph and Maggie could still live happy lives and be saved, even if she was a hopeless cause.

Hustling, tugging her little ones forward, through and around town, she noticed the clenching of her stomach coming with regularity and increasing intensity. She ached for a baby to hold in her arms. The image of the empty cradle would haunt her until she could rock another infant in it. Traitorous but true. She pressed the brooch from Patience against her chest, pinned near her heart, and rubbed her thumb on the worn spot from the last ten torturous weeks.

Maggie slipped, and Ellen yanked her arm up a moment too late. Maggie pulled up the layers of her gown, looked at the hole in her stockings and the bits of blood seeping through, and puckered her lips.

Ellen squatted. "I am sorry. Was I moving too quickly for you?" she said.

Maggie nodded as Ellen attempted to keep her balance despite the fully-grown baby in her womb. Joseph knelt, too, and placed his hand around Maggie's while Ellen brushed bits of gravel from her stockings and buttoned boots.

An intense tightening of Ellen's stomach shot pain around to her back as she arose. She clenched her teeth, cradling her stomach, not fully erect until the contraction subsided.

Joseph squinted at her. "We ought to go home."

Ellen and Joseph took a few steps in the direction of their townhome, then realizing Maggie was behind them, paused. She hobbled on her good leg, keeping her sore one bent out in front of her. Murmuring moans started before she caught up. Ellen crouched again with difficulty and scooped Maggie up, her stomach pulling against the exertion.

Struggling to fit Maggie onto her nonexistent hip, Ellen said, "You sure are growing."

"You are, too," said Joseph, eyeing her middle.

A full, belly laugh burst from Ellen, surprising her, and spurring on another painful contraction.

Joseph's shocked face and Maggie's concerned one stared up at her, and her giggles progressed until they were uncontrollable hiccups. Somewhere in the midst of her laughter, tears started to streak down her cheeks. She could scarcely see through them, but, witnessing the distress of her children, she attempted to slow her breathing. She squeezed Maggie and patted Joseph's head. Her control was not complete until another tightening sensation overcame her. She stabilized herself on Joseph's shoulder.

Still some distance from home, she determined to take slow steps, one at a time, carrying an injured Maggie.

They rounded the corner onto Avenham Road. "Are you able to walk on your own?"

Maggie nodded, and Ellen lowered her down. Straightening her back against the pain, they made slow progress. Still keeping her injured leg almost square, Maggie limped forward with measured, halting motions.

Another contraction doubled Ellen over, stronger and tighter. Taking three times as long as the walk away from home had taken, they rounded the corner to John's shop. Her anxiety at seeing John seemed to spur another contraction into being. She stepped in, closed the door, and leaned against it.

John shot toward them. "What is it?"

A sharp pain in her back left her breathless.

John repeated the question to Joseph, who told him that they had been out for a walk when Maggie hurt herself. Joseph cocked an eyebrow. "I think Mama hurts, too."

John patted Joseph's shoulder. "It would seem so." He called for Mary, who came immediately, and John said, "Stay with Ellen while I find the doctor."

Ellen shook her head. "I should go home. Send for the two Miss Davies, and have them meet me there."

He scowled. "You are not in a proper state for walking." He returned his attention to Mary. "I will fetch the midwives and Alexander."

Mary helped Ellen situate herself as John left.

"Joseph," Mary said, "will you go to the bedchamber and grab the blankets from our bed?"

"Yes, ma'am," said Joseph, appearing smug to be given an important assignment.

"I think this one is coming more quickly than the last three. Thank you for your help, Mary," Ellen said before another pain pulled her into a ball. Mary and Joseph arranged the blankets beneath her and behind her head.

The breaks between contractions shortened until there was no reprieve at all. She squirmed under an unstoppable urge to push, biting down to keep from screaming. The door opened again and the midwives entered with John. After a quick glance around, they pushed up their sleeves and rearranged the blankets. They ordered John and Joseph out, and John lifted Joseph and Maggie into his arms and was walking out when Ellen grunted. "Thank you." Alexander dashed into the cottage in time to give her a quick kiss on the top of the head and be kicked out again.

With two tremendous groans she was afraid might be heard by the children, another Neibaur joined the family.

Miss Amelia wiped the baby off. "A boy!"

Ellen let go of the air trapped in her chest. Relief accompanied the deep, cleansing breath. As much as she loved Maggie, she had hoped for a boy...not to replace Samuel Peretz, because it was impossible to replace a child like a lost stocking, but she missed having a little boy in the crook of her arm, feeding at her breast, and wrapping his hands into her hair when she let it cascade down.

Miss Edith poked her head out to invite Alexander inside once they had Ellen cleaned and covered up.

Alexander knelt beside Ellen, locking eyes with her. She gave a tired but contented smile in response. He reached for their new baby boy and took in his tiny olive face. "He looks like a Neibaur," Alexander said with pride. "Look at his thick, dark hair. We should name him after someone on my side."

Ellen bit her lip. "Alex, I hoped that if we had another boy, we might call him Isaac."

Alexander stared at the nearby wall. He pinched his eyes shut for an instant before nodding. "Ja. That feels right." He put his finger in the baby's palm, which curled around it. "Welcome, Isaac."

15

On a drizzling Sabbath day when baby Isaac was but two months old, the Neibaur family attended church at the Cockpit. Ellen smiled around at the familiar faces she had missed, grateful to be in good company. At the conclusion of the meeting, the rain kept everyone trapped in the entryway, waiting for the deluge to lessen.

Sister Snailham pushed over to them through the crowd, her gathered skirts pressing others from her path. She took the baby from Ellen and cooed at him before glancing down at the other children and with an expectant smile said, "Where is your other little one?"

Ellen's stomach sank like a sailing boat in a gale.

Alexander's forehead wrinkled in pity. "Our son, Isaac, passed away," he said.

Sister Snailham brought little Isaac close to her face and spoke in a baby voice. "Oh no," she said, dramatically jutting out her bottom lip. "I had no idea. No wonder I have not seen your parents for so long."

Each high pitched syllable pricked Ellen's heart like a needle.

Sister Snailham, with eyes only for the baby, still did not look up. "What is your baby's name?"

Alexander placed his hand on Ellen's shoulder and rescued her again by answering in her stead. "His name is Isaac, same as the last."

"Ah, Isaac. That reminds me." She rubbed her nose against the baby's, then met Alexander's eyes. "Have you heard the news?"

Ellen could not move her mouth, but Alexander responded in the negative.

"I fear you both will be shaken by it. I may not be the best person to pass on the little tidbit," she said with a tap to the baby's nose. Despite her words, she appeared thrilled to be the one to share the gossip. "Brother Isaac Russell was excommunicated from the church." Her brows lifted to the clouds as she awaited their reaction.

Ellen tilted her head. "Brother Russell? But he baptized us. Are you quite sure?"

"I remember." Sister Snailham leaned in close to reveal more of her secrets over the sound of the pouring rain and a dozen conversations. "Did you ever hear about his experience before the first Preston baptisms?"

Alexander shook his head again.

"Demonic forces attacked him. He told Elder Kimball he would surely die if Elder Kimball did not pray for him. Elders Kimball and Hyde laid their hands on his head, rebuking the evil spirits, but the spirits did not go without a fight. The elders battled them face to face for over an hour."

Alexander's eyes narrowed. "Sister Snailham, while that is an interesting story, it occurred before we met him. Not only did he preach to us and baptize us, but he befriended us. What has happened to him since we parted company?"

"Well," she said, licking her lips, "he continued to preach on the ship and on his journey from New York to Kirtland, where he found that a great majority of the church members had removed to Far West, Missouri to escape persecution. The Russell family went with them last fall. They found themselves encountering persecution in Far West, too.

"Mobs tried to drive them from Missouri once and for all. Brother Russell, reportedly, led a secret group to apostasy." The word was said slowly and deliberately. "He wrote his cousin, saying he would prepare for them to join him in the American wilderness." Sister Snailham raised one eyebrow and crossed her arms. "Elder Kimball heard about it and sent Elder Richards, who found them out. The church leaders in America met and excommunicated Brother Russell, along with his entire family." She lifted baby Isaac to her shoulder and patted his back. "And to think you named your little ones after him." Her eyes twinkled with the scandal. "Both of them!"

Ellen bit her tongue and observed Alexander, attempting to distinguish his thoughts. He scratched his bearded cheek and moved away from them as Sister Snailham exclaimed at how precious Joseph and Maggie were in their Sunday best. Just as the downpour lightened to a drizzle again, and the conversations around them hushed, Sister Snailham broke the silence in speaking to the children. "I am so sorry for your loss. At least you have a new little one to dote upon."

Ellen took the baby and grasped Maggie's hand. "Alexander," she called, and he joined her straightaway, though he did not meet her eyes.

When they were almost home, Abigale's face appeared in her window before she pulled her curtains tightly closed.

Alexander reached an arm around her shoulder and squeezed. "Do not let it bother you."

She gulped, clenching her teeth against the pain that threatened to explode.

Ellen ushered the children into the house and up to their rooms for dry clothes. "I will follow in a moment," she told them. Then, to Alexander she said, "What do you think about this business with Brother Russell?"

"Words escape me. It is most distressing."

"Words escape the linguist?" she teased in a voice pinched with emotion. "It must be bad." She gazed at nothing. "To be honest, it was not the most distressing part of the conversation by a mile."

Joseph peered at them from the top of the stairs, and Ellen pointed him out to Alexander with her eyes, speaking in hushed tones. "Let us speak later when we better understand ourselves regarding the matter."

He dipped his head and stepped into his study, closing the door behind him and not reappearing until their Sabbath dinner was served.

Ellen's worries swelled like the river at Darwen Park in a squall. Thinking of Darwen Park reminded her of her family and her distance from them. She wished they could move out to the country. Perhaps a shorter physical distance would help them bridge the emotional distance she had created in joining the Saints. While town was varied in its attractions and acquaintances, the country was home and a magical place to be a child, away from the billowing smoke of the cotton factories. They could make a new start and put some distance between them and the fledgling church that was destroying all they held dear.

If Brother Russell could not be trusted, how could they trust any of the Americans? Furthermore, how could they trust their own feelings when Brother Russell had acted as a guiding light leading them into the Restored Church? Were their baptisms even valid if their baptizer was excommunicated?

At the dinner table, Maggie tugged on Ellen's sleeve.

"What is it, darling?"

"I cannot reach my drink," she said, waving her arms to demonstrate that they were not long enough.

Ellen shifted the cup closer.

Alexander put down his own glass and addressed Ellen. "Shall we talk now?"

Before she could answer the query, baby Isaac's whimpers became wails, and she was obliged to leave the table to care for him.

The storms of the day found an exhausted Alexander and Ellen stumbling into bed after the children were settled in for the night. Why did bedtimes always take the longest on days when she felt as depleted as a milked cow?

Alexander scooted to the middle of their shared bed and stretched out his arm.

She quit rocking Isaac's cradle and rolled into her husband, feeling a level of comfort in an instant. "I fear we have made a grave mistake in joining the Mormons," she said. "We have lost friends, business, and closeness with my family for the sake of this church, and now..." She left the words hanging in the oppressively damp, stuffy air.

He rubbed her shoulder. "Now—what—Ellen? What does this change?"

"Everything," she said louder than necessary.

"It changes nothing, and do not wake Isaac."

She leaned up on one elbow, facing Alexander. "As I am the one that cares for Isaac, I will worry about that myself. How can you say it changes nothing? I have seen your distress. This is the reason you have been dour all day. Admit it."

"I am dour, but Sister Snailham's tidbit, as she called it, does not change anything. Not really."

"Are you in earnest?"

He pulled his arm out from under her and stretched, placed his hands behind his head, and stared at the darkness above them. "I am in earnest. We have not made any mistakes...well, not recently. Brother Russell has, but his choice does not relate to us."

Her eyes widened. "How can you be so callous? This matters to you and to me and to my family and to our children."

"While I feel sad for him and his family, we were told by God that the Church belongs to Him. Whether Brother Russell agrees with God or not is irrelevant."

"But we have been deceived, Alexander. The very man who taught and baptized us has left the beliefs he preached to us. He was wrong, thus we were wrong. It is time we listened to everyone who has ever cared for us."

Alexander shifted his head back and forth.

Ellen went on. "I have been thinking about this all the day long. Listen. The Church has already taken so much from us. We must not let it take any more. The Church of England would never demand such sacrifices. We should move out to the country to be near my father. Maybe he will allow us to move into Darwen Park."

"Why does every discussion lead you back to moving to the country? It cannot be done. I live for my work. I love my work."

"Live for me and the kids instead."

Alexander leapt from the bed and glared.

It was the exact wrong thing to say, but the words had burst out like vomit, and they could not be swallowed back down.

Alexander walked out the door, slamming it behind him and shaking the room.

Ellen spoke to the closed door. "I did not mean that. I know you love us."

She considered following him, but sometimes it was better to let his temper simmer down first. Isaac fidgeted and started to fuss, and Ellen lifted him to her.

The sun rose the next morning only to hide behind billowing storm clouds. The anger had dissipated as they slept, but hurt rooted itself in its place. Ellen scooted toward Alexander and watched him sleep until he sensed her presence and blinked.

With closed eyes, he pulled her closer. "Sorry, Ellen."

She swallowed. "Me, too. I know you love us more than your work, but I also know your work is important to you and to our family."

"I do it for you."

"Yes." She agreed. "And for you."

"We cannot be removed from town. Perhaps in a few years, I might be able to open an office on Avenham Street or Church Street, and we will be able to move closer to Darwen Park."

"Thank you for considering it. I regret the difficult situation I place you in whenever I make the request."

They held each other closer. "Ellen, do you truly question our decision to be baptized?"

She took her time answering him. Yes, she questioned it. She would not say she regretted the decision, though they had made many sacrifices, but she did question the wisdom of it.

16

Spring 1840

Ellen put on her flattering cornflower blue morning dress with matching silk slippers. A relic from her days at Darwen Park, it was one of her more elaborate gowns. The few gowns she had had made since her marriage were simpler but still nicer than what some of the Saints wore. Many of them were the poorest of the poor. Would her own family be as impoverished as the rest in time?

Today, along with many of the local converts, the Neibaurs were headed to the railway station to greet some newly arriving missionaries and elders from America. She supposed her apprehension about the manner of dress was really a mask for a deeper concern, having not worked out her feelings regarding Brother Russell. Time had not healed the wound, and there was still the matter of her father, who had scarcely seen Isaac in this first year of his life.

At the station, Alexander and Ellen observed two separate groups awaiting the train's arrival from Liverpool: the Saints on one side and everyone else on the other. The Neibaurs strolled toward the converts, and Alexander greeted a few members with the enthusiasm Ellen lacked before he checked his pocket watch. "Seven minutes," he announced, punching the air with his cane, and the small crowd cheered.

Ellen, feeling guilty over scorning their need, observed their simple, well-kempt clothes and smiles, which brought a measure of peace about the uncertainty in her own future. If Alexander refused to leave their newfound faith, perhaps her children could still have a measure of happiness, though they would likely never live as comfortably as the Breakells. With a glance to the group of scowling Preston parishioners, doubt crept back in. The Neibaurs were set apart from the majority of the town and would be hard-pressed to reintegrate without a full renunciation of the Restored Church.

The train arrived precisely on time. Dependable as his pocket watch, Alexander loved watching the steam engines.

Several members of the Quorum of the Twelve Apostles arrived, including the leader of the Quorum, Brother Brigham Young, who exited the passenger car first. Ellen saw that he was a handsome, broad man with auburn blonde hair, vibrant blue eyes, and a stocky build. His hair was as smooth as his clean-shaven face. He gave a curt nod to the crowd as he stepped out. Others stepped down behind him. Alexander and Ellen were thrilled to see Brother Kimball among the group. Alexander embraced him, pounding his back, and Brother Kimball introduced them to the Pratt brothers, Orson and Parley, who seemed to be educated gentlemen. Alexander would enjoy them. He loved to learn and discuss. Finally, there was a young farmer in his early twenties. Elder Kimball introduced him as Brother George Smith.

The men were obliged to make other introductions, and, after a quarter of an hour, the Neibaurs prepared to leave.

Ellen took note once more of the group of whispering, pointing Prestonians in the station and saw Patience's sister,

Charity. Ellen smiled and bowed her head to her, and she pointedly looked away.

Without stopping to deliberate, Ellen stalked up to her. "How do you do?" she asked.

Charity's head darted side-to-side to her companions, and she swallowed before slipping into a shallow curtsy. "How do you do, Mrs. Neibaur?"

"See, we *can* be polite." Ellen glanced at Charity's well-dressed companions before meeting her eyes. "Pardon, but what is it you find so distasteful about me and the company I now keep?"

Charity opened and shut her mouth with nary a sound, so the gentleman behind her piped up. "We don't want devil-worshippers in Preston." Others chorused in agreement.

"Ah," Ellen said, "Mr. Branson. A pleasure to see you. I assure you we would never--"

Alexander tugged on her arm. He leaned in, tickling her ear with his beard. "You know it is difficult for me to walk away, but it will not help our situation to draw attention to their disdain."

Ellen fumbled away from him and finished her thought. "I assure you we only want to follow God."

Mr. Branson huffed, and Charity disappeared in the crowd.

Young Joseph's eyes were brimming with worry. It would be ill-advised to start a quarrel in front of the children. She allowed Alexander to lead her out of the station with the children in tow. "I know your temper, Alexander," she said as they exited. "How can you stand idly by while being treated thus?"

"It will only make more of a division between the two groups, and we all need them to forget their anger and patronize our businesses."

～

WEDNESDAY AND THURSDAY of the following week were filled with General Conference meetings at the Cockpit. Willard Richards, who had remained in England to preach all this time, was there. John Taylor, Joseph Fielding, Theodore Turley, and Wilford Woodruff were also present. Nearly the whole quorum was in Preston, and the room buzzed with excitement.

Elder Kimball presided over the meetings. Ellen guessed that there were over two thousand members in the old Cockpit today. It was decided that a monthly periodical would be published in England, the Millennial Star. They also planned to print hymns, the Book of Mormon, and the Doctrine and Covenants locally.

Brother Brigham spoke next. He called for the Saints to leave Mother England in small groups and join the Saints in America. Ellen's brows rose, and her stomach simultaneously sank. There were wide, attentive eyes all around trained on the elder. It had never occurred to Ellen that the Church might ask them to leave their homeland.

The room spun, and she would have swooned if she had not already been seated. Was he requiring this move or merely suggesting the Saints should go if they felt so inclined? Ellen's heart quickened.

Alexander fanned her with his hand. "Are you well, dear? You look as if you had seen a ghost."

She willed her breathing to slow and her mind to quiet. "No," she said, her thoughts churning as butter. "I am not well."

Brother Brigham asked that those with the means to do so, help the needy immigrate. Many who had been poor were now destitute because of prejudices against the Church, and, though Alexander and Ellen had more than most, she could scarcely fathom how much such a journey would cost.

And not only monetarily.

Preston was like a cracked acorn. What would happen if

their half, that of the members of the Church, sailed away across the world? Could Preston survive such an upending?

And what of her family? One of the greatest desires of her heart was to mend her relationships with them. Would the Church physically remove her from them forever? Alexander would be able to write them from time to time if paper and ink could be found, but would she ever hear from them if she left?

Crossing the vast depths of the sea was something other people did, not Ellen, not her children. They were content in Preston. She had desired to move out *to* the country, not out *of* the country.

No. The bulk of the Saints may leave, and her life could return to a semblance of normalcy. Perhaps her father would even grow to appreciate Alexander as time continuously clicked forward.

The conference adjourned. Alexander and the children were standing around her, waiting. She blinked to clear her head and stood.

Alexander steadied her. "You look shaken. There is no rush."

"It is this talk of moving to America that has me thus."

"I was likewise surprised, but it does make sense, does it not?"

She scowled at him. "I am not sure that it does. Have they not spoken of establishing the Church throughout the world? Why are they making plans for periodicals and local printings, only to leave?"

He lifted his shoulders. "Maybe only a few will actually make the journey."

Ellen sighed in relief that Alexander did not seem to expect his own young family to up and leave.

He led them outside and down the cobblestones. "Let us hurry out of the chill. I do not want anyone becoming ill."

Ellen smiled gratefully. While not prone to illness, she was petite and delicate, and it bothered her not a bit that he treated her as such. She liked to be protected and taken care of, and they did not want to risk the lives of any more children. Protecting their family was one of Alexander and Ellen's most important responsibilities. Crossing the ocean to America was out of the question. It would be far too dangerous.

When Alexander had promised her adventures, she never imagined that such a tremendous one as traveling to America would be in the realm of possibility. She shook her head. Alexander, who had seen foreign destinations around the world, might be intrigued by the prospect, but she hoped it would not be too difficult to make him see reason.

"You are worrying me with your silence, Ellen. Tell me your mind on the matter."

"My mind is circling like the windmill. I scarcely know my own thoughts."

"Let me put your mind at ease. We will study the options together, pray, and discuss until we know the will of God."

She cringed. "That is what has me frightened. You always do the will of God, not the will of your wife."

He chuckled. "As you know, I have not always done the will of God, but I am trying to forge a better path for our future than I sojourned in my youth. Is your will to stay?"

"Of course it is."

He moved closer and spoke softly. "Even if God calls us to move with the Saints?"

"Has God called us?"

Alexander's gaze penetrated hers. "Not yet, but we do need to ask Him."

She shook her head. "I should prefer not to ask."

"Because you know the answer already?"

"Because I fear what the answer may be."

SUMMER RETURNED, and with it, forty-one souls sailed away for the American Zion, including the Snailhams. As the Neibaurs waved a final goodbye to them from the Cockpit doors, Ellen suspected she would never be in their company again. A small group of Saints next to her spoke of their anxiousness to be next to leave. She hoped her lack of desire to go was a sign they would not be required it of God.

On their walk home, Alexander said, "I have a few appointments with patients this week. These rumors of the Saints leaving may help me find more work."

Ellen nodded, shifting Isaac to her other hip as they walked. "That is good."

"I thought we may be able to give a little money to those attempting to raise the funds to leave."

She hugged Isaac closer. "That is a wonderful idea."

He smiled. "I am pleased you think so. We can save for our own journey after we help some of the more impoverished to leave."

"Alexander," Ellen said with a sigh, "this is my home. I do not wish to leave. This is the perfect opportunity to make amends with my family and with the town and move on. The poorest are likely to find a better life in America, but we have everything we need here, especially if people are becoming more apt to come to you with their dental woes."

He scratched his beard. "Brother Brigham says Nauvoo is a prosperous city, and surely they could use a dentist. It may be an opportunity for us to start over. Did I tell you what Nauvoo means?"

Ellen shook her head and shifted Isaac's growing weight again.

"It is a Hebrew word, meaning beautiful and comely. Do you suppose the Prophet Joseph Smith has an interest in Hebrew?"

"Of that, I have no idea, I assure you."

"It may be a sign from God."

"What is?"

"A Hebrew word calling to a Hebrew man. Do you not think we should stay with the Saints?"

Ellen changed the subject without answering. "Will you write Papa to expect a visit Thursday next?"

"Ja. Will you be bringing the children?"

"Yes."

"I will write."

On the appointed day, they arrived at Darwen Park. Heavy, steamy air dampened their hair and skin. Papa greeted the children, who skipped off despite the oppressive heat.

"Shall we walk through the park?" Ellen asked.

"On a day like today?" Papa asked, then shrugged. "I suppose we can take a short walk to the stone bench in the garden. The oak tree there will provide ample shade."

Ellen nodded, and they snaked through the park to the bench in relative silence.

Papa sat on one end, and Ellen scooted beside him.

"What brings you today?" Papa's voice held a hint of suspicion.

She laced her hand into his arm. "Do I need a reason to visit?"

Papa gazed down the pathway from whence they had come. "We have precious little to say to one another. You have left the Church of my fathers. You no longer see the Bible as the whole of God's word. You do not care for my advice. As soon as you met your foreign dentist, you ceased listening to me." His words were barely over a whisper, filled with resignation, even despair. "What is there for a father to do?"

"And you do not listen to me. You might understand my point of view and see the situation with more respect."

"I do not respect your situation, nor is it right for you to ask me to," he said with increasing volume. "I do not respect that husband of yours who changes religion like a fop changes cravats."

"Papa!"

"What? You want to talk, do you not? Would you prefer to converse about the weather? It is sweltering and sticky. There. Now you may nod, smile, and leave as you are wont to do in your attempts to avoid confrontation." He stood as if to depart but then sat again on the end of the bench with a groan, facing away from her, head in hands.

"I am sorry to distress you so," she said, rubbing his arched back.

Papa sat up straighter. "Actually it is good you have come. I have a matter of business to talk to you about."

She gripped the bench.

"You have betrayed our family, and, having done so, are no longer welcome at Darwen Park." He moved his head side to side like an animal sniffing for food. "You will be forgotten both in writ and attitude. If you choose, as I hope, to return to regular church service at the Church of England and leave the blasted Mormon cult, you will be welcomed once more."

Joseph walked up with Isaac on his hip.

Ellen took Isaac. "Joseph, please find Maggie. Something has come up, and we must leave straight away."

He sauntered away in search of her.

Ellen stared at the trees in stunned silence. She could not believe her Papa had spoken such words. "Why are you doing this?"

His eyes looked pleading. "To teach you that your actions have consequences. To help you see reason."

She rose, her shoulder brushing against his. "I believe you know that I cannot in good faith do as you ask."

"Do I? Sometimes I think you are only following the whims of your Alexander." He spit the name out.

"Perhaps I sometimes do, but I believe the Church is true, Papa. I believe in the Book of Mormon."

He pursed his lips. "Word from town is that some of the Mormons are fleeing to America." He narrowed his eyes, apparently observing her reaction.

"It is true."

He huffed. "Good riddance."

She lifted her chin. "And what if we were to go?"

He opened his mouth and closed it, watching a passing bird before answering. "I would have you stay and rejoin the Church of England, but, if you are to remain one of them, you may as well go. It matters not to me."

The children approached once more, and Ellen turned back and forth between them and her father, brows raised as if to say, "They matter not?"

He gave quick embraces to each of them before they left, and when he held Ellen, he whispered, "Think about what I have said."

Feeling the pain behind her eyes, she said, "Goodbye, Papa."

The final bricks were laid in the wall they had been building between them, tall and impenetrable.

ELLEN MADE appointments for Alexander and herself to receive patriarchal blessings by the laying on of Brother Melling's hands, hoping for some much-needed direction. When it was time to leave, Alexander checked his pocket watch. "Shall we take the carriage?"

"Would you mind walking?" she said with an intentional smile and a quick batting of her lashes. "This evening is perfect for a walk. We must take advantage of niceties for which there is no cost."

In response, he held his elbow out.

"Just a moment," she said. "Where are the children?"

"In the kitchen with Louisa."

"Do I have time to kiss them goodbye?"

He grinned. "If you only allow them one kiss each." She dashed to the kitchen, giving each a quick kiss. Each of the children present, of course. Not the one in Heaven. She rubbed the brooch with Samuel's lock of hair trapped inside like buried treasure.

When she returned to the entry, Alexander, as a statue, was still holding his arm out for her and yawning as if she had taken hours. She gave him a little pinch before accepting his elbow and leaving with him.

The warm summer air rested thick. The lamplighter, about a block ahead of them, lit the lamps on the empty street like glow worms floating in the evening sky. Ellen squeezed Alexander's arm, and he flexed. She laughed and leaned her head on his shoulder.

"Alex, I know life is busy and full of worry, but I hope you still feel loved."

She felt his smile rather than saw it. "And I love you, my Ellen."

A gaunt boy in rags stepped in front of them out of nowhere. "Anything to spare, sir?"

Alexander bent down to the boy's level and reached into his pocket, producing a few shillings.

The boy's dark-rimmed eyes sparkled at the sight of them. Ellen's hand moved to rub at a smudge of coal dust on the boy's cheek, but he swatted at her.

"More for my sick sister, sir?" he said as he pocketed the coins.

"That is all I have with me."

"I may have a coin in my reticule," Ellen said, fumbling to the bottom and producing a shining silver shilling.

The boy dissolved into the night as quickly as he had come.

Ellen grinned at Alexander. "It may not be prudent to keep helping others as our own finances provide little extra."

He lifted both hands, palms up. "We cannot turn them away. If we both died, our children would rely on the grace of others to survive."

She did not want to think of that.

The patriarch greeted them warmly when they arrived at his home. Brother Melling was an older man, about the age of their parents, with mostly white hair and a genial face. He invited them into his sitting room, and Ellen's heart raced. She and Alexander had come fasting, and Ellen hoped they would feel prompted to stay in Preston and build His kingdom locally, but something in her suspected that would not be the case.

"May I offer you a refreshment?"

Alexander shook his head. "Not any. Thank you, Patriarch."

"Very well. Who is first then?"

Ellen volunteered.

"Very well," he said again, moving to stand behind her chair. Ellen removed her bonnet and held it on her lap. The patriarch placed both hands on her head and called her by her Christian name. He told her that she was of Israel through baptism and heir to the blessings of Abraham, Isaac, and Jacob. He said great things lie ahead for her.

In her mind, she asked, "Must we emigrate to America?"

Following the unspoken prayer, Patriarch Melling said, "Thou shalt see glorious things and be brought to that goodly land which was given to the fathers of old." Though the words were contrary to her personal desires, her heart swelled, and a feeling of peace consumed her.

They would cross the ocean to be with the Saints. Her children would be raised there, and her posterity would grow up with a prophet in their midst. It was unusual to think of America as a land given to the fathers of old. Most would say that about her beloved England before America, but she knew the Lord meant for them to go.

When the patriarch completed her blessing and lifted his hands, Ellen opened moistened eyes to meet Alexander's gaze. He grinned at her and nodded his acknowledgment of what they had both heard and experienced.

Patriarch Melling moved around to stand behind Alexander and repeated the process. He said, "Be not dismayed at thy present situation. Neither be too anxious but comely. Wait upon the Lord." He promised Alexander that he would see the temple of the Lord raised up again.

Alexander rose at the end of his blessing and heartily shook the patriarch's hand. "Thank you, brother. What a blessing!"

The patriarch waved his hand. "The words are not mine. Thank Him," he said, pointing heavenward.

"We shall do that, too," Alexander promised.

Back at home, Ellen and Alexander kissed the children goodnight, and Alexander sang them Hebrew lullabies. Maggie pet his nose like she used to do. "Pet the bunny," she said, giggling.

Ellen listened to their laughs from her bedchamber.

As long as the Lord did not take Alexander or any more babies from her, they could weather the upcoming storms, whatever lay ahead.

ELLEN PULLED her cloak tightly around her bosom against the chill of the evening as she went alone to see John and Mary. When they did not answer her knock, she proceeded up to the shop where they were working the handloom. They did not stop when she entered, only looked upon her warily.

She greeted them, stepping close. "Has Papa spoken with you?"

John nodded. "He has forbidden us from continuing our association."

She collapsed to the floor beside him, her gathered skirts billowing around her, and looked upon his pained face. "And will you obey?"

Mary stepped over, took her hand, and pulled her up. "We must, Ellen. He has threatened to remove us all from his will if we do not."

Ellen stared at John, but he refused to meet her eyes. "We are moving to America," she told him.

Shock crossed John's face. "Papa said that might be a possibility, but I did not believe it."

"It is true. It is the will of God."

"And the will of Alexander?"

"Yes," she admitted.

He stopped working and turned his body to face hers. "And is it your will, sister?"

She swallowed. "That matters not, as my will is to follow God."

17

Ellen was in the carriage, headed toward the most unpleasant task remaining before they were to board a train bound for Liverpool tomorrow morning. For the first time, the train would not disappear from their view into the distance. They would follow the tracks and round the bend, leaving Preston forever. Their trunks were full to capacity, but it felt like they were leaving everything behind. Although they had asked Brother Kimball and Brother Young multiple times about Nauvoo and America, Ellen could scarcely imagine it. She pictured it like Preston, because that was all she had ever known.

Ellen had not seen her father since that fateful day six months ago, and he would not welcome her home now. When they arrived in Nauvoo, she would dictate a letter to him, but today her visit would be to Samuel Peretz's gravesite.

Having had Alexander write to Patience, she hoped her once most intimate friend might meet her there, but she knew little hope. Patience had made her position on the Mormons—and their friendship—clear.

Cradling a bouquet of wildflowers, Ellen descended the carriage and strode to Samuel's grave in the churchyard. She knelt beside the gray stone marker, arranging her skirts around her, and placed the flowers at its base before leaning her head onto the cold gravestone and wrapping her arms around it, remembering the way she had spent countless hours running her hand along the empty cradle beside her bed. "I am so sorry I failed you. I am hopelessly lacking, but I am trying not to fail your brothers and sister. Forgive me." She hummed Lavender's Blue before sitting erect and running her fingers along the engraved words and brushing away a bit of dirt that had settled in the curves of the letters.

Someone sniffled and knelt next to her. Patience took Ellen's arm and rested her head on Ellen's shoulder.

"Dear Patience," Ellen whispered. "Thank you for coming."

They sat in the deep silence of mourning. At long last, Patience lifted her head and spoke softly. "Life has been difficult for you if rumors are to be believed." Her gaze pleaded with Ellen. Then she pressed on. "Surely you are not taking your young family to the godforsaken wilderness of America."

Ellen's shoulders rose and fell. "I am afraid the rumors prove true." She fingered the brooch that had been Patience's gift the last time they had seen one another.

Patience nodded, seemingly unsurprised but unready to let go of a lifelong friend. "I would try to convince you not to embark on such a journey if I thought it might make a difference." She met Ellen's eyes from beneath her lashes, then glanced meaningfully at Ellen's once again swollen belly. "Especially in your apparent condition."

Ellen nudged her. "Really, Patience. Ladies do not speak of such things."

"No, but intimate friends might." She smiled warmly.

"Am I not always in this condition?" Ellen used the hem of

her skirt to smooth the dirt around the bottom of the stone. "We are packed. The cemetery is my final stop. We board the train tomorrow. In a few days' time, we will be on the Atlantic."

"So soon?"

"I would try to convince you to join me if I thought it might make a difference."

Patience laughed. "You must be mad."

"Perhaps. I am toting three children to a strange country without so much as a maid of all work. I do not know what I shall do without Louisa." Ellen took Patience's hands. "But suppose I am not mad. I know how you and Mr. Walker feel about the Mormons, but I would be remiss if I did not speak further. Dear friend, please read the Book of Mormon. It has the power to change everything."

"Clearly," Patience said with a teasing smile. She gently broke a browned leaf from one of the wildflowers on Samuel's grave and tossed it into the wind.

"I am quite serious. You will not understand why Alexander and I would willingly give up everything I have ever known unless you read that book and ask God if it is His truth."

Patience bit her lip. "Very well."

Ellen looked at her with surprise. "Will you?"

"I said I would."

"Promise me."

Patience moved her head very slowly up and down. "I promise," she said softly, seeming to surprise even herself.

Tears pricked Ellen's eyes as she nodded. "May I burden you with one more request?"

Patience threaded her hand through Ellen's arm. "Anything."

Ellen swallowed her sadness, leaving an ache in her throat and chest. "I only wondered if you might come to Samuel's grave once in a while in my stead."

With a squeeze of Ellen's hand, Patience nodded wordlessly.

"Thank you. I will continue to treasure our friendship from afar, and it will bring me great comfort to picture you right here in this churchyard. With my son."

"I am sorry we have not seen one another of late. Who knew it would come to this?"

"Not I." Ellen sighed. "Take care, dear Patience."

"And you, as well."

Ellen hugged her friend, attempting to put all her love for Patience and all she had lost and was about to abandon in one final embrace, and, sending a blown kiss to settle over Samuel's coffin in her absence, she said, "Goodbye."

AFTER A TEARFUL FAREWELL TO LOUISA, the Neibaurs boarded the train at twenty minutes past eight o'clock.

Joseph and Maggie were wide-eyed with excitement, naming everything they saw. "There is the station!"

"The platform!"

"The green train! That one has always been my favorite. Is that our train, Abba?"

With trunks loaded, Joseph and Maggie were bouncing in their seats.

"When will we leave?" asked Maggie, who was dressed in her blue morning dress with a matching feathered hat. It was Ellen's favorite outfit on her. When had she grown up? How much of their homeland would Maggie and Joseph even remember?

Isaac squirmed in Ellen's arms, grumpy about being out and about so early. He seemed to sense his parents' anxiety and made everything a touch more trying. Isaac, at nearly two years old, would not remember England at all, nor the family members they were leaving behind.

Ellen placed Isaac in Alexander's lap and angled herself to observe out the window. Throngs of people were embracing and scurrying from place to place.

She hoped they were doing the right thing.

The train lurched forward, and Joseph dashed to the window in front of Ellen, followed by Maggie.

Joseph rapped at the window. "Did you wave to Mrs. Walker, Mama?"

"What?" Ellen's eyes followed Joseph's pointing finger and landed on Patience standing still in the middle of the jostling crowd, holding her hood on her head with one hand and waving vigorously with the other.

"Thank you," Ellen mouthed, placing her palm on the window as the train lurched forward.

The moment passed, and the station, followed by Preston, were forever lost from view. Ellen wiped a tear from her cheek and leaned into Alexander, struggling to keep her emotions beneath the surface. She would never see Patience again.

The train ride from Preston to Liverpool took over two hours, but it passed quickly, due to the excitement of Maggie and Joseph. Rolling hills tumbled by, and England's unknown towns came in and out of sight for the first and last time.

"We are going fast. Are we not, Abba?" Joseph said.

"We are. Before the railway, this two-hour journey to Liverpool took days."

"Too bad there are not any trains across the Atlantic."

They all chuckled.

The countryside gradually turned into a heavily populated city. "Is this Liverpool?" she asked Alexander.

He checked his pocket watch. "I believe it is. We will arrive at Lime Street Station in approximately four minutes."

The impressive station soon came into view, complete with iron gates and a palisade. Ellen undid Maggie's bow under her chin and re-tied it, fluffing out the loops. She pulled Isaac up onto her lap. Their bodies jolted forward when the train lurched to a stop. Ellen and Alexander looked into each other's eyes, both taking a deep breath. Alexander smiled at her and kissed her cheek before grasping his walking stick with one hand and Joseph with the other. Ellen took Maggie's hand and carried Isaac on her opposite hip.

They stepped from the train and searched the crowd for members of their congregation.

Sister Romney spotted them and, waving, called out. "Brother and Sister Neibaur, we are gathering over here."

The large group moved as a herd to Albert dock, where they boarded the *Ship Sheffield*. Chaos engulfed them until Alexander tugged Ellen's sleeve, and they crossed to the edge of the ship where there was a little more space. Ellen gasped at the sight of the vast, endless ocean. Aware of Alexander watching her expression, having seen it before, she said, "It makes me feel tiny as a beetle."

"Sailing across the Atlantic, you might feel more like a crane fly, still small but gliding around the world." He put his arm around her. "I had almost forgotten the salty scent, but our nostrils will be filled with it for some time."

They bundled the children close.

"Can you see America?" Maggie said.

They laughed, and she scowled in return. Ellen patted her hat. "Not for many weeks yet."

"How many days is that?"

Alexander lifted her, so she could see out over the side of the ship. "We do not know," he said. "It depends on the favorability of the winds. It could take anywhere from twenty to forty days."

"I detest wind," Maggie said.

Joseph raised his chin. "We need all the wind we can get, Mags. You want to go to America, do you not?"

She craned her neck to check her mother's face. "I suppose so."

Ellen wrapped her shawl around Isaac. "It is much colder here than in Preston."

"The coast is always colder," Alexander agreed.

"Will all these people be traveling with us?" Joseph asked, observing as over one hundred passengers piled in around them. "Where will we all sleep?"

"It will be a crowded voyage," Alexander said. "We will sleep below decks with a majority of the passengers in bunks three levels high."

"Do I have to sleep with Maggie?"

"I am afraid you may be sleeping with more than just Maggie," Ellen said. "We will all pack in and make do."

"In one bed?" His eyes were wide.

"In one bed."

"I need to go to the Hargraves Railway Office," said Alexander, "to retrieve our luggage. Will you manage?"

"Of course," Ellen said, missing Louisa more with every passing minute.

Alexander withdrew into the throng of passengers, and Ellen and the children sat on the deck of the ship, huddled close, and observed the hustle and bustle.

The *Sheffield* was a packet ship with three large masts of full sails and weighed about a thousand tons. How such an enormous structure could stay afloat was beyond Ellen's capability of imagining.

A majority of the Saints would be sleeping in the steerage area. Some would even be obliged to take turns sleeping while standing for lack of space, packed in like a school of fish for what was likely to be a full month. It sounded less like an adventure and more like a nightmare. How would they maintain any sense of privacy?

"It is freezing, Mama," said Maggie.

"And I am hungry," added Joseph.

This seemed to remind Isaac that he was both cold and hungry, and he whimpered. "Hungy," he said.

Ellen pulled out a hunk of bread and cheese from her reticule and gave each child a piece. "Once you have eaten, we will see if we cannot find something for you all to do. If we continue sitting here, we might just freeze into solid ice."

They ate quickly, and Ellen discovered a group of children sitting in a large circle, playing Hide the Button. The Neibaur children joined in, with Isaac sitting on Maggie's lap. Ellen located the mothers nearby, also in a circle, and went to join their company.

Sister King's leathery face turned up into a worn smile at Ellen's approach, then she returned her attention to Sister Ann Walmsley, who was in the middle of telling a story, with her kind eyes and thin lips.

Sister Romney moved aside, making space for Ellen in their circle. "Have you heard this before? It is a miracle, to be sure."

Sister Walmsley agreed. "First Henry Clegg, who was fifty at the time, lost the footrace down to the River Ribble to the much younger brother, George Watt. Brother Clegg and Brother Watt each hoped to be the first to be baptized in Europe." She swatted the air. "It was no contest. Poor Brother Clegg." Her face was bright. "I was the first woman baptized on the continent, but I certainly was not running any races." She peeked at Ellen. "You see, I had struggled with consumption for years and was too weak to walk into the water on my own accord. My doctor told me that the sudden immersion would likely kill me." She laughed boisterously. "He could not have been more wrong. I trudged right out of that water unaided. When I was confirmed, the consumption disappeared entirely, and I went about doing the chores I had not been able to do for years."

Sister Walmsley's story warmed Ellen's heart and renewed her conviction about the journey they were undertaking.

When Alexander returned, having secured the luggage, Ellen sent him off again in search of the cook shop and a hot meal for her freezing family, which he obtained.

As the day darkened, there was not anything for the frigid little family to do save go to bed and hunker down under a mound of blankets.

Another day of preparations dawned cold and breezy. Though still docked, the rocking of the ship began to trouble Ellen's constitution. The day was not blustery, but a steady wind swept across the ocean, making the *Sheffield* sway gently back and forth like a baby's cradle. Nobody else seemed bothered by it. Was sea sickness worse when one was expecting? Surely there were other ladies on board in similar condition. Determined to be brave, she did not complain despite her growing nausea.

After breakfast, Alexander went to call upon an old German friend, and Ellen took the children to purchase some last-minute provisions. She bought lemons, salt fish, soap, and a store of candles, meandering through the shops as long as the children could stand, as she was not anxious to reboard the rocking ship.

She stalled until the time arrived when the Saints were to meet Brother Brigham at the dock. Alexander found them and presented gifts from his friend. Ellen gasped when Alexander handed out the finery.

"These are lovely. I cannot imagine we will be wearing them for a ride across the Atlantic, though." There was a boa for Ellen, fur gloves for Alexander, and a white muff for Maggie. Ellen took the items to her bosom, feeling comfort in their softness. "I will tuck them into the trunks for safekeeping."

It took some time to quiet the enthusiastic Saints, but when silence reigned, Brother Brigham arose, his usually impeccable hair flapping in the salty sea breeze. "It has come to my attention that some of this company have not yet paid the necessary funds for this voyage. As you know, it is required that each pay the two-pound deposit before the ship will set sail. Others have paid in full. It is not you to whom I speak. Those who have not paid their dues will go directly to 72 Borlington Street. If you have not paid by eight o'clock tomorrow, you and your luggage will be removed from the ship, and you will abide the consequences of your poor planning."

A couple next to the Neibaurs looked at one another with concern written in their faces. Ellen was relieved to know their tickets were paid for.

"I hope you have also brought or purchased the necessary provisions that your journey may be fair. Brother Hyrum Clark, president of this voyage to Nauvoo, will help you organize into companies."

The meeting concluded with a comment from Captain Porter, a small man with a kindly face. "Thank you, Mr. Young. Welcome to the *Sheffield*, ladies and gentlemen. May the winds be favorable and the incidents few."

"Amen," Ellen said aloud.

Alexander squinted in the direction of President Hyrum Clark.

"Is something amiss?" she asked.

Alexander shook his head, but she was unconvinced and waited for an explanation. "I know President Clark has done many things for the good of the Kingdom in serving as a missionary in America. I heard he participated in the daring rescue of Elder Parley Pratt from Columbia Jail."

"Clearly, you are not telling me everything."

"There is nothing more to tell."

James and Lettice Proctor approached Alexander and Ellen purposefully but with some level of trepidation. "Brother Neibaur," James Proctor said. "We are a bit short on passage funds." He wrinkled his nose. "We are selling some extra clothing, the finest ones, to reach the required amount. Will you check our offerings? We do not wish to turn back."

"Indeed," Alexander said, and they followed the hopeful couple to their trunk.

Ellen tugged her blankets up against the chill air just before Isaac began to stir. She brought him to her breast and nursed him, comforting and warming them both. "You will be bumped from your position as youngest soon," she whispered, her lips brushing the soft hair atop his head. "But your father and mother will always love you just the same."

Light crept into their little draped space in the belly of the ship, which would be their humble home for the next several weeks. Ellen opened her eyes again to find Maggie wearing the muff and prancing back and forth like a fine lady. "Put that back in the trunk, Margaret."

Alexander was sitting on the foot of the bed poring over something. "What is that?"

He held up a brown leather-bound book without any writing on the cover. "A journal. I purchased it in town, so I can record the details of our journey." He paused, thoughtful.

Ellen smiled at him. "Will you read it to me?"

Alexander chuckled, and it healed part of her heart. "There is not much to tell yet. My first entry tells of my visit with Mr. Hauk and his generous gifts and of the meeting last evening."

"I am glad you will keep a record. I have a feeling there will be much to tell."

"One day, you may read it yourself."

She lowered her gaze. "You know I cannot."

He shrugged. "I would love to teach you."

"I may not be able to learn."

He looked skeptical. "We shall see."

Alexander nodded and dropped the subject. "The Spirit told me to do this," he said, holding up the book again.

She moved over and kissed him. "Thank you for being so good." Surely he had made up for his past misdeeds. Any mistakes he made were hiccups in a long line of goodness. But she? Her flaws outshone anything good she did. Earning a happy life, not to mention salvation, felt beyond reach. At her core, she was too weak.

The family went above deck as soon as they were presentable and found all in an uproar. Captain Porter barked orders while the crew rushed about preparing the sails. Though he shouted, a smile remained just under the surface. It was clear he enjoyed the thrill. Ellen leaned on the bow.

At precisely 10 o'clock, with passengers lining the deck, a rugged-looking sailor with wavy long hair and an even longer beard called out. "Anchor's aweigh!"

Ellen clutched Maggie's hand as the ship pulled from shore. Alexander began to sing "How Firm a Foundation", and one by one, the Saints joined in until the roaring of the ship and the waves were drowned out by the chorus of refrains. She and Alexander held onto each other and their children as they sang, "When through the deep waters I call thee to go." Ellen choked on the words. Whether the emotion came from the Spirit, from the longing for her family and the familiar, or from the deep ache she felt at leaving her baby buried in the English countryside, she could not say. Clutching at the brooch from Patience, she knew it was a tangled mix of all three. She burrowed into Alexander as the shore blurred with distance and tears.

"Are you sad, Mama?" asked Maggie.

Ellen squeezed her shoulder but did not trust her voice. Biting back her feelings brought her nausea up, and she was sick over the side of the boat. Alexander offered his handkerchief to wipe her face, but as she reached for it, she was forced to turn her face overboard again and repeat the unladylike upheaval of her stomach. She stayed put for some time with Alexander patting her back, then accepted the handkerchief.

Her knees wobbled, and her head pounded with the pitching of each wave. Alexander supported her weight, directing her to their bunk with the children trailing behind like ducklings. They were nearly there when her stomach began to heave again, but nothing came out, and they proceeded. Alexander helped her into their bed where she fell asleep, waking later to an empty room, oblivious to the time of day. A tin bowl rested beside her, and, knowing it was there for her to be sick in, made her stomach flip. "Little one who will never know England, I am doing this for you. You will grow up with the Saints in Zion, not knowing the rejection of conversion. I am doing this for all of us." She rubbed her belly and rolled over.

The next time she opened her eyes, all were settled for the night, and she scooted into Alexander and fell back asleep.

In the morning, it was difficult for Ellen to as much as lift her head. She tried to sit, but a wave of nausea sent her right back to her pillow. Alexander brought bread, cheese, and water, which she nibbled and sipped to no avail. As soon as it reached her stomach, it came back up again. A deepening crease formed between Alexander's thick brows.

Isaac rolled around like a log on the floor, and Maggie and

Joseph were trying to dodge him by jumping whenever he came near. She could not watch the motion without her head swirling.

"How are you feeling?" Ellen asked Alexander.

He shrugged. "Not as well as them," he said, cocking his head toward the children. "But not as poorly as you either."

A crashing wave shoved the ship to one side, and Alexander seized hold of the bed, nearly falling onto Ellen. Joseph, Maggie, and Isaac giggled in a heap on the wood floor.

Ellen grabbed the bowl and heaved into it. Alexander, who had been fighting to keep the contents of his own stomach down, lost the battle when he saw Ellen and threw up in the bowl as soon as her head was out of the way. The entirety of the day was spent huddled together in their berth, and many other passengers seemed to be doing the same. The grunting sounds and increasing odors of the sick made Ellen feel infinitely worse.

After a couple days in the same attitude, Alexander's constitution grew more accustomed to the constant motion, and he was well enough to take the children up on deck.

Ellen awaited the times when they returned with tales of the sailors and animals with anticipation. But, as much as she loved when they sat with her, she had to admit she was also relieved when they departed. Their enthusiasm exhausted her infinitesimal strength. Alexander seemed to sense when she had had all she could handle and would leave with them for hours at a time while she rested.

In the afternoon of their fifth day at sea, Ellen opened her eyes feeling drained and discovered Alexander beside her with a cup of water and a handful of food in his hands.

"You need your sustenance," he said with a frown.

She nodded, and her head pulsed with the motion. Opening her eyes wider, she tried to comfort him by appearing better than she felt and forced a small smile.

"Eat. For you and the baby. Neither of you will ever see America at this rate."

His eyes were moist, and, for his sake, she forced herself into a sitting position and took his hand.

"The Lord did not set us on this path to die," she said, hoping it was true. The words reminded her of similar sentiments before the inexplicable deaths of her mother, brothers and son, but she shoved the thought from her mind.

Alexander seemed more distraught at her saying, and it frightened her.

She squinted at him. "What is amiss? Where are the children?"

He shook his head. "They are well. I left them with Sister Elizabeth Romney."

"She has five of her own darlings to see after," she protested, but her complaint lacked strength, and who was she to talk when she could scarcely sit up? "What are you not telling me?" She shrunk back under her blankets.

"Allow me to be your doctor."

She glared at him. "Tell me of your concern."

"Very well," he said. "I will make you a deal. Eat and drink, then I shall tell you."

A slow breath escaped her, and she let him help her back up and bring a cup to her lips.

"Your lips are chapped."

She cleared her sore throat. "You always were too concerned with my mouth."

"I am a dentist, as well as a man in love." His smile did not reach his eyes. "Promise me you will not get too worked up when I tell you. I cannot bear to see you ill. I should conceal the events of the day for your own safety."

"Nevertheless, you agreed to tell me."

He stared, unfocused, into the room. "Sister King has died."

"Died?" It came out as a hoarse gasp. "But she was perfectly well in Liverpool."

He swallowed. "Yes."

"What was the cause of death?"

Alexander rubbed his beard, as if deciding if he should tell her. "I believe it is from dehydration." He lifted a hand in defeat. "From seasickness."

She groaned, followed by the upheaval of her newly eaten meal.

Alexander held the bucket for her and placed his other hand gently on her back. "See? I should have left you in ignorance." The worry lines around his eyes deepened. "Promise you will not leave me, Ellen."

Breathing through her mouth to keep from smelling the abundance of odors, she spoke. "Who can keep such a promise? Would one such have saved Sister King? It certainly did not save our Samuel. But tell me, what of Sister King's family?"

"The children are nearly all grown. Her husband is, of course, devastated. The Lord does not stay the storms simply because we are doing as he directed."

Thunder clapped, shaking the ship, as if to accentuate Alexander's statement.

"But he does help us when tragedy strikes." She rolled onto her side away from him. "I miss our baby."

He squeezed her shoulder. "As do I, and I refuse to lose anyone else." Alexander's fighting spirit almost convinced her he could prevent such a thing, but they were in God's hands.

The boat rocked forcefully against a wave, and Ellen peered back at him.

"There will be a service for her on deck in a few minutes. Are you well enough to join us?"

Shaking her head sent another wave of nausea into her throat.

"Very well."

She dozed off after Alexander left, but it seemed only moments later that the ship bumped her awake, and she shot up in time to watch a variety of loose articles fly through the air. A woman shrieked, and Isaac started crying before Alexander and the little ones stumbled across the wooden planks to their berth.

"Hurricane," he called between panting breaths. "Started while Elder Clark was saying a few words after burying Sister King's body in the sea." He lifted Isaac onto the bed. Joseph and Maggie climbed in, too, but Alexander protested. "Come. Mama needs her space. Leave her alone."

"You cannot wander about in a hurricane. Besides, I want you here." She reached for Alexander's hand and pulled him over until the whole family was huddled on the small bed, listening to the whipping of the winds.

AFTER THE HURRICANE, a handful of days graced with fresh, favorable currents lifted everyone's spirits, though Ellen was still confined to her berth. Alexander spoon-fed her on her worst days. Her fate would have already been the same as Sister King's if not for her attentive husband.

On the ninth day of their journey, when Alexander stormed in, picked up his pen, and threw it, Ellen smirked, but she tried to arrange her face to look sympathetic. "What is it, dear?"

"The whole ship will be without dinner tonight. Cook drank too much liquor and neglected his duties. Most of us will survive a missed meal, but you may not." He shoved a finger in her direction. "Your body retains precious little these days."

"Missing a single meal never killed anyone. Do we not have a few items remaining from Liverpool?"

He grunted. "Yes, but we should not have to use them, as dinner is supposed to be included in our five-pound fare."

She suppressed a smile.

"I do not see what you find amusing, Ellen."

"And that is precisely what is amusing."

He stomped from the room again. When he returned with the children some time later, he appeared sheepish.

"Have you decided to be amused with me instead of angry?" she asked.

"Not amused." He scratched his beard.

"Oh dear," she said with a question on her face.

"Cook was flogged. Twenty-four lashes."

Ellen scrunched up her nose. "That is terrible."

Alexander nodded as the ship swayed heavily toward the starboard side, knocking his head into a low beam. He cursed in German.

"Mr. Neibaur!" she scolded.

All night, the *Sheffield* pitched to and fro, but thankfully there was a reprieve again in the morning. A favorable wind blew throughout the day, followed by a much-needed calm night, allowing them to rest deeper than they had in days.

Two weeks into the sea voyage, Elder Clark ordered the whole company on deck for Sabbath services. Ellen, sick as she was, was exempt from the order, but she longed to join the others and told Alexander so. Her frail attempt at climbing from her bed confirmed that she would not be able to.

When her family returned, Sister Walmsley and Sister Romney came over, bringing a couple empty barrels to sit on next to Ellen, who tried to smooth the hair that was a tangled nest atop her head.

They glanced at one another, appearing concerned at her apparent weakness. At seven months pregnant, her belly protruded, and it was difficult to get comfortable, owing to the lack of cushion on any other part of her bones. Her arms appeared positively skeletal. Constant seasickness exacerbated the problem beyond her control, and she wondered for the thousandth time why she and her family had set out away from all they had known, at once seasick and homesick. So she could die, leaving her children motherless in a strange country?

But now was not the time to pine for English shores. "I am afraid I will not be able to be a proper hostess, ladies." Her laugh was weak and raspy. "How was the service?"

"Church is different on a ship, to be sure," Sister Romney said. "The breezes blew so strong at times, it was difficult to hear the speakers."

"The hymns are my favorite part." Sister Walmsley folded her hands together in her lap. "My husband opened the service with a hymn, then after the prayer, we sang another. Heaven feels close as the music pours out into the open sky, as though we are closer to God without great cathedral ceilings overhead. God's creations have always been grander than man's."

A beautiful picture of two hundred Saints praising God on a warm, sunny deck sauntered into Ellen's mind. "Sounds heavenly after being in the same attitude for so long."

"To be sure," said Sister Romney with a sympathetic expression. "But I pity those who are still suffering the persecutions of Preston and cannot afford to leave."

Even though the Neibaurs had lost friends and business associates after their conversion, they had always had enough to live on. Alexander had been able to pay for their passage, as well as help others. His services would always be needed. The faces of Preston's street urchins swam before her, and she vowed that her children would never want for bread. "True," she said. "There are always those who are less fortunate."

Sister Romney smiled. "Back to the services. After the hymn, three more of the elders spoke, followed by another song and the passing of the sacrament. It was so refreshing."

Sister Walmsley added thoughtfully, "We will ask the elders to save some consecrated bread and water for you next time."

A comforting warmth that had little to do with her blankets filled her. "Thank you."

Climbing on Ellen, Maggie wanted to be part of the conversation. "Guess what, Mama?"

Ellen shifted under her weight. "I could not. Tell me."

"After I had the sacrament, I saw the crewmen shoot fish."

The idea of smelling fish sent nausea coursing through her, but she managed enough enthusiasm to appease Maggie. "Do you mean they caught fish?"

"No. They shot them with arrows. Two of the fish are bigger than me." She held her arms out wide.

This topic appealed more to Alexander and Joseph than their previous conversation, and they were quick to confirm Maggie's story. Joseph added, "There was a whole school of them, but they still missed their first shots. Their third or fourth rang true, striking a large fish in the side. They shot it with an arrow attached to a long rope and yanked it up. After the first fish, they could not miss. I can hardly wait for supper."

Alexander grimaced. "I understand that your constitution will not allow for fish. I will be sure to provide you with some salt pork."

Sister Walmsley patted her arm. "We will let you rest. We do not want you to overexert yourself."

The following Sunday, Alexander brought some consecrated bread and water to Ellen. Though it turned her stomach like all morsels did, it also brought a small level of peace to her sickbed. Anything would be better than this blasted bunk, but her legs refused to hold her weight, so she was obliged to stay in it.

Every day was nearly the same as the one previous with friends and acquaintances coming and going. She did not enjoy long stretches of being alone as the others went about the boat freely, but when they returned, it was worse. Their increasingly musty smell never failed to force up the contents of her stomach. Her own children often made her sick, but she did her utmost not to let them know that. Weeks felt like years, and Ellen wondered if they would ever reach their destination. Perhaps her baby would dissolve within her and nothing would ever change from her current state.

Thankfully, if there was one thing Ellen could be sure of, it was change. How her life was turning out was a testament to this. It was nothing like the vision she had for herself growing up, with a quiver full of children playing in the countryside near Darwen Park.

But Alexander was her favorite surprise. Maybe America would be, too, if she could only live long enough to step foot on its soil.

19

Though it was only March, and, despite the constant currents sailing across the ship, temperatures rose beyond anything the Englishmen and women had ever felt in their native land, and as is common, heat sometimes brings out the worst in people.

Sister Walmsley and Sister Nightingale were knee deep in a dispute over sleeping arrangements. Sister Nightingale did not think it fair that the Walmsleys had two bunks allotted to their family, but Sister Walmsley, who got precious little sleep as it was, could not abide the thought of crowding into only one.

Ellen agreed that a whole family in a single bed was a tremendous trial—she should know. She did not speak up, though she thought about it a great deal, wondering if she would have entered the fray if she had not been so very ill, but, truth be told, she preferred pondering to contending, even when well.

Alexander had gone to draw a painful tooth from the steward's mouth and would, no doubt, come back with a biscuit and a bit of salt pork. Fresh meat might be a rare treat, but Ellen preferred the salty bite to the pork.

Throughout the day, swelling waves grew stronger and more forceful. Ellen upended in her bowl. How many times had she done so?

Joseph, Maggie, the Romney children, and some others commenced a game of tag despite the waves. Either the rocking did not bother them, or they thought it added to the excitement of running around and dodging one another. Joseph stumbled into a dark-haired boy twice his size when a particularly powerful wave hurled them toward one another. They laughed and bolted in opposite directions.

Ellen's head swelled with dizziness as she observed their antics, darting around barrels, posts, and trunks. She squeezed her eyes shut. If everything could be still but a moment, she might breathe.

A boy wailed, breaking into her thoughts. It was Joseph.

She forced herself from her perch, and, though she wobbled, she stepped with care to her son, yelling for Sister Romney to grab some cool, wet rags. Ellen crouched beside him, and gently took his red, scalded hand in her shaking fingers.

A brother near them said, "Is it any wonder? I am surprised he is the first. How can we be expected to live like this? Boiling pots for food right next to our berths. Children should not be running around in here." His mumblings grew quieter as he stormed away.

Ellen had been watching the game, thinking only of herself, not the danger in which her children played.

Would she ever be a real mother again?

Sister Romney handed a cloth to Ellen and left in search of Alexander.

"Can you stand?" Ellen asked Joseph.

When he nodded, she helped him to their berth and carefully checked and cleaned his wound.

"It hurts," he told her.

"I know, Joseph."

ONE HOT MORNING, Joseph and Maggie barreled in. "Mama. Mama," they squealed.

Ellen rubbed her sleeping eyes. "What is it?"

"A ship. We spotted another ship," Maggie said.

Words sprinted from Joseph's lips. "A crewman saw their colors at half mast through a spyglass. They're American!"

Ellen laughed weakly. "Slow down. I can scarcely comprehend what you are saying."

Joseph took a long breath and repeated himself, but his words were still quick and overly loud. "It is an American ship in distress with its flag lowered. The crew lowered the sails to wait for it."

Ellen spoke slowly to keep from needing her bowl. "I thought the wind had ceased." The gentler swaying was slightly better on her constitution, but, as Joseph had said weeks ago, they needed the wind to keep the ship sailing, and the faster they arrived in America, the better.

A couple hours later, the scene repeated with her breathless, stinky, excited children making another report.

"Mama. Mama," Maggie said. "The ship was all right. The flag was half mass because..."

"Half mast," Joseph corrected.

"Half mast," Maggie said, emphasizing the T. "America has a new president on the throne. His name is President General Harrison. Is that not the loveliest name?" She twirled. "Soon he will be our president."

"I suppose you are right." Ellen swallowed the moisture in her mouth. "Although we will always love our Queen Victoria. Also, I do not believe American presidents have thrones."

Maggie's face fell, clearly disappointed by the news.

Joseph lifted his chin. "The captain realized his mistake, but it was too late. It is dead calm out there, and, though the sails are back up, the ship might as well be anchored. The captain said we must have a Jonah on board for the sea to be so still."

Night and morning passed in calm. Ellen did not mind as it was the first time in a month she did not feel nauseated, though weakness kept her abed. The crew made use of the stillness, touching up the paint on deck until, according to Alexander, the ship gleamed like new.

Sister Walmsley came in late in the afternoon to sit beside Ellen. "There has been another death on the ship."

A tear trickled down Ellen's cheek at the thought of another death, and she did not wipe it away. She wanted to feel it there, a tiny tribute to the fallen. Her own failing body was nearly lifeless. The child in her womb moved more than she did.

"Who?" she asked, hoping it would not be someone she knew, but death always devastated someone. It was selfish to hope she would not be one of the mourners.

"Brother and Sister Proctor's youngest," Sister Walmsley answered.

Ellen shook her head. "Illness or accident?"

"Dehydration."

It could happen to anyone. She might be next. "We bought clothes from them to help with their passage." She scrunched her nose, as if the thought smelled foul. "We tried to help them. I suppose we are partially to blame."

"We did, too. If we had not, they would all be alive and well in England." She sighed. "Why the Good Lord takes some and leaves others is a mystery understood only by Him."

"Will you do something for me?" Ellen asked.

Sister Walmsley answered in a bone-weary voice. "If I can. What is it?"

"Go to my trunk, please. You will see a fine brooch settled upon the blankets."

Sister Walmsley did so, examining it and the lock of hair within. She grasped Ellen's frail hand in both of hers, giving it a gentle squeeze as she handed it over without a word.

Alexander came soon after, sitting in the same spot where Sister Walmsley had been, surveying Ellen with hollow eyes. He lowered his head onto her chest. "Nobody expects to lose a child when they embark on such a journey. I am grateful that when we lost our son, we could not think back to a certain thing we could have done differently for a better outcome. Thoughts of 'if only' will haunt their lives."

She brought her hand to his coarse, curly hair and dug her thin fingers into it, massaging his scalp. "It is no more their fault than ours."

"Does that matter?"

"I suppose not."

"There is more," he said in hushed tones. "Did Sister Walmsley speak to you of Sister Marie Harmon?"

"No. Is she dying, too?"

Alexander shook his head. "Nevermind. There are purple shadows beneath your beautiful eyes. Rest, dear."

She grabbed his hand as he turned to go. "Tell me about Sister Harmon first."

"Not yet. I do not know my own mind on the matter. I will tell you if more details come forward, clarifying the story."

Ellen squeezed his hand and whispered, "With all of us packed in here like cattle, secrets are scarce."

"Too true." He huffed and gave in. "Sister Harmon, as well as some other ladies, are accusing President Hyrum Clark of behaving himself unseemingly toward them."

Ellen's eyes narrowed. "President Clark? Do you believe his accusers?"

He shrugged. "I have had some reservations about him from the beginning, but I did not see this coming."

The children trailed up, and Isaac looked sunburnt.

"Oh, Isaac, you are red as a rose. Come closer. Does your nose hurt?" She pressed a finger softly into his pudgy cheek.

He nodded, tears filling his eyes. "The tops of my feet hurt, too."

Ellen leaned over the side of the bed. Even in the dim lighting, she could see that they were also burnt.

"At least it is not as severe as Harvey Vorough's sunburn," said Joseph.

"Or Henry's blisters," added Maggie.

Ellen kissed Isaac's forehead gently. "Oh dear."

"Is there anything you can do for their burns, Alexander?"

"Not in the middle of the ocean. In Preston, I may have recommended warm milk on it or a paste of some sort. Out here, I can only prescribe time below decks. I shall make sure Isaac does not go out without his hat and shoes."

He looked up at his father with a fat bottom lip.

Ellen half-smiled. "You will look like a common urchin before long."

"You are thin as one, Mama," said Maggie, placing her hand around Ellen's thin wrist.

"No," said Isaac. He raised his pointer finger and poked Ellen's stomach.

They laughed, and, since Isaac enjoyed making people giggle, he continued poking her round belly.

Alexander pulled Isaac onto his lap, smiling. "That will do, Isaac. I will have to teach you not to speak of such things."

"You do not usually care for English propriety," Ellen said.

"True. I was about to become a proper English gentleman when we left. There is no hope for me now." He smirked. "I will have to be a wild American instead."

It was difficult to imagine Alexander working land with his precise, surgical hands. Would Ellen have a maid in America? They would have to employ a cook at the least. Ellen did not know the first thing about preparing meals. Alexander could make challah for Shabbat. That was about it.

The next morning, contention between President Clark and a handful of women peaked. Everyone seemed to be storming about like steam engines, and harsh words were hurled on both sides. Brother Harmon, who sided with his wife, was ready to take up arms against the president. By nightfall, the yelling pounded in Ellen's head.

When the Saints began to settle in for the night, Sister Romney crossed the space to Ellen. "I would tell you all, but I have a feeling you would rather stay out of this nasty business, and I would guess that you have already heard more than enough."

Ellen agreed. "Thank you."

Next morning being the Sabbath, the members of the Church left Ellen for services on deck, and she was grateful for a respite from the noise and chaos. Calming refrains of "How Firm a Foundation" floated on the warm air, and she was reminded of the day, nearly a month ago, when they sang the same chords as they left England behind.

She cried softly without tears and wondered if she was too dehydrated to wet her own eyes.

When the Saints returned, the problems of the past days seemed to have been smoothed over. A wave of peace entered with them, and she eyed the adults as they gathered by the cookfire. She willed herself to sit up, and Alexander came to her aid.

"Are you well today?" he asked, appearing surprised that she wanted to sit up.

"A bit better, I think."

"I see that." Relief relaxed his features. "Do you wish to sit by the others?"

She placed her hand in his. "Yes, thank you."

Alexander, supporting her fragile frame, half carried her over to the small grouping of Saints. Sisters and brothers cheered at their approach, bringing a blush to her gaunt cheeks.

Sister Walmsley placed an arm around Ellen and helped her sit. "It is so good to have you join us," she said, with a gentle squeeze.

"Thank you. It does feel like an accomplishment of sorts. Tell me about the services."

"Before the Sacrament was passed," Sister Walmsley said, "Brother Francis Clark started the meeting in the pleasant shade of the sails with a sermon about righteous and unrighteous conduct relating to the case of President Hyrum Clark. He admonished that any that had to make a confession not partake until they were reconciled. The president rose and begged forgiveness from any he had offended. He cried in depths of humility and many of the others' eyes filled with tears."

Ellen turned to Alexander. "Do you believe him?"

Alexander jutted out his lips. "He seemed sincere."

The Saints reminisced about their homeland while the children skipped about, careful not to come too close to the fire or the boiling pot of beans hovering over it.

The next week took Ellen back to her bed with the ship sailing a solid nine knots an hour. The evening at the cookfire had rejuvenated her somewhat, though, and she looked forward with hope and longing for the day they would step ashore, and she would never have to be seasick again.

ELLEN SLAMMED into Alexander as the tossing of the ship threw her toward him in the bunk, and the weather did not improve from there. Many were confined to their beds due to the stewing storm. The stench below decks became rank, and the children were tasked with emptying chamber pots more often than normal.

Brother King entered the room the next morning with the first smile Ellen had seen on his face since the passing of his wife. "We are near the islands of the West Indies. You can see some of them off the port bow, though at some distance." The company cheered, many from their sickbeds. "It is a fine morning above deck," he continued. "Those who have recovered enough to walk may feel better up there."

Brother King stalked over to speak with Alexander, and Ellen could not help but overhear. "On a darker note, Brother Neibaur, the First Mate spoke to some of us as were up there, respecting the inability of the crew as seamen. He spoke some harsh words."

"Seems late to say such a thing as we have made it this far," said Alexander.

"Maybe," said Brother King, "but I expect the most difficult job for the crew is to bring the *Sheffield* into port."

"Is that what the First Mate is concerned about?"

"Aye."

"I am inclined to trust Captain Porter and the crew. They are a good lot, rough around the edges as sailors are wont to be, but they will deliver us to America safe and whole."

Brother King shrugged. "Not much we can do for it anyway."

Joseph ran in. "I saw St. Dominic and Antigua. How I wish you could see them, Mama. It would do you good. I am sure of it!"

"As do I, Joseph. As do I. Soon enough, we will arrive. How much longer do you expect, Alexander?"

"It could still be a fortnight."

Ellen groaned and rubbed her stomach but tried to appear

optimistic for the sake of the children. "A fortnight is not so long considering we have already survived five weeks." She put on a brave face.

Alexander squeezed her hand. "We will conquer this journey yet."

Ellen awoke to Brother John Alston having words with Sister Alice Standing, and she could not help but think that all parties needed some time and space apart from one another. Brother Alston, an eligible bachelor who usually acted well his part, would never have spoken in such a way to a lady in England. They had all but forgotten their manners.

Thumping footsteps sounded on the deck above, followed by shouting. Alexander yanked on his hat, boots, and jacket and ran out of sight with a herd of other men, leaving Ellen and the children on the bunk.

She could not make sense of the screams and thuds. Her nerves were never helpful for nausea, and her stomach gurgled.

Brother Romney ran back into view. "The First Mate commanded the crew to paint." He took a panting breath, hands on his knees. "Crewman struck him. Thrice! One of the men is yelling that the First Mate had threatened to split his skull last night." The moment Brother Romney finished speaking, he disappeared again.

A few whispers began, and Ellen wished to hear what they

were saying. Not knowing the First Mate or crew as well as anyone else, she scarcely knew what to think. She sat up, protecting her children in her arms.

Moments later, she heard a group of men stomping toward them. A crewman burst in, his head swinging from side to side, his wide eyes searching the room. He bolted to a corner, where he curled up under a bunk and barricaded himself behind a trunk. At the back of the group, Captain Porter stood, brandishing handcuffs.

She held her little ones tighter, tucking them behind her like a mother hen pulling her chicks under her wings.

Two of the more muscular men yanked the trunk away from the offending crewman, who braced himself under the bedposts. Captain Porter stormed out and returned a moment later, sword in hand.

The children peeked around Ellen.

The captain had not even crossed the space before he began to yell. "If any man resists, I will split him in two."

The threat seemed to strengthen the offender's resolve, his wild eyes dashing around the room, but his arms and legs were tightly wound around the posts under the bunk. The two strong sailors each pulled on his limbs, untangling and yanking with little success.

Ellen shuddered, jaw slack, and Isaac squirmed free, moving away from her on the bed.

The group of men with the captain left the steerage area. During their absence, three others entered and sat in front of the offender, arms folded in defiance.

President Clark returned, followed by Alexander. "I need some men. Brother Whithnell, Brother Walmsley, Brother Hardman, Brother Gore. Come at once."

Alexander's shoulders slumped.

"I am glad you have not been called upon," whispered Ellen when he sat by her. "I do not wish to be alone with lunatics."

Alexander straightened. On the other side of him, Isaac slipped from the bed and screamed. The fugitive untangled himself and crept toward Isaac.

"No," Ellen yelled, sitting up and sliding from her bunk.

President Clark and the other brethren returned, brandishing pistols and pointing them at the mutinous men. "It will be better for all of you if you come peaceably."

Ellen swept in, scooping up Isaac and returning to the bunk.

The offenders held steady, so the brethren raised the pistols in their direction.

Ellen held her breath, barely conscious of the children pressing into her from behind.

One of the mutinous men groaned and swore but rose to his feet at length, arms raised in surrender, and the others followed suit. The wild-eyed sailor allowed the captain to clap irons onto his wrists.

Captain Porter waved his sword toward the door. "Take him to the longboat, and contain him within."

The brethren kept their guns raised and directed the sailors from the room.

Captain Porter glanced around over those who were left. His eyes softened. "I would not hurt the hair off any man's head if I was not forced. I say, this ship is in a state of mutiny. Best look out for the safety of your wives and your children."

He bowed and went out the door, and the Neibaurs held on tight to one another.

BABIES DO NOT WAIT for a convenient situation to arrive. Sister Whithnell's time had come despite mutiny and squall. The ship pitched side to side. Some of the sisters created an enclosure of blankets surrounding Sister Whithnell, who was writhing, pulling on a sheet, and clenching her teeth against the pain.

Ellen wished to help, but the movement of the *Sheffield* kept her firmly on her side, clutching her own rounded belly. Who would help her deliver when the time came? She would be an ocean away from her beloved midwives. Would she, like Sister Whithnell, deliver under adverse conditions with only a few women who had never delivered babies before? What if the baby arrived while they were still on the ship? She gulped. It should not be time yet.

The ship heaved, and Ellen was sick in her chamber pot. Her head pounded with Sister Whithnell's cries, and still the baby did not come.

Just as she began to think this would end poorly, she heard a clap, several sighs of relief, and the fragile cry of the newest passenger.

The makeshift curtains shifted, and, between them, Ellen glimpsed the wrinkly pink baby.

Half an hour later, the curtains were removed, and Sister Whithnell was propped up, holding her sleeping baby tight against the rocking of the *Sheffield* when Brother Whithnell stumbled across the room and knelt by them, tears of gratitude in his eyes. "I was afraid to hope for a good outcome in such conditions," he said. He seemed to want to say more, but instead he puckered his lips, kissed the baby's head, and kissed his wife soundly on the mouth.

Ellen smiled and closed her eyes. The cycle of birth and death continued whether on land or on sea, whether the day burned bright or torrential rain pounded and waves crashed, whether it was surprising or as constant as a rising tide.

Alexander and the others filtered back into the room throughout the day, many confining themselves to their beds against seasickness. By evening, the Neibaurs were huddled together.

"Mama, I am going to be sick," said Maggie.

Ellen passed her the pot, and Alexander rested his hand on her back while she made use of it.

The squall was still raging when shouts startled Ellen. She turned weakly toward them.

Sister Standing lifted her head and yelled above the thunderclaps. "The Captain and First Mate are the ones at fault, and I cannot believe you would arm yourself against a man who was being mistreated. Now he is being held in confinement, and I have a mind to sneak out and set him free."

Brother Standing placed his hand on her shoulder, apparently to calm his wife. "All we are saying is that the situation was not handled well."

Brother King's breath puffed out in disbelief. "Would you choose chaos and mutiny over order and safety? Is it not appropriate to arm yourselves in defense of family and friends?"

Brother Standing moved closer to Brother King until they stood nose to nose. "You question my honor. This was not about the safety of my family."

Brother King spread his feet wider and puffed out his chest. "In cramped quarters, threats affect everyone. Maybe you belong in confinement to keep the peace. Shall I find the captain?"

"Tell him to bring the irons," someone else called.

Sister Standing's eyes darted to her husband, and she pulled him away to their berth.

The night dragged as sleep was scarce between the sounds of the storm and Baby Whithnell not being accustomed to sleeping on the same schedule as the other passengers.

The next couple days were intermittently warm and squally as the breezes changed from a southwest wind to a northwesterly. Joseph came to tell Ellen they had spotted Jamaica. "You should see the coffee plantations, and the First Mate caught a barracuda."

"Ship on fire! Ship on fire!" someone screamed.

Ellen shot into a sitting position, but Alexander pressed her back to her pillow. "I will see what is happening."

Brother Whithnell dashed over to his little family, grabbed the infant, and helped Sister Whithnell to her feet.

"Ship on fire!" someone yelled again. Men rushed by, water sloshing from their full buckets and cans as they ran. A sister swooned and hit the floor.

Despite Alexander's words, Ellen rose onto wobbling legs, and, holding Isaac's hand, she led the children slowly toward the door.

The pungent odor of smoke filled the space, and Ellen and the children coughed. Where was Alexander, and how far was Jamaica? Were they to drown? Heaven knew they could not swim, and, if Ellen knew anything after several weeks at sea, it was this: the ocean's many moods were harsh and unpredictable.

Brother Romney met them at the entrance to the steerage deck, coughing. He waved a sheet, cutting through the thick, choking air. "All is well. All is well."

"What about the fire?" Ellen asked.

He shifted uncomfortably and coughed again. "There was a fire, but there was never any danger."

In direct conflict with Brother Romney's words, Brother George Scholes stumbled in with severe burns on his face. Alexander was with him, supporting his stumbling steps to his bunk, then administering to him by wrapping torn pieces of sheets around his wounds. Ellen caught Alexander's eyes, and he nodded to her once, reassuring her that, although all was not well, the present danger had passed.

When President Hyrum Clark came in, head hung low, he walked over to Brother Romney, and they had a whispered conversation. Many of the eyes of the Saints were upon them.

President Clark lifted his hands over his head and cleared

his throat, ensuring the attention he already had. "First, let me reassure you that the fire has been extinguished with minimal internal damage to the *Sheffield*."

Ellen exhaled.

"When I went to draw spirits, the brandy cask caught fire. I am sorry for my carelessness and for the panic I inspired. Furthermore, I am saddened that Brother Scholes was injured and wish and pray for a speedy recovery for him. I personally will be checking on him often and hope you will all do the same. Thank you to Brother Neibaur for your help. Tomorrow, during our Sabbath services, I will be thanking the Lord for his infinite goodness in preserving us this day."

TIME FINALLY BEGAN to speed up. The monotonous days at sea shifted into days of increasing news.

When they came upon a ship called The Julius, Captain Porter spoke to the crew and ascertained that she was also headed to New Orleans—only her cargo was coffee, not emigrants. Sister Hadgsen delivered a healthy baby boy, who cried louder than the Whithnell's newborn and slept far less.

The next day, Joseph and Alexander told her of two more ships, and Ellen's heart pounded with hope. More ships had to mean they were nearing their destination. Toward eight o'clock, the evening being fine, a crewman caught a dolphin measuring almost five feet long, and it was but two days after, when the mate caught a second, nearly as large as the first. As provisions were growing scarce, the dolphins were a boon. Even Ellen ate a few bites without throwing up.

A third dolphin was caught the following day in the Gulf of Mexico, and the remaining provisions were divided up. Unease abounded among the Saints, but Ellen could not find the strength to worry herself. They were so close she imagined she could smell grass and trees. Surely everyone would get along once they had a bit more space to call their own.

After a more restful night, she heard commotion above and waited to be told what was afoot.

At last, Sister Romney came. "The seamen are preparing to lay anchor."

A great breath of relief gushed from Ellen. She had made it.

Alexander and the children came beside her. "You will have to walk up to the deck today, Ellen."

"If it means getting off this ship, I will fly." She straightened, and, though her head swirled, she found her balance and slowly rose to her feet with Alexander's hand tightly around her waist. Her legs trembled.

"Hooray," the children cheered. Others, hearing them, joined in the revelry, much to her embarrassment.

The Romneys offered to help Alexander with their trunks, since she could not walk unassisted. He half-carried her up to the deck where she stopped for a deep, cleansing breath of fresh salty air. She had not seen so much as the surface of the deck since they left England all those weeks ago. Alexander guided her and the children, one painstaking step at a time, through the crowd toward a steamer.

Ellen paused, her face wrinkling in concern. "You did not warn me that we were only leaving this ship to board another."

"I could not, my dear, as I was afraid you would not come, and I cannot live happily in America without you."

21

The morning was frosty, a stark change after weeks of stuffy heat on the open ocean. Ellen gulped the cool, cleansing air as the family cuddled together in the herd of passengers.

It was a grand boat, much smaller than the one that had carried them in its belly all these weeks, but with fine carved details, cushioned seats, and formal dishes and utensils.

"We will have a small cabin to call our own," Alexander said.

What a difference a little privacy would make in the attitudes of the Saints. What a difference it made to her personally, but she supposed it would not take much to please her after so long on the *Sheffield*.

"How long until we reach Nauvoo?" she asked once she settled into her new bed, spent from the exertion of moving from one boat to another.

The children watched their father, waiting for an answer.

He hesitated. Not a good sign. "As it happens, it is a very long river."

Joseph stared. "Surely not as long as the ocean, Abba."

"No. Not that long." Alexander chuckled. "We have about 3 weeks of boat travel yet."

Ellen steeled herself, but Maggie threw herself on the other bed and moaned. Ellen caught Alexander's eye, and they shared a moment of amusement at her dramatic reaction.

He plopped down beside Maggie and pulled her head onto his lap. "These weeks will go more quickly than the last. On the ocean, once in a while we saw a dolphin, a whale, or a ship. Now we are in America, and every day we will see new cities, new landscapes, new people. Things your grandparents never dreamed of."

Maggie burrowed into his chest, followed by Isaac and Joseph. Alexander tickled Joseph's stomach until he cried out for mercy. After Maggie received her tickle torture, she climbed up his back onto his head. Joseph wiggled his fingers on his father's neck.

Alexander attempted to shake them off like a dog shaking water from his fur while it was Isaac's turn to squeal.

Ellen wrapped her thin arms around her protruding stomach and was grateful for her dear husband. Another blessed child would call him Abba.

On a short stroll around the boat, Ellen held onto Alexander's arm. A beautiful New Orleans plantation spread before them. Joseph pointed at the men working the fields. "Look at all the workers, Mama."

Ellen nodded, and Alexander pursed his lips.

"What is it?" she asked.

He answered in a voice only loud enough for her to hear. "When I went ashore to make some purchases, I overheard the steward telling a crewman to take the cook into New Orleans and sell him. They were speaking as if he was livestock. Louisiana is one of the chief slave states."

"I did not know," Ellen said, surprised.

"The day we missed a meal because of the cook was upsetting to me, I admit, but I would not wish a slave's life on anyone."

Ellen squeezed his arm, then acted on a sudden impulse to kiss his cheek. It was so good to be part of everyday life again.

In the evening, all the passengers were to bring their luggage out to be inspected by the officer from the custom house. As the last few travelers brought their belongings out, torrential rain pelted them, and they scrambled to secure their items.

The Neibaurs were lucky to have their luggage placed near an overhang. They shoved their trunks underneath it, and Ellen glanced around, seeing many still trying to get their belongings out of the deluge. "We should help."

"I should get you out of the rain. You are too weak to weather such a storm."

She shook her head and moved toward a family nearby, but Alexander grabbed her hand and pulled her toward him, embracing her.

She looked into his eyes. "We should help," she repeated.

"I almost lost you. We should kiss."

Ellen feigned shock. "In front of the whole world?"

"We are in America. They do not care about such things," and he kissed her squarely on the mouth.

As it turned out, the grand first steamer and its private cabins were a short-lived luxury. After only a few days, they moved onto the steamer, *Moravian*, bound for Quincy, Illinois. Quarters were at least as cramped as on the *Sheffield*. The Neibaurs were obliged to share a cot once again, and some were even less fortunate.

Conditions were made more trying with constant, drenching rain, which prevented the passengers from moving about the steamer as they otherwise would have done. Alexander cooked a tongue he purchased onshore. Ellen was grateful for the fresh meat, and, though her stomach growled, she kept it down.

The rain continued with varying force, sometimes accompanied by claps of thunder. During intermissions between storms, they observed the lush plantations and settlements again.

Ellen was filled with fresh hope. "What do you think of America?"

Alexander grinned. "It shall please me as long as you are by my side."

A SOUPY FOG descended upon the *Moravian*, so the captain stopped along shore to await its clearing. Men boarded, selling vegetables, hardware, jewelry, eggs, apples, and pies. Alexander made some purchases, and they feasted like Queen Victoria that night.

After passing more towns, they landed at Vicksburg, an imposing town built on a plateau. They went ashore, walking slowly on shaking legs. Joseph ran ahead, pointing and shouting. Maggie tripped in her excitement. Alexander scooped her into his arms, brushing dirt from her dress, and they hurried to catch up with Joseph, who was kneeling next to a turtle. He held his hand up to stop them from scaring it, but the turtle stretched its head from its shell and lumbered away.

The high-pitched scream of a lady near the steamer drew Ellen's attention, and they turned in time to watch Brother King chop the head off a two-yard-long serpent. Ellen gasped as she covered Maggie's eyes, whether because she saw the creature killed or at the sheer size of the thing, she could not be sure.

Soon after, a terrific storm arose, terrifying the crew and passengers. Rain pounded while thunder and lightning drew nearer. All eyes were on the storm. Around seven in the evening, a tremendous clap of thunder rattled the *Moravian*, followed by the sound of shattering glass. Alexander sped out to investigate, and, while he was gone, Ellen heard screams.

"Fire! Fire!"

Not again. She clung to the children, waiting for news. Would they ever be safe in a home of their own again, free from persecution and terrors?

Alexander came back, soaked to the bone. "All the windows in the wheelhouse blew out. Sparks are flying everywhere, but the rain is keeping the fire from catching."

"Let us pray," Ellen said, wide-eyed.

He agreed, and the family huddled together, their knees on the hard floor. Every noise made Ellen jump while her husband prayed for their safety.

"What shall we do?" she asked.

"I will go out and watch for signs of danger, in which case I suppose we will have to swim."

She could not speak. The prospect of swimming in such a river was only a touch better than being obliged to swim in the open ocean. She held onto the children, trying to be calm for their sakes, and sang them a lullaby.

Alexander left and returned, and, though the time was short, it did not seem so. "The *Moravian* is anchored," he said upon his return, "and the greatest danger has passed."

This one anyway. There were sure to be more. The Lord's vengeance had built up all these years and was being unleashed upon her.

A FEW DAYS went by without incident, so Alexander cleaned the teeth of some of the passengers and crewmen.

When he approached Ellen afterward, his eyes were smiling. "A full day of work makes a man feel that all is right in the world."

Ellen kissed his bearded cheek.

Alexander pressed his face into her lips to prolong the kiss. "You will never guess what I learned today," he said, leaning back.

"Do not make me guess then."

"Very well. The new leader of America, President Harrison, died of typhoid or something similar."

"But he only just took office."

"Yes. A month to the day. I wonder who the next one will be."

~

On the 15th of April, Ellen and her family left the *Moravian* and boarded a fine new boat, the *Goddess of Liberty*.

"A beautiful name for a beautiful boat, is it not?" Ellen said to the awestruck Maggie.

"What is liberty, Mama?"

Joseph and Isaac listened nearby, and she motioned them over. "I am glad you asked. Liberty is the power and freedom to be able to do as one pleases. It is the ability to make one's own choices of how to worship, how to provide a living, and whom to marry."

Maggie smirked at the mention of marriage, and Joseph wrinkled his nose.

Joseph ran his hand along the woodwork outside the rooms as the *Goddess of Liberty* moved majestically up the Mississippi River.

"I could get used to this," Alexander said, as they strolled the foredeck on a sunny afternoon.

A cool breeze rustled the ribbons of Ellen's bonnet. "Always an optimist. Where are all these people going to sleep?"

"I will make sure you have a bed."

She squinted at him. "And you?"

"I have the pleasure of sitting up with the other men. There are enough berths for about half the passengers." He raised his shoulders. "At least packing in like a bundle of wheat will keep us warm."

THREE DAYS after boarding the *Goddess of Liberty*, they landed near Warsaw. President Hyrum Clark left the boat for Nauvoo and later returned with his wife, daughter, and a splitting smile. The captain determined that the *Goddess of Liberty* could not venture any further due to rapids. He engaged a keelboat to take them the rest of the distance, but it did not arrive that day.

When the *Aster* came, they were ready to make the final stretch to Nauvoo.

Lush greenery met them in every direction. Dense trees filled the sloping landscape with only small patches of cleared land, dotted with homes and crops. A large gathering awaited their arrival at the dock. Ellen made eye contact with a pretty lady on shore who smiled and waved. A group of brethren came up to the boat, helped them unload, and offered lodgings for the night.

Most of the Saints took up habitation in a large, stone building. Ellen and the children were happily situated inside while Alexander and several other men stayed out all night to watch over the luggage and keep a fire burning.

In the morning, Brother Snailham greeted them with a hearty handshake and offered to share their home with the Neibaurs until other arrangements could be made.

While the house was not really adequate for two families, it felt luxurious after the last several weeks. Ellen's family slept on the main floor as she was unable to climb into the loft where the Snailhams resided for the time being.

Alexander and Ellen went in search of Brother Thompson about obtaining land once they were temporarily settled. Standing on solid ground felt strange. The rich earth seemed unyielding beneath their feet, but their sea-legs still wanted to give out beneath them, leaving Ellen dizzy.

At Brother Thompson's house, they were greeted warmly by Sister Thompson, who showed them to the gentleman's office. Alexander told them of their need for some land.

"There is plenty of land to be had," Brother Thompson said. "Do you have means of purchasing some?"

Alexander laughed. "That depends on the cost, I suppose."

"Anything is a start," said Brother Thompson. "Many have nothing when they arrive. What is your trade?"

"I am a dentist, sir, educated at the University of Berlin."

Brother Thompson's brows raised appraisingly, and Ellen held his arm proudly.

"I am also a linguist," Alexander went on, "and have experience with several languages."

The man fiddled with some papers on his desk. "I am not sure how much that will help you obtain land."

"I mean, Brother Thompson, that I will teach Hebrew or German or another language for pay or trade, as needed."

Brother Thompson pointed a finger into the air. "There may not be many who are able to pay for such services yet, but Nauvoo is growing in size and prosperity."

The door creaked as it opened, followed by the entrance of a handsome, blue-eyed man with an elegant woman on his arm.

Ellen felt at once that this was both an important man and a kind one. She smiled at the woman, and the man tipped his hat to them. "Welcome. You must be straight off the boat. I'm Joseph Smith, and this is my dear wife, Emma."

Ellen's jaw went slack, manners failing her, and the Prophet guffawed as his wife blushed.

"It is a pleasure to meet you, Brother Smith." Alexander shook his hand with vigor and introduced Ellen to the Prophet. His blue eyes penetrated hers.

He pumped Ellen's hand. "Call me Brother Joseph, please. Were you part of President Hyrum Clark's company?"

"Yes, sir," Alexander said.

"I'm sorry I was not there to greet you upon arrival." He squinted. "Many expect me to be taller, shorter, older, wiser, calmer, you name it, so I will apologize now if I do not live up to your expectations." Emma smiled at him from underneath her lashes.

Ellen did not know what to say, and it seemed Alexander was in the same state.

"You're not English," Brother Joseph stated to Alexander.

The corners of Alexander's lips lifted in a proud grin. "I am a Jew, born at a fortress on the border of France and Germany. My father served as a surgeon and linguist in Napoleon's army."

Brother Joseph's face lit up. "That does make you different, and are you still a Jew?"

"Once a Jew, always a Jew, but I am also a baptized member of your church."

Brother Joseph was quick to shake his head and raise both hands in front of him. "God's church, Brother Neibaur, not mine."

Ellen smiled at the Prophet, then her husband, pulling him closer.

"Are you familiar with the Hebrew language?" Joseph asked Alexander.

He nodded heartily. "Much better than English."

"God will provide," Joseph said, raising his arms to the heavens.

"Pardon me?"

"I have learned some Hebrew in the past and am in need of a new tutor." He elbowed Alexander. "God provides a way for His will to be accomplished. I would very much like to hear your story, Brother and Sister Neibaur." He turned to Emma. "When will our schedule allow a meal with them?"

Emma smiled graciously. "We are available Wednesday next."

"Perfect," he said. "Will you come then?" He met Ellen's eyes again.

Should she feel something extraordinary? This man was a modern-day Moses. She did not break his gaze, willing herself to know if this man was all he claimed to be. "Our only plan for many months has been to come here. Other than buying land, building a house, planting crops, raising animals, educating the children, preparing meals, and squirreling food away for winter —which, by the way, neither of us have ever done before—our schedules are wide open."

They laughed, with the Prophet chuckling loudest of all.

"Sounds like we are available," Alexander said, tossing his hands up.

Brother Thompson attempted to resume his conversation with the Neibaurs about land, but Alexander waved an arm, cutting him off. "Please, help the Smiths. I will return tomorrow after a little exploration of the city."

22

A fter picking up the children, the family traversed all over Nauvoo, discussing idyllic places in which to build a house.

"How will we find our way back to the Snailham's?" Joseph asked. "There are trees everywhere."

"We shall have to stick to the paths. It is difficult to believe there are thousands of homes here, is it not?" asked Alexander. "And we shall be the proud owners of a pretty little parcel ourselves soon enough."

"Indeed," said Ellen, shifting Isaac to her other hip.

Observing the motion, Alexander took him from her. "Take it easy, my dear. You are still recovering."

After determining they would like to be near the Mississippi River, down the hill from the temple lot, they spent the next few days preparing lumber at the sawmill for a fence. Soon, they had in their possession a quarter acre, in their preferred location, which also, as it turned out, was near the Smith residence.

The Sabbath was a blessed reprieve from the hard labor of building the fence. The damp air weighed heavily after a forenoon rain. Ladies lifted their skirts to an appropriate height to avoid dragging them in the squelching mud but could do little to save their shoes. As they climbed the hill to the Grove below the temple lot, people flowed to it from all directions.

Alexander took Ellen's hand, and she gently fingered the hardened calluses in his palm through her gloves. The skin on her own hands had already lost its petal softness, though Alexander spared her from the hardest tasks. Stronger than she had ever been, and certainly a good deal healthier than she had been on the *Sheffield*, she reveled in feeling well. She slid her hand up to Alexander's elbow and squeezed his muscle. "All this exertion is not all bad," she said, and he flexed for her.

Isaac clung to Ellen's skirts, intimidated by the sea of strangers. "Is it not odd to think we live in Nauvoo?" Ellen said.

"Indeed," said Alexander. "We spoke of this foreign land so many times. Now we are here, beginning a new life." He placed his free arm on Maggie's shoulder and spoke to the children. "Are you pleased with America?"

"It beats the boats," Joseph said, and Maggie and Isaac heartily agreed.

"And how do you feel it compares to England?"

Maggie sighed dramatically. "Preston seems so far away and long ago. It is difficult to remember."

"What?" Ellen said. "Do you not recall our happily-situated home in the Old Cock Yard or your grandparents' home in the country?"

"And playing in the yard with Uncle Richard?" added Joseph.

"Yes," Maggie said. "I remember, but when I think of our Preston house, there are so many doors, and I am no longer sure where they all led."

Ellen hugged her. "Let us vow to remind one another of our favorite memories often enough that we will never forget."

The Neibaur family squeezed onto a log bench next to the

Whithnells. Ellen reached for their baby, Nephi, and thought about the approaching day when she would again have another of her own, squeezing her finger.

Brother Whithnell leaned forward to speak to Alexander around the ladies. "I hear you have begun to build at the end of Water Street, across from the cooper's place."

Alexander smiled proudly. "And you?"

"Not yet. It will take us some time to purchase a lot. I will be doing some odd jobs for Brother Joseph tomorrow. I believe he is still short a few workers. Care to join me?"

Alexander searched Ellen for approval, and she gave it but asked, "Do we not need to begin planting our garden?"

Alexander rubbed his beard, but, before he could answer, Ellen continued, fear lacing her words. "I do not know the first thing about planting, preserving, or preparing food." She lowered her head and grimaced at Sister Whithnell. "Do you?"

Sister Whithnell shook her head. "No, but I have time to learn before we have a space of our own."

Brother Whithnell smiled compassionately at Ellen. "The cooper and his wife have an impressive garden. Perhaps they will help you get started."

The meeting was beginning with an opening prayer, silencing their conversation.

A brother by the name of John Bennett spoke after the opening song. He talked of his own respectability as a doctor. Alexander perked up to hear from one of a similar profession, but Ellen wondered why he was not speaking on a more spiritual matter. His entire speech seemed to be meant to prove his respectability to the congregation, which in and of itself, made her question his motives. She leaned to her husband, "Clearly something is amiss that we are not privy to."

Alexander clenched his teeth. "There must be some serious accusatory rumors spreading about his character for him to defend himself so."

Brother Law's speech, which followed, had a condemning tone to it. "Unrighteous acts will lead you to be cut off from the church," he bellowed.

The Prophet stood up next, and the congregation straightened as one, pointing their full attention toward him. With a determination shown through strong language, he put down all iniquity, and, though Ellen's heart pounded with the passion of the words, she squirmed as Darwen Park popped into her mind, and the events of the past year wound through her mind like John's cotton mill, thousands of miles away.

A one-hour break ensued shortly after noon, and Ellen fed the children, and took them to relieve themselves in a thicket of trees while Alexander went about introducing himself and making friends, as was his way. Manners were so different in Nauvoo, she did not know how to behave. In England, it was appropriate to speak with those with whom one traveled, but the connection would cease at the end of the journey. Appropriate connections always began by means of an introduction through a mutual friend. Different customs made her feel like a fish floundering on dry land.

A brother by the name of Green spoke for a couple hours on the principles of the gospel. Though she agreed with his sentiments, she was happy when he closed the meeting. The children were tired of sitting for several hours, and, if she was honest, her own expectant body was stiff and uncomfortable, and she relished a small stretch as she stood.

While Alexander worked for Brother Joseph the next day, Ellen made a visit to their future neighbors with a gift of leftover challah from Alexander's Shabbat loaves. Peeking into their door, she saw their small log home filled with barrels in various stages of completion.

"Good day," she said. How did one introduce one's self? She cleared her throat, shifting her feet. "My name is Mrs. Neibaur. We will be your closest neighbors once our home is built."

"Ah! Welcome. We are the Jones family, and I am Harriet."

Whether Harriet was likewise with child or simply pleasantly plump, her round face was highlighted by twinkling eyes and rosy cheeks.

Ellen was invited in. "My husband, who is a Jew," she said, "makes a couple loaves of braided bread for the Sabbath each week, except when we were on the ship, of course." She handed Harriet the hunk of bread. "I assure you it is as delicious as it is beautiful. Next time I will bring some while it is still warm."

"Thank you. Please do not hesitate to ask if you need anything."

Ellen glanced at her boots. "As a matter of fact, I have come to solicit your services if you are willing." She met the woman's kind eyes.

"What can I help you with?"

Her cheeks warmed. "Will you teach me how to plant a garden?"

WITH HELP FROM THE CHILDREN, Ellen tried to follow Harriet's instructions with exactness. They first cleared the garden plot of wild flora.

Maggie squatted with a huff, her gathered dress poofing up around her. "Mama, I mustn't help you. I wish to be genteel."

Ellen half-smiled. "I know, dear. Here is the problem. If we do not plant food, we will not have anything to eat when winter arrives."

"I never planted in England, and we always had plenty to eat."

Ellen bent in front of Maggie. She was about to take Maggie's hands, but, seeing her dirty fingers, she thought better of it. "We are not in England, and Papa cannot do everything. We must be the workers."

Maggie bit her lip, and tears flooded her eyes. "I want to be a lady, Mama."

"And you are. Even in Preston, you saw me work sometimes. Besides, in America, ladies are allowed to work."

Maggie's eyes opened wider. "They are?"

Ellen nodded. "As a matter of fact, they must." She motioned for Joseph and Isaac to come closer. "Look. I will show you all what to do."

Sister Snailham asked Ellen to fetch an onion, a basketful of potatoes, and some pickled cherries from the cellar. "Oh, and a tomato," she added. "Doctor Bennett says they keep us healthy when the weather turns hot." A blush rose to her cheeks.

The smell of wet earth and vinegar accosted Ellen when she opened the heavy wood door. Shelves lined with fresh produce and preserves spread before her, many she could not identify. She found the potatoes and tomatoes in baskets, the cherries on a shelf of jarred fruits, vegetables, and meats, and the onions hanging overhead.

Back in the kitchen, Sister Snailham took the food from her and laid it out on the table. "Will you make the soda biscuits while I boil the potatoes and onion?"

Ellen stared. "I am not sure how to make biscuits. Will you show me?"

Sister Snailham jutted out her hip and put a hand on it. "How about you do the potatoes then?"

"I am afraid..."

"For heaven's sake, how do you expect to survive? All you have to do is boil water in the pot over the fire and put the potatoes and onion in until they're soft."

Ellen could count the number of times she had boiled her own water on her fingers. She would have to learn all she could while with Sister Greenwood, but she needn't be treated as a scullery maid.

The potatoes plopped into the pot one by one. "How long do they boil?"

Sister Greenwood huffed. "Until you can stick a fork in," she said, then mumbled something about *fine* English ladies.

THE NEIBAURS PUT on their best clothes to sup with the Smith family at their beautiful residence. Supper was served by a servant with great attention to detail, and Ellen could almost imagine they were back in her beloved England at the fine home of family friends. Homesickness lumped in her throat and was difficult to dislodge. While the Smiths were clearly American, Emma's grace and Brother Joseph's friendliness made her feel at home.

After the men spoke for some time about the Hebrew language and culture, Brother Joseph said, "Will you help me with Hebrew? I would also be interested in learning some German."

"I would be honored to be of service in any way possible," said Alexander with a glowing smile. "I do not want to be presumptuous, but I may be able to provide another useful service to you."

Brother Joseph's eyes sparkled with amusement, as he leaned and rubbed Major, his mastiff, between the ears. "It is not everyday that I find someone so serviceable. What else can you do for me?"

Alexander cleared his throat. "I have noticed that you have a bit of a whistle when you speak."

"Ah, yes. A souvenir from the mob at Brother Johnson's farm. In their attempts to force poison down my throat, they chipped one of my teeth." He opened one side of his mouth and tapped his tooth with his nail.

Maggie gasped, and Ellen shook her head sharply to remind her of her manners.

Alexander stepped around the table to Brother Joseph. "I am sorry to hear that. My people have faced oppression throughout history. They were God's people. Now, you have started a new people, and they likewise are persecuted for their God. I would be happy to take a look at your broken tooth and do my best to repair the damage."

Brother Joseph patted his dog before shaking one of Alexander's hands in both of his. "I would be grateful. I am glad you are one of us, Mr. Neibaur."

Emma gracefully set her spoon on the table and met Ellen's eyes with a pleasant smile. "How about you, Mrs. Neibaur? What secret talents are you hiding?"

Ellen squirmed in her chair, not knowing how to answer.

Joseph laughed. "Do not be shy. I am sure you have much to share, as well."

Ellen lifted her head. "I fear it is not shyness that has silenced me. I would not have claimed a great number of talents in England. Here, in America, I am completely out of my depth. I lack all the talents necessary for life in this country."

Emma tilted her head and smiled. "You will adjust. I am certain."

"Thank you. I hope so."

After a lovely dinner party with the Smiths, Ellen took Alexander's arm, and they returned to their temporary residence with the Snailhams. Despite their immense kindness in letting Ellen's family take over the main floor of the house, she could not wait to put a little distance between them and have a place of her own again.

"I must say I am rather intimidated to tutor the Prophet," Alexander said.

Ellen nodded. "I would be terrified, but he would remind you he is only a man, and a rough one at that."

"But can I teach such a man?"

"It is as Brother Joseph said. The Lord brought you here at this time for this purpose. You will do the job well, because it is what the Lord needs you to do."

He lifted his hat and ran a hand through his hair. "Is that why we are here, do you think?"

"Indeed. I am sure there are many reasons, but this is one of them, and heaven knows I am not going to be of much service. It will take a miracle for me to perform the most menial tasks to satisfaction."

IN THE NEXT WEEK, two of the passengers that came over on the *Sheffield* with the Neibaurs died of disease. It felt unjust to travel halfway around the world only to expire upon arrival. If the Neibaurs were grateful for their situation before, they felt a renewed desire to make the most of whatever time they had. After all, they had experience with death, and it came at the most inopportune times.

After an exhausting day of working the land, Ellen awoke to labor pains in the early hours of the morning. She missed her midwives, but the birth proceeded without a hitch with the help of Sister Snailham and Sister Jones. A baby girl was born around eight in the morning on the twenty-second of May, and, according to tradition, they named her Alice after Ellen's mother. It was difficult to think that Alice Breakell would never meet her namesake as Joseph Neibaur had never met his, but it still felt like a long, invisible thread tied these beautiful children to their grandparents somehow.

Alexander, Joseph, and Maggie finished planting corn, potatoes, and beans while Ellen was in confinement, and, to her amazement, with the help of some new and old friends, they were able to get a basic house structure raised. Within a couple weeks of Alice's birth, they moved in. The rudimentary structure was their new home, and Alexander was proud of it as he rested his hand on the wall and leaned against it.

As hospitable as the Snailhams had been, Alexander and Ellen went to bed with smiles on their faces in their new home overlooking the Mississippi.

"I wish I could be of more help," Ellen said in the darkness.

"Your doctor demands that you care for yourself and his little girl for now. We are managing."

She giggled. "I guess I must do as my doctor orders."

"I have a bit of taxing news for you, though."

"What is it?"

"Brother Joseph and Brother Hyrum, as well as Brother John Bennett and Brother William Law were arrested in Quincy, Illinois, having a writ from the Missouri government. Many of the brethren went to see him by horseback. They have returned, saying there is a flaw in the indictment, and all will be back in Nauvoo in no time. The good news is that the devil's plan has been frustrated."

"What is the bad news?"

"The bad news is that the devil does not give up. I fear Nauvoo will not be free of the persecutions we fled."

"Heaven help us."

23

When the morning light filtered through the grease paper windows into the house, and baby Alice began to fuss, Ellen hung over the side of the bed and rocked the wooden cradle.

Alice fell back to sleep long enough for Ellen to observe Alexander since he had not been feeling well the night previous. He had dark purple bruise-like circles below his eyes, reminding her of Samuel when he was ill.

She tiptoed from the room, and as the older children woke up one by one, she sent them outside to keep the small home quiet. Around noon, she went in to check on him again, carrying Alice in her arms.

He peeked beneath his lids. "Do not fret over me. Keep the children healthy, and I will soon be well."

Departing from the room, she handed Alice to Joseph and returned to her husband's bedside with a wet cloth. As she washed Alexander's head and neck, he dozed in and out of consciousness.

Over the next few days, Alexander became progressively worse until the bones in his face protruded in contrast to his sunken eyes. Ellen prayed over him night and day when she could step away from the work that needed to be done.

"Father in Heaven, please do not take Alexander from me after everything else we have been through," she whispered. "Please. We left everything but each other in coming to America, and I cannot do this without him." She balled up the folds of her dress in her palms and squeezed.

Alexander wordlessly placed his hand on top of her clenched fist.

With great effort, she relaxed and sat quietly while he rested.

"Father, is there anything I can do to help him?" she silently prayed. Ellen was careful not to move her hand and disturb his sleep. She sat perfectly still until Alice started to cry, at which time, she extracted her hand.

He stirred but did not wake.

While she nursed Alice, a repeating thought kept popping into her mind. Alexander needed a Priesthood blessing.

But should she leave him in search of help? She determined she must, for she could not stand by while he continued to wither away.

Grabbing the baby, she left the house without a certain destination in mind and followed Water Street up the hill, quickening her step when she spotted a gentleman coming her way. As he approached, she knew a moment of panic at the thought of meeting a man alone in the road, but the choice had been made before she left the house. It had to be done.

Relief and gratitude warmed her as his features formed into clear lines, and she saw Brother Hyrum Smith.

He was still tipping his hat to her when her words poured out. "Alexander is ill. I am searching for someone to give him a blessing."

He touched his hat again. "I will stop by the cooper's and

ask Brother Jones to join me at your home right away," he said, bowing.

"Thank you." She lifted her skirts and ran back to the house.

Before long, the brethren were there, laying hands upon the head of Alexander and, with strong cries to the Almighty, demanding that the illness leave his weakened frame.

Ellen gasped as Alexander immediately sat up and shook their healing hands. The pallor of Alexander's sunken cheeks looked less gray. "To think I was the one trained at University to be a healer."

Ellen collapsed in a heap of gratitude onto the bed beside him, and Alexander rubbed her back.

Brother Hyrum moved to steady her, and she thanked him repeatedly. "Please, take some challah and butter with you as a small token of my gratitude." Her eyes went to the floor. "Sorry. Jewish bread is the only recipe we know how to make."

They bowed, and Brother Hyrum laughed. "It looks delightful. We were happy to be of service."

They showed themselves out while Ellen heated broth for Alexander and tipped it into his mouth.

His eyes locked on hers above the rim of the bowl, and, when she lowered it, he said, "Blessed be the name of the Lord God of Israel."

"Amen," she agreed.

WHEN ALEXANDER RECOVERED FULLY, he began to tutor the Prophet in Hebrew and German. After one such meeting, he opened the door a crack from the outside. "Children, come," he called into the house. "Everyone."

They scampered over, and Isaac tried to peek around the door.

Alexander laughed, "I have a surprise. Only guess what it is."

"Ribbons," said Maggie.

Joseph puffed out a breath. "No one wants ribbons."

Maggie scowled at him. "I do."

The hidden surprise barked behind Alexander, and he set a white puppy on the floor and followed in after it. The puppy yipped and hopped around the giggling children.

Only Maggie stood a few steps back, observing. "What shall we call it?"

The puppy knocked Isaac over and licked his face, causing him to roll on the floor, laughing. "Down, Pippy, down."

Ellen grinned. "Sounds like he just named it Pippy."

Alexander fingered his beard. "Not as tough as the Prophet's dog's name, Major, from whence he came." He chuckled. "But I suppose Pippy will do." He scratched the dog's head. "Welcome to the family, Pippy."

ANOTHER GROUP of Englishmen and women arrived in Nauvoo. The whole population arrived at the dock to welcome them. Brigham Young, Heber Kimball, and John Taylor were in the company. Their joy quickly turned into mourning, however, when they saw how many of the Saints were sick from their journey and were informed about all those who had not survived.

Most of the brethren and sisters who arrived ill were nursed back to health and were well enough to attend the grand celebration that took place on America's Independence day soon after. Ellen's family watched the Nauvoo Legion march in full regalia. At three o'clock, the artillery announced the arrival of the Lieutenant General, and they marched through the town.

Citizens from other towns were also in attendance, witnessing the magnificence of the army.

Alexander bent to Ellen. "I am not sure it is wise to show off the power of the Legion like this. It appears to make some of the other Illinoisans uncomfortable." He gestured with his head toward a small, rougher-looking crowd of men who did not seem to be enjoying the demonstration and were growing increasingly raucous.

Alexander took Ellen's hand, motioned for the children to follow, and led the small party away from the rambunctious men.

When the display ceased, other festivities commenced. Baked goods, produce, and beautiful handmade items were being sold at tables along the whole street.

Brother William Cross and his family approached the Neibaurs. "Dr. Neibaur, what a pleasure to see you again."

"You, as well, sir. This is my wife, Mrs. Ellen Neibaur, and these are my children, Joseph, Margaret, Isaac, and baby Alice."

Ellen flinched as she always did when they introduced their children. It still hurt to think of the one missing. She attempted to shake the gloom and be gracious to the Crosses, who were now being introduced. Ellen sought Sister Cross's cooking advice while Alexander and Brother Cross talked business, and, out of the corner of her eye, she observed her husband growing animated, his arms flailing, as they spoke about filling a need by starting a matchmaking business.

When they stepped away, Ellen said, "Do you not have enough work with the homestead, tutoring, and dentistry? Are you seriously considering another venture?"

Alexander's eyes were on fire. "There are not many who know the chemistry behind making matches, yet they are so convenient. Everyone will love them." He threw his arms up.

Ellen smiled skeptically at his enthusiasm.

From a calico-draped table, a charmingly round woman

called out to her. "Hello there, Sister. We are having a beauty contest. Would you like to enter? There will be a prize." She winked. "I think you have a real shot at it."

Ellen shook her head and moved to go, but Maggie and Alexander directed her right back to the table. "You won a beauty contest before, Mama."

"That was some time and a world ago, Maggie, before I had children."

"And you are more beautiful than ever," said Alexander. He looked at the stranger. "She will do it."

The lady's smile glowed.

After Alexander signed her up, Ellen hissed, "You are biased, you know. I will not be winning any more beauty contests."

"You might be surprised, but if you do not win, it is only because the judges' eyes do not work."

She elbowed him.

Later in the afternoon, the crowd gathered for some lively entertainment and dancing. Some of the dances were new to her, but they were simple enough. The lady from the booth climbed onto the podium after one of the songs ended. "Ladies and Gentlemen! The grand prize for today's beauty contest is this delicious pie, provided by the Scovil family's bakery." She rubbed her stomach. "If anyone knows how delicious their pies are, 'tis me."

The crowd erupted in laughter. "Ladies, please come up here, and stand to my left."

Ellen leaned into Alexander. "I almost forgot. Now I am all flushed from the exertion of the dances."

"You have never been more stunning. Besides, the touch of red on your cheeks is most becoming."

Ellen crept through the crowd, embarrassed and feeling presumptuous. At least it was not a talent contest.

Beautiful women stood on either side of her. Some were

older and some younger. While she had often been called a real beauty, she no longer felt like she had when she was younger. She used to turn heads wherever she went, always aware of the eyes of strangers and acquaintances taking in her face and figure, and while she sometimes enjoyed it, other times it made her uncomfortable. The eyes of some men lingered in certain places a bit too long to be considered respectable and left her feeling unseen, like she was only a body to be admired as opposed to a person to be loved.

She lifted her chin, knowing negative thoughts could alter her appearance for the worse. Remembering her lessons about ladylike posture and expression, she stood erect and smiled just enough.

"We will judge the contest based on the cheering of the crowd. Decide now who you want to see win. More than one of these ladies look like they could use a pie or two on their bones." She pinched the arm of the young woman beside her, and the crowd erupted again.

The announcer came down the row, one lady at a time, and the crowd cheered for each of them. Ellen was nearly the last, and it seemed that the applause grew with each person. Surely, the final lady would win the greatest cheers.

When she stopped before Ellen, she pointed and waggled her eyebrows. "How about this one?"

The applause was thunderous. The ruffians they had seen at the parade earlier hooted and hollered for her, and she averted her eyes, locating Alexander in the crowd, whistling through his fingers. She fought the urge to hide her face beneath her bonnet.

The next two contestants received polite cheers, but Ellen was the clear winner. She accepted the pie, blushing, and the announcer said, "I told you you might win. Enjoy!"

Ellen weaved her way back, aware of the eyes of curious strangers. "That was flattering but humiliating."

"Nonsense," said Alexander. "Now, you must believe me when I tell you that you are the most beautiful woman I have ever seen."

She shoved into him with her shoulder.

"Dance with me, my gorgeous wife."

Ellen handed the pie to Maggie, and Joseph eyed it. "We shall see if this pie is still around when you are done," he teased.

Taking Alexander's arm, Ellen was led toward the ring of dancers. She tugged on him to stop, but he pulled her until they were right in the middle of everyone. "Truly, must you always be the center of attention?" she asked.

"I must show off my prize-winning bride."

As they danced, Ellen kept one eye on the children, who were still ogling the pie.

Alexander leaned forward and kissed her cheek.

Raised voices carried over the music for but a moment before the band ceased playing, and the crowd's attention turned in unison toward the commotion.

The unkempt men who had cheered for her moved as a pack of wolves just to the left of her children. Ellen let go of Alexander's hand and dashed toward them, sensing his feet pounding only a pace behind.

"You're all fools," a man yelled, his words slurring together.

Ellen positioned herself between the men and her children.

"If you want to take over our state," he said, looking at Ellen and licking his lips, "we should get something in return." He leered at her while his companions slapped each other on the backs and laughed.

Alexander darted in front of Ellen, and she backed away, forcing the children to step back, as Alexander spread his arms to the sides. "Leave us alone," he called.

The man wobbled back with a raised brow, his body rolling like a wave, and mocked Alexander, who was much shorter.

"Not just fools. Foreign fools. You let any kind of riff-raff in this town you call Nauvoo."

"Not the likes of you," Alexander retorted.

The man lunged toward him, but his companions grabbed his arms and held him back. "Save it. We will come back for them. Today we are outnumbered, but next time we will come with reinforcements."

ALEXANDER BEGAN MAKING matches to supplement their income, and, after speaking with Brother Brigham Young, took out an ad in the local paper, The Times and Seasons. He waved the paper above his head. "My ad has been printed. Let me read it to you," he told the family over dinner.

Alexander Neibaur - Surgeon Dentist

From Berlin, in Prussia, late of Liverpool and Preston, England

Most respectfully announces to the ladies and gentlemen and the citizens of Nauvoo as also of Hancock county, in general, that he has permanently established himself in the city of Nauvoo, as a dentist, where he may be consulted daily in all branches connected with his profession. Teeth cleaned, plugged, filed, the scurvy effectually cured, children's teeth regulated, natural or artificial teeth from a single tooth to a whole set inserted on the most approved principle. Mr. Neibaur having had an extensive practice both on the continent of Europe, as also in England, for the last 15 years, he hopes to give general satisfaction to all those who will honor him with their patronage.

Mr. Brigham Young, having known Mr. Neibaur (in England) has kindly consented to offer me his house to meet those ladies and gentlemen who wish to consult me. Hours of attendance from 10 o'clock in the morning to 6 at evening. My own residence is opposite Mr. Tidwell, the cooper, near the water. Ladies and gentlemen attended at their own residence, if requested.

Charges strictly moderate."

After placing the advertisement, Alexander saw an increase in work and spent much of his time at the Young home. Ellen was grateful, but she also felt a loss after being together for so many hours and days.

While she was at the Smith's Red Brick Store with the children, shopping for a few necessary household items, she heard that Joseph and Hyrum's younger brother, Don Carlos died of malarial fever and would be interred with military honor on the seventh of August. "Oh, I am so sorry for Joseph and Emma," Ellen said.

The funeral turned into a grand affair, and it hurt Ellen's heart as funerals were wont to do. She did not like to admit that the pain came from her own guilt and losses as much as compassion for the family of the deceased. Each time, her heartache came to the forefront until it was difficult to breathe. Abandoning Alexander and the children, she fled the funeral for respite in the quiet of the woods, smacking at the mosquitoes that found her exposed skin.

Would she ever cease to grieve? If she could only earn atonement for all her faults, perhaps she could put it behind her.

Days later, the same crowd reconvened for another sort of gathering. A tribe of Native Americans, who had been encamped at Montrose, crossed the river on the ferry and two flatboats. The military band stood on the banks, ready to receive them, but, when Chief Keokuk saw that Brother Joseph was not present, they refused to come ashore.

Maggie tapped Ellen's elbow. "They are naked, Mama."

There were easily a hundred men, plus their wives and children. The company was in full native dress, adorned with beads, teeth, and feathers. Some heads were crowned with elaborate headdresses.

Alexander averted his eyes with a smirk toward Ellen, who returned his gaze, knowing her face registered both shock and amusement, as well.

"Mama," Isaac said. "Are they people like us?"

Ellen's mind churned like butter. "They are both gloriously different and the same. They are children of God, like us, and are sons and daughters of Adam and Eve. Their ancestors are the characters of The Book of Mormon. On the other hand, I have never seen a culture so opposite from my own."

The boys nodded, but Maggie shook her head. "I find them terrifying. Look at their faces, and *that* one." She pointed. "Look at all the teeth he is wearing. His painted face is mean, too."

Ellen observed the warrior. "Maybe he is Chief Keokuk's bodyguard, so it is required of him to appear fierce."

"I believe we are as frightening to them as they are to us," said Alexander. "It is natural to be afraid of the unknown."

Maggie grimaced. "I disagree. My dress and bonnet would not intimidate a soul."

"On the contrary, little lady. There was a time I was rather afraid of Englishmen and women." Alexander said. "They spoke and acted differently than my own family and people. When I met your mother, I was petrified."

Maggie's eyes darted back and forth between her parents' faces.

Ellen's own knees bounced with nervousness. "I heard these are Sauk Indians." She steadied her voice. "They are known to be friendly to settlers."

Brother Joseph and Brother Hyrum arrived, and the Sauks joined them on the landing, where Joseph Smith introduced his brother and guided them to the Grove for a meeting of Sauks and Saints alike.

The mayor, Brother John Bennett, greeted Chief Keokuk

and the others. The Nauvoo Legion marched, dressed in uniform, and Ellen pointed out that the terror in Maggie's face was mirrored in the eyes of some of the native women and children. Musicians from the Legion performed a musical number before the Prophet arose and addressed the gathering. The air felt heavy with humidity and charged with anticipation. "We welcome our Sauk brothers and sisters. The Lord has revealed unto me many things concerning the forefathers of your people. The Book of Mormon is their record and makes promises specific to you. I will offer a bit of advice. Cease killing and warring with other tribes. Keep peace with your white brothers."

The chief came up to Joseph and said he still had a copy of The Book of Mormon, given to him years earlier by Joseph himself. "I believe you are a great and good man. I look rough, but I also am a Son of the Great Spirit." He brought his arm proudly to his chest, as the two faced each other, leaders of separate tribes, but one in heart.

After the conversation, spoken for all to hear, a great feast was presented by the townspeople, including dainties and melons, pies and game.

When Alexander threatened to take Ellen to speak to some of the Indians, she escaped with the children to a group of Saints instead. The conversation hushed as she approached and ceased when she stepped in. One of the sisters frowned at her but continued to speak. "He calls it spiritual wifery and says that the Prophet taught it to him in secret."

Others shook their heads in disgust.

Sister Romney put her arm up. "Do not bring Brother Joseph into this. I am certain it has nothing to do with him."

Ellen was lost and considered leaving, but Sister Whithnell met her eyes. "What do you think, Ellen?"

"I know not of what you speak."

Sister Snailham joined in. "Have you not heard the rumors?

It is said that our esteemed mayor has been caught in the beds of some of our sisters."

Ellen's hand shot up to cover her mouth. "That is a mighty accusation. I hope you do not spread it without cause."

"On the contrary. He is said to have been with multiple women." She lowered her voice to a harsh whisper. "He is telling them that, as a doctor, he will terminate any resultant pregnancies so nobody will ever know."

"No." Ellen stepped back, feeling ill and shifting Alice to her other shoulder. "What can be worse than that?"

Sister Romney took Alice into her arms. "Sisters, we must not gossip. However, I do think it necessary to spread the word to be wary of John Bennett and stay away from him as much as circumstances allow. It may be advisable to take special care about where and when you step out alone."

Ellen could hardly believe it. How could such things happen in Nauvoo regarding people as respected as the mayor? Should the true Church be riddled with such debauchery?

When the feast tables were nearly emptied, she found Alexander and whispered the news.

He clenched his teeth. "I have heard these rumors, but Brother Joseph trusts him. I stand with the Prophet."

Ellen felt a measure of peace at his saying, and together they watched as the Sauks entertained the crowd with dancing unlike anything Ellen had ever seen. "We are a world away from England, my dear."

24

Alexander swallowed a large bite of pork, and as he forked the next piece, he said, "You are becoming quite the cook, dear."

"Words I never expected to be pleased by. That would not have been a compliment a few short years ago."

He chewed and grinned intermittently.

"Try the soda biscuits, too," she said, proudly.

"I shall." He brushed a bit of food from his beard. "It appears you were right to be leery of John Bennett. He was excommunicated from the Church today and is resigning as mayor."

Ellen cocked her head. "I am in shock."

"Are you?" He pursed his lips. "It seems the rumors have been just, and this may not be the first town where he has wreaked havoc."

Good riddance. "Will he stay in Nauvoo?"

"I believe he will leave as soon as circumstances allow."

ELLEN SAT on a bench in the Grove, surrounded by her sisters in the gospel and in this singular life they had all given so much for.

The women, under the direction of the Prophet, had begun to organize themselves into a cohesive group, namely the Female Relief Society of Nauvoo, with Sister Emma Smith as president.

This was Ellen's first meeting, and she relished the feeling of camaraderie among them, having spent the winter cooped up in their small house, keeping everyone warm, fed, and generally alive.

The women began by singing, "Awake, Ye Saints of God, Awake", and Sister Sarah Cleveland, counselor to Emma, gave a beautiful opening prayer.

Sister Emma arose, proposing that the Society raise funds to help build houses for the poor. She rejoiced in the growth and union of the Society and expressed hope that the sisters would live right before God, themselves, and the world.

Sister Cleveland then spoke powerfully, saying that all must live by faith alone. Many of the sisters around Ellen nodded in agreement. "The powers of darkness are arrayed against us, but I am not afraid!"

Ellen felt a thrill shoot through her chest.

Sister Cleveland continued. "We should be extremely careful in handling character. Be merciful." She expressed a desire that the sisters would be inclusive with one another, slow to judge those who were objected to by others. "We must also take care not to speak ill of the Prophet."

All appeared to be comfortable until Sister Emma spoke. "I propose that a circular go forth from this Society, expressive of our feeling in reference to Dr. John C. Bennett's character."

It was not that anyone disagreed, but Ellen shifted in her seat at the mere mention of the loathsome man. A petition went around, which would be sent to Governor Thomas Carlin, stating in no uncertain terms that Bennett was an unvirtuous man and a most consummate scoundrel, a stirrer up of sedition, and a vile wretch unworthy of attention or notice.

After the meeting, some of the sisters gathered in a circle, and Emma spoke to Ellen. "Have you heard that Brother Orson Hyde made it to Jerusalem where he is serving the Lord and dedicating the land?"

Ellen shook her head. "I have scarcely been outside for months. It feels wonderful to be out."

Emma nodded. "Be sure to tell Alexander about Brother Hyde."

"I will, and I am sure my husband will find the first opportunity to invite him to dine with us when he returns."

MONTHS PASSED, and temperatures were cooling once again when Brother Hyde returned to Nauvoo. As Ellen expected, Alexander welcomed him and his family over at their earliest convenience. Sister Marinda Hyde arrived with her husband. Both were handsome with dark hair and vibrant eyes. Their children, Nathan, Laura, and Emily, also came, and the Neibaur children were excited to play tag with them outside, leaving the adults to visit.

Alexander scooted to the edge of his seat, leaning toward Brother Hyde. "Tell me about Jerusalem."

Orson chuckled and addressed Ellen. "Many have been anxious to hear about my mission, but no one more than your husband."

Ellen nodded conspiratorially. "I know it, sir."

He laughed again. "What do you want to know?"

Alexander threw his arms above his head. "Everything."

Orson beamed and took Marinda's hand. "Where to begin?" He rubbed his chin and neck. "I have spent the last eight months or so in Palestine. I planned to set out with Brother John Page, but when he did not arrive in New York at the appointed time, I proceeded alone. Brother Joseph wanted me to travel to several European cities, sharing the gospel and gleaning all the information I could, especially about your people." He waved his hand toward Alexander. "I preached that the Jews had been scattered amongst the Gentiles long enough and that the time had come for them to gather to the Holy Land again."

"I knew it." Alexander said, arms moving with each word. "What was their reaction?"

"Slow down," Orson guffawed. "On a late October morning, I climbed the Mount of Olives, which is now a cemetery. I knelt there, overlooking the Holy Land and the Garden of Gethsemane, overcome by the Spirit of the Lord. Do you know why the Spirit is to be felt on that holy mountain?"

"Ja. It is a sacred place for many reasons. Messiah, Himself, taught his disciples there, which makes it like unto a temple, and when He returns, He will come there again, and the mountain will split in two."

Orson had a faraway look on his face. "I wish all could step foot on that mountain and experience what I felt that sacred morning."

Marinda patted his leg, and he took her hand in his.

"I dedicated the Holy Land with a prayer given to me in vision." He pulled out a worn sheet of paper and unfolded it. "I will read a portion of it to you." His eyes moved to the creased paper in his hands. "Thy servant has safely arrived in this place to dedicate and consecrate this land unto Thee for the gathering together of Judah's scattered remnants, according to the predictions of the holy prophets—for the building up of Jerusalem again after it has been trodden down by the Gentiles so long, and for rearing a Temple in honor of Thy name.

"O Thou, Who didst covenant with Abraham, Thy friend,

and who didst renew that covenant with Isaac, and confirm the same with Jacob with an oath, that Thou wouldst not only give them this land for an everlasting inheritance, but that Thou wouldst also remember their seed forever. Abraham, Isaac, and Jacob have long since closed their eyes in death, and made the grave their mansion. Their children are scattered and dispersed abroad among the nations of the Gentiles like sheep that have no shepherd, and are still looking forward to the fulfillment of those promises which Thou didst make concerning them."

The party was still, absorbing the sacred words that infused Ellen's heart and soul. They smiled at one another with mutual affection as they enjoyed the stirrings of the Spirit together.

"After I spoke the words of the inspired prayer, I built a small altar of stones unto the Lord."

In an unusually quiet voice, Alexander said, "I thank you on behalf of my people."

After more time passed in silence, with only the distant sounds of children playing in the yard, Orson changed the subject. "Marinda also had some interesting things happen while I was away."

She folded her arms and shifted her weight away from him. "Not now, Orson."

"Have you heard of polygamy?" he asked Alexander and Ellen.

Ellen and Alexander shook their heads.

"Well, I do not know how you can live in Nauvoo and not have heard of it. Spiritual Wifery?"

"Ah. You refer to the treachery of John Bennett," said Alexander.

A question hung in Orson's eyes. "Have you heard only what has been spoken publicly concerning him and no others?"

Ellen recalled hearing the Prophet, himself, tied up in the rumors.

Orson waved an arm toward her. "Our sister here has heard

more. I see it in her eyes. Some of the brethren are practicing polygamy, also known as plural marriage. It has been relatively secret, but Alexander, you must know about Brother Brigham, working from his home, as you are."

To Ellen's surprise, Alexander nodded slowly, cautiously. "I did not want to alarm you," he explained to her with a shrug.

Pippy scooted between their legs on the floor, and Alexander stroked his head.

Ellen scowled at Alexander. "Tell me now."

"Brother Brigham, who was completely averse to the idea of multiple wives, has taken a second wife. When he first heard of the practice, he desired the grave, but he seems to have gained a testimony of it now."

Ellen grimaced as if she had eaten something sour. "What would prompt him to do such a thing?"

Alexander defended him. "It is not at all the same as what John Bennett is guilty of. Brother Brigham has taken Lucy Ann Decker to wife. You know her non-member husband abandoned her."

"You work in the Young home and kept this from me? How does Mary Ann feel about it?"

His shoulders lifted and fell. "I believe she is taking it in stride, knowing it is Lucy's only chance for an eternal marriage."

"There are plenty of unmarried men in this town," she said, her words laced with disdain.

Orson's head moved back and forth. "On the contrary, there are many women who lack the support of a husband. I will likely take a second wife. That is, if the Prophet instructs me to do so."

Ellen's eyes widened. How could Marinda sit calmly by, while her husband spoke of marrying another? The whole topic shook Ellen to the core and made her long for the relative safety of Preston. Would this be another test she must endure to prove herself?

"Marinda has another husband, too," Orson said.

"Another husband?" Ellen said, dumbfounded.

"Tell them," he said, gesturing to Marinda to speak.

"I did not know if or when Orson would return, so I was sealed to the Prophet to ensure access to the Celestial Kingdom."

Ellen and Alexander met eyes. How could they respond to such an unusual notion?

Orson answered their unasked questions. "Brother Joseph preaches to his inner circle that everyone must be sealed and connected to one another to attain the highest degree of Heaven, also known as the Celestial Kingdom. Being connected to Joseph assures Marinda a place there."

His words seemed amiable enough, but a slight edge to his voice indicated an undertone of bitterness, and Ellen had to wonder if his threats to marry a second wife were an attempt at revenge.

Long after the Hydes left, Ellen reposed upon her bed with a heavy heart.

Alexander scooted up behind her. "Are you awake?" he whispered.

She nodded against the darkness and scooted closer to him, listening to his breaths. Although they slowed and deepened, she whispered, "Do you believe plural marriage could have possibly come from God?"

He yawned. "I believe in the Prophet."

"How can you if he believes in this abhorrent practice?"

Alexander wrapped his arms around her and ran his fingers along her arm. "You know I support Brother Joseph no matter what."

"No matter what? Is it possible for a prophet to stop being a prophet?"

"Perhaps," he said, with another yawn. "There may even be a scriptural basis for that in David, but Joseph has not fallen from grace. The Spirit still testifies to me of that."

Ellen had to agree. The Spirit continued to testify that Joseph Smith was the Lord's mouthpiece.

The words cycling through her head would not move to her lips, and Alexander was asleep before she could utter them. Would he marry a second wife? She knew the answer. If God, through Joseph Smith, asked him to enter into a plural marriage, he would do so. He was nothing if not loyal and faithful to his God.

———

25

E llen was not being fair to Alexander the next morning. She had never even asked him if he would be willing to take a plural wife. Nevertheless, she believed he would do whatever the Lord asked, even if it petrified her. The resulting mix of fear for their future and frustration at the unknown had kept her from getting any decent sleep during the night.

She avoided superfluous interactions with Alexander throughout the morning, and by the afternoon, he seemed to be choosing to steer clear of her as well.

After dinner, when she found herself alone with him, she rose to leave and check on Alice, but Alexander grasped her hand and pulled her onto his lap. "What is amiss, Ellen?"

She was unsure how to answer him. He had not done a single thing to deserve her anger, but that did not lessen the hurt in her heart, which she knew to be valid.

"What cause have you to be upset with me?" He said it with such love that her heart filled with guilt.

"It is nothing. I love you." Tears betrayed her, welling up in her eyes. She tried to stand, but Alexander wrapped his arms tighter around her.

"It is not nothing. Tell me so I can make it right."

She buried her head into his shoulder. "It cannot be made right."

He rubbed his beard and waited for more.

"It cannot be made right because, frankly, it is part of who you are."

Disappointment registered on his face. "What about me do you oppose?"

She kissed his cheek through his coarse curly beard. "It is not a bad thing, strictly speaking."

"Your treatment of me today says otherwise." He narrowed his eyes. "Does it have to do with the Hydes?"

She pursed her lips and blinked rapidly, convincing him he was on the right track.

"Did I say something that upset you?"

Sweet Alexander was trying so hard. Why was it impossible to form the words she needed to say? "You did nothing wrong. Our conversation scared me. That is all."

His brow furrowed. "Are you afraid I will leave for Jerusalem or go on a mission somewhere?"

The idea struck her. She should have worried about that. "The thought had not even occurred to me," she admitted. "While that would be difficult, it was our other conversation that left me floundering."

Alexander was quiet as he put the pieces together. He placed a gentle kiss on her forehead. "I have no intention of taking another wife."

She angled her face away from him. "Your words, though heartfelt, are as empty as the vinegar jar. You may not *seek* a second wife." She swallowed hard. "But if Brother Joseph asked you, in the name of the Lord, to enter a plural marriage, what would you do?"

Alexander pursed his lips.

They both knew the answer. He would obey the call from the Lord.

She rested her hand on his chest. "I told you it was not something you would change."

"Then let us hope that such a thing will not be asked of us."

Alexander kissed her, and her lips moved in time with his, tentatively, aching with hurt and love, and gradually deepening into a passionate, cleansing kiss.

All would be well. She prayed that the Lord, after all He had asked of them, would keep this one trial far from the marriage they treasured.

ALTHOUGH ELLEN WAS able to put the topic of plural marriage aside for the time being, it was not going anywhere. More of the people they knew were entering into these covenants. If Alexander was hesitant to bring it up before, now he avoided the subject completely, although Ellen suspected that, like her, he heard the circulating rumors.

The perpetuation of the gossip extended beyond the membership of the church, and persecutions picked up their pace.

"Alexander," Ellen said, "Trouble has been increasing in town, as you know, and I wondered if you might accompany us to the Red Brick Store. We are in need of vinegar and a few other little things."

He closed the book he was reading and went for his boots.

Though the roads were deeply trenched with mud due to heavy rains, the day was the warmest in some time.

Joseph carried the empty stone vinegar jug, swinging it as he hopped over the deepest puddles. At the entrance of the store, they stopped at the sight of a tanned man with cropped hair and a scruffy blonde beard yelling and cursing the name of the Prophet Joseph.

Alexander took the stone jug from their son and moved to shield Ellen and the children, who stood just outside the doorway. A few members of the church waited stock still inside the store, watching the cursing man, who seemed to be growing in volume and boldness as the Saints waited.

"That blasted Joe Smith is a womanizer. Best keep your wives and children away from him, or he'll be taking each and every damn one into his own warm bed, same as that Doctor Bennett." He spit out of the side of his mouth onto the plank floor.

Ellen froze, peeking around Alexander's shoulder, grateful she had asked him to come along.

"Joe Smith better watch where he steps," the man continued. "We are making plans." He rubbed his hands together. "It will not be long now before we send him to his grave."

Alexander stomped directly up to the man and growled, "What do you know of the Prophet Joseph Smith?" He swung the jug, bringing it down hard, and breaking it over the man's skull.

Ellen gasped and pressed the children away from the building. She spoke to Joseph. "Take the little ones home. Go. We will be right behind you. Go now."

They did not need to be told twice.

Women came running out of the store as the Neibaur children sprinted away, and Ellen moved against the current, entering in time to see the man, with his nose gushing, swing and hit Alexander in the mouth, in the stomach, and in the face again.

Both were bleeding and moving around like drunkards. Alexander, still holding the broken jug, punched the man with it again, slicing into the flesh of his arm.

"Crazy fool," the man said, holding his arm with one hand

and hobbling out the door. "You haven't heard the end from us!"

Ellen rushed to Alexander. "I need a clean rag," she called to nobody in particular.

One of the Smith girls brought her a scrap of cloth and a bucket of clean water, and Ellen dabbed at his wounds.

He gazed up at her. "I won."

She let out a breath. "Nonsense. Nobody wins this sort of thing."

Alexander stuck out his bottom lip, and she kissed it, tasting blood.

"You were brave," she admitted. "You may have done worse to him than he did to you." She grabbed the handle of the broken jar and gestured toward it with her other hand. "I suppose we need a new bottle with our vinegar."

Alexander chuckled, then clutched at his stomach. "That hurt."

Ellen shook her head and helped him up. "I have to agree with that man about one thing. You are a crazy fool."

DESPITE GROWING tensions between the Saints and the outside world, Alexander and Ellen began to feel settled in Nauvoo. Friendships deepened, crops grew, and it was not long before Ellen found herself to be in the family way again.

Alexander was able to provide a comfortable living, mainly through his dental work at the Young home, and he continued to supplement his income with matchmaking and tutoring, but nothing brought him joy like discussing the Hebrew language and practices with Brother Joseph.

Ellen's pregnancy was easier this time around, and she was able to keep up with her household duties better than before.

Alice, a busy toddler, still occupied much of her time, as did the others.

Joseph, at the age of eight, was quite the little man, and Ellen keenly felt the passage of time when he started school and was baptized in the waters of the Mississippi.

Their sixth child, Bertha Breakell Neibaur, was born in December before their world rotated from autumn to winter again. Bertha had golden hair and a fair complexion, but she was not the content child Alice was.

Mealtimes were a sight to behold, with lively Joseph, chatty Maggie, inquisitive Isaac, little Alice, and discontent baby Bertha, so when Alexander said one evening, "We should invite the Smiths over," Ellen's jaw went slack. She glanced around at the piles of bread crumbs surrounding Alice, bits of jam on Isaac's forehead and left ear, and the crying baby in her arms with stained clothes from the food Ellen had dripped on her while trying to eat and rock simultaneously. With exasperation and maybe a little too much fire, she said, "This is not the time to suggest such a thing to me."

Alexander turned side to side and erupted into laughter. "The Smiths can contribute a couple children to the chaos."

Ellen knew a pang of guilt at the comment. "And they are missing more of their babies than we are. I can scarcely imagine what they have been through, losing four. If you would like to invite them over, they are always welcome, as long as they know what they are getting themselves into. We are a far cry from England, where a maid would keep the children out from underfoot during a dinner party." She directed Alexander's attention to the jam on Isaac's ear with a nod of her head.

Alexander caught Ellen's eyes, and they commiserated in a moment of understanding.

"Is this not better, though?" he asked. "I prefer to be surrounded by the joy of little ones. Why send them away?"

Observing the disaster once more, Ellen was not sure she

would not mind a proper English party, with its multiple courses made by a cook, but once again, the thought of losing a child made her grateful for the ones she still had.

Joseph and Emma Smith, with their young children, Julia and Joseph, came over a few weeks later for supper. Hyrum and Jerusha also came, bringing their little ones, Lovina, Mary, and John.

As they alighted from their buggies, Ellen directed them into her humble home, where the main room was full to bursting.

Ellen had picked out a pig's head from the smokehouse, and the enticing smell as it cooked over the fire, mixed with that of freshly baked bread, brought smiles to the faces of the company the moment they entered the house. She was proud of the presentation of the meal, considering the circumstances, though her mother would have been appalled. The ladies worked to feed the little ones before the children were sent out to play, and they had their turn at the table.

Emma brushed a few crumbs into her hand. "What do you think of the Female Relief Society?"

"It is wonderful. I attend whenever possible," Ellen said.

Emma smiled graciously. "Have you heard about the penny box?"

"I have not."

Jerusha cleared her throat. "Sister Mercy Thompson was praying, asking the Lord how she could help build the Kingdom and felt inspired to start a penny donation box. Sisters may contribute one penny each week to go to the building of the Temple."

Ellen clasped her hands in her lap. "How perfect."

The men had grown quiet and seemed to be listening. Brother Joseph said, "Rumor has it, they have quite a collection started. Will you contribute?"

"Of course," answered Ellen. "Whenever I am able."

"And you, Brother Alexander, will you help build up the structure?"

"As you know, I am not a large man. If I challenged you in a stick-pull, you would probably throw me across the room, but I will do my part." To add emphasis, he pounded his hand on the table.

They shared a laugh.

Ellen remembered the rumors about Brother Joseph taking additional wives. It comforted her heart somewhat to see the evidence of affection between Emma and him. It was clear they were a love match. Hyrum and Jerusha were also a loving couple, and being with them made Ellen want to inch a little closer to Alexander.

The women cleaned up the meal before joining the men near the fire where Joseph was speaking. He gazed up with his piercing blue eyes, standing and pausing as they took their places, then continued. "Sister Ellen, thank you for sharing your husband with me. If I had the time for it, I would spend days on end picking his brain. Right now, I am seeking political advice, as I'm considering a presidential run next year. As you know, Nauvoo is one of the largest cities in Illinois. It would help the cause of our people, as well as the country as a whole."

All were nodding in agreement.

"What are you views on slavery, Alexander?" Brother Joseph asked.

"My own people have been slaves at times. I think all people are children of the Most High, and it is wrong to treat them as anything less."

Brother Joseph agreed. "Here is my thought. They are technically property, and we should respect property, but as you said, they are first and foremost, children of God. I believe the sale of land should be used by the government to pay the slaveholders and free the slaves."

"A marvelous idea," Ellen said. "I wonder why no one else has proposed it."

Joseph had a persuasive way about him. If he were to be elected President of the United States, it would greatly help the situation of the Saints. Persecutors would all but disappear, and Ellen said so.

A laugh boomed from Joseph. "Satan does not give up that easily. However, I am the greatest advocate of the Constitution of the United States there is on the earth."

Alexander grinned. "I am pleased to be here in Nauvoo with God's Prophet. The Holy One of Israel sent me visions all those years ago, so I would know the truth when I found it. My dreams of a golden bible and a beautiful building led me here. That beautiful building, the temple, is progressing. I hear some have received their endowments already."

Emma looked at her husband before turning to Alexander. "It is wonderful. I received the endowment of power from Joseph and am authorized to perform it upon others."

"I could say the same about being here in Nauvoo," said the Prophet. "My life would be completely different without visions sent from God. You are indeed one of us." He cleared his throat. "Speaking of visions, the Spirit bids me to share with you first-hand what we now call my First Vision. Of course, at the time, I was a young boy and did not know what the future would hold."

"I would like that very much," Alexander said. "Would you mind if I wrote your words in my journal?"

"Not at all."

Alexander went for his notebook and returned to the table. He and Ellen moved to the edge of their seats, sensing the sacredness of what they were about to hear.

"There were many Revival Meetings at the time," Joseph said with a glance to Emma and a squeeze of her hand. "Religion was a topic of much interest and debate. My mother, brother, and sisters found churches to join, and, though I wished to find one, I felt unsettled. I wanted to feel and shout with the rest but could feel nothing. With these thoughts, I opened my Bible and the first passage that struck me was James 1:5, which states, 'If any man lack wisdom, let him ask of God, who giveth to all men liberally and upbraideth not.'

"I went into the woods to pray, but when I knelt down, my tongue cleaved to the roof of my mouth that I could not utter a word. It felt a little easier after a while. Then I saw a fire toward Heaven come nearer and nearer. I saw a personage in the fire with a light complexion and blue eyes. A piece of white cloth was drawn over His shoulders, and His right arm was bare.

"Another person came to the side of the first. I asked, 'Must I join the Methodist Church?'

"One answered, saying, 'No. They are not my people. They have gone astray. There is none that doeth good; no, not one. This is My Beloved Son. Hearken ye unto Him.'"

Ellen's heart beat with joy. To think they were in the presence of a man that had seen God.

Joseph let that sink in. "Fire drew nigh, rested on a tree, and enveloped the Son of God.

"Comforted, I endeavored to rise but felt uncommonly feeble. I got into the house in time. I later told the Methodist Priest, who said that this is not the age for God to reveal Himself in vision and that revelation ceased with the New Testament."

Although Brother Joseph seemed to be done speaking, Ellen held her breath for more.

Silence ensued, save the scratches of Alexander scribbling notes into his journal. When he finished, he spoke. "Thank you," he said in hushed tones. "Thank you."

They stood, shaking hands and embracing.

"Thank you," said Ellen. "I know you are the Prophet. That knowledge makes everything we have done to be here worth it."

"God chose me, but I am only a man who asked a question. Thank you for your friendship. Heaven knows many are losing their faith and turning against me."

WHEN ELLEN and Alexander climbed into bed that night, Alexander asked how the rest of her visit had gone.

"It was a perfect evening. I am so happy you insisted."

"Me, too. There was a bit of distressing news, though, while you and the ladies were cleaning up."

Ellen leaned up on her arm. "What now?" she asked with a groan.

"Strange story about First Presidency counselor, William Law."

"Oh?" She was not sure she wanted to know.

"Apparently, William Law and his wife desired to be married for eternity. They wanted Brother Joseph to inquire of the Lord concerning the matter, but he would not. Sister Law wanted to know why Joseph refused to seal them, but Joseph was not willing to wound her feelings."

"Brother Law is one of the prominent leaders of the Church. How is it that he cannot be sealed to his wife?"

Alexander breathed out, and it blew one of Ellen's loose curls into her face. "Joseph said he is an adulterous man."

Ellen spread her hair above her head in a halo. "That cannot be. Were it true, Joseph would publicly denounce him as he did regarding the mayor."

"I do not know the particulars," Alexander said. "But when Joseph went to his office recently, Sister Law was waiting alone inside. She drew him into her arms, asking if he would seal himself to her since he would not seal her to her husband."

"So many convoluted stories, Alexander. How are we ever to know what to believe?"

"Through the Holy Spirit. The same one that testified to us as the Prophet told us of his glorious vision." Alexander continued his story. "Joseph pushed Sister Law aside, refusing to do as she asked. When she saw her husband later that evening, she told William that Joseph wanted to marry her. Brother Law was furious, as you can imagine."

"And you believe Joseph is honorable in this?"

"Completely."

She burrowed into him. "If only we all had your believing heart."

26

Maggie, who sometimes went by Margaret now, turned eight in February. The Neibaurs waited until the ice melted from the Mississippi for Alexander to baptize her. It was a day full of friends, family, and the gifts of the Spirit. When Maggie emerged from the water, her brightly colored dress muted and heavy, her smile could not have been brighter.

"I feel light," she told her family over dinner. "Like new. I want to keep this feeling forever."

Pride poured from Ellen's heart as she combed through her daughter's hair, wishing time would stand still, but like Alexander's pocket watch, it kept ticking forward. "That is how I feel when the Prophet speaks."

Alexander interrupted their conversation. "I want to join our army, the Nauvoo Legion."

"If that is your desire," said Ellen, with a question in her voice.

"Trouble is stirring. I might be able to help."

"You never struck me as a soldier, dear."

"True, but I know more about battle than most. How many

times did I sit at my father's table listening to him talk about serving under Napoleon?"

"If that is your desire," Ellen said again with more conviction.

He swallowed. "Are you aware that Brother Brigham has taken more wives?"

She directed Margaret up to bed before answering. "How many wives can one man handle?"

"Apparently Brother Brigham can handle five." He laughed. "He must be a better man than me."

Ellen's eyes widened to saucers, and Alexander continued, "And that does not include his first wife who died before he married Mary Ann. Do not you worry, though. We both know I can scarcely handle the one I have, the only woman I will ever love."

She stood, melting into his arms, pulling herself into his embrace. He felt her protruding stomach, and they kissed long and hard until he directed her to their room.

ALEXANDER SPENT the next day training with the Nauvoo Legion. He came home with a new gun and a splitting grin. "It feels good to know we can protect our families, despite the mounting troubles."

Each night that week, he hummed happily in the evenings when he was home and helped Ellen around the house.

On Sunday, the brethren spoke defensively about Church leadership, warning against false teachings and rumors and calling Brother Joseph's accusers, including William Law, mobocrats.

Brother Miles Romney spoke to the Neibaurs after the meeting. "Take care," he said. "I know your family will be loyal, and it is difficult to know who to trust. I wanted to let you know that about three hundred so-called Saints have started holding meetings led by William Law. Be ever watchful."

After expressing gratitude, Ellen and Alexander clasped hands and turned toward home, feeling that the air was charged with trouble. As Miles had said, it was difficult to know who to trust. Although the majority still stood with the Prophet, even prominent leaders were susceptible to deception. They caught each other's eyes, as the kids ran ahead, and Ellen sighed deeply.

Alexander spent more time with Joseph Smith over the next few weeks, sometimes in the morning, sometimes in the evening. They read Hebrew and German together whenever they could fit it in.

One afternoon, Ellen took the children to see the progress on the temple while Alexander was working there. Although the basement had been done for a few years and many baptisms for the dead had already been performed in the space, the main walls were just going up. The limestone, quarried nearby, sparkled in the summer sunshine. The base was quite large. Although the temple was far from complete, the Spirit testified to Ellen that they were on sacred ground as they watched the workers lifting stones onto the tops of the walls.

THE SICKNESS ACCOMPANYING pregnancy hit Ellen again, and she rested in bed while Alexander busily worked for their living and helped build the temple, in addition to training with the Nauvoo Legion. The strain of such a busy life drained his bodily resources, and after a hot day at the temple, he came home ill, crawling into bed beside her.

The next day, both Ellen and Alexander stayed abed, while Joseph and Margaret acted the part of caretakers.

Significantly better the following day, Ellen went about her tasks, but Alexander was no better, and when Brother Joseph stopped in to check on him, he was alarmed to see Alexander so altered in such a short time. The Prophet pronounced a blessing upon Alexander and promised provisions from the Church farm. Before he departed, he told Ellen that his enemies were recruiting, and he appreciated his loyal friends more every day.

When Alexander was well enough to sit at the table, Ellen found him writing frantically.

"Is something amiss?" she asked, trying to make sense of the squiggles on the page.

"No. Shhh!" he said, waving her away.

Ellen raised an eyebrow at him.

"I am writing a hymn, and I need to concentrate." He spent the rest of the day, bent over a piece of paper, covered in letters and scribbles, humming to himself.

SHORTLY THEREAFTER, Alexander resumed his full schedule. He had never been one to sit idly by.

"Are you not going to read with the Prophet this evening?"

"I am not," he said with a frown. "Brother Joseph spent the day at the jail in Carthage, being accused of fornication and adultery. The prosecutors did not have a case against him, and he was released. I only hope we have seen the end of the ordeal. Besides, Emma needs him to herself tonight as she is not feeling well."

Another evening, Alexander came home from a visit with Brother Joseph in deep distress. It was early June and already very hot and humid. Ellen stood before him to stop his pacing, feet shoulder-width apart. "What is it?"

Alexander punched the log wall. "A newspaper," he threw his hands in the air. "They call it the Nauvoo Expositor. It is slandering the name of the Prophet, claiming to expose the truth." He snorted. "That treacherous William Law is behind it. It is a ridiculous four-page paper, filled with wedding announcements and poetry, and this 'Statement from the Seceders from the Church at Nauvoo'."

Ellen handed him a ladle of water. "Sit down. Have a drink. You must not work yourself up about it. We cannot handle any more sickness around here."

"I must work myself up about it," he argued. "You know how the citizens of Illinois will take this! They will read it as fact and take up arms against us. Only two of the Twelve are even here as they are campaigning for Joseph to become president. How can he run for office when he is being accused on every side?"

Ellen moved closer to him and rubbed her fingers through his hair. "Surely he cannot. You and the Nauvoo Legion will protect us. No other town has such protection. Besides, the Lord is on our side. All will be well." The words sounded hollow to her own ears. Only God knew what the future held for them, and she knew from experience that He often let them fall on very difficult times.

She would have to try harder to do everything just right.

Alexander attended a City Council meeting where the Nauvoo Expositor was discussed. He returned, appearing a bit more buoyant. "The City Council declared the Expositor a public nuisance," he told her. "The City Marshall marched hundreds of us over to the building that printed the Expositor, and the press was destroyed, the type scattered about."

She sighed. "I am grateful to know they will not be able to print further slanders and half-truths."

"As am I," Alexander agreed. He fell into a chair, scratching Pippy behind the ears and began to sing part of the hymn he wrote, with the dog howling along.

"O, never shall our harps awake,
Laid in the dust for Zion's sake,
Forever on the willows hung,
Their music hushed, their chords unstrung;
Lost Zion! City of our God,
While groaning 'neath the tyrant's rod."

His rich voice rang out, praising God and mourning the difficulties of Zion while Ellen rubbed his shoulders and silently prayed for their safety.

TWO DAYS LATER, Brother Joseph was arrested and tried for the destruction of the Expositor.

Alexander stormed about the house once more. "We were justified," he said repeatedly. "They will not find him guilty. The Expositor was defaming his name. They are the ones at fault."

"Do you believe the law is on our side?" Ellen said.

"Absolutely. I have a mind to attend the trial. Do you want to join me?"

She agreed, and the following day, seventeen others were also named for the trial, which occurred at a municipal court in Nauvoo. Alexander and Ellen attended and were pleased to find charges dropped after many testified that the press was destroyed peaceably.

On their way home, Ellen laced her hand into Alexander's arm. "That is that. Thank goodness."

His expression was one of surprise. "Remember when Joseph was talking about running for President of the United States and said the devil would not give up?"

She nodded gravely.

A short time later, Joseph put the city under martial law,

declaring that he was willing to sacrifice his life for their preservation. Alexander ceased his other responsibilities and began to exclusively train with the Legion, coming home exhausted each night after full days of marching.

Ellen did her best to care for him and their home.

He told her that Governor Thomas Ford had sent a messenger who promised bail but insisted that Brother Joseph face trial in Carthage for the destruction of the press. "There is talk of him going into hiding with Hyrum and Willard. They may even attempt to go to Washington and appeal to the government, or they might head west."

"What will become of the rest of us?" Ellen asked.

Alexander shrugged. "If the Prophet leaves, the mobs may come anyway." He rubbed at his temples.

As it was becoming more dangerous to go out, Ellen did without small necessities. Alexander seemed pleased when he told her that the brethren had decided to go into hiding, only to find out that they had returned by nightfall and planned to leave for Carthage the following morning.

Ellen massaged his neck. "We must have faith."

"Ja. In Carthage, Joseph and Hyrum submitted themselves for arrest for rioting, but when they met with Governor Ford, they were charged with a capital offense: treason for declaring martial law. A trial date has been set for June 29th."

"Is there anything we can do?" she asked.

Alexander let out a slow breath. "Only pray, dear. Only pray."

A couple days before the appointed date, Alexander came home earlier than usual. "Governor Ford would speak to the Saints. Shall we all attend?"

"Is it safe, Abba?" asked Joseph.

"With the Governor there, I believe so."

Ellen scrunched her nose. "Has the Prophet not counseled

us to stay in our homes and avoid gathering for the time being?"

"He has, but I am anxious to know what side the Governor will take. Would you prefer to stay? I can go alone and let you know what he says."

"No. Let us go together."

At the Grove, where they had so often listened to the sermons of Brother Joseph and the others who were now with him, Hyrum, John Taylor, and Willard Richards, Governor Ford said, "A great crime has been done by destroying the Expositor press and placing the city under martial law."

"Great crime, indeed!" Alexander hissed.

"A severe atonement must be made, so prepare your minds for the emergency." He warned of an extermination if the people rebelled.

Alexander scowled at the Governor and the soldiers with him, muttering to Ellen. "I guess we can expect no help from him."

Ellen's breath caught, her chest refusing to hold air. She pulled Bertha close with shaking fingers. "An extermination? Like they did in Missouri?"

Alexander squeezed his cane until his knuckles went white.

Ford continued. "Depend upon it. A little more misbehavior from the citizens, and the torch which is now already lighted will be applied." The governor gave a sharp nod, then led the troops in a march down Main Street.

"Look," Ellen said, pointing. The soldiers had drawn their swords and were swinging them threateningly toward the Saints as they passed.

Ellen and Alexander stepped away from the procession with their children and did not stop to talk with anyone. They clasped hands, and, moving as quickly as they could with small ones, hurried to the relative safety of their home.

Before the sun rose the next morning, Ellen awoke to the sound of a rider yelling from Water Street. She shook Alexander awake, and he launched from the bed, pulled on his trousers, and bolted for the door. Pippy followed barking and howling.

Ellen stood behind Alexander, leaning into his back and straining her ears.

"It's Porter Rockwell," he said, opening the door.

Brother Rockwell saw them, raised a hand, and pulled on the reins of his horse with the other. "Joseph is killed! They have killed him! They have killed him!"

"No," Alexander screamed, stumbling outside and falling to his knees. "It cannot be." He rubbed his face, then looked up at the brother towering over him. "What news of the others?"

Porter Rockwell stopped directly above Alexander, his long hair swinging forward. "Hyrum has also been killed!"

Ellen knelt beside her husband, wrapping him in her arms as Brother Rockwell rode off to spread the word as if it were a plague, leaving them in the dust.

27

A lexander slunk against the wall of their main room, and Ellen shut the door before sliding down next to him. They held their knees to their chests and stared into nothingness. It could not be true. Time passed in a blur until the children awoke and, seeing their parents in such a state, remained quiet.

"What is it, Mama?" asked Margaret after observing them.

Ellen wiped at her hollow, puffy eyes and focused on her daughter's inquisitive face. "Bring everyone here, and we shall tell you the news."

The young family gathered on the hearth rug, and all eyes turned upon Ellen, who swallowed a large lump in her throat. "As you know, Joseph and Hyrum Smith were taken to Carthage Jail a few days ago." Tears filled her eyes, but she kept them in check long enough to form the words: "They have been killed."

Upon seeing young Joseph's anguished face crumple, Alexander opened his arms to him. Then everyone was there, gathering in a huddle on the floor, crying together, and Pippy licked the childrens' tears from their cheeks.

At length, Ellen spoke. "I should check on Emma."

"Let us all go together," said Alexander, petting Pippy before staggering up to his feet.

When all were dressed to step out, they closed the short distance to the Mansion House without a word.

A solemn crowd had gathered there. Ellen whispered to Alexander. "Looks like others had the same idea."

Sister Snailham stood amongst the teary Saints, and Ellen went to speak with her. "What is happening?"

Sister Snailham enveloped Ellen's hands in hers. "Little is known. Joseph and Hyrum were shot by a mob, but you probably know that. Brother Taylor and Brother Richards may yet be alive. The Smith family is holed up in the house, not receiving visits or condolences, but if you watch long enough, you will likely see Sister Lucy Smith pacing in that window, gazing out like a ghost."

Hours of quiet later, Ellen and Alexander remained outside the house with the mourners. The children had run off with others to play while the adults stood idly by, unsure what to do. It would be impossible to go on as if nothing had happened.

The slow, steady pattering beat of approaching wagons drew the heads of the solemn crowd. Willard Richards and Samuel Smith were each directing a team at a careful, deliberate pace toward the Mansion House.

"Thank Heaven Willard made it out alive," Ellen breathed.

The teams and wagons were followed by, it seemed, everyone in Nauvoo who was not already abreast of the Smith home. The wagonbeds were piled high with brush, and the congregation parted like the Red Sea as they passed. Alexander pursed his lips, and Ellen sucked in a breath as realization hit.

"Do you suppose...?" She could not voice the question. Were Joseph and Hyrum under that brush?

Alexander nodded and removed his hat with a sweeping motion as a sob burst from lips. Tears flowed freely, and Ellen did not see a dry eye in the group. She clutched her brooch, a symbol of her personal experiences with death, and hoped Patience remembered her promise to visit Samuel's grave.

Willard, with sunken cheeks in his usually cheerful face, climbed from the wagon, onto a platform where Joseph had spoken to them only days before. He pleaded with them not to retaliate, claiming it would bring additional violence upon the town. "Leave vengeance to the Lord."

Brother Snailham murmured something about "atoning for the blood of the Prophet" and several men, including Alexander, nodded with hardened expressions.

The next morning, a crash in the kitchen awakened Ellen, and she tore from the bed to find Alexander in a heap, cradling a broken crock, with Pippy climbing into his lap and nuzzling into him.

Ellen crouched beside Alexander, patting Pippy before pushing him away and pulling Alexander's head onto her lap while his body convulsed with sobs.

At length, his breathing returned to normal. "I feel so angry." He grimaced. "I broke your crock. I am very sorry."

Ellen stroked his hair, unsurprised, cradling his head until he sat up abruptly, wringing his hands.

ELLEN and her family waited in a line of thousands of Saints to pay their respects at the Mansion House, filing slowly past the bodies of Joseph and Hyrum, like two hollow trees whose occupants had moved on.

Parallel moments materialized before her eyes. Thomas, William, Mama, Samuel.

None taken for any apparent misdeeds. Some were too young to even have the ability to understand right and wrong.

Joseph and Hyrum would join them. Surely Heaven's gates had been thrown open wide at the expectation of their arrival.

At William's funeral, Ellen's hopelessness had consumed her, certain she would never see him again because of her damning choices.

Samuel's funeral was further evidence of her personal treachery.

Now, she worked and sacrificed every day in hopes of making up for the enormous deficit she owed.

Though the skin on the Prophet's face seemed stiff, his countenance was serene. Was there a sliver of hope she would one day find serenity in death?

The brothers who brought about the restoration of God's church had not been taken for their wrongdoing or those of their loved ones. Faithful until the end, they would be hailed as heroes.

"Lord," she thought, "I will give my all to Thee."

A PUBLIC FUNERAL WAS HELD, and Ellen did her best to keep the children reverent while John Taylor spoke, defeated and weak. To think of the horrors Brother Taylor had been through as a firsthand witness of the martyrdom of his friends. Having been shot, he had teetered on the edge of life and death and was unable to return to Nauvoo right away. "Joseph lived great, and he died great in the eyes of God and his people, and like most of the Lord's anointed in ancient times, has sealed his mission and his works with his own blood, and so has his brother, Hyrum. In life they were not divided, and in death they were not separated!"

That was one thing to be grateful for, Ellen supposed. But what of all their loved ones who were separated from them? Their poor, unfortunate wives! And their pitiable mother losing two sons at once! She would not have survived being deprived of two boys on the same day.

William Phelps spoke, his deep-set eyes grim above his high, prominent cheekbones. His voice, as was typical for him, was full of fire, and though he had sent a letter days previously calling for peace, his words passionately spoke otherwise. "The blood of all the prophets, shed from Abel to Joseph must be atoned for; the debts must be paid, whether in blood for blood, or life for life. It matters not. When man takes what he cannot restore, let him die the second death. When there is weeping and wailing and gnashing of teeth, learn our perfect rule of right, that no murderer inherit eternal life.

"The great day is at hand. The master trump sounds; wake the world for the conflict of power. Let the spirits of the damned enter their comrades as the legion did the swine. Amen!"

Ellen's stomach stirred with anxiety, but she raised her voice in unison with the passionate crowd when they spoke as one with a solemn but solid amen.

As Ellen's middle grew, so did the unrest both in and out of the Church. The Saints' enemies had hoped that the fledgling Church would quickly fade into nothingness without its head, but they seemed to realize this was not the case and doubled their efforts.

Work continued on the Temple, services were held, the Twelve were returning from missions, and the efforts of salvation steamed forward. Mourning the loss of the Prophet and wondering which way to look for a new leader left Ellen and the Saints stumbling.

"Alexander, suppose we all walk to Brother Lyon's Drug and

Variety Store to pick up some things." She gestured to the children, who were lying about. "We could all use a bit of fresh air."

He glanced at them and nodded. "I could use some tools and medicinal herbs that Brother Windsor keeps on hand."

Windsor and his wife, Sylvia, were both working in the store when the Neibaurs arrived, and Alexander entered a passionate discussion with the brother about the availability of certain herbs. Ellen would have more than enough time to peruse the latest foodstuffs, crockery, glass, hardware, and paints.

Pleased to see Alexander speaking animatedly about something other than the murders of Joseph and Hyrum, she stepped up to admire a blue and white crock that would make a lovely replacement for the one Alexander shattered.

He had been fighting his own internal battles, seemingly caught between the desire to avenge their deaths and the need to peaceably move forward. A scintillating discussion with another medical professional was precisely what he needed.

Sister Lyon gave each of the children a piece of candy.

"Mama, may we wait outside?" Joseph asked.

"I suppose, but stay in sight of the store."

They did not wait for another word.

Sylvia, an attractive New Englander with dark hair pulled into a tight bun, came to offer assistance to Ellen and make conversation. Her baby was wrapped to her back with a long piece of cloth.

Hugging Ellen's shoulders, she said, "How are you holding up, Sister Ellen?"

"As well as any, I suppose," Ellen answered truthfully. "And you?"

"It has been difficult. I loved Joseph, you know." She choked back tears.

"We all did." Ellen rested a comforting hand on the woman's shoulder.

Sylvia nodded, dabbing at her eyes with a handkerchief. "I am grateful to have been sealed to him."

"Oh." Ellen tried not to allow shock to register on her face. "Oh," she said again, attempting a smile. "I did not know."

"Yes. It occurred during the time Windsor was excommunicated. I feared for my salvation without a worthy husband, so I was sealed to Brother Joseph."

Ellen shifted her weight. Although the reason made sense, she prickled with jealousy on behalf of Emma. How could a man split himself between multiple wives, even if only in the hereafter? And what of Windsor? How did he feel about it?

Sylvia caught Ellen's sidelong glance at Windsor and guessed her thoughts. She swatted at the air. "Fear not. He knows, and he loves the Prophet. He hopes to testify against the murderers when the time comes."

"Pardon, but how is it that Brother Joseph can be sealed to married women as well as unmarried ones?"

"Ah. Like most, you see marriage and sealings as the same thing, but that is not how Brother Joseph saw them. Sealings are for the eternities and trump any civil marriages made on earth. Marriage is part of earth-life and without a sealing, it means nothing hereafter. All must be sealed in the New and Everlasting Covenant to be exalted."

"Curious," was all Ellen could say in response.

As if the topic had not been heavy as a sack of flour, Sylvia brought up another. "What is your opinion on who should lead the Church in Brother Joseph's absence? I am asking everyone who comes to the store. A sort of survey, I suppose."

"I hope the Twelve will lead."

"Ah. An answer without giving an answer." She raised her pointed finger into the air. "So, I will ask further, who shall lead the Twelve?"

"Can they not work as one body?"

Her eyes stared at the ceiling as she appeared to consider

the answer. "No. I do not think they can. A leader must rise to the top like cream."

Ellen silently pleaded with Alexander to come to her rescue with a pointed look, so he made his purchases and led Windsor to them.

Sylvia cleared her throat. "I was asking Sister Neibaur who should lead the Church now that dear Joseph and Hyrum are...gone. Sometimes it feels as if the store is the center of happenings. I have heard many opinions on the subject, but I have not been able to come to any sort of conclusion."

Ellen raised her brows to Alexander, as if to say, "See why I needed you?"

Alexander, in his ever-faithful way, said, "The Lord will provide. In the old stories, another prophet always arises."

Sylvia smiled, nodding with vigor. "You are of the belief that there will be a new prophet. I agree."

Windsor puffed out a breath. "It was a long time between the scriptural prophets and the birth of Joseph Smith. We may not see another in our lifetime."

"No." Alexander waved his arms as he spoke. "Joseph spent the last eight months of his life preparing the Twelve and the Church for his death. He knew it was coming, and the Lord prompted him to give all the keys of the priesthood to the brethren for such a time as this. The Church will continue to roll forward like a wagon down a never-ending slope!"

Ellen nodded curtly and took his arm. "Shall we go? We should find the children."

He shook his head. "Not yet." He turned back to Brother Lyon. "Who are the frontrunners to lead the Church according to your customers?"

Sylvia lit up. "Hyrum would, of course, have been the natural choice if he had survived. God rest his soul. Their brother, Samuel, may have also had claim to lead had he not died last week from complications of that same dreadful night.

"And William Smith wants only to succeed as Patriarch. It does not seem anyone considers him a real possibility anyway. As for Joseph's sons, they are far too young to lead anything. Poor dears have long fatherless lives ahead." She wiped at her brow. "That leaves us with non-familial relations with claim to leadership. Oliver Cowdery or David Whitmer might have been good choices if they were actively following Brother Joseph's teachings, but they are not currently in good standing.

"Most seem to agree with me that the most likely choices are Sidney Rigdon, as the surviving member of the First Presidency, and Brigham Young."

Ellen nodded. One of these great men would lead the Twelve and, therefore, the Church. What would that look like? Either of them would lead in a different manner than Brother Joseph. She wondered if either could be a visionary like their beloved martyred Prophet or if they would simply strive to continue what he had begun.

"Is Brother Rigdon not in Pittsburg?" she asked.

Alexander shook his head and gestured to Windsor. "He informed me that Brother Rigdon has recently returned to Nauvoo. Since he went to Pennsylvania to be eligible as Joseph's running mate in a presidential campaign, there was no need to remain there." He clenched his teeth.

Windsor agreed, placing his hand on Alexander's shoulder. "If my sources are correct, and I believe they are, Brother Rigdon is offering himself as Guardian of the Church until the glorious day when Joseph is resurrected. He has called a prayer meeting on the 8th."

The idea of having a guardian over the Church pleased Ellen, but Alexander did not appear convinced. "I am not sure Brother Joseph would have entrusted the Church to Sydney."

"Why would he choose to run as president alongside a man he did not trust?" Ellen asked.

Nobody could answer the question.

"This proposed meeting," she said. "Should it not be held when the rest of the Twelve can be present?"

Windsor nodded. "That would be ideal, but I do not believe Rigdon wants to wait that long."

"And what of Brigham Young?" she asked. "Has he returned?"

"Not yet," said Sylvia. She turned to Alexander. "You know Brother Brigham well. Would you endorse him as the new leader?"

Alexander paused before answering. "He is a good man and a stalwart one, but he is so different from Brother Joseph, it is difficult to picture."

Sylvia frowned. "If it is him, I fear for his life. It is not a secret that he has multiple wives. How many brides has he taken?"

Alexander shifted his feet. "A few."

"Do you not know how many?" asked Windsor.

Alexander turned, answering with his eyes on the wall of tools. "Five. I believe he has five wives, not counting Miriam, his first. She joined the Church with Brother Brigham in New York and died shortly thereafter, leaving their two young girls in Brigham's care."

Ellen was not sure she sympathized with a man who lost one wife and married five new ones.

After the drug store, they located the children and made a quick stop at the post office where Alexander was thrilled to find a letter from his parents. Ellen knew a moment of sorrow at her own lack of correspondence from England.

Oblivious, Alexander was all smiles on the way home until they spotted a familiar figure strutting toward them on Hotchkiss Street. He puffed out his chest. "William Law," he muttered. "He is the last person I wish to run into today."

Ellen groaned. "Stay calm, dear."

"He does not deserve calm."

"Your children do." She turned behind to the children. "Run ahead to the end of the street. We shall catch up."

Brother Law sauntered up as if there was nothing wrong with doing so and wished them a good afternoon. Having been increasingly vicious in his attacks against the Church, and worse yet, possibly instrumental in the death of the Prophet, Ellen was surprised he dared show his face around town, let alone speak to them.

He grinned and reached out to shake hands with Alexander, who kept his arms firmly to his sides. "William Law, I never give my hand to a traitor."

A humorless laugh burst from the man, who looked like he might strike. "If you think I am the traitor, you deserve what's coming to you."

28

The all-too-familiar fire in Alexander's eyes caught Ellen's attention one day when he returned from his shift at the temple. He was circling the room, and Ellen wondered if he might throw something again, so she redirected him to the table and handed him a sheet of paper and a pen. "Put your passion into this."

He opened his mouth as if to speak, but shut it again, huffing through his nose.

She prepared the children for bed, and when all was quiet, she sat next to him, pleased to see he had taken her advice and was writing furiously. Taking up her basket of mending, she began to stitch quietly.

Soon she was yawning so much, it was difficult to focus through moist eyes, and she retired to bed, leaving Alexander alone with his paper and ink.

In the morning, he shared his creation with the family. So much heart had spilled onto the page that he had to stop more than once to contain his emotions.

Blessed the people knowing the shout of Jehovah,
In the light of his countenance they will walk.
How can we, a people in sackcloth,
Open our lips before thee?

They have rejected and slain our leaders,
Thine anointed ones.
Our eyes are dim, our hearts heavy;
No place of refuge being left,

Redeem the people that in thee only trusts;
There is none to stand between and inquire;
Thou art our helper,
The refuge of Israel in time of trouble.

O look in righteousness upon they faithful servants,
Who have laid bare their lives unto death,
Not withholding their bodies;
Being betrayed by false brethren, and their lives
    cut off,

Forbidding their will before thine;
Having sanctified thy great name,
Never polluting it;
Ready for a sacrifice; —standing in the breach,

Tried, proved and found perfect,
To save the blood of the fathers;
Their children, brothers, and sisters;
Adding theirs unto those who are gone before them;

Sanctifying thy holy and great name upon the earth;
Cover and conceal not their blood.
Give ear unto their cries until thou lookest

And shewest down from Heaven—taking vengeance

And avenging their blood—avenging thy people and
    thy law,
According to thy promises made
Unto our forefathers, Abraham, Isaac, and Jacob.
Hasten the acceptable and redeeming year;

Shaddai; remember unto us thy covenants;
All this heaviness has reached us;
Can anyone be formed to declare
What has befallen us?

All this we bear, and the name of our God
We will not forget, nor deny,
The "Hebrews' God" he is called,
Thou art clothed with righteousness,
But we are vile.

Come not in judgment with us.
Before thee nothing living is justified by their works.
But be with us as thou wast with our fathers.
Help us, O Father; unto thee

We will lift our souls,
Our hearts in our hands;
We look to Heaven,
Lifting our eyes unto the mountains,
From whence cometh our help.

Turn away thine anger,
That we be not spoiled.
O return and leave a blessing behind thee.

HE TORE his gaze from the page, and Ellen clapped her hands along with the children. "A perfect tribute, my dear," she said with a kiss to his whiskered mouth.

Joseph wrinkled his nose. "Must you do that in our presence?"

"Indeed." Alexander dramatically rubbed his hands around on Ellen's back and made a loud smooching sound, scattering the children.

Ellen blushed. "Poor Joseph."

Alexander chortled. "Nonsense. Now I have you to myself." He kissed her long and hard.

THE MORNING BOILED like stew despite a strong wind that billowed across the Grove as they found their seats at Brother Rigdon's prayer meeting. If Alexander was not so particular about his pocket watch and being on time, they would not have been lucky enough to find a place to sit at all. Nearly half the crowd was obliged to stay on their feet.

Brother Rigdon spoke, but a gale threw his words back into his face. He held up a hand to indicate a brief break and moved around to the back of the congregation to speak in the same direction as the wind, standing upon a wagon bed.

The usually dynamic speaker lacked fire this morning, and when Alexander checked the time, Ellen peered at it and was unsurprised that Brother Rigdon had been speaking for over an hour. At long last, he concluded his words. "I am calling for a vote to be taken as to whom should take the position of Church Guardian. All in favor of…"

Another booming voice rang out, interrupting him from the front of the Grove, which now at their backs. "I will manage this voting," the voice said, as the crowd, almost in unison, swung around to see Brother Brigham. "Brother

Rigdon does not preside here. I will manage this flock for a season. Do you not feel that something is amiss in this hurrying spirit?"

With a spirit of relief, Ellen leaned to Alexander, whose grin was wide. "Did you not know he was returned?" she asked.

"No. He must have just arrived."

Brother Brigham quieted the onlookers. "This meeting is adjourned until two o'clock," he called before being surrounded by well-wishers.

Ellen chanced a glance back at Sidney Rigdon, whose lips were drawn down.

During the afternoon meeting, the apostles sat on a stand at the front of the Grove. The men were seated according to their priesthood office, as this meeting would be a special one and required a vote.

Brother Brigham arose, clearing his throat. The sound reminded Ellen of Brother Joseph. Brigham spoke for hours about the organization of the Church, reassuring the people that the keys and authority rested with the Twelve.

Ellen closed her eyes and found that the voice of Brigham did not sound like him at all. It sounded like Brother Joseph. Strange. Though it was Brigham speaking, it was as if the mantle of Church leadership fell upon him, cloaking him in the spiritual voice of the Prophet. Ellen opened her eyes, and rubbing them, found that he *looked* like Joseph. She elbowed Alexander, who was too riveted to react, and she wondered if he was hearing and seeing the same thing. Her heart burned within her as it had done the day Brother Joseph related his glorious vision to them.

Brigham was clearly the Lord's choice to succeed as prophet. Gratitude for that knowledge swelled in Ellen's breast.

Hours later, when they lay abed, Alexander pulled her to him. "It was as if Brother Brigham transformed before my eyes into Joseph. His voice, his mannerisms, his very appearance was Joseph, yet my physical eyes knew they were deceived as my spiritual eyes gloried in the testimony of the Holy Spirit."

Ellen scooted into the crook of his arm. "The Lord provided as you knew He would. Why do I ever doubt you?"

Alexander held her closer. "The Lord is good."

While he dozed off, Ellen rested against him, her mind spinning with Alexander's last words like a cotton loom. Could it be as simple as that? If the Lord was good, why was life packed with suffering? Were trials always the result of transgression of God's laws? Was it possible for her to be good enough to not only repent for past misdeeds but also forgo future tribulations?

MOB THREATS INCREASED in frequency and intensity as word spread about Brigham Young taking the Church's leadership upon himself. It was evidence that the intended outcome of their enemies had not come to fruition.

In November, Ellen gave birth to a perfect baby boy. After so many babies, her body knew the process, and the delivery, while not painless, was quick and relatively easy.

The first time Alexander held the tiny infant in his gentle hands, his eyes glistened. "I was hoping for a boy. Shall we call him Hyrum Smith Neibaur?"

Tired, Ellen blinked and grinned. It was perfect. "Another Hyrum is just what the world needs. And we already have our own Joseph."

Alexander rubbed baby Hyrum's head and spoke to Ellen without tearing his eyes away from the baby. "Our enemies have convinced the Illinois government to revoke the Nauvoo Charter. They do not want us to be able to defend ourselves." His forehead wrinkled when he finally met Ellen's gaze. "We shall have to return all of our government-issued arms."

Ellen sucked in a breath. "Will you still be able to defend Nauvoo?"

Alexander pursed his lips. "We will try."

THE SUN FILTERED through the tops of the sycamores, elms, and birches as the Neibaur family marched up the street to the temple along with thousands of fellow believers. The nearly white limestone walls were complete and glistened in the early morning light. Thirty pilasters stood tall along the walls, intricately carved with a moonstone at the base and topped with a sunstone. Above these, stars of stone and vibrant blue and red stained glass shone.

Alexander moved behind her and lifted his eyes to see where she was looking. "Do you know why the stars are upside down?"

Ellen shook her head. "But I am sure you will tell me." She laughed softly.

He wrapped his arms around her. "It is a symbol of Jesus Christ and the five punctures to his body during His crucifixion. The same symbol graces the Notre Dame Cathedral in France and at Marketirche in Germany. It is a symbol of protection against evil."

"I hope it saves us. We need all the protection we can get."

Alexander tightened his embrace around her. "Do you remember the dreams I had all those years ago? The ones that led us to meet the missionaries and join the Church?"

She rested her head back against his shoulder. "How could I forget?"

"Do you remember that, in addition to being about a gold Bible, they featured a beautiful building and some of the practices that would take place inside?"

Ellen raised her eyebrows and turned toward his face, inches from hers. "The practices?"

"Ja. This is the building of my dreams, and I know some of the glorious gifts of power that will be bestowed upon us here."

Ellen inhaled the brief reprieve of peace. "And today we will watch the placing of the final capstone." She pointed out the windows to the children. "Did you know that we helped purchase those by contributing to the Relief Society's Penny Fund?"

They nodded, and Alexander said, "If only the Prophet was here."

Ellen placed her hands on his arms, which were wrapped around her. "He is. He would not miss this for anything."

A sea of people gathered near the southeast corner of the building, and the Nauvoo Brass Band played a spirited tune. Alexander, still holding Ellen, rocked back and forth to the beat. Brother Brigham, with several others, set the capstone. Despite the number of people, only the wind whispered as they watched in awe.

Brother Brigham paused before speaking. "The last stone is laid upon the Temple, and I pray the Almighty in the name of Jesus to defend us in this place and sustain us until the temple is finished, and we have all got our endowments."

Ellen whispered to Alexander. "What will happen once it is done?"

He rested his head against hers. "Only the Lord knows, but I do not think we will be permitted to stay in Nauvoo."

"Now we shall give the Hosanna Shout," Brother Brigham said, "as introduced by Brother Joseph at the Kirtland Temple."

"I was hoping we would do that," Alexander said. "It reminds me of the Hebrew Feast of the Tabernacles. God is restoring His ancient church."

Brother Brigham raised his arms to direct the words of praise.

The third time the crowd repeated the sacred refrain was powerful, and Ellen felt a thrill of hope as the words reverberated through the air, into the trees, and beyond.

The structure was finally complete. If only the mobs would leave them alone long enough to make use of it.

29

Ellen was hanging laundry on the clothesline when Alexander returned from the trial of some of the Prophet's murderers. She could tell the moment she met his dull, disheartened eyes, that it had not gone as he hoped. He walked up, shaking his head gruffly, and hugged Ellen while he wept anew for his friends. "There will be no justice on Earth," he said. "Brother Lyon and others testified, but there was never any hope of a fair trial. The jury acquitted the murderers, saying that Brother Joseph's death was the will of the people, therefore no particular person or group could be blamed."

Seemingly emboldened by the lack of consequences for the deaths of the Prophet and the Patriarch, reports of mobs burning homes, mills, and farmland on the outskirts of town grew in frequency and intensity.

The Saints from Lima, under direction from church leaders, moved to Nauvoo and its relative safety after mobs burned some of their homes and drove them out.

"It is only a matter of time before they attack here,"

Alexander said one night. The younger children had gone to bed, and he was cleaning his rifle.

Ellen poked her thread through the sock she was darning. "What shall we do?"

He lifted his shoulders. "Defend ourselves until we are driven out, I suppose."

"Driven out? But where are we to go?"

"Joseph spoke of moving the whole of the Church out to the Rocky Mountains." He sighed. "That is the most likely place."

"The Rockies?" Ellen said in disbelief. "Is that not beyond the borders of the United States?"

"Ja. Over 1,000 miles west of here."

She rocked back, placing her work in her lap. "Mercy. We could never survive a journey like that with the children."

"There may come a time when trekking across the wilderness is fraught with less danger than remaining in Nauvoo."

"What I would not give to sit in an English parlor tonight surrounded by my family and dear Patience and play on my old pianoforte."

"What I would not give to hear it," agreed Alexander. "Perhaps one day out west in the Rockies or far out in California or wherever we go, we will settle for good and save up the money for an instrument."

That felt as unlikely as returning to Preston. "Perhaps."

"Do you remember playing at Mama's parents' house when we were young?" Joseph asked Margaret.

"Maybe. I seem to recall running and screaming from Uncle Richard and Uncle James."

Ellen laughed. "Dear boys. I wonder what has become of them. I wish we, on occasion, would hear from the Breakells as we do from your grandparents in Germany."

Joseph sat beside Alexander, studying the parts of the gun. "Are we safe here, Abba?"

Alexander appeared thoughtful before responding. "I

cannot be sure, but I will do my best, along with the other men, to protect our family and our home."

"Are we not right at the edge of Nauvoo?" said Margaret. "If the mobs come here, will our home not be the first target?"

Ellen gave Alexander a warning look. She did not want them becoming overly concerned.

"Do you remember the story of Captain Moroni?" he asked.

They nodded and moved to kneel at his feet beside Pippy.

"The Lord is on our side as he was with Moroni, because we are fighting for our homes and liberties, our wives and children, and the right to worship the God of Israel. Like the Nephites, we may be called upon to defend our families unto bloodshed."

Ellen raised her brows to Alexander, willing he would stop there.

"What?" he said. "They are old enough to understand the gravity of the situation."

If only they could stay blissfully safe and ignorant.

Alexander spent the following day marching with the men of Nauvoo. Ellen, trying to occupy herself, worked around the house. She cared for the animals, did the wash, churned butter, weeded and picked vegetables from the garden, dressed and fed the children, and baked bread, all before the sun was directly overhead, and while carrying Hyrum, who was no longer an infant.

Scanning the house for more work to occupy her hands and mind, she noticed some dust in one corner near the fireplace and went for the broom, but when she surveyed Joseph and Margaret, sitting quietly at the table, and the other children, Isaac, Alice, and Bertha playing quietly on the floor, she knew what to do. She rested the broom against the wall and knelt beside Isaac, still holding Hyrum. "Let us put our frowns away. Shall we make shaped cookies or play a game?"

The little ones barreled into her, and she wrapped her arms

protectively around Hyrum so he would not be pummeled in their excitement.

"Hoop Roll!" Isaac said, but, at the same moment, Alice said, "Marbles!"

Bertha climbed onto Ellen's lap. "How about you, Bertha? Hoops or marbles?"

"Tookies!" said Bertha.

She smiled up at Joseph and Margaret. "And you two? Care to vote?"

Margaret shrugged. "Anything is fine with me."

"I would venture a guess that you would like to go to Lyon's to look at their inventory of ribbons."

Margaret's face lit up like a candle, and Ellen chuckled. "I thought so."

"And you, Joseph?"

"Hoop Roll or marbles is fine."

"Let me see," Ellen said dramatically. "That makes two votes for hoops and two for marbles."

"Tookies!" Bertha said again.

"Very well. Let us do them all. If we do not get to one of the activities today, there is always tomorrow."

But surely there was not *always* tomorrow. She knew that from experience.

"Is it safe to go to the store, Mama?" Margaret said.

"We will be extra cautious."

They played the games and shopped for ribbons, all the while being reminded throughout the day that Bertha wanted to make "tookies". After dinner, Margaret fed Hyrum soup and bread and put him down for a nap while Ellen and Joseph cleaned the dishes, with some not-so-helpful help from Isaac and Alice.

"Tookies!" reminded Bertha.

Ellen squeezed her. "I know, darling. It is tookie time at last." She placed a big wooden bowl and spoon on the table and retrieved the necessary ingredients, sending Joseph to the cellar to fetch the lard.

Isaac went out to the hen house for eggs and had not yet returned when the sounds of marching soldiers pounded toward the house. Pippy growled at the door until Ellen bolted outside, fearful for Isaac, with the dog at her heels.

The former Nauvoo Legion men were marching. Releasing a deep sigh of relief, she swung the door open wider, allowing the children to parade out. Alice was the first to spot her father.

"Abba," she yelled. "Abba!"

"Where is he, Alice?" Ellen asked, and Alice tried to point him out. "Joseph, Maggie, do you see him?"

After another minute, they discovered him in the group, and pride washed over Ellen from head to toe when he smiled at them. Isaac joined with eggs in his arms, and they waved, watching until the soldiers were well out of sight before returning to the house to bake.

It was not an efficient nor pristine process with each of the little ones taking turns adding ingredients, but they enjoyed the activity nonetheless. Bertha stirred with a bit too much enthusiasm, sending puffs of flour and sugar across the table. A bit of the snowy powder landed on Margaret's comely nose.

She stomped her foot, which made the rest of the party laugh. The giggles were small at first, but, because laughs are contagious, they grew until all were nearly rolling. Margaret remained stern-faced, making them giggle all the more until she finally joined in the revelry.

Isaac laughed himself right into the container of flour, and a bit of it landed on Margaret's arm. Ellen's laughs became heavy and forceful, and after a day, actually months, of stress, the emotions were too much and turned into sobs.

The mess only grew when they cut shapes out of the ginger and molasses dough. They were elbow deep when Alexander returned. His worry lines melted away as he sniffed the delicious scent. "What is the occasion?"

Ellen kissed his cheek and took his hand. "We needed some light-hearted family fun, and that resulted in…"

"Tookies," said Bertha.

Alexander lifted Bertha up, sticky hands and all, and twirled her around. "I would love a tookie," he said, tapping her nose. He turned to Ellen and spoke softly. "A mob was descending on Nauvoo from Warsaw, and our guard chased them out. They retreated all the way to Missouri, so that is something to celebrate."

Ellen whispered, "Will they not come back?"

"You can be sure they will."

Each day for the next week, Alexander stood guard with the former members of the Legion. The only respite came when Brother Brigham hoisted a white flag for the Sabbath and preached to the Saints. Ellen warily kept one eye on the surrounding areas, watching for would-be persecutors.

Brigham spoke of preparing to move west, and Ellen knew in her heart that it must be. The opposition to the Church would continue until the Saints were beyond reach. She recalled similar feelings when Brother Brigham gave his speech about leaving England.

Was there a place far enough that persecution would not follow them? Why did the Lord not stay the hands of their oppressors?

Was this the life they deserved?

ELLEN HELPED Alexander put on his coat.

"Are you sure you and the children will be well while I work on the temple?"

"For the hundredth time, Alexander, we will be fine. There is nothing more important you can do."

He brought her hand to his lips. "I worry about you while I am away. It looks like an agreement with Governor Ford is forthcoming. We will all have to leave Nauvoo by spring."

"It is no surprise." Ellen sighed. "But how are thousands of Saints to prepare to leave in a matter of six months?"

He grimaced. "You have not seen the 'Bill of Particulars' yet. The required provisions are extensive." He dug through his coat and into the pockets of his pants. "Here it is." He unfolded the paper and read the list to her.

"1 good strong wagon well covered with a light box, 2 or 3 good yoke of oxen between the age of 4 and 10 years, 2 or more milch cows, 1 or more good beefs, 3 sheep if they can be obtained, 1000 lbs. of flour or other bread, or bread stuffs in good sacks, 1 good musket or rifle to each male over the age of twelve years, 1 lb. powder, 4 lbs. lead, 1 lb. tea, 5 lbs. coffee, 100 lbs. sugar, 1 lb. cayenne pepper, 2 lb. black pepper, 1/2 lb. mustard, 10 lb. rice for each family, 1 lb. cinnamon, 1/2 lb. cloves, 1 dozen nutmegs, 25 lbs. salt, 5 lbs. saleratus, 10 lbs. dried apples, 1 bushel of beans, a few lbs. of dried beef or bacon, 5 lbs. dried peaches, 20 lbs. dried pumpkin, 25 lbs. seed grain, 1 gallon alcohol, 20 lbs. of soap each family, 4 or 5 fish hooks and lines, 15 lbs. iron and steel, a few lbs. of wrought nails, one or more sets of saw or grist mill irons to company of 100 families, 1 good seine and hook for each company, 2 sets of pulley blocks and ropes to each company for crossing rivers, 25 to 100 lbs. of farming and mechanical tools, cooking utensils to consist of bake kettle, frying pan, coffee pot, and tea kettle, tin cups, plates. knives, forks, spoons, and pans as few as will do, a good tent and furniture to each 2 families, clothing and bedding to each family, not to exceed 500 pounds, ten extra teams for each company of 100 families.

"In addition to the above list, horse and mule teams can be

used as well as oxen. Many items of comfort and convenience will suggest themselves to a wise and provident people, and can be laid in season, but none should start without filling the original bill."

Ellen's jaw hung open. "They cannot be serious. How is anyone to procure so much? We are better off than many, and I do not think we can."

"Have faith, Ellen."

She lifted her shoulders. "Thousands of families will be trying to find the same items, and if we all try to sell our homes at the same time, I do not expect them to sell for much."

He bit his bottom lip. "In that, you are surely right. Buyers will know we are about to abandon our properties if we cannot sell. They will have little incentive to pay for what will soon be readily free for the taking. But the Lord will provide."

Ellen wished she had the faith to match his. The Lord did provide, sometimes in miraculous ways, but He was also known to take away. Her hand moved up to the brooch. She stroked it and remembered all she had lost and given up.

E llen pressed her fingers into the sweet-smelling bread dough as she studied Alexander, sitting by the fire. "Do you suppose we shall be able to receive our endowments before we leave?"

His tired eyes moved heavily to Ellen. "We must. Who knows how many years it will be before we have another opportunity—or if we shall have another chance at all." He fingered his beard. "Brother Brigham has scarcely left the building in weeks. I hear he is only sleeping four hours each night to endow as many with power as he possibly can before our journey."

She flipped the dough over, tucking the edges around to smooth the top. "Do you suppose the mobs will leave us alone?"

"Maybe for a time. They see we are doing all we can to leave the country."

"Are we, though? With the leaders and Saints spending so much time worrying about their ordinances? Would the temple not be the perfect place for the mob to attack?"

Alexander crossed the room to her. "There is no need to fear."

Her eyes returned to the dough. "But there is, and I know you are worried, as well."

He cupped her face in his calloused hands. "Our enemies are not brazen enough to attack the heart of the city. The cowards only attack on the outskirts where we are weak."

"And we practically live on the outskirts." Ellen set the bread pan aside to rise while they slept. In their room she removed and hung her wrapper and knelt beside their bed. The cold of the wooden planks seeped through her nightdress, sending a shiver up her body.

She heard Alexander blow out the candles and enter the room while she prayed.

"Since you brought up the ordinances, I wondered if we could go to the temple tomorrow and see if we cannot get in."

Ellen silently said, "Amen," and she opened her eyes against the darkness where she could barely make out Alexander's figure standing on the other side of the bed.

She arose. "It may take all day. Will the children be safe?"

"Ja. Our Joseph is practically a man, and he and Margaret can handle the chores. Hyrum does not need to nurse anymore."

Excitement bubbled up in Ellen's chest. "I think you are right. It is an important enough reason to leave, and we can tell them to see Sister Jones if there are any problems."

The next morning, Ellen peeked out the glass window. The ground glistened with frost. "Today will be a bitterly cold day to line up outside the temple with the other hopeful Saints."

Alexander yanked on his boots and smiled up at her. "I will warm up some stones in the fire to help me keep you warm."

"Very well." Ellen parted the curtain that hid her clothes and chose her nicest dress and shoes, remnants of days long past.

She served hotcakes, milk, and sausages to the family, and she and Alexander ate quickly.

"Keep a close eye on Hyrum," Ellen reminded Margaret.

"Yes, Mama. I know."

"And keep everyone inside with the door latched except to care for the animals."

"I know that, too."

Ellen pulled her cloak tightly around her when they stepped out the door, but her teeth chattered anyway. Alexander wrapped one of the blankets he was holding around her shoulders and dropped warm rocks in the pockets of her apron.

It was afternoon before it was their turn to enter the temple. Ellen paused in the entrance and took in the room which was still under construction. "Though it is not finished, I feel as if we have walked through an invisible veil into a sacred space," she whispered, tingling with joy and gratitude.

The endowment, unlike anything she had ever experienced before, renewed and enlightened her spirit. "I am grateful you insisted upon coming," she said when it was over. "I could listen to the ordinance a hundred times and not fully under-stand it, but the Spirit testified of its importance, and at some small level, I understand and am grateful."

He placed his hand on her back and directed her through the crowds and debris on the main floor toward the exit where he spread his arms out. "I have an advantage there. It is not the first time I have heard these things."

She squinted at him, the biting cold whipping under her bonnet when they walked outside the grand temple doors.

Alexander stalled and pulled her around to face him. "I dreamed it. The endowment was familiar to me because I have been through it in my sleep."

Her eyes widened. "You said before that you had seen some

of the processes from inside in your dreams. Was it what you expected?"

"It was."

Ellen gazed into those handsome, faithful eyes. "I love you, Alex."

"I love you, too."

Surrounded by waiting Saints on the steps of the temple, he kissed her.

Less than three weeks later, Alexander and Ellen entered the temple again, and, kneeling across the altar from one another, they were sealed for time and eternity in the New and Everlasting Covenant.

It was a day they would never forget.

WHEN ALEXANDER FINISHED WRITING a list of items they still needed before moving west, he drove Ellen in the wagon to Lyon's Drug Store. They handed the list to Sylvia, and, while she measured out coffee, Ellen fingered the calicos. "We have been so busy making preparations that we have scarcely been about. What news have you?"

Sylvia tied the top of the coffee bag closed and placed it on the counter. "Brother Brigham planned to leave town with the first company a week ago, but seeing the faces of so many hopeful Saints at the temple melted his resolve. He has delayed his departure multiple times, but there are always more people asking to receive their ordinances before embarking on such a perilous journey. It cannot be long now, though." She turned to find the next item on the list.

Ellen gazed out the window. "I fear spring is arriving early, and our enemies will be anxious."

Alexander shook his head. "The Lord will make the elements work in our favor."

Sylvia gathered a few more items and set them on the growing pile on the counter. "Does your family have the animals you need?"

Alexander nodded vigorously. "Yes. Thank you."

"Have you sold your home yet?"

"No." He paid for the goods and lifted the heaviest bag, carrying it out to the wagon. "But I have little hope of doing so."

Ellen picked up the large sack of flour and a wave of heat and nausea flowed up from her stomach to her throat, leaving her to lower the heavy sack to her feet.

Alexander came back in, and, seeing her bent there, he rushed over and put a hand on her shoulder. "What is it?"

She forced herself to breathe slowly, and the sensation passed. Her eyes flicked to Sylvia. "It is nothing." Straightening her shoulders and lifting her head, she reached for the flour, but Alexander hefted it up and carried it out.

Sylvia studied Ellen while the latter grabbed a couple smaller bags. Alexander stood in the wagon box, and she handed the packages up.

"You look pale," Alexander said. "Let me lift you in, and I will get the rest." He jumped down, and, without waiting for an answer, helped her up before disappearing into the store again.

Could she be pregnant for the eighth time? It would be a terrible time to be ill. How would they prepare to leave if she was stuck in bed? How could she bring another little one into the dangerous world in which they lived?

The weather warmed over the next several weeks, and Ellen's nausea increased, confirming her suspicions. Every day, Alexander reported to her on which families had crossed the Mississippi. Busy with preparations, he left her in Margaret's charge. Ellen had been confined to bed for weeks when the blossoms on the trees made way for late spring's green foliage, and she was well enough to move about the house again.

Alexander entered with an ear-to-ear smile one day, waving a packet of papers in his hand. He hung his hat and crossed the room, placing a kiss on the top of Ellen's head. "How are you, my dear?"

Sitting by the fire, she set her mending in the basket beside her rocking chair. "Past the worst of it, I believe."

"I hoped you would say that. The Nauvoo Temple is complete, inside and out. Do you think you can come to the grand opening?"

She tilted her head and breathed in. "Maybe."

Dropping the small packet into her lap, Alexander knelt beside her. "Say yes. These are the tickets. I purchased them at a dollar a person. The money will be given to the temple workers to assist them in procuring what they need for the journey, now that they are done working on it."

"It is complete only to be abandoned." She glanced around at the hopeful faces of the children. "We shall go to the opening of the temple to say our goodbyes to the Lord's house."

Ellen helped young Hyrum fold his arms and bow his head before doing the same. Elder Orson Hyde rose to give the dedicatory prayer for the temple. "We thank Thee that Thou hast given us strength to accomplish the charges delivered by Thee. Thou hast seen our labors and exertions to accomplish this purpose.

"By the authority of the Holy Priesthood, we offer this building as a sanctuary to Thy Worthy Name. We ask Thee to take the guardianship into Thy hands and grant that Thy Spirit shall dwell here and may all feel a sacred influence on their hearts that His Hand has helped this work.

"Accept of our offering this morning. Let Thy Spirit rest upon the laborers that they may come forth to receive kingdoms and dominions and glory and immortal power."

Ellen and Alexander's eyes met at the prayer's conclusion, and they reveled in the Spirit of the moment, together with their growing family.

On the third day of the dedicatory services, Elder Hyde rose again. "We, the leaders of the Church, propose that this Temple of God be sold to provide funds for the poor to join the main body of the Saints in the West."

Ellen sucked in and covered her mouth, an instant knot tying in her stomach.

"All in favor, show forth a sign in the affirmative with the raising of the right hand," Elder Hyde concluded.

With tears of unbelief slipping from her eyes, Ellen raised her hand with the rest. The Lord had stayed the hands of their enemies until the temple served its purpose, and now their time was up.

31

A lexander returned from guarding the temple and told Ellen the latest news while she swept the day's crumbs into a pile.

Instead of being appeased by the dwindling number of Saints, the mobs were increasing in audacity, knowing that Nauvoo's defenses had crumbled. Farms and homes were being burned and the animals scattered, stolen, or killed. "Rumor is they have caught and lynched a few of the brethren."

Ellen rubbed at the skin around her eyes. "We cannot stay here."

Alexander shrugged. "You are not well enough to leave." He gazed out the small window. "There is more. While so many are moving away, others are still arriving penniless from the East and beyond, and, having exhausted their funds to get here, they must proceed with nothing."

"Is there anything we can do?"

Alexander shook his head. "All *you* can do is gain strength."

∾

Ellen put on a brave face for the children but found herself jumping at every sound. What if Alexander was killed? The Saints were more outnumbered every day.

If she had not grown so close to her confinement, they would have left Nauvoo by now, but it was not to be. On the hottest day of the year, with the town feeling ever the more deserted, Ellen gave birth to a healthy little girl with the help of only Margaret.

"Is it my turn to choose the name?" Ellen asked Alexander when he held the wrinkly, sweet-smelling newborn in his arms.

He nodded, then shook his head. "What a frightening world we brought this little one into."

"May God protect her." Ellen took the baby back. "How do you feel about calling her Leah?"

Alexander beamed at the infant and touched his nose to her soft, tiny one. "It is a good, Hebrew name."

She smirked. "I thought you would like that."

"If this is Leah, the next will have to be Rachel, for Rachel of the Bible follows Leah."

"Mercy," said Ellen. "Let us try to keep the ones we already have alive before we speak of having another."

He raised his shoulders and glowed with pride. "You still have plenty of child-bearing years ahead."

"Thankfully, they cannot come much faster than one per year."

He laughed.

Ellen was still in confinement when she heard three distinct fires of a cannon and shot up in bed. It sounded so close. Not as close as the barn, she would guess, but close.

"That is it," she said to no one but herself. "We must leave this place, confinement or not." She arose, strapped Baby Leah to her front, and went about doing chores.

When Alexander came home and saw her up, he chastised her. "What are you doing out of bed?"

"The mobs will burn us out if we do not go soon. They could be here at any moment, Alexander. I cannot lounge about as I would have in England. We must go."

He took her shaking hands. "What brought this on?"

She slowed her breath but could not halt her trembling. "I heard a cannon."

"Ja." He scowled. "The mob fired on Joseph's farm."

"But that is so close to here. Will they not let him rest in peace?" She stared at him with half-lidded eyes. "And what of Emma?"

"She and the children are alive, but they still refuse to leave town."

"She is a braver woman than I. How can she bear it? And without a husband."

He scratched the back of his head. "She has no desire to follow Brother Brigham. They are not on friendly terms anymore. According to her, the Church as good as robbed her."

"But it is too dangerous here. It is clear that the mob will not give up until we are all evacuated or dead. I cannot bear to stay another day. Will they not kill her and her family?"

He helped her to a seat and took the baby, shrugging. Leah started to fuss and rooted against his shoulder, so Ellen took her right back and fed her. She stared at the perfect, tiny forehead.

Ellen and the children settled in for the night as Alexander went out to stand guard against a growing force of eight hundred men. The total number of Saints left was not half so many.

Between worrying and breastfeeding, Ellen slept but little.

Alexander did not return when the sun arose, nor when it

set again. She could think of nothing else, sitting in her chair with Leah. Throughout the day, they heard shouts and reports of guns. "Joseph, come away from the window," Ellen said.

"But look, Mama. The mob is at our house!"

She bolted over, pushing him aside. Hundreds of men marched nearby, moving toward her home, toward her babies. She latched the door and blockaded it with chairs. "Come. Help me move the table," she said to Joseph.

They watched through the window as the men broke through their fence and stomped across her garden. Her heart pounded against her chest. What could she do to protect her little ones against so many men?

"I should be fighting," Joseph said.

Ellen frowned at him. "Thank the Lord you are not. I could not bear it. Besides, who would protect us here?"

He appeared at least partially appeased. "Are they coming here, Mama?"

The mob continued past the house. "No, Joseph. Look."

She fell into her rocking chair, but not long after, shots rang out once again, and she covered Baby Leah's ears against their terrorizing echoes.

After taking the children to bed, Ellen sat alone at the table, which Joseph had helped move back to its rightful place, with only an alert Pippy to keep her company.

Her knitting had long since been abandoned when a noise sounded at the door, and she jumped. "Alexander?" she called.

"Yes, Ellen. It is me," he said.

Ellen let him in and bolted the door before throwing her arms around him. "I am so thankful you are alive." The lantern light exacerbated the stress lines and deep shadows beneath his eyes. She directed him to where she had been sitting and stood behind him, rubbing his shoulders and neck, pressing deeply into the knots with her thumbs.

"I watched my friends bleed from bullet holes today."

She paused and looked at the ceiling, then resumed rubbing his neck. "We must leave."

"As soon as you are well enough, we will."

"I am well enough."

The following day, Ellen was grateful for Alexander's presence when a sharp knock sounded on the door. She opened it to find a large group of soldiers outside. They parted, and a massive man rode through the middle on horseback, sword drawn, right up to the doorway. Ellen watched, paralyzed.

Alexander came up beside her, and the leader yelled to him. "Were you in the fight yesterday?"

Alexander lifted his chin. "Yes, I was."

"Have you a gun?" the man yelled again.

"Yes, I have."

Ellen shook her head frantically, thinking he should have answered in the negative despite the truth. A memory of the day she first laid eyes on this handsome man of hers flashed before her as Alexander stood bravely, stubbornly in opposition to a crowd that could instantly take his life from her.

"Bring your gun to me. The general wants every gun that was in that fight."

"Find my gun if you want it," Alexander said in defiance, stepping out of the house.

Ellen covered her mouth, expecting to hear the cocking of a rifle or the swing of a sword.

The men were looking at one another, but Alexander appeared unafraid. "Take me to your general. I am quite willing to see him."

Ellen walked out, taking her place beside her husband and bending her head back to look up at the man on horseback.

"That will not be necessary," the soldier said. "Bring me your weapon."

"I will not."

Ellen took his hand.

The two men stared at one another, unspeaking and unmoving, until finally the soldiers turned to leave.

Ellen held her breath as she and Alexander went back inside and shut the door. "Do you think they will come back?"

He wrapped his hand around his beard and pulled. "We had better not wait to find out."

Less than a week later, fever and chills racked Ellen's body while she helped Alexander put the cover on the wagon, atop their provisions. Though ill, she dared not complain if it would delay them even an hour. The thought of Saints being beaten or thrown in the river and vacant homes being ransacked kept her moving. She would not allow any of those things to happen to her family.

Alexander handed Baby Leah to Ellen and lifted Bertha and Hyrum into the wagon, where they sat between legs of furniture and bags of foodstuffs. He spoke to the older children. "Take care of them." With his help, Ellen climbed onto the wagon seat, her arms shaking with the weight of the baby.

With a final glance at their log house surrounded by its trampled garden and broken fence, she turned to face the next chapter in their lives.

32

Dizziness rocked Ellen, and it took all her strength to stay upright. Before heading left on Parley Street, Alexander pulled the team to a halt. "Whoa."

They faced the abandoned House of the Lord, standing like a great, glowing monument on the hill, and she remembered her experiences within. "Do you think we shall ever see it again?"

"No, but we shall build another."

"And will we leave that one, as well?"

"I hope not, but the Lord's ways are not ours." He shook the reins. "Giddap."

ON THE BANKS of the Mississippi, Ellen collapsed upon the ground, weighing heavily against a rear wagon wheel, while Alexander determined how long it would take until their turn to ferry across. The remaining several hundred Saints had made a temporary camp along the river.

Ellen shifted her head from one side to the other with

effort, observing the forlorn refugees with threadbare blankets, standing ankle-deep in mud. The movement of her head made it pound, and she rested it atop Leah's in her arms, blinking her eyes to clear them. "Do you think she is cold?" Ellen asked Margaret.

"No, Mama. She is bundled well."

Chills trembled through Ellen's arms and legs, so Margaret took hold of the baby, and Ellen scooted under the wagon and slept in the mud.

Alexander broke into her fractured rest. "Ellen! Ellen! It is our turn to cross."

She peeked at his crouched frame beside the wheel, driving rain pouring down upon him and pooling in a recess of the ground, and crept out, allowing the rain to rinse the dirt away from her face and water-logged dress. The deluge continued as they crossed the wide river and did not stop when they stepped foot on Iowa soil.

Food was scarce when compared to the sheer number of refugees. Thankfully, they had been able to gather the required items, but many had been in the camp for months already, and their provisions were already wearing thin. An elderly woman near Ellen poured her heart out in supplication to God, weeping and begging His mercy between hacking coughs.

In the morning, Ellen stirred and squinted at the sky, the sea of blue was dotted with black in every direction. The dots grew larger and closer, forming into birds. She watched as quail descended from the sky as manna from Heaven. The birds seemed slothful and out of sorts, hobbling around within reach. Margaret stepped right up to one and grabbed it in her hands and carried it over to Alexander and Joseph, who also had their hands full of quail.

Ellen came to a stand, shaky at first, and helped Alexander pluck the quail feathers and cook them over a fire. The scent of roasting meat and cookfires permeated the camp. Alexander divided the cooked quail among the children while Ellen laid under the wagon, sweating, hoping her illness was pouring out with every drop.

A blessed woman with a tender heart cared for her and Leah until they were fit to travel again. After only progressing another mile and a half, they were taken in by another gracious family in Farmington, where they resided for a few weeks.

They settled in Bonaparte for the winter with yet another family. Ellen helped around the house as much as she could with seven children under eleven. Mr. and Mrs. Crockett became the grandparents her younger children had never known, and Alexander worked at dentistry as often as he could in the main room of the house to pay for their stay and save for their travels. The start to their long journey was moving along painfully slow, but Ellen was grateful to be in full recovery. Besides, what could be done with another winter approaching?

One afternoon, Alexander arranged his tools beside his cup of water at the other end of the table where Ellen was peeling potatoes. He was preparing to extract a dead tooth for a patient from the town. The man placed his pistol on the table next to the tools and took a seat.

The children were playing outside, excepting Leah, who was wrapped against her mother's chest.

Alexander cleaned and dried the inside of the man's mouth before stretching his back and taking a drink.

The man opened and closed his jaw, rubbing his cheek. "They say you come from Nauvoo. You ain't Mormon, are you?"

"I am," Alexander said with a single nod.

Ellen's fingers tightened around the potato she held.

"I don't want no Mormon putting his filthy hands in my mouth," he said.

Alexander waved toward the door. "You are welcome to leave if you no longer desire my services."

The man growled. "Maybe that's not enough. If Illinois is

too good for Mormons, so's Iowa. You ain't welcome here." He stood, towering over Alexander, who was still seated.

Ellen set the potato down but held tight to her paring knife and placed her free hand protectively on Leah's back.

"Sir," Alexander said, "Iowans do not have anything to worry about. We are only passing through."

The man scrunched his nose but nodded curtly. "Good. 'Cause you're all cotton-headed for listening to that lyin', cheatin', devil of an imposter, Joe Smith. There ain't no room for your kind of stupid here in my town."

Alexander rose, though he only came up to the man's crooked nose, chest heaving, and pointed at the door. "Leave this house. I will not stand in the presence of anyone who defames Joseph Smith's name," he said, his voice crescendoing with every word. "He was my leader and friend, and I will defend him to the grave."

"Shut up, or I'll send you to your grave now," said the man, wrapping his hand around his pistol.

Alexander placed his feet shoulder width apart and tipped his chin up to the man. "There has never been a man as good and devoted to God as Brother Joseph. He sacrificed himself for his love of God and friends."

"Alexander," Ellen said in exasperation. Did he not see the danger before him?

The man snorted and cocked his revolver with shaking hands. "I said, 'Shut up.' He didn't sacrifice himself. He was killed, and I am going to kill you." He lifted the gun with a shaking hand and aimed at Alexander's heart, right there in the kitchen, and pulled the trigger.

"No," Ellen screamed, dropping her knife and throwing herself toward her husband. Her eyes and hands ran over his body, searching for the wound.

Alexander took her by both shoulders and pressed her down to a chair behind him, inching away from her and Leah.

The man pulled the trigger again, and it clicked, but it lacked the reverberating sound of a shot. And again.

Alexander's pocket watch ticked impossibly slowly, but Ellen's leaden feet were slower as she lunged for the man who was trying to kill her husband.

Click. Click. Click. The man brought the pistol close to his face, inspecting it with a scowl. He groaned, stepping backward toward the door.

Alexander was still standing.

Ellen's head whipped back and forth between him and the shining pistol. The man opened the door, stepping just outside, and fired a round into the sky. The report reverberated through the walls of the house as thunder.

Ellen bolted the door, and, when Alexander peeked out the window, she shoved him away from it.

Mrs. Crockett blinked rapidly. "That man tried to shoot you in my kitchen." She plunked down in a chair and stared at Alexander. "In my kitchen! Why aren't you dead?"

His chest heaved, and he stared at his hands, rotating them back and forth. "Perhaps I have a guardian angel."

"Perhaps the man whose memory you defend so bravely defended you," said Ellen, leaning heavily into the table to stabilize herself.

Alexander fell to his knees and thanked his God.

WITH TEARS of gratitude and love, they bid farewell to the Crocketts at the end of June, having sold their horses and bought a yoke of steers for the wagon, they were ready to plow toward Winter Quarters, Nebraska, over two hundred miles and a month of travel away.

When skies were clear, they slept on the soft earth under the endless stars, the moon providing their only light. On stormy nights, they slept under the heavy covered wagon, shoulder to shoulder. Days were filled with endlessly flat prairies, with only rolling hills to change the horizon from time to time. Prairie grasses provided plenty of food for the cows. When Alexander was in a particularly good mood, he sang while he steadily prodded the team along.

When he started singing a song Ellen had not heard before, she looked up at him in the wagon seat while she walked beside the animals. "Is that a Jewish song?"

His eyes twinkled. "It is a Jewish song, but no other Jew but yours knows it."

She raised an eyebrow and waited for him to explain.

"It has been coming to me in bits and snatches."

"You wrote it?"

He chuckled. "Not strictly speaking as I have no paper, but I have sung it." He laughed again.

> *Come, thou glorious day of promise;*
> *Come and spread thy cheerful ray,*
> *When the scattered sheep of Israel*
> *Shall no longer go astray,*
> *When hosannas, when hosannas*
> *With united voice they'll cry.*
> *Lord, how long wilt thou be angry?*
> *Shall thy wrath forever burn?*
> *Rise, redeem thine ancient people;*
> *Their transgressions from them turn.*
> *King of Israel,*
> *King of Israel,*
> *Come and set thy people free.*

"I do not know how you do it." She grinned up at him. "It is beautiful."

"It lacks an ending, but the Lord will provide."

"I hope he provides a pleasant end to our journey, as well."

Alexander motioned to the open land around them, dotted with wagons. "He will. Hopefully in this life, but, if not, in the world to come."

Each step was a testament to her faith. Was God requiring this of them because it was what she needed to do to at last come to a pleasant end? Could she risk the hope of being with her Samuel once again?

THE BULLOCKS WELCOMED Ellen's family to their cabin in Winter Quarters, having been there for several months previous. Alexander and Ellen shared food and other necessities in exchange for lodging in their cramped log home. Having sustained themselves on cornbread from a time, the Bullocks were grateful for a little variety. Food would need to be tightly rationed, if they were all to survive the winter.

While he helped them settle, Brother Bullock said, "Brigham Young and a small group of pioneers left earlier in the year to scout out the trail, and the rest of us are awaiting word."

Ellen nibbled a piece of salt bacon on a chair in the warm summer sun, trying not to throw up due to her latest pregnancy, when the sounds of yelling and hooves pounding through the grass penetrated her ears. Alexander popped his head out of the house, and they exchanged glances before surveying the prairie.

Several men sprinted by after a handful of Native Americans on galloping horses. "Those belong to the Saints," Alexander hollered, running after the others and waving his cane.

Ellen knew the efforts of the Saints had been in vain when

she saw Alexander's expression. "We cannot spare supplies," he said, "especially not our animals."

Ellen pulled out a chair for him at the table and motioned for him to sit. Alexander pulled her onto his lap, and she looked guiltily at Sister Bullock, who swatted the air and smiled before going outside to allow them some privacy.

"Why some of the tribes want to trade with us while others want to steal from us or worse is beyond me."

Ellen leaned into him, cradling her belly. "Will they welcome us in the Great Salt Lake Valley?"

Alexander shrugged. "We can hope, but we have not been permanently welcome anywhere."

He set his arms atop hers, surrounding her stomach. "Are you eating enough for two?"

Ellen closed her eyes. "There is scarcely enough for me to eat for one. You know, I would give about anything to bite into a crisp apple right now."

The baby kicked at their arms, and Alexander shifted his hand to feel the motion. "The baby agrees. It must be excited at the thought of an apple, too."

GOOD NEWS ARRIVED when it was needed most. Brother Brigham returned to Winter Quarters, and Ellen and Alexander were invited to meet with him. When Brigham spotted them approaching, he broke away from a crowd and clasped hands with Alexander. "It is so good to see you. We have exciting things to share tonight. Hold onto your horses."

"I sold them." Alexander smiled broadly, and Brigham laughed.

"Hold onto your wife then," Brigham boomed, turning to Ellen. "How are your little ones?" His eyes flicked to her rounded middle for the briefest moment, and he failed to conceal a smile.

"Well enough, though to be honest, conditions are not ideal. You will find many with blackleg or worse as produce is scarce, and fevers are rampant throughout the settlement." She watched a bird pass by before meeting his eyes. "How are yours?"

"Very well," he beamed. "Very well. My family is ever-growing. We shall all settle in the Great Salt Lake Valley. The Lord has shown us the way to do so. With proper guidelines and preparations, we shall flourish there. You shall see."

33

Increasingly frigid temperatures contrasting with decreasing provisions created a dire situation by December when Ellen felt the familiar pangs of labor earlier than expected. She sent Alexander away with the children, save Margaret, and called for Sister Mary Ann Young to assist her. Mary Ann brought along her daughter by the same name to help.

Upon their arrival, Ellen said, "Thank you for coming. I know you have been scurrying about caring for the ill. You must be exhausted at every conceivable moment."

"It is only the ones who do not survive that leave me truly exhausted, body and soul, so let us be sure there is none of that today."

The labor was more difficult than the last. Ellen endured hours of fierce pain, and, though she pushed with all her strength, gripping the edges of the bed and biting on a rag, the baby did not crown. Her contractions were close, one after the next, coming over and over again, until she was too drained to be of any use.

Mary Ann sent her daughter and Margaret out for more

water and clean rags, then, placing her hand on Ellen's arm, she said, "I know you are exhausted, but you cannot give up until this baby is out."

Ellen swallowed and squirmed against the pain. "Something is wrong."

Mary Ann pursed her lips. "That may be, but that does not make a difference right now. We have to get that baby out. Shall I lay my hands on your head and pronounce a blessing by the gift of the Spirit?"

"Please."

Mary Ann placed her palms on Ellen's matted hair. "Ellen Neibaur, I bless you in the name of Jesus Christ to be well and to deliver this child."

Margaret returned with a drink and a crust of bread, but pain engulfed Ellen, and she could not swallow more than a few spoonfuls of water. She pushed four more times before Mary Ann said, "I see the top of the head," and breathed a deep sigh of relief. "Now we are getting somewhere."

Ellen kept pushing, bearing down in a squatting position, but the baby still would not come. "It is no use. I cannot do it."

"You must."

At length, the head came down far enough that Mary Ann coaxed it out, pulling while Ellen pushed.

Ellen crashed back against the bed in a moment of respite.

"The cord is around its neck," said Mary Ann, yanking on it.

Ellen stretched her arms helplessly toward her tiny, purple infant while Mary Ann took a knife and sawed through the cord. Blood spurted out, and Ellen held her breath. When the final slice cut through, Mary Ann unwrapped the baby's neck and threw the cord aside. "It is a girl," she said, sadness lacing her words as she wiped the baby and handed the little bundle to Ellen.

The baby's pallor was like a gray-purple sky, with big, midnight blue eyes. Ellen held her close and whimpered.

Mary Ann blinked quickly. "I will fetch Brother Neibaur."

Ellen stared at the baby without responding. She kissed her head and her gray fingers and toes. She put the baby's soft cheek against her own and listened to her labored breathing. She closed her eyes. "Stay with me," she whispered. She tried to breastfeed, prying the baby's small mouth open and stuffing her nipple into it, but the baby failed to suck. Ellen tried again and again, and tears began to flow. She expressed a little milk onto her fingertip and rubbed it on the baby's tongue.

Alexander stood in the doorway, observing silently before joining them on the bed. He stared at the little girl.

"Rachel," Ellen whispered, gulping back the fear.

His trembling hand cupped the baby's face. "A good, Hebrew name," he said, leaning his head against Ellen's. "Were you feeding her?"

Ellen did not pull her gaze from the baby's face when she shook her head. "She is not strong enough to eat."

"Maybe she will improve. What can I do?"

Baby Rachel's hollow, bare chest moved in and out quickly in time with her rapidly blinking eyelids.

Her breathing stopped, and Ellen held her own until the baby's shallow breaths resumed. "Give her a Priesthood blessing, Alexander." Her voice cracked. "Please."

He nodded. "Do I have time to get oil?"

"I do not know."

He kissed Rachel's tummy. "I will be right back."

Ellen tried again to feed Rachel, inserting her nipple into her mouth as far in as she could and holding it there, but Rachel's mouth did not close around it. "Oh Lord," Ellen prayed. "Do not take this child from me. If I have demonstrated sufficient faith, grant her the breath of life. Give her strength of body and appetite. Lord, please, please, please, let her live."

Tears poured down her cheeks, and she left them there as a testament to her pain.

Alexander returned, holding a container of olive oil. "Where shall I anoint her?"

"I think the problem is in her chest."

He poured the smallest drop of consecrated oil onto her ribcage and rubbed it tenderly with his index finger before cupping the top of her head in his hands. "Rachel Neibaur," he said, swallowing hard.

Rachel's rasping quieted, as if she too were holding her breath to see what the Lord had in store for her.

Alexander blinked and began again. "Rachel Neibaur."

Ellen tore her eyes from Rachel and studied the face of the man she loved. His brows were wrinkled in pain. He blinked, his eyes locking on Ellen's, pleading for forgiveness before he closed his eyes again. "We send you, little one, with all the love in our hearts, back to the loving arms of the God of Jacob, and to His Son, Jesus Christ." He balled one hand into a fist and pressed it against his lips. Tears squeezed from his closed eyes and trickled into his beard.

Ellen cradled Rachel firmly against her chest with both hands, fingering the peach fuzz at the nape of her neck. She shut her eyes against the pain, against reality, against a God who could steal a baby from her praying parents.

Again.

But God had not forgotten her in her sorrow. She envisioned her Savior standing in the air an arm's length away, Samuel standing on his right, half hidden behind the Lord's robe, peeking out at her. Jesus Christ, glorious and loving, had one hand on the boy's head and was reaching toward her with the other, palm up, as if to say, "I will care for her." His blue eyes were filled with love that enveloped her soul.

She opened her eyes and saw Alexander watching her, light shining from his dark eyes, as if he had seen something similar.

Baby Rachel gulped, and Ellen, placing one hand behind her head and the other under her bottom, held her out in front of them, and they watched her take one final breath.

ALEXANDER PLACED his hands on Ellen's shoulders. "You should not be up and about yet. Lie down."

She shook her head determinedly back and forth.

"Your body needs time to recover," he insisted.

"If I had a reason to sit, I would, but I must keep my empty arms busy. In truth, I do not want to move about the house. I want to move west and never return. I cannot bear to live in this cemetery of death and disease any longer." She angled herself away from him.

"I will do everything I can to make sure we leave with Brigham Young in his next company. We have all the necessary provisions. All we lack is a functioning wagon and the teams of oxen, as ours are being used by others."

She laughed with disdain. "Those are pretty important."

Why had it been so difficult to tear herself away from her son's grave in Preston? Staying in Winter Quarters near Rachel's grave was like trying to keep a whipped horse from bolting. Perhaps it was because this was never intended to be a permanent abode, and Preston was never meant to be a temporary one.

Ellen said a silent prayer that Patience remembered her promises.

Every morning was more frigid, and there were increasing reports of sickness and death, but Ellen's heart was numb. Whenever she heard about another death, she simply nodded, unfeeling and unsympathetic.

Everyone lost loved ones. God did not spare His people from heartache. He never had. Alexander's forefathers could attest to that. Knowing the widespread nature of tribulation only added to the guilt that rolled through her mind like a wagon wheel. How many women, like Emma Smith, had lost even more children than Ellen? They moved on and kept living, smiling, laughing. How? Why was she the only one who could not accept what was?

Sometimes, if she was honest, she felt the peace only God could provide, but most of the time, she dug into the pain and mourned without comfort. At times she felt carried, but at others, she was swallowed in the sludge, barely able to keep her head from disappearing under.

Spring could not come soon enough.

ALEXANDER WENT to discuss the matter of leaving with Brigham the next day and reported that, while Brigham first said to keep working until he was properly outfitted for the journey, Alexander had quickly convinced him to see the matter his way. Alexander told Ellen about the conversation. "'Brother Brigham,' I said, 'I never turn back after I have put my hand to the plow. Besides, if I do not get my wife out of this place, I believe I will be burying her beside our baby before long.'

"'God be with you,' Brigham said. 'I wish I could see every Latter-day Saint show the same determined spirit.'"

Alexander blushed at the telling.

Brigham had advised him to go to the widow, Sister Lydia Knight, and ask if they could use her wagons and teams and send them back with the payment of an extra cow once they reached the Salt Lake Valley.

Ellen scrunched her brows together. "Maybe we should wait until we find teams of our own. Sister Knight is a crotchety woman. I fear she will not like the idea."

"I will ask her." Alexander placed a hand on her hollow

cheek and rubbed it tenderly with his thumb, then he coaxed her head up. She kept her eyes averted before meeting his. "I will take you from this place," he said earnestly.

She swallowed the ball in her throat and returned her gaze to the floor.

Alexander left, and she was alone with her torturous thoughts. She curled up on the bed, holding her knees, and sobbed, clutching her blankets and burying her face in them. When her eyes ran out of tears, she rolled onto her back, placing her hands on the loose, empty skin of her stomach, and stared at the ceiling.

She stared and stared and stared. Hours and days went by before finally, something inside began to shift.

Opening her heart to light, it gradually filled her soul like a new day as the sun peeks over the horizon. Tears dried on her cheeks, and, though her face felt stiff, she tested out a small smile. Her babies were in the care of the Lord.

Spring would come again, but she knew from experience that the pain and memories would stay locked in her heart forever.

34

By the end of May, with a bright sun overhead, Alexander and Ellen, along with their seven living children, readied themselves to make the last and longest stretch of the journey with the teams they had on loan from Sister Knight.

The wagon box was a cheery red, and Joseph and Ellen still had speckles on their hands from painting it. Alexander had applied wax over the red paint, in addition to the arched bow and canvas over the box, to provide some protection from rain and river water, making it smooth to the touch. Ellen ran her hand along it whenever she checked on Bertha and Hyrum tucked between trunks, the butter churn, and sacks of grain. Alexander, Isaac, and Alice were riding up front with Alexander. Carrying Leah, who, at almost two years old, was no lightweight, Ellen walked alongside the wagon with Joseph and Margaret and directed the lead cows. Pippy also trotted along beside them, dashing ahead and running back. How was it that he had so much energy?

"How long have we been in this wagon, Abba?" asked Alice.

Alexander pulled out his pocket watch. "One hour."

"And how many hours until we get to Salt Lake?" asked Isaac.

Alexander raised his eyebrows at Ellen, and they laughed. "I have no idea, Son. Calculate four months' worth of hours, take away sleeping time, and you might be close."

"How long is four months?" called Bertha.

"Sixteen weeks," Joseph answered proudly, and Ellen smiled at him.

Hyrum popped his face out of the opening in the canvas next to where Alexander sat. "Will we be there by dinnertime? I'm hungry."

Alexander faced Ellen. "This reminds me of the *Sheffield*. I think we have a mutiny on our hands, dear." He rubbed Hyrum's bushy hair. "We will have many dinners from the wagon before we arrive at the valley."

A tall hill rose in front of them, and Alexander kept the oxen lumbering forward.

Ellen's breathing deepened as they neared the top, and she shifted Leah's weight to her other hip.

A thunderous crack came from the wagon, which began to roll backwards, detaching from the yoke of oxen next to her.

Isaac slid from the bench and somersaulted down the hill. Alexander leaped from his falling seat and ran after the runaway wagon box.

Ellen squealed, and, handing Leah to Joseph, sprinted after Alexander as the wagon crashed backwards and rolled to its side. "Is anyone hurt?" she screamed, the image of the wagon morphing into a coffin in her mind.

Alexander reached them first and gathered up Alice and Bertha in his arms, and, after feeling their limbs and heads, passed them to Ellen.

"Hyrum," he called.

No response.

Ellen held her breath, straining to hear something.

"Hyrum," he said again, hefting a trunk out of his way. "Where are you? Answer me. I need you to answer!" Ellen heard the edge in his voice.

Wind whistled through the wagon, winding its way through their upturned provisions.

Ellen moved to the back end of the wagon and worked her way through the wreckage while Alexander came toward her from the front end. They discovered little Hyrum at the same time, curled into a ball, holding onto a sack of sugar for dear life. His eyes were wide, and when he caught sight of her, his bottom lip quivered.

He was alive. She reached for him, curling her trembling lips over her teeth to keep from bursting.

Alexander held up his hand. "Wait. Do not move him yet." He inspected Hyrum's arms and legs, his back and front, and his head before pulling him into a careful embrace while Ellen stroked his hair.

"What happened?" Ellen said, her voice quavering.

"I think the falling tongue broke."

"The falling tongue?"

"Ja. The wooden piece that connects the wagon to the yoke."

Joseph peeked his head inside. "Did you find Hyrum?"

"Yes," said Ellen. "He will be covered in bruises, but he is fine."

They climbed out and observed the wagon and teams. The oxen were nibbling grass, but the wagon box was cracked, and one of the rear wheels broken.

Alexander leaned his head into his hand. "We will have to go back to Winter Quarters."

"Do we not need to meet up with Brigham Young's company?" Joseph asked.

"Ja. We do, but we cannot go another mile without a new wheel. Thankfully, we did not make it far."

Ellen laughed without humor. "Thankfully? That is an interesting thing to be thankful for. I would have preferred arriving in the valley before breaking down, or better yet, I would prefer to be in my father's parlor, blissfully unaware of the plight of the American Mormons."

Alexander met her eyes. "Truly, Ellen?"

"How could I wish otherwise?" she said, stubbornly, drained from difficult times with no end in sight. "Would you rather be here on this godforsaken journey, heading back to a place full of disease and death?"

He tilted his head to one side, eyeing her. "I would rather be in Zion, and we shall be there soon."

She shook her head. "Soon? How many more children are we to lose in the process? How much more is the Lord going to require before we have given enough?"

Leah fussed in Joseph's arms, and Ellen picked her up, still waiting for an answer from Alexander, but he had none to give.

"Must I walk?" Hyrum interrupted.

"Yes," Ellen snapped. "The wagon is broken."

His tears joined Leah's, and Ellen, feeling a prick of guilt, pulled him into a hug. "Are you well enough to walk?" she asked him.

He nodded bravely, but Joseph said, "He can ride on my shoulders," and Hyrum cheered.

Alexander detached the broken wheel while Ellen checked through everything before they turned around, leading the teams of animals away from the wagon back in the direction of Winter Quarters, Alexander carrying the large wheel.

In one week's time, they were ready to try again and headed out to meet with Brigham Young's company. After five miles, they were all caked in a thick layer of dirt. When they stopped to camp for the night on the open prairie, Ellen washed down the animals and fed and watered them while Alexander and the boys built a fire to cook dinner. The children looked like little natives dancing beside the flames with their red-brown faces.

Rising at five o'clock the next morning, Ellen turned the cattle out to feed before a long day. Finally, it felt like they were really on their way. She wondered what the Salt Lake Valley would be like. She had never seen a desert. Would they be able to grow crops and survive there? And what about the Indians that had already claimed the land for their own? She shook the worries from her head.

Pounding rain and clapping thunder was an unwelcome guest on the second night. They crowded inside and under the wagon, but, sometime in the blackness, Alexander, Joseph, and Isaac loosened the canvas on the end of the wagon and clambered inside, groping their way through bodies and provisions in almost perfect darkness. Joseph accidentally stepped on Margaret's foot, who had been dead asleep. She squealed and moaned, and Ellen turned onto her side to make a space for Alexander to squish beside her. As he nestled in, moisture seeped through her nightclothes from his.

"Alexander," she cried. "Your clothes are soaked."

He chuckled. "Our bed of grass became a veritable creek."

She attempted to squirm away from him, but not a millimeter of space remained on any side. "Come here, boys," she said with a noisy yawn. "You must not sleep in wet clothes. You will catch a cold. Or worse." She cringed at the thought.

Thunder crashed, and Ellen could not be sure anyone had heard her, but she did not repeat herself, bone-tired as she was after two long days of travel.

Isaac clambered over Alexander, and she swiftly undressed him and wrapped him in her own blanket. "You, too," she said to Joseph.

"Mama," he said, in an exaggerated tone from somewhere near the bags of dried beans, "I am perfectly capable of undressing myself."

Ellen smiled into the darkness. "Very well, but be sure to do it." She rested her head on Alexander's bare shoulder, and he snickered, which tickled her ear. Rustling came from Joseph's corner as he stripped off his wet clothes.

"Do you feel the extra blankets over there?" Ellen asked.

"It is not cold, Mama."

"It is plenty cold if you are wet. Shall I find them?"

"Good luck getting over here."

Despite the crowded quarters, exhaustion won, and Ellen slept sitting up against Alexander until sunlight illuminated the canvas over their heads. The morning smelled of wet grass and mildew. Her hips hurt from sitting cross-legged through the night, and she clambered out into the early light of day. Facing the rising sun, she stretched her arms, shoulders, and back. She was stretching her hips when she caught sight of Alexander watching her, waggling his eyebrows.

"Do not stop on my account," he said, climbing from the wagon with an enthusiastic smile.

He wrapped his arms around her waist like a corset, pulling her in and kissing her squarely on the mouth. She flushed and glanced around for spying eyes from any of the hundreds of neighboring wagons or from their own. The only eyes she saw gazing back belonged to an ox, so she giggled and kissed him back heartily.

"Whoo-eee," said Eleazar Miller, as she pulled away from his grasp. "Looks like a good morning to you, Brother Neibaur."

Ellen's cheeks grew hot, but Alexander squeezed her hand. "There is not a place in this world I would rather be," he said, tipping his hat. "Good morning, Brother Miller."

The smell of wet grass hung in the crisp air, and the first order of business was to hang out all the dampened clothes and blankets. Ellen milked the cows and turned them out to graze, dressed the younger children and fed them, replaited her hair, then the girls' hair, and finally sat by Alexander to have a bite while the children found some friends and played Drop the Handkerchief.

When it was his turn, Hyrum grabbed the dropped hand-kerchief, left the circle of children, and dashed away in the wrong direction.

Ellen giggled and said to Alexander, "The little ones never understand that they are to run once around the circle and sit in the spot their chaser vacated. Either they do not understand, or they love the chasing part too much."

"Probably both," he said, watching her. "I am pleased to see you smiling."

She met his gaze and lifted her shoulders. "What is there for us but to keep moving forward?"

Days plodded along with the oxen, and her children grew browner by the hour. She was grateful they had their father's tanning skin, for while she would rather have them be fair, brown was better than sunburnt. Their skin grew tougher, and their feet became accustomed to walking mile after mile even as their clothing and bodies thinned.

By night, though they were tired, their favorite travel days culminated in a lively prairie dance, while the worst ones ended with mothers and fathers burying their children. On one such trying day, Alexander was obliged to help dig a grave and bury the body of eight year old Maria Kay. He returned with swollen, bloodshot eyes and stretched his arms out for Leah to toddle into, filling his empty lap. Before bed, Ellen noticed he intentionally spent a moment with each member of the family, one on one, and during family prayer, he thanked God aloud that they were together on this journey, begging the Lord to let it remain so. Ellen squeezed Alexander's hand in solidarity.

Sundays were Ellen's favorite days. While chores still had to be done—after all, animals and children still had bellies to fill —travel ceased on the Sabbath, and they listened to the preachings of Brigham and others, such as Brother Kimball.

Time blended in a blur of walking, milking, cleaning cows and children, and attending to bug bites. May turned into June, and June transformed into hot, dry, sunny days where the dust filled their mouths and clumped in their throats, at times making it difficult to speak or breathe.

Ellen's shoes were more holes than substance, and when she tired of holding them on with her toes, she bent down, yanked them from her sore feet, and tossed them aside into the deep prairie grasses like an apple core.

In the morning, she tore long strips of fabric from worn sheets and wrapped them around her blistered feet.

When she sat to her scant supper at the end of another tiring day, she lifted her skirt. The dirty fabric on her feet was streaked with blood, and she grimaced.

"What is it?" Alexander asked with concern.

"I had a morbid thought you would rather not hear."

He scooted closer and waited for her to go on.

"The bloody rags on my feet reminded me of my favorite scarlet slippers in England." She lifted her feet and wiggled her toes. "Papa had them made special in London, and I wore them the day you proposed marriage, and we..." She swallowed.

Alexander knelt before her and gently unwrapped her feet, working gently at the bits that had adhered to her feet. "The day you pushed me in the River Darwen?" he asked.

"I ended up as wet as you."

He fetched a bucket of water and scooped some out with a tin cup, pouring it over her feet and rubbing them gently until they were clean. "If you ended up as wet as me, it is only because you jumped in. I was too much of a gentleman to push you."

She smiled into the distance. "That was a world away and a lifetime ago."

Running the remainder of the water from the cup over the fabric scraps, he scrubbed them together and set them on the grass to dry. He lifted one of Ellen's feet to his lips, and then the other, and his beard tickled her toes.

Her eyes flicked to Joseph and back to Alexander. "The guilt from that day is gone at last. To think it has taken so long. I do not know what we do without Joseph."

"I am glad." He looked up at her. "But if you are pining for another water fight, I would be happy to oblige." He held up the tin cup, and they laughed.

Later that night, the dog would not stop barking. "Hush, Pippy," called Ellen. She could see his dark outline standing nearby, facing some unseen threat. Pippy groaned, then obediently quieted, but other dogs of the camp took up the howling where he left off, and soon he was rejoining in their refrains.

"Could it be wolves, Abba?" came Margaret's shaking voice through the darkness.

"No. I think if there were wolves we would hear them howling with the dogs."

Alexander arose, grabbing his gun, and patrolled. He walked up to another man's dark figure and started talking. Ellen strained to listen and heard Jacob Peart's voice in quiet conversation with Alexander. His dog was barking as well. After a few minutes, the two men walked in opposite directions, scanning the prairie. A quarter of an hour later, he returned to his makeshift bed.

"What is it?" asked Joseph.

"Nothing," he answered, but the dogs did not stop.

Sleep was closing in on her again when she and Alexander bolted upright at the report of a pistol, their shoulders bumping into each other. Leah started to fuss, so Ellen reached for her as Alexander leaped out of bed to investigate, the shot was still ringing in her ears.

"Indians," whimpered Margaret, and she was joined by other scared mumbles coming from the starlit darkness.

Brother Peart's voice came again, and Ellen tried to make

out his form as she rocked Leah and rubbed her back. She stepped over the children with care, and Pippy came to her side with a growl.

"What is it, Pippy?"

He growled again.

"Where is Abba?"

He yipped and led the way. She wondered what dangers lie ahead and if it would not be more prudent to leave Leah with the others.

Joseph called to her. "May I come?"

"No. Protect the others."

Alexander's form, along with another, soon came into view beside a mound. Pippy ran ahead to them and took his place beside his master. Alexander and Brother Morley became clearer as she approached.

She paused. The mound consisted of Brother Peart draped over his bleeding dog, their moans mixing into one mournful sound.

"What attacked it?" Ellen whispered to Alexander.

"A man," he said through clenched teeth.

Her heart pounded against her bodice.

"Seems to have been a man from the camp, upset about all the barking."

Ellen rubbed at the front of her neck. "Is there anything we can do?"

"No. It was a fatal wound. Take Leah back. You will not want to be here for what happens next."

She nodded in the still night.

As she climbed into bed, a second shot rang out, but this time it did not surprise her. This shot was made, not out of anger, but out of mercy.

35

"Are the wagons stopping ahead?" Joseph asked, pointing to a clump of trees.

Alexander twisted his beard. "Must be the Platte River."

When they arrived, they discovered that Brigham had ordered a ferry to be built from cottonwood during his vanguard trip. A few men had stayed to man the ferry, charging $3 cash or $1.50 worth of provisions to all nonmembers. Though the crossing was still dangerous because the river was over 100 yards wide, all were able to safely cross.

They made camp on the other side. Wolves howled through the night from every direction, so they kept Pippy close and urged him to keep quiet.

"Have you seen my pocket watch?" Alexander asked Ellen.

She told him she had not, but she helped him look for it in the morning. They were rummaging through their things when Porter Rockwell arrived from Salt Lake and advised the company to recross the river, though it was the Sabbath, as miles of heavy sand on this side would be too hard on the cattle.

Alexander offered his arm to Ellen, breathing heavily. "I suppose my pocket watch found its final resting place in this sand somewhere."

"I am so sorry, Alexander. I know how you have loved it."

Ferrying all the company, wagons, and animals back across the Platte took the majority of the day as misfortunes plagued their efforts. Captain Goddard's oxen yoke cracked, Jacob Peart broke a wagon bow and a drag rope, and while making way through a ravine, the Neibaurs' log chain broke. As if that was not enough, Jacob Peart sliced his finger while the men were preparing buffalo meat for the company to eat. As they distributed the meat, a child fell out of a moving wagon, which promptly rolled over his leg. Thankfully, the leg did not break.

At day's end, when Brigham gathered the Saints, Brother Bullock said, "So much for traveling on the Sabbath!" and Ellen nodded heartily.

ON ONE OF the hottest days of the year, a few families continued their trek to the Salt Lake Valley while the Neibaurs and most of the company bivouacked, sending wagons and cattle they had borrowed back to Winter Quarters and waiting for horses, wagons, and oxen to be sent from the valley.

Meanwhile, Sarah Ann Kimball was confined of a baby boy, and Ellen went to visit her. Though she tried to be happy for Sister Kimball, the pink infant pricked at her heart, reminding her too much of her own losses. She could not bear to spend long in their presence, and she took a serpentine route back to her family, giving herself time to be alone and feel the pain without an audience.

Plopping onto a large rock, she rubbed at her dirty face, both relishing and detesting the loneliness. She allowed herself to cry out, sobbing for herself and for all she had given up, both intentionally and without choice. Had she earned her place in Heaven? She had worked to that end ever since that condemning day at the River Darwen with Alexander, even leaving the comforts of England and her dear father, siblings, and friends.

And what of Alexander? He committed some of the same crimes, yet she could not believe he would be damned for all eternity. He was too good. Had he earned his reward?

Why was she convinced she could never be good enough?

EVERY MUSCLE ACHED from walking and carrying Leah. Hyrum complained constantly of hunger while the older children ceased to say much of anything.

Would it be so bad to crash on the side of the road, close her eyes against the world forever, and never open them again? Life was so endlessly exhausting.

Would the Savior spread His arms to her as he had done for her little ones? Everyone made mistakes.

Her legs shuddered beneath her, and she nearly collapsed, heart and head pounding, but she did not stop stepping. Though she could never earn her own salvation, she would keep trekking forward.

Thoughts beat in rhythm with every step of her sore, bleeding feet. Left. She would never be enough. Right. She was less than dirt. Left. She was nothing without Jesus. Right. But with Him?

Overwhelming peace spread from her center, tingling to her fingers and toes. Left. She was worthy of joy. Right. She was worthy of love. Salvation could not be earned. It was a gift the Savior had been holding out for her all along.

And she would embrace her babies again.

IT TOOK the company two weeks more to travel to Fort Bridger. Setting up camp after another full day of walking seemed impossible work. She wished she could crash to the ground, but she washed the animals while Joseph built a fire. The night was cold, and her toes were colder. The tips of the grasses were stiff with prickling frost beneath her, and dust sprinkled the mountain tops with snow.

As the first stars appeared, Ellen pointed at some peculiar tents on a ledge nearby. "Who lives there?"

Alexander shook his head.

"Do not try to protect me now. What is it?"

He pursed his lips. "Snake Indians. Their tents are called wigwams."

"Frightening name. I hope they do not come after our food-stuffs. We have none to spare."

"Do not you worry, dear. I shall sit up and protect the camp."

"All night?" She frowned despite her gratitude. "Are you sure?"

"Quite sure."

Before the sky was fully lit the next morning, a group of the Snake Indians marched toward the Saints. Ellen and Alexander braced themselves between the children and the Native Americans.

Ellen squinted and saw they were carrying trading goods and not weapons and relaxed in relief. If only her family had something to trade for boots.

EACH NIGHT, with shaking hands, Ellen carefully detached the bloodied rags from her feet and rubbed until her toes had color again. Every blanket and bit of tattered clothing was used to keep her family from freezing solid as they curled together like a litter of kittens in a basket. Sleep came quickly, due to exhaustion, but never lasted long enough.

Mountain fever infiltrated the camp, and Ellen did what she could to nurse the ill back to health, praying they would not lose anyone else before they reached the valley.

When help arrived, they packed their belongings into a wagon and pressed forward. Rough mountainous terrain and thin elevated air left them gasping for breath as they climbed up the trail.

Though the leaders told them they were getting close to their destination, it felt to Ellen like they had walked an eternity, and the rest would continue equally as long.

At the end of September, the exhausted, travel-weary company made their way up Big Mountain Pass, a cool breeze pressing against them.

Carrying Leah on her hip, Ellen's legs and feet burned with every step upward. Hyrum rode in the wagon next to Alexander, who took care not to let him fall out. Bertha walked, albeit slowly. Every bit of their energy and faculties was needed to keep their feet plodding forward.

Ellen dropped behind the wagon with her five older children.

Alexander reached the top first and called back to them with arms waving, "I see it, Ellen! I see the valley." He threw his hands to the heavens. "Praise God! We have made it!"

His excitement traveled toward them on the wind, renewing their energy, and they all pressed to the top, where they stepped off the path, out of the way of following wagons, and stopped to admire the view, brimming with trees of red, gold, and plum-purple, surrounded by majestic snow-capped mountains.

"Praise the Lord," Ellen said. "Another week, and we would have run out of food."

Alexander lifted Hyrum onto his shoulders, and Joseph put Bertha on his.

"We are high," said Bertha.

"On top of the world," said Alexander with an exultant laugh. He slipped an arm behind Ellen's waist and squeezed her toward him. "Welcome home, my dear," he said, kissing her on the cheek.

Ellen filled her lungs with a deep breath of crisp mountain air, and with it, a confirmation that this was the right place for them.

DESCENDING the pass into the valley proved to be even more challenging than the ascent. Rain drizzled on the company, making the path slippery. Noting broken wagons on every side, Ellen realized they were not the first company to struggle here.

But with the valley in view, their spirits remained high, and slowly, slowly, the company plodded its way down and across the valley floor to the fort that would be their temporary shelter. It consisted of hundreds of buildings, as well as sawmills and grist mills.

A few days after their arrival, Alexander procured a tent and signed for a piece of land. "Brother Brigham spent a great deal of effort planning out the city with wide, straight streets," he told Ellen. "A new temple will stand at the center. We shall build a homestead two blocks south and two blocks east of the temple lot."

"Sounds wonderful," she said, wrapping her feet in clean rags. "Do you think we shall be happy here?"

"I do." He embraced her. "I believe we are here to stay."

Preston had been a different life altogether, full of niceties. She thought back to her early days with Alexander, to the passion that had gone too far and changed their lives forever. Would she have left England if she could have foreseen the trials that awaited them in America? She doubted she would have had the courage, but now that she was here, it all felt worth the effort somehow.

ON DRY, sunny days, Alexander, Ellen, and Joseph spent their time making adobes for their house by mixing clay, sand, straw, and a bit of water. The resulting mud was poured into wooden forms about ten inches by fourteen inches and left to dry. A five-gallon bucket of sand produced about three bricks, so making enough for a home was a painstaking job.

Ellen was helping Alexander pour mud when a couple sisters strolled up. "Good day. Word has reached us that you, Brother Neibaur, are a dentist. Will you be practicing here in the valley?"

"Ja," he said, swinging his muddy hands with excitement. "May I be of service?"

They nodded. "We are hoping to have our teeth cleaned."

He held his palms out to them. "My hands are not as smooth as they once were, but let me clean myself up."

The Grands sisters were pleased with Alexander's work and news spread that the first dentist in the area was open for services. A week later, after several more appointments, Alexander came home whistling.

The money he made went toward materials for the house and keeping the family alive. They were all pretty desperate for shoes, Ellen worst of all, but she was prepared to be the last to obtain some.

During the first week of October, a General Conference was held. It was a time of great celebration. The population of members of the Church in the valley had blossomed to over 3,500. Ellen was overwhelmed by the beauty of seeing thousands of Saints gathered on a stunningly colorful and warm autumn day.

When it was proposed that Brigham Young be sustained President of the Church, Ellen's heart swelled within her breast, and she knew it was right. A powerful witness filled her soul as she raised her right arm to the square in confirmation of her willingness to follow him.

She smiled to herself, remembering her horror when he had taken multiple wives. Now that she had seen their family in action, it seemed to work, though she was grateful not to be living in such a situation herself.

As the meetings concluded, the clouds opened up their stores and began to pour on the Saints.

"Brothers and Sisters," called Heber through the rain, "we will put off the rest of our planned festivities of feasting, dancing, and singing until tomorrow." He ran over to his family as the rain increased its fury.

Alexander lifted his shoulders. "Well, Lord, we do need rain." He grabbed a couple of the closest children and made his escape.

They tramped through the mud to their bit of land, and Ellen helped the children remove their muddy clothes before entering the tent.

"I'm hungry," Isaac said.

Supplies were dwindling, and they would have to ration their foodstuffs to keep everyone alive through their first winter. "We will eat in a bit," Ellen said. "Shall we play a game?"

Isaac nodded.

"Will you be the leader and help the others choose what to play?"

He sat up straighter.

Alexander was last to stumble in. She waited until he situated himself before scooting toward him. "I have been thinking about something."

"Time for another baby?" he asked with a twinkle in his eyes.

She grinned at his mischievous expression. "That will likely not be long knowing us, but this is another matter." She had his full attention. "I know we are busy preparing food for winter and making adobes for a house." She shook her head. What was she thinking? "Nevermind, some other time."

"Ellen," he said, grasping her hand. "What is it?"

She swallowed. "I want to learn to read and write."

Alexander's face split into a smile. "I have wanted to teach you for so long. Shall we start now?" he asked.

She laughed. "What else are we to do, trapped in here against the rain?"

"Well, I can think of a few things..."

"Shhh. The children," she said, playfully covering his mouth.

He tickled her waist in defense, and she chuckled and squirmed away.

Then, right there in a leaky tent full of children, Ellen had her first reading lesson.

36

Winter whipped in, strong and fierce, and the valley, being a desert, provided little in the way of food for its booming population. It had taken most of what they had to get there. On a chill and stormy night, the family was settling into their tent a bit earlier than usual. Their provisions long gone, they had resorted to eating wild plants from the frozen ground around their camp, but even those were increasingly scarce.

With nothing to fill their bellies and thick, gray clouds hiding the sun before sunset, they climbed into their blankets in hopes of receiving the necessary warmth their thin, frail bodies could not provide.

A moaning sound came from one of the children, and Ellen's ears perked up at the sound as she tried to decipher from whence it came. The moan came again, and she wrinkled her nose, realizing it was one of their empty stomachs. Her own stomach groaned in hunger as she rolled into Alexander. "How are we going to feed them?" she whispered. She felt rather than saw him shake his head.

"I do not know how you and Joseph are still able to make

adobes on so little." She shut her eyes and interlocked her
fingers, hoping the Lord would forgive her for praying without
rising to her knees. Her energy was spent. She licked her
chapped lips and prayed silently as gusts of wind attacked the
tent, and Pippy, curled up next to them, howled at it. "Lord,
Thou art kind and good. I know Thou dost mourn with those
that mourn and comfort those that stand in need of comfort. I
have felt the enabling power of Thy love and know Thou art
aware of our suffering. Wilt Thou lessen our burdens? Grant
that we may find food to last us the rest of the winter. Please,
Lord. Provide for us in our want. Nevertheless, if it is not Thy
will to nourish our bodies and provide meat, bless us with the
strength to carry on."

The words to "Come, Come, Ye Saints" drifted into her
mind with the frigid wind.

> *And should we die before our journey's through,*
> *Happy day! All is well!*
> *We then are free from toil and sorrow, too;*
> *With the just we shall dwell!*
> *But if our lives are spared again*
> *To see the Saints their rest obtain,*
> *Oh, how we'll make this chorus swell—*
> *All is well! All is well!*

The wind howled harder than before, pressing on the tent
and whistling through the seams. The little ones slept fitfully,
but Ellen could tell Alexander was still awake with his arms
wrapped around her.

A flash of light lit his face and only a breath later, thunder
roared. Rain turned to hail, beating on the canvas above
them. Another gust fought against the tent and won, lifting
the stakes out of the ground. Ellen yelped as it collapsed
around them. She jumped up, pushing the fabric high above

her head and saw Alexander, Joseph, and Margaret doing the same.

Alexander spoke to Joseph. "Grab the hammer, and see if you can stake it back down."

Joseph opened the tent flap, and moments later, they heard him hammering.

Ellen caught Alexander's eye, and he grinned. She shook her head in exasperation, but his smile only grew.

"Be careful of the hail," Alexander called to Joseph. "It can knock out a grown man if it is large enough."

Joseph completed his task and returned, shivering. Alexander clapped him on the shoulder as thunder boomed overhead.

"Strip off your wet clothes," Ellen said, "and take my blanket, so you don't die of a chill."

"I am not taking your blanket, Mama. You need it."

Ellen tossed it to him anyway. "I will share with your father."

"Ew," Joseph said, pulling his damp shirt over his head, and making Ellen chuckle.

Wind and hail combined against the tent again, and the stakes pulled free once more. Joseph moaned and stood, holding it back up with his hands over his head. "I hammered them all the way down, Abba."

"I believe you did," said Alexander. "This time you hold up the canvas while I hammer."

Joseph started to protest, but his teeth chattered, and he nodded.

The clinking sounds of metal on metal mixed in with the pounding of the storm. "Lord," Ellen said. "Wilt Thou stay this storm?"

The heavens continued to pour rain and hail upon their crowded tent and did not let up until the wee hours of the morning, but the stakes stayed rooted in the ground.

The clouds obscured the sunrise, keeping the tent dark late into morning. An icy breeze whispered through the cracks and pores of the canvas, and frozen water droplets shimmered above them. Ellen might have stayed tucked up in bed forever and closed her eyes ready for her final judgment, except a sudden lurch of her stomach sent her crawling to the door, which she opened as quickly as possible and dry heaved into freshly fallen snow. She lifted a handful of the freezing snow in trembling fingers, cleaning her face, and swallowing a bit to clear the bitterness from her mouth before crawling back into her blankets. Alexander's eyes never left Ellen's face.

She felt his lips move into a smile against her cheek, and she nudged him with her shoulder. "What are you so happy about?"

"I am thinking of the cause of such an upheaval as the one you just had the pleasure of...upheaving."

She grunted and pressed her back into him, but even as she did so, she realized it was probably true. Did her body not understand that a starving mother cannot provide the right conditions for making a child? They could not feed the seven children already in this tent.

She groaned. Make that eight. An eighth was coming. Again. If her body could produce a healthy child in such circumstances.

When they grew restless enough to endure the cold outside of their blankets, Alexander and Ellen knelt up in quiet prayer. Alexander whispered, "God of Abraham, Isaac, and Jacob. We need Thy everlasting help. We have nothing to eat. These children will starve to death and join their brother and sister in the arms of Jesus if we do not find them something. We have roasted the remaining pieces of our boots for sustenance and eaten our animals, save Pippy. The plants are all hibernating. What shall we do?"

As they opened their eyes, Brother Cahoon's voice called from outside the tent. "Brother and Sister Neibaur?"

Alexander peeked through the flap, a streak of cold blowing in.

A gentleman who resided nearby towered above them. "This morning, as I prayed, I knew I needed to give you some potatoes and corn. I know you have many mouths to feed."

Ellen reached out and shook the man's hand. "You are an angel of mercy coming in our great hour of need. Thank you!"

The children, excited by the prospect of a bite to eat, slipped from their blankets and cheered. Alexander hummed while he started a fire, which was no easy task since most of the wood was soaked through. Once it was ablaze, Ellen filled the stockpot with water and set it over the flames, placing the precious potatoes and corn into the boiling water. Ellen's mouth salivated as the smells augmented into the air.

Breakfast had never tasted so good.

SPRING CAME SLOWLY, and Ellen's stomach grew rounder, even as the rest of her body thinned. She was heedful not to imagine a new bundle in her bony arms. After all, Rachel had not survived, and life was at least as desperate here as it had been in Winter Quarters. If the child did live, how would they feed another when they already did not have enough to go around?

On afternoons when the weather was anything short of blizzard conditions, Alexander worked. She was little use to him in her state and without shoes, so she practiced reading when her head could handle it. On dry days, Alexander and Joseph began to stack the adobes of what would become a twelve by fourteen foot hut. Even with its dirt floors, it would be a palace compared to their tent that was wont to blow over.

On a cool, clear day in March, the Neibaurs woke to yelling

and the barking of the dog. Alexander grabbed his gun, face grim as he climbed out of the tent. Ellen stumbled out behind him and stretched her back and neck.

Brother Cahoon growled at them. "One of the tribes came and killed some of our cattle."

"I should help," said Alexander, and with a nod from Ellen, he and Brother Cahoon were gone.

Ellen did not hear from them until late in the evening when she saw Alexander approaching and went out to meet him.

Alexander hugged her close. "Four Native Americans were killed. None of ours."

Four natives? Surely there would be repercussions. "How can they feel justified in killing our animals?"

"They want us to leave. Anyway, in their view, we are probably stealing their land, fish, and animals. Of course, we cannot allow it. When they destroy cattle, they are taking food from the mouths of our hungry children."

Relationships between the groups grew as cold as the foot of powdery snow blanketing the ground. Another band came and destroyed more of the cattle, slitting their throats in the night. An armed company of Saints, including Alexander, marched against them again.

He was away for two weeks, and when he returned, he recounted the battles to Ellen and was overheard by Joseph and Isaac. "A few days after we left, we engaged in battle for ten straight hours. Four of our men were wounded. The very next day, the battle resumed. Joseph Higbee was killed and several others wounded. After that, they retired to Spanish Fork, but by morning, they were ready to fight again. Some of them were killed in the skirmish. We brought quite a few prisoners back with us."

"What will be done with them?" Joseph asked.

Alexander shrugged. Ellen's eyes pleaded with him, and he said, "We must protect our family, Ellen."

At last, the adobe hut was ready, and they moved in. Full of gratitude, Ellen scurried about making everything just so in their new little house. Food gradually became more available as trees, plants, and flowers blossomed and animals came out of hiding and fattened up.

"I believe the time of my confinement has arrived," Ellen told Alexander above the sound of the drizzle, only days after they had moved into the hut.

"Can the little one not wait for more ideal weather?" he said, smiling. "Shall we leave right away?"

"This is the tenth time my body has experienced labor. I do not think it will take long—if all goes well."

He nodded, kissing her on the forehead, and busied himself, getting everyone ready to leave. Joseph helped Hyrum dress, Margaret helped with Leah, and Alexander hurried the others along.

"Where will you go? You cannot merely wait outside on a day like today."

"We will go to the Youngs' home, and I will send Sister Young to assist you."

That made sense. It set her mind at ease to know they would all be cared for.

She was alone for some time, her contractions growing steady and strong. She compared every feeling to what she had felt when she birthed Rachel. Was this what it felt like with her? Would this baby be born dead or, like Rachel, only live a short time and slip away? Alone with her thoughts, she decided, was not a safe place to be, so she got up and walked laps around the inside of the little house, wishing she could go out.

The consistent rain did not stop for hours, and right around the time Sister Young arrived, the adobe walls began to sweat.

Water droplets gathered into streams that flowed down the walls, turning them muddy. The dirt floor became a muddy puddle of water. "Come to my house. You cannot deliver a baby in this."

Ellen fetched the strips of fabric for her feet, and with great difficulty lifted one leg onto her other knee to start wrapping. An intense contraction stopped her, and she allowed her foot to fall back to the muddy floor. "The baby is coming too soon." She clenched her teeth against the pain. "This is a little better than birthing outside in a deluge, and I do not think I would make it to your place."

Sister Young lifted a quizzical brow. "Are you sure?" she asked with another glance around the muddy little hovel.

"Quite," said Ellen, clutching her stomach as a contraction doubled her over.

"At least we know there will be no lack of water," she said, grimacing.

The baby arrived twenty minutes later, and Mary Ann took care to keep Ellen and the baby out of the mud. "A girl," she announced.

"How is she?" Ellen said, panting and trying to see the baby's coloring through the blood.

The howling cry of a newborn came in reply. It was the hearty cry of a healthy child.

37

Ellen finished reading the story of the brother of Jared and closed the Book of Mormon, lifting it to her chest and rocking back in her chair. "Alexander, do you know Doctor Anderson?"

"Of course."

She cleared her throat. "I hear he is seeking an assistant."

He wrapped his hand around her knee and squeezed. "I have more work to do than I have time for."

"I know." She hesitated. "While I do not have medical training, I believe I have watched and assisted you enough to be of some help to him."

Alexander twisted his mouth to one side and rubbed his beard. "You want to work?"

"Only until we have recovered some basic necessities and stored a bit away for winter."

"What about the children?" He shook his head. "I am too busy to attend to them day and night."

"I know. Margaret can handle them."

"Even baby Sarah?"

"Even Sarah if I come home to feed her regularly."

He lifted his hat and scratched above his ear. "I never wanted it to come to this, but if you want to, you should."

She kissed his cheek. "Thank you."

ELLEN RUBBED her feet after a day of work, feeling the toughness of her skin as she unwrapped them.

Alexander frowned and knelt before her, meeting her gaze with intensity. "All of the money you make assisting the doctor must first go toward obtaining a pair of leather boots for you."

She imagined new shoes on her feet but shook her head. "Isaac needs shoes first."

Alexander appeared exasperated. "Did we not obtain shoes for him a few months ago?"

"Yes, we did, but the boy is growing faster than the corn, and Joseph's old ones are completely falling to pieces."

"I cannot stand to have you working with Doctor Anderson and gallivanting around town without even a pair of shoes."

"My dresses keep my feet covered." She flicked her hem to cover her toes. "I had ever so many pretty shoes in England."

He smiled mischievously. "And I recall you being a bit too attractive for your own good."

She shoved him playfully. "I was not."

"You must be getting old and losing your memory, dear. You were irresistible."

"Old? You better not say another word. And am I not attractive anymore?"

He pulled her into his arms. "Judging by the constant growth of our family, I would say you still are too attractive for your own good." He met her eyes and spoke tenderly. "A new pair of boots needs to be our highest priority." He placed his palms gently on both of her cheeks and choked back his emotions by clearing his throat. "I am serious. I have taken you away from your family, your friends, everything that could have given you a comfortable life. This is not what I promised you."

She cupped her hands around his. "I would not go back, Alexander. There is more peace and joy here in this hut than in all the Queen's riches." To prove her point, she kissed him soundly.

AFTER WORKING for pay as much as possible, Ellen at length had enough money for a pair of shoes.

With a pleasant autumn breeze dancing through her skirts and around her bonnet, she and the whole family paraded to the shoe shop. None of the pairs were as fancy as those she wore in England, but they were a good deal sturdier. She chose a well-fitted pair of black, high-top patent leather button-up shoes, and along with the blue and white striped stockings she had knitted while nursing, they were perfect.

Sunday was General Conference, and she strolled along with a spring in her step. Entering on Alexander's arm, her feet felt comfortable as a cloud.

Brother Brigham arose to speak, but before he formed the first words, she noted the deep wrinkles of distress on his face and sat forward on the bench.

"As you may have heard," he said, rubbing his forehead beneath his hat, "a large handcart company is headed our way. As it is late in the season, we were unaware they had set out. It has come to my attention that they are in dire need, stranded and dying on the plains of Wyoming." He looked directly at Ellen in the crowd. "I am asking you to help." His gaze traveled through the congregation. "We need to send sixty mules and horse teams right away. I am asking for forty young men and twelve tons of flour. Send whatever you are able to spare in terms of shoes, clothing, and blankets, as well."

Ellen stared at Brother Brigham, her brow wrinkled in worry. How could the Saints spare so much with winter approaching? Would their children starve their way through another season of bitter cold?

"I mean to forego this meeting," Brother Brigham said. An abrupt nod emphasized the words. "The Holy Ghost urges us to make haste!" He motioned with his arms for everyone to stand.

A buzz of chattering grew around them as families discussed what they could send. Ellen met Alexander's crinkled eyes. What could they possibly spare? Alexander's shoulders slumped forward. "I shall have to tell them we have nothing to give."

Ellen stopped him, placing her hand on his chest, and shook her head, her bonnet strings swinging back and forth. "We must give something. We have known more desperate times than we are now in. Surely there must be something."

Her eyes swept over the children in their mended clothing. She bowed her head to the floor and sat back on the bench, her unfocused eyes resting on the new stockings and boots she had worked so long and hard to obtain. Could someone need them more than she did?

She had made the trek with her feet in rags. Others could do the same.

If she gave them up, she would be obliged to wrap her feet in rags for the foreseeable future. At least her feet had grown tough and weathered. She wrapped her arms tightly around herself.

She had to give something, and her shoes were all she had. People were dying out there.

Ellen unbuttoned her boots with shaking fingers and slipped them from her feet. She removed the striped stockings, one at a time, and, after folding them neatly, tucked them into one of the boots.

"Mama," protested Margaret, "You must not give your new

shoes. You need those. Besides," she said, looking scandalized, "you are showing off your ankles."

Ellen reached for Margaret's hand. "All is well." She took the boots and stockings over to the relief wagon that was being piled high and watched Sister Romney reach under her skirts.

Seeing Ellen's curious expression, Sister Romney explained. "I am trying to remove my petticoat to donate it without being too improper."

"Ah," Ellen said with a vibrant smile. "May I be of assistance?"

"You may," she said. "What would my mother think to see me like this? She's probably rolling over in her grave."

They chuckled. What indeed would their proper English families think to see them now?

Margaret stepped up to her mother, pulling the hood from her head and handing it to Ellen, who took it with a nod and added it to the donations.

ELLEN WRAPPED her feet in clean rags, and the family, along with nearly all the settlers in Salt Lake, stepped out to greet the weary travelers and provide assistance. Over a hundred wagons from the stranded company were expected to roll into the valley.

Medicine and food were laid out for the arriving companies in front of the tithing office near where Ellen stood. Wagons and handcarts plodded by one-by-one, full of weary travelers, as the crowd cheered.

Ellen dipped her head, trying to view each woman's feet to see who had ended up with her prized leather boots and stockings. At long last, she discovered them half-hidden beneath the bottom of a woman's threadbare calico skirts. Her eyes trailed up to the face of the woman. She blinked and squinted, stepping forward as if in a dream. "It cannot be."

She dropped Alexander's hand, grabbed her skirts in her palms, and sprinted, and though she heard Alexander call to her, she did not pause until she reached the woman whose face was as dear to her as any sister's. She placed her hands on the woman's bony shoulders, staring into those familiar eyes of long ago, into the face that had shared every joy and sorrow of her childhood. "Am I dreaming? Dear Patience, is it really you?"

The frail woman nodded, and Ellen pulled her into her arms and wept.

THE END

EPILOGUE

Alexander would soon pass to the other side of the veil to join his dear Ellen. He was surrounded by his posterity when one of his boys said, "You have been telling us of your long and hard experience, and we have listened with intense affection and interest. But let me ask you, is it worth it all? Is the gospel worth all this sacrifice?"

His dim eyes brightened, and he strained to be sure the words came out clearly. "Yes! Yes! And more! I have seen my Savior. I have seen the prints in His hands! I know that Jesus is the Son of God, and I know that this work is true and that Joseph Smith was a prophet of God.

"I would suffer it all and more, far more than I have ever suffered, for that knowledge, even to the laying down of my body on the plains for the wolves to devour." He swallowed, exhausted from the exertion of sharing his testimony.

A short time later, he lost his ability to move his limbs.

For three weeks, his family attended to him, when suddenly, a bright, warm light shone above him, and he opened his eyes to it.

"What is it, Father? What do you see?"

"Joseph! Hyrum!" He reached his arms to the heavens and stepped through the veil.

AUTHOR NOTES

While this is a work of fiction, most of the story's plot points and even a little bit of the dialogue come from Church history, family stories, and journals. However, historical records are, for the most part, silent about how these people felt about the things they went through and how they reacted.

Chapters One to Three: Ellen Breakell attended the Church of England with her family in Preston. They were wealthy landowners. While we do not know much about her growing up years, there are a few clues. The story about her getting in trouble in church and having to stand at the front in a white garb is told in a family story. Another story says she worked in a cotton spinning factory for a while to be with friends, though her family did not need the money. This story and others show that Ellen cared deeply for her friends.

We do not know if Ellen and her siblings could read, but she and her sisters signed marriage certificates with an X, indicating that they could not even write their own names. Their younger brother was able to sign his name.

Alexander was born at a fortress at Ehrenbreitstein, Prussia. Because of the changing of ownership of the fortress, various records call him German, French, Prussian, and Polish. His father, a linguist and surgeon for Napoleon Bonaparte, wanted him to be a rabbi, and Alexander was taught accordingly. He learned several languages in addition to a deep study of the Law of Moses. As a teen, he decided to go to the University of Berlin instead and become a surgeon-dentist. He converted to Christianity and traveled Europe, settling in Preston, where he set up his dental practice.

Alexander and Ellen Breakell married on September 16, 1834 and had their first child, Joseph, on January 6, 1835. You can do the math. There are, of course, other explanations for this than conceiving before they married, but this seems the most likely scenario.

Chapter Four: Ellen's brother, William, died in July 1834 at the age of thirteen. Cause of death is unknown. He was the second Breakell son to die and be buried in Longton.

It seems that Ellen had difficult pregnancies. This idea will be expanded in later notes.

Chapters Five to Six: Alexander and Ellen married at St. Laurence Church in Chorley, Lancashire, England in September 1834, as mentioned in a previous chapter note. The marriage registry calls Alexander a Dentist Bachelor of Preston and Ellen a Spinster of Chorley. Ellen's brother, James, and her sister, Margaret, were the witnesses. Ellen and Margaret signed with X's, while Alexander and James signed their names. The record says they were married by licence, as opposed to banns.

Chapter Seven: Ellen first heard about the American missionaries from a neighbor while she was whitewashing her front porch. When the neighbor said the ministers claimed that an angel had given them a gold Bible, Alexander poked his head out the window and asked, "What was that you said?"

He was excited because he had had dreams about an angel with a golden Bible. After finding out the ministers were preaching in the Old Cockpit, he said, "I must see and hear them. Are they in the Cockpit now?"

The neighbor did not know.

Ellen could not believe Alexander was interested in speaking with them. She said, "You're not serious? You actually want to waste time listening to such nonsense?"

He grabbed his coat and hat. "They may have the answer to my strange dreams! They may be the key!"

He ran down the cobblestone street (which is still there) in the Old Cock Yard, and he met Heber C. Kimball, Willard Richards, Orson Hyde, and Joseph Fielding at the Cockpit. He asked them, "You have a book?" They replied in the affirmative and gave him a copy of the Book of Mormon.

Chapter Eight: Alexander read the Book of Mormon in three days. Ellen was less enthusiastic at first and didn't think of it as more than a nice story. Alexander wanted to be baptized right away, but the missionaries told him to wait.

Moses, Elias, and Elijah appeared at the Kirtland Temple in 1836 while Jews around the world celebrated Passover.

Chapter Nine: At one of the meetings in Preston, someone spoke in tongues. Alexander recognized it as Hebrew and translated for the congregation. He told them he did not translate by the Gift of the Spirit, but rather as a natural-born Hebrew.

Chapter Ten: Ellen dreamed that the sky was covered with small white clouds which came together. At the center was the face of Willard Richards. The clouds fell to the earth. She believed this dream meant that God had sent Brother Richards and the other missionaries to preach His gospel.

At the General Conference on April 8, 1838, Elders Kimball and Hyde were set apart to preside over all the churches in England and about 100 children were blessed.

Alexander and Ellen were baptized on April 9, 1838 in the River Ribble by Isaac Russell.

Chapter Eleven to Thirteen: The first railroad station in Preston opened on October 31, 1838 and was part of the North Union Railway. It connected Preston to Wigan, twelve miles south, linking London, Birmingham, Liverpool, and Manchester.

During this time, persecution was mounting for the members of The Church of Jesus Christ of Latter-day Saints. Alexander and Ellen lost friends and business associates.

It is unknown how Ellen's family reacted to her choice of husband and their baptisms. The only possible hint is that, while there is evidence Alexander continued to receive letters from his family once in America, I have not found evidence that Ellen corresponded with her family.

Chapter Fourteen: Isaac Neibaur died just before his first birthday. His name was later changed to Samuel Peretz after Alexander's maternal grandfather. Their next son was also named Isaac and lived to adulthood.

Chapter Fifteen: Isaac Russell was excommunicated for apostasy in May 1839. The news shook the Saints in Preston.

Chapter Sixteen: A multitude gathered at the railway station in Preston to greet Brigham Young and others in April 1840, prior to meetings at the Cockpit, where he proposed that the British Saints begin to move in small groups to Nauvoo. The first company left less than two months later.

At the same conference, Peter Melling was called as the first Patriarch in Great Britain. Alexander and Ellen received patriarchal blessings from him. The short quotes in the chapter come from these blessings. Ellen was given a second patriarchal blessing about five years later.

Chapter Seventeen: Alexander started a journal in time for their journey to America. The family boarded the 8:20 am train from Preston to Liverpool. From there, they boarded the ship, *Sheffield*, bound for New Orleans. Alexander wrote, "went directly on board the ship where we found a number of emigrants - the ship all in an uproar, luggage, men, women & children all huddled together. A number of us went to the Hargreaves Railway Office for our luggage, got this on board, got something from the cook shop for our families as it was very cold. Went to bed at dark."

The Romneys, Walmsleys, Nightingales, and Proctors were some of the 235 Saints on the *Sheffield*, though most of their actions and conversations in this book are created for the purposes of the story. The Kings are fictional characters.

Alexander's journal says that "some went to purchase provisions, some lemons, some salt fish, soap, candles, &c. I went to see a friend of mine, Mr. Hauk. He gave me a present for my wife, a boa, a muff for my daughter, and a pair of fur gloves for myself."

Later, Brigham Young chastised those who had not yet paid for their passage, and Brother Proctor was forced to pawn his clothes for the needed funds.

Chapter Eighteen: Ellen was so sick as they crossed the Atlantic that she was obliged to stay in bed below decks for the seven week journey. It was likely a combination of pregnancy and seasickness that gave her so much trouble.

Alexander kept a daily record about events including births, deaths, quarrels, injuries, and weather conditions.

While Sister King is a fictional character, Alexander noted that on the fifth day after they set sail, "one of the passengers from Preston, a woman dangerous ill died about 12-1/2 o'clock. Several of the ship's crew came to look at her as it was the first that died on board the *Sheffield*. One of our own company sewed her up in a sheet. Buried about 2 o'clock in the afternoon." A few hours later, while Brother Hyrum Clark, president of the voyage, spoke about her burial, the ship heaved, and everyone hurried to their berths ahead of a hurricane.

The stories about the cook being flogged with 24 lashes and the crewmen shooting fish are recorded in Alexander's journal.

Chapter Nineteen: Alexander recorded that at least two children were scalded by boiling pots and that Sister Nightingale and Sister Walmsley were in a dispute.

The *Sheffield* stopped when a ship came by with its flag at half-mast, only to find out that the flag was lowered in honor of the new president. While the sails were down, the winds ceased.

While the sea was still, Ellen felt better, but they also received the news that one of the Proctor children died.

Chapter Twenty: Alexander mentions more disputes in his journal, and on March 17, he wrote, "About 8 o'clock as the first mate came to the men to give orders about the painting, one of the men struck at him 3 times, the mate having threatened the previous night to split his skull for having pulled the sheet off him. The captain came up with handcuffs to confine the offender, but some resistance being offered to him, he went to the cabin, fetched a sword and said he was determined to support his authority, and any of the men resisting him, he would split him in two if he had strength in his arm. The offender went down to his place refusing to come up. The captain then said he would not hurt the hair off the head of any man except he was forced. He said, 'Passengers, the ship is in a state of mutiny, look out, your wives & children's life is in danger.' He went to the cabin, called for Elder Clark.

"Elder Clark came out calling the passengers on the after deck; he then said, the captain wishes some to come forward as volunteers to stand by him in securing the offender. Hyrum Clark said he was willing to take up arms, Richard Whithnell followed, Thomas Walmsley, James Bennett, John Hardman, William Gore. They all 6 of them went up to the captain's cabin when 6 stands of arms was brought out, charged and given to them, they then went up to the men's cabin, and the captain ordered the men to come to the quarter deck, when he again addressed them, and said it would be better for them, and he would advise them and the offender (as a friend) to deliver himself up peaceably. The offender then delivered himself up, when he was put in handcuffs and ordered to the long boat, which served as a place of confinement. Order was then restored—a number of passengers finding fault with the parties that have taken up arms for doing so."

The next day, Sister Whithnell had a baby during a squall.

A few days later, Alexander wrote, "a cry was raised, ship on fire, many of the passengers and crew hastening...Running to the forecastle, some crying, some almost fainting. This ship is on fire; some hastening with buckets and cans of water. It was soon discovered that there was no danger, the brandy cask having caught fire by Elder Clark drawing some spirits, wanted to see how much there was, and so the accident happened. One man, George Scholes, by endeavoring to put it out had his face very ill burned. At night, close reef being opposite Jamaica."

Another baby was born, and tales of catching dolphins come from his journal.

Chapter Twenty-One: The Neibaurs enjoyed the first grand steamer they boarded to travel up the Mississippi, but after only a few days, they moved onto the *Moravian*. Alexander wrote, "A heavy rain, thunder and lightning. No fire on board, no breakfast. About noon the custom house officer came to inspect the luggage. All was now in uproar everyone hastening to secure their luggage, the rain coming down in torrents. About 9 o'clock the mate came around to order our berths or sleeping places. We had iron rails for bedsteads all being huddled together, some slept in hammocks; others was forced to sit up all night having no place, some 6 and 7 sleeping in a bed. Rainy day and night...Rainy morning thundering and lightning passed a fine settlement. About 8 o'clock at night being very foggy stayed to take in wood." Several men came on board to sell vegetables, eggs, apples, pies, etc. a fire kindled on shore."

A week later, "a terrific storm shook the boat, the captain and his men being frightened almost out of their wits, sparks of fire flying about in the steerage. Many of the passengers were awakened by the fear of fire. The captain gave orders to stop the engine and make for the land until daylight appeared, the cook's window being blown out of the kitchen. It was terrifying. Broke all the windows in the tophouse."

Things calmed down after that, and Alexander was able to clean the teeth of some of the passengers and crew.

The Neibaurs heard that President Harrison died exactly a month after taking office.

They next boarded The *Goddess of Liberty*. Alexander wrote that, while it was "a fine new built boat, ...there was confusion, all being crowded together more than ever. Berths being prepared, but as there was not room for above half the number of passengers, many were forced to sit up. It was a very cold night."

Finally, they boarded the *Aster*, which took them the final distance to Nauvoo. The journal says the Saints "kindly offered their houses, many slept in a large stone building belonging to one of the brethren, myself & William Gross, with some others kept up a large fire all night and stayed with our luggage. Some of the brethren that had come here before us kept us company. Early in the morning a number of the brethren came to inquire whether all of us had obtained habitations. We got in very comfortable with a brother."

The Snailhams are a fictitious family, as I do not know who took the Neibaurs in.

On April 21, 1841, Alexander wrote "was in company at Br. Thompson's with Joseph Smith, came to order some false corals for his wife, asked about some land, if I had means could get plenty."

Chapter Twenty-Two: The situation of the Neibaurs' land in the story is accurate, and they started to prepare wood for their fence right away.

On April 25th, the journal states, "Showery forenoon; went to the preaching in the open air, a fine spot of land near temple thea platform for the speakers, seats prepared for the congregation. Br. Bennett spoke first in respect to his profession, all character being injured by some of those who professed to be Saints. Br. Law followed on the principles of righteousness and unrighteousness, there having been some depredations being committed by some that once had been saints but was cut off from the Church for misconduct. Elder Joseph [Smith] the Prophet followed in very strong language determined to put down all iniquity. About one o'clock the meeting broke up for about an hour in the afternoon. Assembled again. The meeting was addressed by Elder Green on the principles of the gospel until 4 o' clock when the meeting broke up. After the meeting the Nauvoo Legion was called to come and volunteer for Secret Service in detecting thiefs, &c."

Joseph Smith loved his white English Mastiff, Old Major, who was given to him at Zion's Camp. The dog and owner were very protective of one another.

The story about the Prophet Joseph's cracked tooth is also true. Alexander tried to fix it, but some stories about Joseph say he had a slight whistle for the rest of his life, so Alexander may not have been successful.

It is recorded in Alexander's journal, as well as in Joseph Smith's journal, that Alexander taught the Prophet lessons in Hebrew and German until close to the time of Joseph's death.

Alice Neibaur was born on May 22nd, on the 25th, they planted corn, potatoes, and beans, and on June 1st, the family moved into their new house.

Notes about the trials and arrest of Joseph Smith and others with him come from Alexander's journal.

Chapter Twenty-Three: A couple days after the Neibaurs moved into their new house, Alexander was dangerously ill. He received a Priesthood blessing and made a quick recovery.

All accounts of the Neibaur's dog are fiction.

Many of the Saints coming to Nauvoo died on the journey, and Alexander wrote about a few that died shortly after arrival.

On July 4, 1841, many people gathered to celebrate America's Independence Day in Nauvoo. While it was probably not at this celebration that Ellen won a beauty contest, family stories say that she won three over the course of her lifetime: one in Preston, one in Nauvoo, and one in Salt Lake.

It seems that Alexander was fascinated by people of different cultures as he often noted them in his journal. Before

Nauvoo, he mentioned Black people, and in Nauvoo and beyond, he speaks of Native Americans relatively often.

On August 12th, a tribe of Native Americans, led by Chief Keokuk, crossed the Mississippi in full native dress. The events of the day, including the words spoken by the Prophet Joseph and the chief, are accurate and can be found in the Joseph Smith Papers.

Alexander's ad in the Times and Seasons is quoted directly.

Chapter Twenty-Four: The sad tale of John Bennett can be read in many places, and the Female Relief Society meeting is based on real events.

Orson and Marinda Hyde's conversations are true to things they experienced, though there is no evidence of any such discussions with the Neibaurs. They are included here because, as a Jew, it is likely that Alexander was interested in Elder Hyde's experiences regarding Jerusalem.

Because plural marriage was increasing during this time, and Alexander worked out of Brigham Young's home, it is likely that it was a topic of interest for the Neibaurs.

Chapter Twenty-Five: Alexander went to a store to buy vinegar when he heard a man cursing the Prophet Joseph. He swung his empty stone jug and broke it on the man's head, and yelled, "What do you know about the Prophet Joseph Smith?" Other details added to this story are fiction, but it is what led me to believe Alexander may have had a bit of a temper.

In addition to dentistry and teaching languages, Alexander started a matchmaking business.

Bertha Breakell Neibaur was born in December 1843.

The story about the penny fund is based on facts, as is Joseph Smith's presidential campaign. The things he says about the Constitution are direct quotes. I am not sure that the Smiths ever all visited the Neibaur's house or had conversations about these topics, but Joseph Smith was in the Neibaur home at least once while Alexander was ill, and Alexander was in their home often.

Though we do not know the circumstances surrounding it, Alexander wrote about Joseph Smith's First Vision in his journal after hearing it from the Prophet, though it may have been recorded sometime later. It is one of only five accounts written by Joseph Smith's contemporaries. Each one has a few unique details. The account written into this story is based on Alexander's journal.

Chapters Twenty-Six to Twenty-Seven: Margaret was baptized at the age of 8, according to a family story.

Alexander spent a lot of time training with the Nauvoo Legion.

He was a poet and wrote multiple hymns. The only poem in this book that was written by Emily Beeson is Alexander's poem to Ellen during their courtship.

The account of the destruction of the Nauvoo Expositor and resulting trials and speeches are based on facts recorded in Alexander's journal and in many other Church history accounts.

Along with the rest of the Saints, the Neibaurs were horrified to hear that Joseph and Hyrum Smith had been killed at Carthage Jail.

Their trials, deaths, and funeral services are based on true accounts of the events.

The story about Alexander refusing to shake William Law's hand is true. He said, "I never give my hand to a traitor."

Chapter Twenty-Eight: The poem here was written by Alexander after the death of his friends, Joseph and Hyrum.

Many accounts were written about the prayer meeting Sydney Rigdon held in hopes of becoming the Church's guardian and the experiences of the congregation when Brigham Young took over. It is unknown whether Alexander and Ellen were there (but seems likely) or if either of them had a spiritual experience that day.

Descriptions of the temple and the laying of the final stone are based on accounts by Alexander and others.

Chapter Twenty-Nine: Accounts of the Nauvoo Legion and the mobs are based on Alexander's journal entries during this time.

An agreement was made between leaders of The Church of Jesus Christ of Latter-day Saints and local governments that the Saints would leave in the Spring of 1836. The Bill of Particulars is quoted from Church history sources.

The Saints spent the winter preparing to leave and completing work on the Nauvoo Temple. Alexander was one of many men that worked there.

Chapter Thirty: The account of Brother Brigham Young delaying his journey multiple times and working in the temple around the clock to give the endowment to as many Saints as possible is based on historical accounts. More than 5,000 Saints received these ordinances at the Nauvoo Temple.

Alexander and Ellen Neibaur received their endowments on January 5, 1846 and were sealed on the 22nd.

In early February, some of the Saints began to leave Nauvoo.

The temple dedication occurred on May 1-3, 1846. The details in this book are based on historical accounts.

Chapter Thirty-One: Tension continued to mount, though many of the Saints were leaving. Ellen and Alexander were expecting their eighth child. Because of Ellen's difficult pregnancy, the Neibaurs were some of the last Saints to leave Nauvoo. Alexander spent a lot of his time marching with the former Nauvoo Legion and standing guard at the temple.

Leah Neibaur was born on August 29, 1846, and, though Ellen was sick with fever and chills, the family finally left their home ten days later.

The story about Alexander standing up to the soldier has been passed down in the Neibaur family, including the dialogue between them.

Chapter Thirty-Two: Crossing the river, stopping in Montrose, and boarding with various families are based on Alexander's journal entries and family stories, though the Crockett family was created for this story.

Alexander stood up for the Prophet in the face of danger. "He was practicing dentistry at a small town in Iowa. A client came in and placed his pistol beside him on the table. The man in the chair began to blaspheme in the most awful and blood-curdling manner against the church leaders. Elder Neibaur rebuked him. The patient grabbed his pistol and threatened to shoot him. He pointed the pistol at him and snapped off every barrel. For some strange reason not one bullet fired. The brother of the patient came in from an adjoining room, picked up the pistol, and emptied every barrel by firing into the air outside the door."

Family stories also say that Alexander wrote the hymn, Come, Thou Glorious Day of Promise. Current hymn books now say the text comes "from Pratt's collection", but the family story claims that Brother Parley P. Pratt helped him make some small edits, and Alexander no longer claimed it as his own, though he had written it.

Chapter Thirty-Three: Records of the dire conditions at Winter Quarters can be found in many sources. Mary Ann Young went about helping the sick. While there is no account of Mary Ann blessing Ellen, it was common practice at the time to bless a mother before giving birth, not by power of the Priesthood, but by the healing gift of the Spirit.

FamilySearch says, "Due to hunger, cold, and all of the conditions of the camp at that time, Ellen gave birth to little Rachel Neibaur, on December 12, 1847...but sadly she was still-born. Rachel is buried in the Mormon Pioneer Cemetery in Grave #276."

Chapters Thirty-Four to Thirty-Five: Because the Neibaurs traveled with the Brigham Young Company, and Alexander and others kept journals, the events of their journey west are based on real accounts.

Though they must have been thrilled to finally reach the Salt Lake Valley, it was some time before their conditions improved.

Chapter Thirty-Six: That first winter was extremely difficult. Food was scarce, they lived in a tent that sometimes blew over during the night, and Ellen did not have any shoes.

One time when the family was starving, they knelt in prayer, and when they finished, a neighbor came with food.

Accounts of skirmishes with the Native Americans are based on entries in Alexander's journal.

Sarah Ellen Neibaur was born on May 21, 1849. She later wrote, "Through the winter, Father, with the help of his eldest son, fourteen years of age, made adobes enough to build a hut twelve by fourteen feet, with mud roof and floor. In that hut, I was born...with a big rainstorm and mud running down the walls and under Mother's bed in streams."

Chapter Thirty-Seven: Ellen began to work with Doctor Anderson, and also went about caring for the sick, while Alexander established himself as the first dentist in Utah territory and continued to teach and make matches.

And now we come to the author's favorite part. Based on family stories, Elder Gerald Lund wrote the following: "After they reached Salt Lake, traveling in the second company with Brigham Young in 1848, her husband became a teacher. She took in laundry. For the next eight years, any time she could save a penny or two, she put it aside. After eight long years, she finally had reached the point where she could buy a pair of commercially made shoes from a mail order house. She ordered a pair of high-top patent leather button shoes. They arrived sometime in September 1856.

"Just a few days later, on October 4, a company led by Franklin D. Richards of the Quorum of the Twelve rode into Salt Lake with some very disturbing news. They said, 'President Young, we have two more handcart companies stranded out on the plains, with over a thousand people.' Brigham Young was stunned; three companies had already come in safely, and he assumed that was it for the season. He had no idea there were more, so he had called all the supply wagons back to Salt Lake.

"The news reached him on Saturday afternoon, October 4. In General Conference on the next day, October 5, Brigham Young stood up and said, 'I will now give this people the subject and the text for the elders who may speak to-day and during the conference. It is this. On the 5th day of October, 1856, many of our brethren and sisters are on the plains with handcarts, and probably many are now seven hundred miles from this place, and they must be brought here, we must send assistance to them. The text will be to get them here.' President Young then called for teams, wagons, food, and clothing to help those who were stranded. And Ellen Neibaur, after eight years of waiting, had not lost sight of what the covenant was and what mattered. She took that brand-new pair of shoes down to the wagon team and gave them to the rescue effort.

"It was customary, when a new company came into the Valley, for all the Saints to go out and line the streets and greet them. When this particular company came in, everyone went out to greet them, because this was the first of the two besieged handcart companies to be rescued. Ellen Neibaur went out. Normally the Saints watched the faces of the people coming in to see who they were. What do you think Ellen Neibaur was watching that day? She wasn't looking at faces. She was looking at feet. She wanted to know who had gotten her shoes.

"Now, here comes the beautiful end to this true story, a great example of faith and covenant, and an example of the power that follows. When Ellen Neibaur saw her shoes, she looked up and, to her absolute amazement, wearing them was an old friend from Preston England, who had joined the Church since Ellen had left England!"

The donation record shows that Ellen Neibaur contributed 1 pair of shoes, 1 set of stockings, and 1 hood.

Epilogue: Alexander and Ellen had 14 children. The account of Alexander's words on his deathbed is true and has been passed down through his posterity.

BIBLIOGRAPHY

"Alexander Neibaur Journal." The Church of Jesus Christ of Latter-day Saints. https://history.churchofjesuschrist.org/overlandtravel/sources/4585/alexander-neibaur-journal-1841-february-1862-april-26-38

Beacon Fell, Lancashire. Wikipedia. https://en.wikipedia.org/wiki/Beacon_Fell,_Lancashire

Bergera, Gary James. "John C. Bennett, Joseph Smith, and the Beginnings of Mormon Plural Marriage in Nauvoo." The John Whitmer Historical Association Journal

Vol. 25, 25th Anniversary Edition, 2005.

"Brigham Young Company." The Church of Jesus Christ of Latter-day Saints. https://history.churchofjesuschrist.org/overlandtravel/companies/4/brigham-young-company-1848

Colvin, Don F. "The Dedication of the Temple." *Nauvoo Temple: A Story of Faith.* Provo, UT: Religious Studies Center, 2002.

Cook, Lyndon. "The Apostle Peter and the Kirtland Temple." Provo, UT: BYU Studies Quarterly: Vol. 15 : Iss. 4 , Article 18., 1975.

Esplin, Scott C. "Remembering the Impact of British

Missionary Isaac Russell." *Regional Studies in Latter-day Saint Church History: The British Isles.* Provo, UT: Religious Studies Center, Brigham Young University, 2007.

Evans, Richard L. *A Century of Mormonism in Great Britain.* The Deseret News Press, 1937.

Fish, Rick J. "Orson Pratt in Nauvoo 1839-1846" May, 1993. http://jared.pratt-family.org/orson_histories/ orson_pratt_in_nauvoo1.html

Galbraith, David B. "Orson Hyde's 1841 Mission to the Holy Land." *Ensign.* October 1991.

Hawley, Gregory L. and William G. Hartley. "Before the Arabia Sank: Mormon Passengers up the Missouri in 1856." http://mormonhistoricsites.org/wp-content/uploads/ 2013/05/NJ10.2_Hawley.pdf

Hebblethwaite, Cordelia. "Mitt Romney's Mormon roots in northern England." June 13, 2012. https://www.bbc.com/news/ magazine-18422949

Hewitson, Anthony. *History (from A.D 705 to 1883) of Preston, in the County of Lancaster.* Preston: The Chronicle, 1883.

Hoag, Karen. "Pioneer Recipes." Jul 23, 2002. https://www. heraldextra.com/lifestyles/pioneer-recipes/article_3f57d8ff-572c-5282-97f1-b528212765e7.html

Holy Bible. King James Version. Salt Lake City, Utah, U.S.A.: The Church of Jesus Christ of Latter-Day Saints, 1989.

"Isaac Russell." The Church of Jesus Christ of Latter-day Saints. https://history.churchofjesuschrist.org/missionary/ individual/isaac-russell-1807?lang=eng

Jenkins, Stanley C and Martin Loader. *The London, Midland and Scottish Railway Volume Two Preston to Carlisle.* Amberley Publishing Limited, Oct 15, 2015.

Joseph Smith Papers. https://www.josephsmithpapers.org/

Kane, Kathryn. "The Regency Way of Death: Furnishing the Funeral." October 19, 2012. https://regencyredingote.

wordpress.com/2012/10/19/the-regency-way-of-death-furnishing-the-funeral/

Knight, Gregory R. *Journal of Thomas Bullock. https://byustudies.byu.edu/content/journal-thomas-bullock*

LDS Living Staff. "What We Know About Joseph Smith's Dog + How It Protected Him in Jail." July 26, 2018. https://www.ldsliving.com/What-We-Know-About-Joseph-Smith-s-Dog-How-It-Protected-Him-in-Jail/s/88975

Lund, Gerald N. Selected Writings of Gerald N. Lund: Gospel Scholars Series. Salt Lake City, Utah: Deseret Book Company, 1999.

Newbold, Bruce Alan. *The Life and Times of Alexander Neibaur: Journey of the First Mormon Jew, 2nd Edition.* Lulu, 2015.

O'Neill, Therese. "How to Give Birth (100 years ago)." December 18, 2013. https://theweek.com/articles/454290/how-give-birth-100-years-ago

Pratt, Parley. *The Autobiography of Parley Parker Pratt.* Russell Brothers, 1874.

"Prayer of Orson Hyde on the Mount of Olives, Sunday morning, October 24, 1841." History of the Church, Volume 4, Salt Lake City, Utah: Deseret Book Company, 1950.

Proctor, Maurine Jensen and Scot Facer Proctor. *The Gathering: Mormon Pioneers on the Trail to Zion.* Salt Lake City, UT: Deseret Book Company, 1996.

Rennie, Claire. "The Treatment of Whooping Cough in Eighteenth-Century England." University of Leeds.

Saints by Sea. "Liverpool to New Orleans 7 Feb 1841 - 30 Mar 1841." https://saintsbysea.lib.byu.edu/mii/voyage/331

Smart, Paul F. "The History of the Early Members of the Church of Jesus Christ of Latter-day Saints in Preston, Lancashire, England." Provo, UT: Brigham Young University, December 1989.

Smith, Joseph, Junior. *The Book of Mormon.* Palmyra: E. B. Grandin, 1830.

Temple House Gallery. "The History of the Nauvoo Temple Star Windows." https://templehousegallery.com/nauvoo-temple-star-window-history

Times and Seasons. BYU Digital Collections.

Walker, Ronald W. "Six Days in August: Brigham Young and the Succession Crisis of 1844." *A Firm Foundation: Church Organization and Administration.* Provo, UT: Religious Studies Center, Brigham Young University; Salt Lake City: Deseret Book, 2011.

www.familysearch.org/

Zucker, Lewis C. "Joseph Smith as a Student of Hebrew." University of Utah. https://www.dialoguejournal.com/wp-content/uploads/sbi/articles/Dialogue_V03N02_43.pdf

ACKNOWLEDGMENTS

Thank you for reading *In Ellen's Shoes: Based on the inspiring true story of Ellen Breakell and Alexander Neibaur*. If you loved this story as I do, please leave a review on Amazon.com.

I would like to thank my family for supporting me in this endeavor, even when it meant eating less home-cooked meals, especially Grace, who has been one of my greatest supporters and was the first reader of this book.

I am also grateful to my critique group members, Martha Keyes, Jess Heileman, and Kasey Stockton, who taught me a lot about 19th Century England and gave me the courage to cut the parts that needed to be cut and to self-publish.

My editor, Jenny Proctor, also made suggestions that made this story stronger than it would have been without her, and I appreciate her honest feedback and encouragement.

ABOUT THE AUTHOR

Emily Beeson is the fourth great-granddaughter of Ellen Breakell and Alexander Neibaur. She treasures being a wife and mother to five children. She is a lover of stories, music, people, and chocolate cinnamon bears.

This is her first published book, but she is busily writing others. She can't help it.

She and her family live near Church history sites in Missouri, and she dreams of traveling to Europe to explore the foreign places she writes about.

Find Emily on Instagram @emilybeesonwrites

Made in the USA
Monee, IL
10 March 2023

29578083R00213